THE BLACK CALADRIUS

NACUSTI CHRONICLES VOLUME II

J. R. DOUGLAS

· Firepost Press ·

THE BLACK CALADRIUS: NACUSTI CHRONICLES VOLUME II

Maps by Jared Douglas

Cover design by Kelly Carter

 Published in the United States by Firepost Press.

The characters and events portrayed in this book are fictitious. Any similarity to real persons, living or dead, is coincidental and not intended by the author.

ISBN 979-8-9905538-2-8 | Ebook ISBN 979-8-9905538-3-5

First edition 2024

For Makenzie, my sister and the first adventurer I followed.

Lion District

Wasp District

The Center

1

2

3

4

5

6

7

8

Farm District

Market District

Crock Disctrict

1 - Entrance Portal	5 - Training Courts
2 - The Archives	6 - The Dormitory
3 - The Center Castle	7 - Den of Darkness
4 - Temple of Light	8 - Soldier Barracks

Wastelands
Pywell Mountains
Merinthia's Pass
Darlangson
Anguis River
Nalawin
Republic of Evartia
Janlaka
Masdaan
Karanadee River
Regadensia
Weslinton
Tor'alan
Gort'haal
Lindomer
Valecium
Southern Isles
Bernadooth
Densba

CONTENTS

Chapter 1

New Routines

Light faded fast, making it difficult to spy on the clearing. Zak's thighs twinged, tight from crouching behind shrubbery. How long had he been there? Leaning forward, his eyes narrowed, trying to discern more of what he saw.

A scattering of tall, dead trees spaced oddly apart reminded him of a grove that hadn't been tended in some time. The crisp air ruffled the leaves on the bush where he hid and sent a shiver to the base of his neck.

A figure perched in one of the trees—it was small, maybe a bird. His vision blurred as if peering through mottled glass. A whisper brushed his ear, and he turned fast to the right, but nothing was there except thick darkness that could blot his hand before his eyes.

"*Nacustiiii.*" The whisper became a growl and Zak's breath quickened his heartbeat.

It sounded hollow, like a voice echoing down a long hallway. It grew louder and louder until finally it shouted, "*NACUSTI!*" and Zak yelped, tumbling into the bush.

"Nacusti? Are you all right?" a gentle but firm voice

asked.

Zak jumped, out of breath, surrounded by books, shelves, and tapestries. He was not in a clearing or tangled in a bush. He was in the Archives, in the Center, in Tor'alan.

He was safe.

Archivist Tinora stood a few feet away, an armful of tomes and scrolls perched expertly on her hip. A shock of white hair wove into a tight braid resting over her shoulder.

"I fell asleep, Archivist," Zak stammered. He winced more in embarrassment than pain as he peeled damp parchment from his cheek and crumpled it, offering a weak smile.

Archivist Tinora didn't move, her eyes never leaving Zak's as she seemed to evaluate his entire reason for existing. Then her gaze softened, and she said, "Two times in as many weeks—don't make it more of a habit. Haven't you somewhere to be?" She turned, not waiting for an answer and began carefully replacing tomes and scrolls in their rightful places.

"Yes, thank you, Archivist." Zak's cheeks flushed as he shuffled sheets of parchment together, cramming them into the leather bag hanging from a chair. Slinging it over his shoulder, he picked up the stack of books and started toward the front desk.

The Archive was a circular wooden tower with the distinct scent of old, somewhat moldy books. Sorwin, his magus, described it as euphoric; Zak found it tickled his nose. The ends of tightly packed bookshelves met in the middle of the structure and grew in size as they spiraled to the outer walls. Each shelf contained as much knowledge as any scholar could dream of exploring. Smooth beige tiles joined together seamlessly on the floor, and as Zak moved, he was astonished at how little sound his quick footsteps made. He needed to ask Sorwin about the charms that must be present to dampen noise.

Scattered tables glowed in the gentle morning light, waiting for eager visitors to sit and read through the Archives' treasures. Zak tottered around them and descended three flights to the ground floor, dropping the stack of books at the front desk with a *thud*. Answering the attendant's withering gaze with a timid smile, he moved toward the banded front doors.

Outside, the light wasn't as gentle. Zak held a hand up, squinting at the sky. The sun was higher than he thought, adjusting for Tor'alan's elevation as a floating city.

He was late.

"Three Fires," he cursed under his breath. He clutched his bag and took off at a full sprint, feet banging hard on the cobblestone path.

Luckily, he didn't have far to go. He bounded across the open courtyard connecting the buildings in the Center. The smooth stone pathways criss crossed over lush green lawns dotted with trees and sculptures. There were not as many pedestrians in the Center as in the city proper. A tall stone wall circled the perimeter, limiting the area to League of Kingdoms mages and soldiers. Yet Zak still encountered enough people to manage a few near-collisions. He dodged a gaggle of chattering mages and shouts sounded in his wake as he disturbed their morning routines. He offered a backward wave and apology as he scurried up the broad stone steps of the Dormitory.

Pushing through the sizeable wooden door in the entrance hall, he crashed into a solid mass and sprawled backward, parchment crunching against his back as he landed on his bag.

"Oi!"

Zak groaned, gingerly finding his footing. A big-boned mage stomped toward him. Zak had run straight into Rauffe. "By Cerevita's grace..."

"Oi!" Rauffe repeated. "In a hurry, *Nacusti*?" He spat the honorific, towering over Zak with folded arms. He was at least a full head taller.

"Actually, I am." Zak brushed off his breeches and readjusted his bag. "If you'll excuse me." He moved to sidestep Rauffe, not wanting to linger, but was pushed back by Rauffe's oversized palm.

"You mean to assault me, then walk away without as much as an apology?" Rauffe let out a single, loud laugh and turned to a smaller man behind him, who Zak hadn't seen behind Rauffe's bulk. "Can you believe this?"

Zak didn't know the smaller man, but his greasy smile meant he was no friend, and he looked several years older than Zak, same as Rauffe. *I'm going to be even later now.* Zak sighed. "Listen, Rauffe, I know we got off to a bad start a few weeks ago—"

Rauffe's boorish smile disappeared as his demeanor shifted. He took two quick steps forward, shoving a giant finger in Zak's face, nearly up his nose. "YOU MEAN WHEN

YOU GOT LUCKY! I didn't *lose* that match, *Nacusti*, and I'll prove it right here, RIGHT NOW!"

Before Zak could react, Rauffe shoved him into the Dormitory wall. Brown fire danced in his fists as he began an incantation, and Zak instinctively raised his hands in defense.

"Rauffe Werbeggen!" A clear, high voice cut through the air.

Rauffe stopped his spell at once, brown fire fizzling out.

Inguma Foucher strode toward their small group. Her deep lavender hair jutted at all angles to circle her face, almost like a frame would a painting—if the frame was shaped like a bouquet of wildflowers. Blue half-moon glasses perched on her round nose, right below her arched eyebrows. Her robes—if they could be called that—were many folds of fabric that sprouted and intertwined in random patterns of reds, silvers, oranges, and yellows.

"Rauffe," Inguma said again, stopping a few feet away with clasped hands at her waist. "That wasn't an offensive spell I saw you aiming at a fellow mage, was it?" Her tone was polite, but a fierce glint lit her eyes.

"I...no, he—" Rauffe stammered, leveling another finger in Zak's direction.

Inguma held up a hand. "Elemental magic is forbidden in the Dormitory, Rauffe. I'd expect an Adept such as yourself to be aware of this. The last thing we need is overzealous mages burning down our housing. Again. And," she continued, her gaze flicked momentarily to Zak. "I'd also expect an adept to offer an acolyte some guidance. Remember, 'For balance in Nature, we must balance our nature.'"

"Yes, Magus," Rauffe said through gritted teeth.

"On your way, you're late for the morning session."

Rauffe and the smaller man shot scathing looks at Zak while trudging out of the Dormitory.

Inguma tilted her head toward Zak. "Here only a few weeks and managed to make quite the enemy."

Zak's cheeks burned for the second time that morning. "We, uh, had a bad start."

"I know, I saw," Inguma said. "It isn't often a new acolyte floors an adept in a sparring match. Though, we've never had a *Nacusti* as an acolyte."

Zak half smiled, half grimaced at the praise mixed with the title he fervently disliked. "Thank you, Magus, for interrupting when you did. I'm not sure what would have happened."

"I am sure, and you are welcome. I was serious, though; I'm responsible for the Dormitory. I won't have it ruined as my predecessor did. Try to avoid needing the interruption in the future?" Her eyebrows arched even higher to assist her questioning tone.

"Of course, Magus." He dipped his head in acknowledgment.

Inguma did the same. "Now, off you go as well. I *know* you're late for Sorwin." She walked by with a smirk.

"Of all days..." Zak cursed again. He spun on his heel and sprinted toward the spiral wooden staircase in the corner of the building, skipping several steps at a time. On the second floor, he burst through the third door on the left.

His room was small, just big enough for a single bed on

the right side, a dented trunk at its foot, and a simple wooden desk and stool next to the head of the bed. The desk sat under the single window in the room, a rounded, lattice-framed glass that swung open with a large brass handle. Zak flung his bag on the red and yellow quilted bed, using both hands to lift the heavy lid of the trunk, its rusty hinges squealing against the movement.

Zak didn't have many belongings, and when they all fit inside one trunk, searching for specific things became a little chaotic, especially in a hurry. He pawed through several layers of books (required reading per Sorwin), a cloak he had bought with his first wages as a League mage, a spare pair of boots, two dirty uniforms (the odor was pungent), and finally found his last clean uniform near the bottom.

He stripped his dark blue tunic and brown breeches, gave them a hasty toss, and hopped on one foot as he finished pulling on the red acolyte uniform.

"Where is it..." he thought aloud. He dashed to the desk, shuffling through scrolls, books, and several pages of notes in his own slanted writing as he searched for his schedule.

There's an easier way to do this, Parignis. The deep, reverberating voice of Jolsu sounded in Zak's head.

"Shut it, wyrm," he said aloud, not responding telepathically. The dragon would be too satisfied by that.

A wave of smugness came from Jolsu. For some reason, the dragon enjoyed getting a rise out of Zak, and Zak wanted nothing to do with him. Not after what he did to Olivia.

Zak stopped, huffing in his haste and annoyance, and stepped back from the desk for a moment. Even though it had been several months since Sorwin found him in Densba, his small hometown in the Southern Isles, Zak sometimes forgot he was a mage. But he had studied magic daily for those several months, and that wasn't for nothing.

He closed his eyes, steadied his breath, quieted his mind, and reached for his magic. It was there instantly, like a comforting, reliable friend. Zak pulled just enough of his magic for a simple spell. "*Invepati* schedule," he whispered.

A small stream of green light ignited in Zak's hand and darted through the air. He followed the light, scrambling over academic debris, and pulled the corner of a page pinned between the desk and the wall. The green light faded as Zak gripped the parchment and turned it over, smoothing out the well-worn folds to scan the neat script for perhaps the hundredth time.

Tor'alan
The Center
Elemental House Dormitory
Second Floor, Third Door on the Left
Zakolor Keldin

Dearest Zakolor,

Am I right in thinking this is your first Firepost? Quite exciting, I should say! It's a simple and highly functional piece of magic.

Anyway, please find enclosed your schedule. Typically, Tansil handles the administration and training of Elemental mages, but since we have a history and you're a rather unique case, he's given the go-ahead for me to direct your tutelage personally.

I hope that's alright with you, though I suspect a familiar face in a strange, new city would be welcome. Look at that! I can ramble rather well on paper, too. My mother called that being "multifaceted."

Right! Onto the schedule. We'll see a lot of each other, so should you have queries, they'll be answered posthaste. Do connect with Inguma Foucher for your Acolyte uniforms and any housing needs.

I am happy you felt comfortable staying in the Dormitory. I have rather fond memories there myself. Of course, it was a bit different before the last burning. Oh, yes, it has burned down more than once! A story for another time, perhaps.

Yours,

Sorwin Darlangson
Second Prince, Kingdom of Darlangson
High Magus, House of Elements

SCHEDULE FOR ZAKOLOR KELDIN
HOUSE OF ELEMENTS—ACOLYTE
MAGUS: SORWIN DARLANGSON

Morning Session
Instructor: Sorwin Darlangson
Focus: elemental magic, telekinetics, spells, and charms

Midday Session
Instructor: Kaleb Deidaku
Focus: weapons, combat, and strategy

Afternoon Sessions
Onesday: Sparring—Center courts
Twosday: ~~Free study~~ Archives research
Threesday: Sight magic, Instructor Shira Motchit
Foursday: Supervised visitation with Kalbick
Fivesday: ~~Free study~~ Archives research

It was Threesday, which meant triple sessions. Checking his schedule had become a ritual as he seldom had time to return during the day, hadn't yet memorized it, and didn't dare remove it from his room for fear of permanently losing it. The morning and midday sessions were always the same, but the afternoon sessions still confused him. He could have asked for another copy from Sorwin if it was misplaced, but he didn't want to bother his magus more than necessary.

Sorwin, Kaleb, Shira, he silently repeated the order for the day. Snatching his bag and leaping out of his door, he wondered at the fact that it had been almost a month since he plunged into his training. Almost a month since the *indagomius* teleported him away from the safety of Tor'alan. Almost a month since he rescued Kal. Almost a month since Jolsu cursed Olivia.

He stumbled down the stairs, catching himself with the railing.

Kal and Olivia. They were his reasons for falling asleep

in the Archives, researching anything remotely resembling a cure. Nothing else mattered when Kal and Olivia were suffering through two very different ailments, but with one common cause.

Me.

Rescuing Kal had been his goal all along, the main reason he joined Sorwin and the League of Kingdoms. When he finally found his friend, he barely recognized him. His expressions, movements, and even his voice sounded strange like someone else wore his body.

And when he tried to save Kal, to purge the darkness from his mind, Zak didn't have enough time. The Consortium closed in, and Olivia protected him, but it wasn't enough. Karazul ran her through.

She should have died, he knew that now. The one good thing about Jolsu's curse was that it kept her breathing.

But Jolsu destroyed her life, too.

The *vitaligo* bound her life to her magic. Her powerful, devastating magic was the reason she left her family, the reason she excelled within the League, the reason she earned a sponsorship and worked for Euphemius. And now she couldn't use it without draining her life, and in its absence, anger inflamed blame, and she hurled it at Zak.

Zak blamed himself, too. He had screamed at Jolsu, asking him why, why, why a thousand times. The dragon never answered, but he couldn't hide everything from their connection. It had only strengthened since meeting in Zak's mind. He felt Jolsu's hatred for all the *Nacusti*, all except the first, Adrastus. The dragon was passed from mage to mage in Zak's bloodline, in a prison of his own making, cursing the world that forced his sacrifice to win the Guardian War.

The sun was higher, warmer. His bag jostled against his back as he sprinted across the courtyard.

Zak had saved Kal at a high cost. *But did I really save him?* Seeing Kal in the healing wards, thrashing under the Consortium's wicked magics, he thought not.

Blame and guilt bolstered Zak's resolve to find a cure for Kal's condition and Olivia's curse, which was why he spent every free second he had in the Archives. If there were an answer anywhere, it would be in the near-endless shelves of knowledge. It had to be.

If not, his only other hope was Cerevita. He met a god! It was still unbelievable, the feeling of her presence, the sheer power she exuded overwhelmed his thoughts and senses. They didn't speak long, mere moments, but it was enough for Cerevita to promise her help in defeating Zandorn—which was equal parts warming and terrifying. If Zandorn was dangerous enough to garner the gods' attention, what chance did Zak have of stopping him?

Tansil still owes me an explanation. Cerevita shouldn't have been able to appear, not with the Contract barring gods from the physical plane. The elf had promised to explain everything, and he was taking his time doing so.

In his reverie, Zak had almost made it to his session with Sorwin. A white stone wall gleamed while a dozen iron-banded plank doors hung in stark contrast, spaced a few yards apart. Behind each door was a closed training court, and as he crossed to the one with a golden seven nailed above its handle, dampened explosions and thudding emanated from nearby.

When he entered and closed the door, a bright purple and white shimmer raced across its surface as the sealing charm took hold. Everything outside the room fell away as if this was the only space in the world. Even after several weeks of daily training, the unnatural quiet still made Zak uncomfortable. Stacked stone walls stood on all four sides, and tidy grass ran the length of the room, crunching under his footsteps. There was no ceiling, leaving the room seemingly open to the sky, but a simple yet effective barrier domed the room, keeping spells or other projectiles in and any number of unwanted things out.

Sorwin perched on a smooth stone bench near the right wall, wearing a deep blue, iridescent velvet tunic draped over a silken white shirt. His brownish-gold hair was short, though it was longer now than when Zak first met the mage. It gave the subtlest hints of curls as it grew. Sorwin's jeweled belt and sword leaned against the wall beside him as he read from a thick book. An easy smile broke his focus as Zak approached.

"I was beginning to think you succumbed to a bit of test anxiety," Sorwin said, gently closing his book and setting it on the bench. "Ready for your exam?"

CHAPTER 2
PROGRESS

"Sorry, Sorwin. I had a run-in with Rauffe." Zak dropped his bag and dug out a day-old hunk of bread, stomach rumbling as he took a bite and again cursed his oversleeping. He had missed breakfast.

"Still giving you trouble? I could have a word with him or ask Tansil—"

"No," Zak said, more forceful than he intended. "Thank you. I can handle Rauffe." Being the *Nacusti* with a unique training arrangement was bad enough, and rumors still swirled through the Center about his sprouting scales and wings while fighting the Consortium. More attention and special treatment wouldn't help. The other acolytes and adepts already gave Zak a wide berth, unsure if he was friend or foe, mage or demon.

"As you say, Zakolor. Shall we?" Sorwin's eyes were kind—bright and attentive and curious. They often soothed Zak, even when there were plenty of things to be anxious about.

"I did have one thing to mention. I, er, had the dream

again last night." Zak pretended to adjust a few belongings in his bag.

"This is the third time, yes?"

"Yes. Nothing different, still a lot of darkness and fuzzy shapes. I saw a bird, I think."

A few silent moments hung in the air before Sorwin spoke. "Explore the dream with Shira today, and perhaps spend some time researching the bird the next time you sleep in the Archives."

Zak whipped around toward Sorwin. "How did you—"

Sorwin looked amused as he stood, pointing to the sky. "You're not the only one who has seen a bird recently."

Far above their heads, a hawk circled, making calculated dips with its wings to stay aloft in the air currents.

Of course, Zak thought.

Croi, Sorwin's familiar. She kept an eye on many things for Sorwin—Zak included—and she was frightfully good at it given how well-informed Sorwin always seemed to be. Croi also contributed significantly to Sorwin's nickname as the Hawk mage.

"I'll give it some thought," Zak conceded. He *had* been spending all his time researching Olivia's curse, and the last time he ignored one of his dreams, Kal was kidnapped. He didn't think it wise to do so again. He glanced at Croi. "When can I get a familiar? Is it difficult?"

Sorwin walked into position on the court. "It can be difficult or easy. That depends on you. A familiar is a bonded creature, one we make a pact with for life. They only respond to a mage that fully knows and accepts themselves. Can you say that you do?" His head tilted in curiosity.

"I...I'm not sure." The sudden depth of the question surprised him. Flashes of Kal's and Olivia's faces passed before his eyes, and the responsibility for their maladies weighed heavily on his shoulders. He tensed, feeling the edges of Jolsu's consciousness, and a surge of anger rushed through him.

"I think you have your answer, at least for now."

Zak's hands tightened into fists as he tried to release the images of his friends and his anger for Jolsu. He had a lot to do before he fully knew *or* accepted himself.

"Shall we begin?" Sorwin asked, bringing Zak's attention back to the matter at hand.

He moved, placing a few dozen paces between them. "Can you remind me one more time how this works?"

"Zandorn will likely continue to pursue you and your power. Therefore, our main goal is to continue your expedited education. Simply learning magic is not sufficient, we also need to learn *control* over our magic. That is why the League instituted certification exams. You'll recall that each magical house has ranks for its mages. Before ascending to the next rank, you'll need to pass the exam, just like every other mage in the League."

Just like every other mage, Zak thought. *Finally, a sense of normalcy.*

Hah! About as normal as a mountain goat sleeping in a dragon's nest. Your naivete is amusing, Parignis. Jolsu's thoughts poked into Zak's consciousness against his will.

He sneered as a wave of satisfaction emanated from the dragon. If he focused, Zak could shut Jolsu out, tucking him neatly away in the cave he crawled out from. But the more Zak's magic developed, the more difficult it became.

"...and since you're at the acolyte rank, we'll assess your control of fire and basic telekinetics today. Passing scores will advance you to adept. Are you ready?" Sorwin had continued his explanation, unaware of Zak and Jolsu's interaction.

Zak rolled his shoulders, shifted his weight, and nodded, almost as if physical movement could shake Jolsu from his thoughts. If only it were that simple.

"First, telekinetics. We're testing for accuracy and power." Sorwin snapped his fingers, and an arrow appeared in midair. Zak snatched it up without thinking. Confused, he looked at Sorwin, who now had an apple on his head and an uncharacteristically devious smile.

"This can't be the test," Zak said, catching on to Sorwin's idea. "There's no way Tansil approved shooting an apple off your head as a standard exam."

"Of course he didn't," Sorwin replied. "He also didn't prescribe my examination methods. I hold you to a bit of a different standard, Zak. You've already seen more conflict than the average acolyte, and what good is the skill of accuracy if you can't perform it under pressure?"

His eyes flicked between the apple and the arrow several times, considering his options. "What happens if I miss? I'll be responsible for killing one of the five Mageri!"

Sorwin waved dismissively as the apple wobbled. "Oh nonsense, you won't miss. And if you do, shouldn't a Mageri be able to handle it?"

Zak sighed. This unique exam was inevitable. Sorwin—to his credit—gave Zak plenty of autonomy whenever possible. But when a specific idea burrowed in his mind, Zak found it impossible to dissuade him, and this seemed like one of those moments.

"Right, well, try not to move too much?" Zak squared his shoulders and raised his right hand, letting the arrow lie flat in his palm. The wooden shaft was smooth and light. He barely felt it as he exhaled and reached for his magic, which met him effortlessly, and pulled the smallest amount to channel into the arrow. It floated, spinning to point straight at the apple. Zak held his breath, saying a silent prayer as his whole body went taut, like *he* was the bowstring.

Breath came first, then the twist of his wrist. The arrow shot through the air so fast the swish of the fletching was almost silent. In less than a second, the arrow crunched into the flesh of the apple, carrying it a few feet as it fell to the ground.

"Well done!" Sorwin cheered and clapped his hands. "You see? You're up to the challenge, and I knew you would be."

Zak leaned forward, resting on his knees. "I'm not convinced 'risk of shooting my magus in the eye' was the right challenge for an adept exam, but thanks all the same."

Sorwin chuckled and snapped his fingers again. The arrow and apple disappeared while a large boulder manifested in the middle of the court. "Accuracy achieved! Ready for power?"

"You really love exams, don't you?" This was Zak's first one as a mage, but it was obvious *Sorwin* was thoroughly enjoying himself.

"I love *learning*, Zakolor, and that includes facilitating learning for others. Do you not enjoy the merits of your progress?" His light and playful tone sounded as if he knew the answer to the question—or what it should be—but Zak thought they would have very different answers.

Zak gestured to the boulder. "What do I do with this? Roll it?"

"Oh no, that would be too easy. Please lift it," Sorwin said.

"What? Do you know how much that thing must weigh?" Zak's jaw hung open as he took in the enormity of the boulder. It was at least half the size of his house in Densba.

"I know exactly how much it weighs; I just conjured it, didn't I?" Sorwin walked around the boulder with the same playful smile, hands clasped behind his back.

"Fine." Zak was starting to find Sorwin's "love of learning" a touch annoying.

There was no possibility that lifting an object this size was part of the standard adept exam. He exhaled, breathing the thoughts away. As his magic heeded his call, he widened his stance and raised both arms.

Telekinesis was an exact magic. The further an object was from the mage, or the heavier the object, the more magic it took to move. There was a formula Sorwin taught Zak to calculate the amount of magic needed to move an object given distance and mass, but the calculations mystified him. *Kal would be excellent at this,* he thought.

Instead, Zak worked with intuition. He had a knack for

feeling out the right approach with magic. It had worked so far in his training, anyway. A grunt escaped as he pushed more magic through his hands toward the boulder, forehead prickling with tiny dots of sweat. A little more. The boulder lightened. Heat flooded his head and chest. He lifted his arms further with one final push. The boulder rose a few inches, hovered momentarily, and then fell with a thud. The ground shook, and Zak almost toppled from the vibrations.

"Another excellent mark—power achieved!" Sorwin patted the boulder like they were old friends before it disappeared. "Ready for the fire portion of the exam?"

"As long as there aren't more surprises." Zak wiped the sweat from his brow.

"You mean *creative examination choices*, Zakolor. And no, not for this part. Since all mages can use fire magic, all adepts—whether in the House of Elements, Temple of Light, or Den of Darkness—take the same standardized exam."

"Mages in the Temple and Den don't learn the other elements?"

Sorwin shook his head. "No, the Temple focuses on physical magic and the healing arts while the Den practice demonic summoning."

"What's physical magic?"

"Zakolor," Sorwin smiled. "I appreciate your sudden curiosity in the other magical houses, but perhaps we should return to your exam?"

"Uh—right." He hadn't meant to become distracted, but he hadn't learned much about the Temple or Den since arriving in Tor'alan.

"You can ask Bazil about the Temple and Shira about the Den if you'd like to learn more," Sorwin said. "Now, when it comes to fire, we test on four aspects to determine control: production, manipulation, destruction, and defense." Sorwin directed Zak back to the middle of the court now that the giant boulder was gone. "Produce a flame in your hand when you're ready to begin."

Telekinetics was not Zak's strength, but fire felt safe, easy. With barely a thought and a flourish, emerald flames appeared in his palm.

"Production achieved. Now for manipulation."

He followed Sorwin's instructions, some simple and a few odd. At first, they primarily focused on movement, like pushing the flames to cover just his right arm or hovering them in a ball exactly eleven-and-a-half paces away. They gradually became more abstract, like shaping the fire into his favorite meal or childhood home.

"You want me to make a self-portrait? With fire?" Zak exclaimed. "I thought you said this portion was standardized."

"It is," Sorwin said calmly. His brow furrowed. "Manipulation relies heavily on Thought as a casting mechanic. It is key to demonstrating mastery."

"Alright," Zak said, shifting his attention back to the flames. It was an uncomfortable exercise, picturing his own visage. He pulled a sliver of magic and projected it into the flames. They moved and danced into a rough representation of his face, though his nose pointed sideways and his hair stood straight on end. A glance at Sorwin told him it was not ideal, and he relinquished the effort as the image faded.

"Manipulation achieved, though definite room for improvement." Sorwin's previously giddy mood retreated into pensive consideration. "Destruction next."

With a wave of his hand, Sorwin conjured a square wooden box and a sculpture of a hawk that stood about waist height and looked like orange glass. "See if you can destroy the box and melt the statue. It is made of amber, so the melting point is not too high."

Zak ignited flames in both palms and engulfed the box in jets of green fire. In seconds, nothing remained except ash scattering on the overheated air current.

Without stopping, his flames covered the amber statue. It stood firm for almost a minute, then began slumping. The hawk feathers dripped like honey, and the head tipped forward in a slow, dramatic fall. After two more minutes, the sculpture was an orange and yellow puddle on the ground.

The tiniest twitch of a smirk danced at the corner of Sorwin's mouth. "Destruction achieved, which just leaves defense. Produce a shield when you're ready."

Easiest for last, Zak thought. He had proven to have quite the affinity for shields in his studies over the last few weeks—not to mention in his previous encounters with the Consortium. He gathered his magic and pushed both arms wide as he incanted: "*Tegoperignis.*"

A domed torrent of emerald flames erupted around him. It was perfect; the flames moved slowly, but not too slowly, in unison without any gaps. The surface was smooth, almost reflective like the polished metals Zak admired in his father's smithy as a child.

Sorwin lobbed conjured items and spells at the shield, testing its strength. A wooden cup disintegrated on impact, a sword deflected and bounced harmlessly to the ground, and even spears of water hissed before evaporating. Nothing pierced the shield or harmed it in the slightest.

"Defense achieved. You can release the spell," Sorwin instructed.

The emerald dome swirled out of existence as Zak released the flow of magic. He couldn't help but sigh with no small amount of relief now that the exam was over.

"Well, I believe you've been keeping track, but mostly top marks all around. It's my pleasure to officially recognize you as Adept Zakolor in the House of Elements." Sorwin approached, clapping him on the shoulder in congratulations with his usual, easy smile returned to his face. A small gesture with his hand brought a waterskin from the nearby bench flying through the air.

Zak caught it and gulped, the cool water quenching his thirst. "Thanks, Sorwin. You don't know how much this means to me." He was an adept! A jolt ran through him. He had almost forgotten the entire point of today amidst the chaotic morning. His dream of joining the League and ascending its ranks was finally coming true, yet a pang of guilt dampened his joy. "I'm sorry about asking so many questions in the exam. I think I was more nervous than I realized."

"I'd be surprised if you weren't nervous, truthfully," Sorwin said. "You should now have a good sense of what future element exams will entail. They all follow the four-part structure of testing production, manipulation, destruction, and defense. We'll also add more spells and charms to your education, so expect to demonstrate a wider array of magic in the future." He took a breath and paused before continuing. "To that end, I'll encourage you to revisit *A Mage's Manual for the Mechanics of Making Magic.* Millicent Murgood is the foremost authority on casting with Word, Guide, and Thought, and the mechanics will be increasingly important as you progress."

Zak bit his lip, recalling his miserable attempt at a self-portrait. "I'll give it a thorough reread," he said, handing the waterskin back to Sorwin. A thorough *first* read would have been more accurate, but he was sure he had at least skimmed the manual. Most likely.

They chatted for a few more minutes, Sorwin giving finer points of feedback and praise from the exam. Zak was as attentive as possible, asking clarifying questions when needed, though his thoughts kept wandering back to his dream. There was something odd about the bird and the clearing.

"Can I ask an unrelated question?"

"Of course, always," Sorwin replied, and Zak knew he meant it.

"Druids tend groves, right? Or, they used to? I know there aren't many left now, but what happened to their groves?"

Sorwin's face set in an expression that Zak was very familiar with, one that said, "We are about to have a historical-and-possibly-philosophical discussion."

His magus didn't disappoint. "They did tend groves, and some may still, though more covert than before Zandorn and the Consortium appeared. Groves without a Druid may survive if they are out of reach of the Rot."

Zak shuddered at the mention of the Rot. The curse still swept across Valecium, killing everything in its path, from the tiniest blades of grass to the most extensive forests. There had even been reports of towns and villages overrun, streets and houses crumbling into dust and darkness. The League hadn't yet found a way to remove the Rot or to prevent its spread.

"It's just, in my dream, it seemed like the bird was in a Druid grove, but everything was dead. I don't think it was the Rot because the bird was there and alive." The more Zak articulated his dream, the more confused he felt.

"Druids ensure that nature is balanced, so without them, a grove could die of natural causes. Perhaps researching Druid groves is an excellent candidate for your next Archives visit?"

Zak took the hint and conceded—again—to diversify his research. Even though Sorwin approved of his goal to help Olivia and Kal, he had made it clear Zak shouldn't spend all his time doing so. Sorwin was many things, and subtle was not one of them.

The talk of Druids spurred another question.

"What of Terasi? Have we found out where he's being held?" The memory of Renna—Zandorn's daughter—pulling the Druid into a portal and disappearing still haunted Zak. He was responsible for Terasi's capture, just like he was responsible for what befell Kal and Olivia.

Sorwin sat on the stone bench, tapping his knee with his fingertips. "No news yet. I'm afraid we'll only find him when we find Zandorn and the Consortium. We know they're hiding in the Wastelands, but we can't penetrate the Rot far enough to find them. They know its secrets, how to move safely through it, and we do not."

"How do we—" Zak started, but Sorwin cut him off.

"Look, Zak, I know you are concerned for Terasi, as you were for Kal when he was taken. I would prepare yourself in the event we cannot rescue Terasi."

His quick shift into stern pessimism threw Zak. It wasn't like Sorwin at all.

"We saved Kal," he countered. "We can save Terasi if we figure out how to fight the Rot."

"We're trying, Zak. We've been trying for decades since the spread began in earnest. Research is slow, and we're working with a substance that has no known precedent and destroys magic at the slightest touch."

"What about portals, then? Zandorn figured those out, too. Have we? Couldn't we make a portal and avoid the Rot altogether?" He wasn't used to Sorwin resisting ideas—quite the opposite; he normally encouraged them.

"We're also working on portal magic and closer on that front. Tansil and I have made some progress in the last few months."

Some progress. He crossed his arms and huffed. "It seems Zandorn is ahead of us at every turn."

"Yes, he rather is. One of the difficulties of opposing a genius, I suppose." Sorwin's posture sagged forward, and his gaze cast downward, looking somehow fixed and distant.

Zak shifted his weight, uncomfortable with his thoughtlessness. Who was he to judge Sorwin, Tansil, and the

League? They were doing everything they could to fight Zandorn—they had been for years, and in Tansil's case, for over a century.

"Sorwin, I'm sorry. I didn't mean to...I'm sure we'll figure it out soon." He offered a supportive clap on Sorwin's shoulder, much like the one he received minutes ago.

His magus nodded and lifted from his deep contemplation. "We will. In the meantime, perhaps we attend what remains within our control. We've used the Firepost charm to exchange letters locally. I think it is time for you to send one a bit further." With a flourish, Sorwin plucked parchment out of the air and handed it to Zak. It was blank except for a few lines at the top:

Isle of Carshandyn
Densba
Blacksmith Forge
Ageric and Clairise Keldin

"My parents..." Something within him tightened as their inked names glistened beneath his touch. "Can a Firepost go that far? All the way to Densba?"

"Of course! With the help of a Fire Post," Sorwin said matter-of-factly.

"What?" Isn't this a Firepost?" he asked, waving the blank letter back and forth.

"Ah yes, words," Sorwin nodded with understanding. "This," he continued, flicking the parchment, "is a *Firepost*, a colloquialism for a letter due to its means of delivery. Now, if we look up there." He guided Zak by the shoulders, shuffling to the middle of the court and pointed over the stone wall. From there, Zak saw the top third of several towers in the Center. High atop one of them was a tall iron pole. "We can see its namesake, the Fire *Post*."

They watched, and within a minute, a small flame streaked through the sky and collided with the post, encasing it in bright red flames. The fire blinked out as suddenly as it appeared, and a breath later the same tiny flame soared away in a different direction.

"One of the early needs after the League formed was for more efficient and long-distance communication. Hence, the Fire Post was created. Posts, technically. They are scattered throughout Valecium, directing letters to and from nearly anyone. The charm is very simple, so even untrained individuals can use it with a descriptive location, incantation, and a spark of magic. After you write your letter, use the charm and it will find its way to your parents in Densba."

"I will, thank you, Sorwin." He smiled. Magic filled him with awe like a child at their first Year Festival. The depth and breadth of magic, the sheer delight it inspired, never traveled to his remote hometown of Densba. They did not need letters or Fire Posts, and no one was knowledgeable enough about magic even to know they existed. And that worked for Densba, beautiful in its simplicity, but since glimpsing the wider world and all its splendor, Zak hungered for more magic, more knowledge, more wonder.

And thank Cerevita for that, because he had much more to learn if he hoped to stop Zandorn and the Consortium.

As he tucked the letter into his bag for later, a loud *crack* boomed like thunder. Zak looked to the door, familiar with the alarming sound of the sealing charm on the court breaking. Kaleb, Bazil, and Olivia entered.

It was time for midday lessons.

Chapter 3

CALL AND RESPONSE

There was always a moment when Zak felt light and dizzy when he saw Olivia, like he could float away with the slightest breeze. Her auburn curls were fastened with a leather tie, and the red and silver elementalist uniform fitted to her every movement. After the battle with the Consortium, Olivia no longer attended the general training sessions since she couldn't use magic without draining her life. Many didn't know of the *vitaligo*, but it became apparent *something* happened. Whispers wondered if she still qualified as a mage. However, once her physical injuries recovered, she wore the uniform every day, and no one had openly questioned her status.

Zak smiled, proud of her for sending a clear message without uttering a word.

It faded as Olivia neared. She fixed her gaze on Sorwin, pretending Zak didn't exist—a strategy which began soon after Karazul almost killed her and Jolsu performed the binding. It was almost impressive how she avoided him in close quarters for weeks.

Impressive, and frustrating.

Try as he might, only a few of his words found her ears in recent weeks. How could he apologize again or share his determination to find a cure when she barely even looked at him? *I guess I should worry about actually* finding *a cure first,* he thought.

Unlikely that will happen, Jolsu jabbed.

A frustrated grunt escaped him as Olivia, Bazil, and Kaleb deposited gear and prepared for Zak's midday session: weapons, combat, and strategy.

"Prince Sorwin, Acolyte Zakolor," Kaleb said in his quiet yet authoritative voice. He turned to them after adjusting a staff, spear, and bow to lean against the stone wall. There was no outward trace of his injuries from the battle with the Consortium mere weeks ago.

"It is *Adept* Zakolor as of a few moments ago. And please, Kaleb, just 'Sorwin' is preferred, as I've said before." Sorwin turned a bright pink, as he did whenever Kaleb was near.

"Ah—congratulations, Zakolor." Kaleb's dark eyes met Sorwin's. "Apologies, my training ingrained formality into my every thought." Zak figured this must be true as he couldn't tell if Kaleb felt much of anything beyond the rigid devotion he gave to the League.

"Was it *really* the training? I thought perhaps you were born with a uniform," Sorwin quipped.

"All right, then?" Bazil asked, interrupting Zak's eavesdropping. The priest tied jet-black braids behind his head.

"You passed?"

"Top marks, according to Sorwin," he said with a toothy grin. "Well, mostly top marks."

"The fire portrait get you?"

"The fire portrait got me."

"Eh, that's normal," Bazil said with a casual wave. "At the adept rank, you're not supposed to be skilled with Thought casting. You should have seen mine. It looked like a sad horse."

Zak recounted some of the highlights of his exam as Bazil listened. Out of the corner of his eye, he thought Olivia's expression changed a few times as if she listened too, but whenever he glanced, her attention wandered around the court, searching for something interesting to study.

As Kaleb broke away from his conversation with Sorwin and rounded them up to begin, the *crack* of the court door sounded once again. The High King's advisor, Limba Dar, poked his thin face and hooked nose around the edge of the door, clearing his throat before he spoke.

"Magerus Sorwin, Major Deidaku, good day," he said with a nod to Sorwin and Kaleb. "My apologies for the interruption. High King Marius has called the council meeting early today regarding an urgent matter. He'd like you both to attend, along with the *Nacusti*."

Zak scowled, and he didn't try to hide it. Limba Dar had cornered him more than once during the last few weeks, and the encounters always involved long-winded descriptions of the state of the League and how much High King Marius would benefit from his overt support. He didn't want to be used as a political game piece and started avoiding the man with moderate success, changing his routes and patterns through the Center as much as his schedule would allow. Yet Limba Dar always devised new ways to track him down. Playing the role of messenger seemed to be his tactic today.

"Why?" Sorwin asked in a sharp tone. The advisor was one of the only people Zak knew Sorwin to be openly rude to.

Limba Dar's head continued to hover at the edge of the door as he cleared his throat again with a phlegmy cough. "The matter is quite urgent, you see. The High King requested you three specifically."

Sorwin's eyes flicked to Zak and Kaleb, and his shoulders dropped slightly. "Fine. We'll be right along."

"I was told to bring you to the council chambers immediately," Limba Dar insisted.

"Fine!" Sorwin yelled. He gathered his things from the bench and stomped toward the court door.

Zak shouldered his bag and followed Sorwin—with less emphasis on his annoyance. Kaleb's footsteps were close behind him.

"Oh, and Olivia, Euphemius would like you to come as well," Limba Dar said, offering one last directive.

Olivia pushed off the wall she had been leaning against, falling into step with the small group.

Zak wanted to turn around and talk to her, to ask if Euphemius had been honoring his agreement to sponsor her, especially without her magic. He wanted to ask how she felt, if she could ever forgive him, or to tell her about his research on a cure. Heat rushed through him at the thought of facing her now, empty-handed, and decided it was better to wait until he *had* something to share.

"Guess I'll be on my way, then," Bazil grumbled. He was apparently not invited to the council meeting, and though he may have felt left out, Zak thought he had the better end of the arrangement.

As Limba Dar led the small group through the pristine pathways of the Center, his pace slowed, so he walked next to Zak. The tall man attempted a smile, his grin crooked and forced as if the movement physically pained him. "Good day, *Nacusti*. How is your education progressing? I heard you had the adept exam today. How did it go?"

"Fine." Zak took Sorwin's approach, giving Limba Dar as little as possible in hopes of ending the conversation sooner.

"Oh good! Good. That means you passed. Well, congratulations are in order. Perhaps I'll organize a small gathering to celebrate. I know High King Marius would *love* to show his appreciation for your dedication to your studies and—"

"No thanks."

Limba Dar looked surprised for half a second, but recovered his composure just as fast, trying another painful smile. "Oh, come now, *Nacusti*, our successes should be honored. Think of what good could come from you and the High King sharing a meal with select officials and dignitaries."

"I'm not interested," he said. "If the High King needs me, he can summon me like he's doing right now."

"His Majesty *can* do that. I think he would prefer that you *want* to support the League."

"That's enough, Limba Dar." Sorwin turned with a glare

that made the thin man bristle. "He said no. And his very presence here means he *is* supporting the League."

Limba Dar gave a single, deferential nod to Sorwin. "Yes, my apologies, Magerus. The *Nacusti* is, of course, entitled to decline offers of mutual benefit."

Zak would have laughed hearing Limba Dar's prickly voice lose its fake cheeriness, but it was unsettling how easily a venomous tone replaced the niceties. Before he or Sorwin could react, Limba Dar continued.

"Let's not keep them waiting."

At the Center's castle entrance, the stalwart doors parted as mages moved as if pulling invisible ropes. A cool breeze rushed from inside as Zak crossed the threshold, a refreshing change from the warm Autumn air. Footsteps echoed in the vestibule as the group filed straight into the council chamber.

He had been in the large room several times in the last month, summoned for the odd meeting appearance. The paintings and tapestries cluttering the walls were becoming more familiar—most presented capital cities and notable landmarks of each country in the League of Kingdoms. Sorwin advised him to learn their names and histories as much as possible.

Being the *Nacusti* seemed to have a few responsibilities beyond destroying the Consortium.

What names did he remember? *Regadensia, Darlangson, the Republic of Evartia*, he thought. There was one more...

He racked his memory as he approached the octagonal table, intricate carvings smaller than a thumbnail danced through the wooden grain. One high-backed chair occupied each of the eight points in the table, flanked by two smaller ones. Tansil sat in one of the large chairs, and Zak took the small one to his left. Sorwin should have taken one of the oversized chairs to represent Darlangson on the council, but he always claimed the small one at Tansil's right.

The rest of the council members shuffled into their seats, and Zak shifted his silent memory game to recall their names before the official attendance was recorded. He was surprised he remembered more names than he expected.

He knew Euphemius Van Ilia, of course. He was Olivia's sponsor and one of the League's wealthiest independent benefactors. His short stature made it look like his salt-and-pepper mustache formed a seam with the table's edge when he sat.

There was Archalium Vermig, leader of the Den of Darkness. His shapely brown beard contrasted with his plump bearing. He spoke with fervor to General Lupa, who stood next to him.

Further down the table, Archlumen Sashina was silent, her gaze far away as she absently twirled one of the rings on her hand. She led the Temple of Light. Bazil didn't speak of her much, but Zak was getting to know her a little as she oversaw his weekly visits with Kal. She was a renowned healer, and if anyone had a chance to understand Kal's affliction, it was her.

An attendant called the meeting to order. Leaders of the four countries, the three magical houses, armies, and industry all sat as one around the sizeable octagonal table. Zak silently scolded himself for names he couldn't recall as each attendee identified themself for the official record.

"Thank you all for coming with haste, yet again," High King Marius began in his trembling tenor. Urgent council meetings were becoming a regular occurrence since Zak arrived in Tor'alan. Tansil *did* predict his presence would accelerate the conflict between the League and Consortium. So far, that prediction held true.

Limba Dar stood behind Marius, leaning to whisper in his ear. The High King nodded as he listened before addressing the council again.

"As King of Regadensia and High King of the League of Kingdoms, I call this meeting to order. You'll notice that we are missing a few key council members. That is part of our urgency today. We'll get to that in a moment. First, I'd like to tie up one lingering matter." He tapped a stack of parchment on the table. "We finally have all the accounts and reports from the skirmish between the *Nacusti*, a Druid, the League, and the Consortium."

Zak's stomach clenched, thinking he had heard the last of this encounter. Where was the High King going with this?

"At this point, everyone here is privy to most of the events that transpired that day. However, after a thorough search of the area where the Consortium ambushed Zakolor and the Druid, our mages found something. A small bronze lizard encased in a rather advanced shield spell. After initial testing, we believe the magic is the work of the Druid."

Marius' eyes focused on Zak, and the rest of the council did the same. The collar of his uniform tightened around his neck.

"Zakolor, you detailed a conversation with the Druid in

your report. Did he mention this lizard to you? What it is, or why he protected it so thoroughly?"

Was it his imagination, or was Marius more confident than usual?

"He, um, didn't mention the lizard. We had little time to talk before Burvenin and Karazul attacked."

"I see." Marius leaned toward another whisper from Limba Dar. Zak thought he heard Sorwin scoff. "Well, we had the lizard moved to your office, Tansil, as you're the most familiar with Druidic magic. Perhaps you can learn more about the spell and the creature."

"I will share my findings as they occur," Tansil said.

Zak exhaled as the subject seemed resolved.

"On to the more pressing matter for today," Marius said. "It is obvious we are missing two important council members." He motioned across the table to two vacant, high-backed chairs. "King Gyrnavo of Weslinton and Minister Jeppida Qor of the Republic of Evartia."

Weslinton! Zak silently recognized the name of the country he had forgotten. His excitement was temporary as nervous glances and whispers spread around the large table. Even Zak knew it was irregular for the council to convene without representatives of all four member countries of the League.

Marius thudded his mallet on the table to hush the murmur of questions. "I'll ask you all to give Limba Dar your full attention as he explains the situation, and then we'll discuss what may be done."

Limba Dar gestured to an attendant standing guard near the chamber wall, a young man in the blue and orange livery of Regadensia. He scurried to Limba Dar's side, and the advisor leaned over the back of the High King's chair, spitting instructions.

The young man nodded and walked to an open space on the table, pulled a parchment from a stiff cloth pouch on his belt, and pressed its edges into the table. As he leaned on the parchment, he uttered an incantation Zak couldn't hear. In the middle of the hollow table, tiny grains of sand and beads of water manifested in midair, swirling and darting around as if they had somewhere specific to be. They collected, forming the likeness of a riverbank with one city on either side. The sand and water vibrated and flowed, a living, miniature landscape hanging in the air.

"The Karanadee River," Limba Dar said in his grating voice, gesturing to the map, "serves as the border between Evartia and Weslinton. The two cities of Janlaka and Masdaan have enjoyed close ties for thousands of years." Limba Dar stalked around the table as if he were delivering a history lesson to children.

Zak resisted rolling his eyes. The scheming man clearly enjoyed the spectacle.

"Janlaka and Masdaan grew together over the centuries, trading resources and sharing the fishing rights in the Karanadee. Now, it seems the previously plentiful fish population is dwindling. As the remaining schools migrate up and down the river, they swim in and out of each city's territories. Representatives from Janlaka and Masdaan lodged complaints that their territory was invaded by the other, and the situation escalated to King Gyrnavo and Minister Qor.

Hence, they both left Tor'alan to resolve the matter."

"That doesn't explain why we are hearing about it now." Sashina tracked Limba Dar's circular path around the room.

"Quite right, Archlumen," he replied. "King Gyrnavo and Minister Qor entered negotiations with the best intentions, my informants tell me, yet they could not come to an arrangement that suited both parties. In fact, it seems negotiations devolved into shouting, by all accounts, and both leaders sent separate Fireposts calling for the intervention of this council."

"Fishing rights?" Vermig sneered. "We're discussing *fishing rights*? This must be a joke, King Marius." He directed his frustration to the seated noble.

"*High* King Marius," Limba Dar corrected, "is well aware this matter seems trivial, yet it is deeper than you realize."

"Unless these fish can clear the Rot and fight the Consortium, we can't waste time on 'em," General Lupa said, thick arms crossed over his chest. "We lost half a regiment not two days ago to some new beasts Zandorn cooked up."

Limba Dar's face scrunched tighter as control of his temper loosened with each interruption. "We are aware of Zandorn's new tactics and are working with the Temple, House, and Den to address the matter. We'll have even more resources if we solve this disagreement between Evartia and Weslinton. They are two of the four countries that comprise the League of Kingdoms. We cannot afford infighting amongst ourselves; it only strengthens Zandorn and the Consortium."

Zak exhaled, overwhelmed as more suggestions and questions were lobbed with increasing ferocity. He squirmed in his seat, remembering Tansil and Sorwin's belief in his ability to unite the League. How could he rally countries, mages, soldiers, and merchants together when their leaders couldn't agree on a simple thing like fishing rights?

"Send a representative of the League to mediate the negotiations," Euphemius said, his tall hat bobbing as he spoke. "This matter doesn't require more time from this council than has already been given."

"Those were my thoughts, too," Marius said, finally chiming in. "Who would be an ideal candidate to negotiate?"

"If I may, High King," Limba Dar started with his crooked smile. "Less than a year ago, Evartia became a republic after their revolution, and it has raised a few concerns. Minister Qor's predecessors, Queen Ymona and King Yuri—who used to sit on this council—weren't the most vehement of League supporters. That is certainly no secret. Yet they upheld the League's required monetary and supply donations and regularly scouted for new mages and soldiers. And when Minister Qor assumed the mantle of power, there were no donations for the first six months, and they've been inconsistent since.

"Before you say it," Limba Dar held up a hand, calling for continued silence, "of course, a fledgling nation bruised from civil war would need allowances and time to recover. But a full year on, and now they are embroiled in this fiasco with Weslinton when they can ill afford another battering. What should we expect from them? What if this situation worsens? What if they decide they *cannot* resume donations and begin to pull away from the League entirely?"

A cacophony of protests and outrage sounded from all sides of the council table. Zak almost covered his ears to dampen the noise, but resisted to catch snippets of the arguments railing against Limba Dar's audacity.

"How *dare* you accuse Minister Qor of treason?"

"On what grounds, Sir?"

"...hasn't provided a shred of evidence!"

The council collectively seemed to dislike Limba Dar as much as Zak and Sorwin did. Maybe there was some hope these leaders would agree on *something*.

Marius whacked his mallet on the table for half a minute before the room quieted again, his face ashen as he cleared his throat. "Limba Dar, what prompted this belief, or concern, as you name it, that Evartia may leave the League?"

"It is a concern for now, High King, and should not be taken lightly. Look around. Are we not absent two leaders? Are we not seeing the effects of erosion already? I suggest the League and Your Majesty take this opportunity to show strength. Demonstrate to all Valecium and Zandorn that no cracks threaten the foundation of the League."

"How would you have me do this?" Marius asked.

Limba Dar smiled, a predator ensaring his prey, and Zak was nauseous at the sight. "Move Tor'alan near Masdaan and Janlaka so this council may mediate the negotiations. If we succeed, this council will be stronger and more united than ever."

"Your Majesty, I must object," Tansil said in his steady voice. "We have dozens of mages and several regiments in the field at this very moment. Moving Tor'alan will leave them vulnerable and compromise their current orders." More than a few council members nodded and agreed with Tansil's assessment.

"There are other fortifications within the League, Archmagus," Limba Dar said. "Our forces may be redirected with a few simple Fireposts. Tor'alan is a symbol, and its power is needed in the east to preserve the future of the League."

Marius nodded as his thoughts seemed to connect. "General Lupa, redirect our soldiers in the field to check in at the nearest fort, village, or city as necessary. And have a security assessment conducted on Masdaan; it is closer than Janlaka, so we will make our way there for now. Limba Dar, send word to King Gyrnavo and Minister Qor that this council will mediate their disagreement personally." He cleared his throat, and Zak again noticed an unusual confidence in Marius, one that grew with each decision and order he gave. "Everyone else, make any preparations needed. Tor'alan moves in two days." The High King gave his gavel a final *whack*, adjourning the meeting.

CHAPTER 4

SIGHT

Mutterings and grumbles accompanied the nearly two dozen council members and attendants that rose from the octagonal table. Some lingered in the grand room, others hurried away, but all shared hushed opinions on the High King's decision. The Archs congregated a few paces from the table, and Zak overheard their conversation as he followed Sorwin toward them.

"Baltenebris blast him, Tansil! Marius is a puppet, and you know it," Vermig bellowed, his face reddened with frustration. "He may as well sign a mountain of death notices now and send them to the families of our mages and soldiers."

"Easy, Vermig," Sashina said, smoothing the sleeves of her lilac robes. "You speak treason and have too little faith in our forces. They'll make the best of this, and it is our responsibility to guide them forward."

"I agree, and so should you, Archalium Vermig," Tansil said. "Tor'alan moving far to the east is not ideal for any of us, but the High King made his decision."

"Did he?" Sorwin interjected. "It sounded like Limba

Dar making decisions for the High King."

"You see!" Vermig raised his voice again, wagging a finger at Tansil. "Even your apprentice agrees with me."

"And what of your thoughts on the matter, *Nacusti*?" Sashina asked. Her expression was neutral as she shifted her attention to Zak, yet her eyes seemed to search for something.

"I...thoughts on what, exactly?" He wasn't expecting to participate in the conversation.

"We all agree that Tor'alan moving east puts our forces at risk. What opinion would you have voiced in our meeting, had you the chance?" Sashina rephrased, and all three of the Archs and Sorwin looked to him, waiting for an answer.

"Well..." His mind raced. Why did this singular question feel more intense than his entire adept exam? He tried thinking like Kal. His friend would analyze the situation first. "It sounds like a question of priority, doesn't it? Is the disagreement between two countries and their leaders more important than the lives of League forces? And is the response from the council equal to the priority?" His heart beat in his throat as he spoke.

A small smile found Sashina's face. "Well-reasoned, *Nacusti*. A wise leader asks many questions."

Zak dipped his head in a grateful bow, his pulse slowing to a more reasonable rate. The Archs and Sorwin shifted the conversation into preparations for Tor'alan's move. He paid as much attention as possible. Sashina's question proved that the League was looking for him to step into a role of some kind, though it seemed they weren't sure exactly what they wanted from him. All he could do was learn from the examples of those he admired, like Kal, Sorwin, Tansil, and Sashina. Would that be enough? Would he ever be what the League needed him to be?

"*Nacusti*," a firm voice interrupted Zak's contemplation. He turned to see Euphemius with Olivia a step behind, looking anxious.

"Mr. Van Ilia." Zak greeted the man, unsure what to say. He didn't have long to think as Euphemius continued.

"You're responsible for Olivia's condition, aren't you?" he stated more than asked.

Ambushed again, Zak thought. He was unprepared to have his guilt lobbed somewhat casually into his face. "I am," he answered in as steady a voice as he could muster. His gaze moved to Olivia. "I'm responsible, and I'm so sorry." Her eyes didn't meet his, but at least she heard him this time.

"'Sorry' does nothing for me, *Nacusti*." Euphemius' mustache twitched. "But I am a reasonable man. Since you damaged my investment, I'll let you pay for my lost value."

"Damaged your—what? Olivia's a *person*, not an investment!" He shouted at the short man, heat flooding his veins.

Euphemius remained unmoved, his hands resting on a dark-varnished cane before him. "My contract for her sponsorship would disagree."

"What's going on here?" Sorwin asked. He had drifted over when Zak shouted.

"I am due compensation for damages wrought, Magerus. Olivia is sponsored based on her status as an exceptional mage. Now, because of the binding, she cannot perform magic without draining her life. I've come to collect from the perpetrator of said binding." Euphemius gestured to Zak with the tip of his cane.

Zak spun. "He called her an *investment*, Sorwin! She's not a *thing*!"

Sorwin hesitated but remained poised as he patted Zak with a comforting hand and eyed the short merchant. "What are you asking for, Euphemius?"

"Olivia's contract is clear: services are to be rendered through the end of this year. Approximately 2.3 Gold Marks in service value remain between now and the Year Festival. So, *Nacusti*, how shall you be paying? Monthly, or in one lump sum?" Euphemius asked without a hint of sarcasm.

Zak fumbled as he tried to think and speak at the same time. "That's...over two hundred Silver Marks!" he exclaimed. "I don't have that kind of money." He barely had ten Silver Marks to his name. Between buying supplies and sending some wages home to his parents, he hadn't saved much yet. Even with his promotion to adept, he'd only make two Silver Marks a week.

"I was afraid of that, truth be told." Euphemius sighed, his eyes narrowed, and he seemed to fight a smile. "In the absence of payment, service transfer is the other option. You could fulfill Olivia's duties for the remainder of the contract."

"You mean, work for you?" Zak clarified.

"Precisely," Euphemius confirmed.

"Zakolor," Sorwin said. "I know you have refused money in the past, but let me front the cost for the contract. You can pay me back over time if you want and—"

"No," Zak said. He looked at Olivia, and this time, she

returned his determined gaze with her nervous one. "Thank you, Sorwin. This is something I'm responsible for and something I have to fix."

Even though Zak didn't perform the binding himself—Jolsu did—the dragon was part of him whether he liked it or not. And that meant he was responsible for the *vitaligo*. He had heard stories from Olivia about Euphemius' short temper, demanding orders, and callous nature. He knew how hard it would be to work for the merchant. Maybe this was what he deserved, what could earn him penance.

"Excellent," Euphemius said, no longer resisting a smile as nearly all his teeth were visible under his salt-and-pepper mustache. Zak had a feeling this was the outcome the man wanted from the beginning. "I'll have the transfer of services drafted and sent for your signature. Every Fivesday afternoon, you'll work for me." The merchant tipped his oversized hat, turned on his heel, and strutted away, a triumphant gait accentuated by the *tap* of his cane each time it struck the floor.

"You're a fool," Olivia hissed as she passed.

"Maybe, maybe not," Zak said under his breath.

After all, those were the first words Olivia had spoken to him in weeks.

Zak hurried through the cobblestone streets of Tor'alan toward the Market district. The afternoon was warm, and sweet scents of freshly baked pies and mulled ciders floated on a crisp breeze. The Autumnal Equinox was a few days away, and the city buzzed with preparations.

It was an important holiday for the House of Elements which represented life, the balancing force between light and dark. Red banners with half-suns and half-moons waved from magelight posts lining the streets. Above, balconies overlooking the streets were dressed in garlands of leaves and late-blooming flowers, adding vibrant red, orange, and yellow hues to the city.

Flyers posted on shop windows and notice boards advertised contests—many asking for feats like running with an egg on a spoon or walking across narrow beams and tightropes. It sounded more extravagant than any celebrations in Densba, and Zak hoped he would have time to enjoy the festivities.

Sidestepping a cart laden with fresh produce from the Farm district, he kept a fast pace, partly due to his lateness for Sight lessons and partly because of his frustration.

He knew working for Euphemius was a terrible idea. If half the stories Olivia had told him were true, it was only a matter of time until he provoked Euphemius' notorious temper. He hadn't even made it through their conversation minutes ago without his own temper getting riled.

You do *keep things interesting, Nacusti. I'll give you that,* Jolsu jeered. *I wonder how long you'll last with the little merchant?*

Zak could almost hear his fanged smile. *It's something I have to do to make up for what* you *did, wyrm.* He was more impatient with Jolsu's incessant quips than usual.

A smile washed his annoyance away, darting down an alley. Not long ago, he had wandered aimlessly through the well-organized streets because in Tor'alan, all directions were meaningless—the traditional ones, anyway. In an ordinary city, buildings and streets had specific—and generally unchanging—relationships with north, south, east, and west. Where the sun rose and the stars glittered was constant, predictable. But in a floating city that may move or turn in any direction at any moment, navigating was a unique challenge. What was east today could be west tomorrow.

Two fixed points—the entrance portal and the Center—served as directional anchors. The Market district was *foreboard*, meaning if standing on the entrance portal, it was toward the Center and to the right. The Artisan district was *aftport*, away from the Center and to the left. It was a tricky mindset to adopt at first, but Zak's time on the *Swift Star* learning nautical language had helped some.

The alley spit him onto the main road and with a quick left after that, Zak arrived at a three-story brick building. He pushed through a door next to a glass shopfront with dozens of herbs, balms, and poultices on display. Taking the stairs two at a time, he arrived at the second floor, rapped on the door, and entered as it swung open.

The room beyond was dark. Filtered sunlight fought through layers of heavy curtains covering every inch of the windows overlooking the street below. Plush pillows and cushions, woven tapestries, and a mixture of simple and intricately detailed wooden furniture filled the rest of the small sitting room. A low flame heated a kettle in the brick hearth on the opposite wall, adding a cozy warmth. Shira sat beside it in an overstuffed armchair, pushing a needle through a pile of fabric.

"You're late," Shira said in a sing-songy voice without looking up from her work.

"When did you know I would be?" he asked, crossing the room to sit on a couch upholstered in a startling purple.

"A few minutes ago. I saw you almost run into that vegetable cart." Shira winked at him over spectacles that danced with the fire's reflection.

They had started this game a few weeks ago. In the first lesson, Shira explained that Sight was a rare gift, and unique as the mage that wielded it. She demonstrated her Sight by predicting a few questions Zak wanted to ask, pointing out where a bird would land on the windowsill two minutes before it happened, and handing him a napkin right before he spilled his tea. She called her gift Near Sight, viewing things that occurred within the next few seconds or minutes. "On a good day, I can see as far as ten to fifteen minutes," she had said.

"That never gets old." Zak grinned, envying her clarity and control. He never saw anything while awake, and struggled nightly with blurry birds in dark forests.

"You'll see much more than me in time," she said. With a wave of her hand, the kettle hanging over the fire floated to the low table between them and poured near-boiling water into two prepared mugs with small metal strainers. The clear water darkened as it swirled through the herbs, the rising tufts of steam pulling vibrant flavors and aromas into the air. Shira always had the best tea.

"Maybe I'll see further. I don't know about more." He

had what Shira called Far Sight, seeing several weeks into the future. Or at least, there were several weeks between his first dreams foretelling Burvenin's arrival and his kidnapping of Kal. That was the only timeline he had to judge from.

Until now.

"I started seeing something," Zak said. Three days had passed since he first saw the bird. How many weeks did he have until the dream of the future became the present?

"I heard, Sorwin told me." She gestured vaguely to assorted Fireposts on the table. A strand of Shira's dark hair slipped from the haphazard bun on her head, and she tucked it behind her ear. "A bird in a tree? Shall we try to see more?"

Perhaps he should have been annoyed that Sorwin kept close advisors in Zak's life updated on many happenings, even when he instructed Zak to deliver messages (hadn't Sorwin *just* asked him that morning to tell Shira about his dream?). Instead, he gave a silent thanks to his magus for staying a step ahead when he needed him the most.

He nodded his assent and closed his eyes. Zak's magic practically vibrated at his fingertips, eager to be put to purpose. Shira found hers across from him. It sprung to life as a bright purple light in his mind.

As their energies met, things became complicated. Their Sight was very different, which made the partnered readings they attempted difficult. Shira was the only other Sight mage in Tor'alan, so he had no choice in a teacher—and he wouldn't want anyone else anyway.

He tried explaining the exercise to Kal once while visiting him in the healing wards. "Imagine steadying a telescope for someone, twisting the dials while they peer through the lens, hoping to view a faraway object you can't see." It wasn't an accurate description, but it was the best he had come up with.

Shira's Near Sight cleared his mind, as visible as the mug of tea before him. But it didn't extend much further. He pushed against its boundaries, trying to expand Shira's clarity with the range of his Far Sight. It was stubborn today, unmoving. The best result was a week ago when they foresaw Limba Dar trying to corner him in the Center on his way to his room. It was an hour into the future. With the forewarning, Zak took a circuitous route back to the Dormitory that night.

It was exciting progress, but it wasn't enough. Zak didn't have time to see so little of time.

He shifted in his seat, the heat from the hearth thickening the air as the minutes ticked by. *Why is this so hard?* The bird from his dream hovered far off in the distance, waiting for him. Why couldn't he move *closer* to it? Maybe if he actually had a telescope, he could at least see it.

And then it was all so simple, so obvious.

"Shira, can we try something?" he asked, eyes still closed.

"By all means." She sounded calm but a little deflated. At the start of their lessons, she admitted this was an experiment for her as much as it was for him. Sight mages were so rare she hadn't had the chance to try partnered readings before. They were both working on instinct.

"Instead of expanding your Sight, what if you focused mine?" He concentrated on the image of the bird with everything he had. His whole body shook with the effort, imagining he was seeing it through the end of a telescope, blurry, distant. The bird may have been far, but the telescope was near, right in front of him.

"What about this?" he asked. "Can you see it?"

"Oh!" she exclaimed. "You clever little adept! That *is* a bird." Her Sight narrowed to the telescope, the image coming in and out of focus.

It wasn't the same as his dream. It didn't feel like he was there, hiding in the bushes, cold nipping at his skin. But with Shira's help, the one image he recalled became clear as glass.

Resting in one of the many twisted branches of an ancient tree was indeed a bird. Its black feathers were darker than the scarcely lit foliage behind it, and two small, ribbed horns emerged above blue eyes, curving into sharp points behind its head.

Zak studied the bird and the tree, committing every detail to memory before withdrawing from the connection. When he opened his eyes, Shira handed him a cloth and his mug. He dabbed his sweaty brow before sipping the clove and ginger tea.

"We did it! We *actually* did it!" He celebrated, bouncing up and down on the purple couch. He reined in his excitement after nearly spilling his tea.

"That we did, Zakolor!" Shira mirrored his delight with a broad smile and hearty chuckle. "Three Fires, I was starting to wonder if we'd ever see further than an hour. Where'd you get the idea for the telescope?"

"It was how I tried describing our readings to Kal once. And today, when we finally had a specific image to focus on, I thought it would be helpful to have a telescope. So I thought, 'Why don't we?'" His grin stretched to his ears.

"Why don't we, indeed!" Shira raised her mug in cheers and took a deep swig of the herbal brew. She let out a contented sigh before speaking again. "Though I can't say I'll be much help now, I don't recognize the bird or the tree. Do you?"

"Not yet," Zak said. "But I was already planning to research them in the Archives. Now I have a lot more to go on."

"I should think so. Not many horned birds come to mind." She sat for a minute with a contemplative look. Then Shira placed her mug on the table and rocked in her armchair as her hands dug into several pockets in her robes, searching for something. She produced a small, blue orb with swirling dots of colors. Greys, yellows, reds, blacks, and others swam inside the glowing surface. A single yellow dot followed her finger as she dragged it around the orb. After circling several times, she yanked it free, pointed to the floor, and yelled, "Ubba, *daematerial*!"

A jet of purple smoke surged, dissipating to reveal a small, rodent-like creature with leathery wings. Its beady eyes darted around the room before the creature sneezed three times. When he recovered, he flapped to Shira's shoulder, gently nudging her and rubbing his nose between two paws.

Zak jumped, startled at Ubba's sudden appearance. "So that's how you call them, your demons?" He had seen the tiny imp before but hadn't witnessed a summoning.

"Oh, yes," she answered, holding up the blue stone. "This is a *lapidaemas*, a demon stone. It connects a mage with their contracted demons." She explained the basics of the stone as she moved around the room, donning a cloak and picking up a sculpted iron staff that leaned against the wall by the front door. She turned to Zak. "Shall we go?"

"Go? What do you mean?"

"To defend the city, we're under attack." She gestured toward the window with the staff.

"What? How?" He leaped to his feet, stumbling over several questions yet unable to form a coherent one. *Shira must have glimpsed something*, he thought.

That was when the first screams from the street below pierced the hazy comfort of the sitting room.

CHAPTER 5

DARK SHAPES

Distant explosions and a grim chorus of yells bombarded Zak's ears as he bounded through the streets of Tor'alan. Shira, moderately short and stout, moved with surprising speed, hiking her robes up in one hand and iron staff in the other. Ubba flitted ahead, his pink and bulbous nose raised high as he sniffed and sneezed wildly.

"Ubba can smell all kinds of magic and should lead us to the nearest active source," Shira called to Zak, a little breathless. The imp sneezed a few more times before flapping faster. "His sensitive nose also yields incurable allergies, the poor dear."

Pandemonium enveloped the main road of the Market district. People disappeared behind slamming shop doors and scuttled down side streets, perhaps finding their way home or a safe burrow to hide in. Zak couldn't see what or who they ran from, but more yelling and the sound of spells ahead told him the battle wasn't far. Ubba led them closer to the Center.

Zak saw them overhead first. "Look!" He pointed skyward. Dark shapes—creatures of some sort—flew outside a translucent shield that stretched over Tor'alan. Tiny bolts of lightning crisscrossed wherever the creatures crashed into the shield, and they burst into flames, leaving nothing behind. Seeing one of the many defenses of the city spring to life left him awestruck. "If they're outside the shield, why are people panicking?" he asked.

"Looks like they're not all outside." Shira pointed straight ahead with the tip of her staff.

A regiment of soldiers and mages fought with the amorphous dark shapes. Some creatures clung to cloaks, arms, and faces, while others jumped over swords and ducked spells, seeking their next victim.

Zak watched in horror as a creature wrapped around a mage's arm not ten paces away. A bright light passed between them, and the mage sunk to the ground, grey and lifeless. The creature hissed, slapping dark appendages on the stone street as it slithered straight toward Zak.

He stumbled back, loosing jets of flame at the creature. It was fast, bouncing over and sliding under his attacks. It reached with a globby, hand-like shape and gripped his shoulder. Immediately, a coldness rippled through him and frigid pain wrenched at something deep within his core. The creature was taking his energy—his life—emptying him like a cracked vessel spilling its contents.

Shira spotted the creature and shot a funnel of purple fire from the tip of her staff, knocking it back and breaking the connection. Zak fell to his hands and knees, gasping for air.

The creature oozed around Shira's flames. "It doesn't seem to be working!" She yelled, cutting off the stream of fire and swinging her staff. It hit with a squelching thud, pinning the monster. But Shira was right—the creature didn't seem bothered by the magic or the solid iron as it squirmed, trying to wriggle free.

Zak didn't have a novel idea. It was all he could do to keep from panicking. If he had a moment to think, he would have realized this was only his third real battle. But he didn't have a moment. Instead, training and instinct took over. He regained his footing, connected with his magic, and spouted emerald flames at the creature. The dark shape sizzled and wheezed a scream-like noise before it solidified under the heat, cracked, and flaked into dark dust. Zak released the spell and coughed, shaking off the cold that had seeped into his bones. "That seemed to do it."

"Well, that's curious. There's no time to explore why your flames work and mine don't." Shira paused for a moment, catching her breath. "Right, new plan: I'll trap them, you fry them." Ubba clung to her shoulder, cowering beneath the hood of her robes.

Zak followed Shira as they worked their way through the melee. Her iron staff effectively trapped the dark shapes against the stone street and kept them at a safe distance from the life-draining creatures. When they clung to soldiers or mages, she yanked them off with expert maneuvering of scattered debris and telekinetics, hovering the creatures in midair for Zak to burn them out of existence. Shira directed any soldiers or mages they found still alive to help the wounded in their wake.

"Bazil!" Zak spotted the priest near the Center's main

gate, short blades in each hand. He ran toward his friend as he stabbed and danced around one of the creatures. With Bazil holding its attention, Zak rushed behind and buried it in a surge of flame. Like the others, it disintegrated into ash.

"Light's peace, Zak. Good timing. How did you do that? My fire didn't bother it a bit."

"I don't know. It was the same with Shira. My fire destroys them for some reason."

"Another *Nacusti* mystery, I'd guess." Bazil surveyed the square. "There's a handful left. Let's help the others."

Shira and Bazil pinned or levitated any remaining creatures they encountered, giving him a clear shot at incineration. In minutes, the last remains turned to dust and scattered on the wind.

"Is that all of them?" Zak asked. Craning to look at the shield over Tor'alan, he saw no more bursts of lightning.

"Seems to be. The better question is what *were* they." Shira leaned on her staff, dabbing at her brow with a handkerchief. "I should have trapped one to study, but they were oddly resistant to magic. Well, most magic."

"Wait! There's one more. Look!" Zak pointed across the street, where a single dark shape was slinking away toward the entrance portal.

"Quick! Find a box or something with a lid!" Shira yelped as she chased the creature.

Zak bent down, digging through the stone and brick blasted from the sides of buildings. Plants, woven baskets, leather goods, and other wares that had been stacked neatly in shopfronts covered the street in debris. He picked a careful path outside a glass and pottery shop, stepping over hundreds of pointed shards until he found an unbroken glass jar with a cork top. He snatched it up and ran to Shira, who had pinned the creature under her staff. It struggled and squealed against its restraint but didn't escape.

"Will this work?" he asked, waving the jar at Shira as he trotted over. Bazil followed empty-handed, his search for a vessel less successful.

Shira's eyes darted to the jar momentarily as if she didn't want to look away from the creature for too long. "Yes, that should do. This will take some coaxing. Bazil, hold the jar here. Yes, just like that. Now, Zak, I'll begin an incantation to trap the little beast. Use your flames to scare it toward the jar, and be sure *not* to destroy this one."

Shira began muttering under her breath. A chunk of the creature swirled toward the jar as a strong wind buffeted it toward the opening. It clawed at the ground, squealing in its desperate struggle to crawl away. Zak pulsed a few flames just ahead of it, trying not to hit it but to get the fire close enough to threaten. The creature retreated as each flame licked close to its strange appendages.

The pull of Shira's incantation finally picked the creature up. She lifted her staff, and its oozing body gushed into the jar. Bazil snapped the cork on the top and held tight as the creature ricocheted around its new container.

"Best get that to the Center, Bazil, and see if they can identify it. And don't let go of the cork. I have a feeling even a magic seal won't contain that thing for long," Shira said. Bazil nodded and jogged toward the Center's main gate.

"You've never seen anything like them before?" Zak asked.

"No, not a once," she said. "They resist magic but aren't immune. That's a tricky wrinkle. Lucky for us, your flames worked just fine."

"Yes, lucky," he agreed. Another oddity added to the growing list of things he didn't understand about his magic. "What should we do now?"

"I will help the survivors get to the healing wards." She eyed him up and down as she brushed soot from her robes. "You should head straight there as well to get looked over. Didn't one of those creatures grab you?"

"I'm fine, just tired." He straightened his uniform, hiding a shiver.

"Hmph. Then you should go to the Dormitory. You've done plenty here today, Zakolor. I'll deliver my report; I should expect you'll be asked a few questions once the League begins an investigation." With a kind smile, she bustled down the street, stopping every few paces to help a mage or soldier to their feet.

Zak breathed deep for the first time since leaving Shira's apartment, the air stretching his aching chest. It *had* been one thing after another, from waking in the Archives and rushing to the adept exam, the surprise council meeting, Sight lessons, and then this attack. It was a wonder he had the energy to stand, especially after the creature drained him.

Ambling toward the Center, he quickly passed through the mess hall to grab bread and fruit for dinner before climbing the Dormitory stairs and flopping into bed.

Despite his exhaustion, Zak found little sleep that night. Every time he slipped into unconsciousness, he jumped awake, thinking one of the dark shapes was crawling up his leg.

He gave up as dawn's yellow light peaked through the window's edge. No sleep meant no dreams, and a few months ago, that would have been a good thing. Now, he depended on those dreams—the glimpses of the future they offered—to understand what to do next.

Or maybe what to avoid.

Moving to his desk, he pored over musky volumes and notes from his last visit to the Archives. His eyes studied the words, but his mind wandered. Between lessons with Sorwin and Kaleb, research to cure Olivia, Sight lessons, visiting Kal, and now working for Euphemius once a week, his responsibilities threatened to pull him apart. And after yesterday's attack, he seemed to be the only mage capable of stopping the dark creatures, and his role as *Nacusti* became even more vital.

How? he wondered. How could he keep doing it all? He felt the same now as he did while learning to swim in the salty waters near Densba. He was fearless back then, but small, and when the shallow currents swept him too far from the beach, his tiny limbs struggled against wave after wave, crushing him beneath the foamy tide. For mere moments, he knew what it was to drown, sinking into the airless depths. Then Ageric's solid arms plunged through the water, ripping him to the surface with a gasp, clutching him tight, warm and safe.

But his father wasn't here, and Zak wasn't drowning, even though the same choking sensation now flooded his lungs. How much more could he take before he went under completely?

A knock at the door jarred his spiraling thoughts, and he shuffled his weary body to answer.

No one was there. A rectangular package wrapped in brown paper and twine floated in the air. He blinked at it for a moment before noticing a small parchment attached to its corner. Pulling it free and unfolding it, he found a note inside.

Zakolor,

I hope you don't mind. I heard the good news about your promotion and sprung for your new uniforms. Your old ones have been confiscated and thoroughly destroyed. Do remember that laundry is a free service in the Dormitory. I strongly urge you to take advantage of it in the future.

Yours,

Inguma Foucher

Zak winced at the scolding. Even in writing, Inguma was a force. Yet her words carried truth; his old uniforms had developed a particular aroma over the last few weeks. He picked up the floating package and placed it on his bed, unwrapping the twine and paper to find three pressed adept uniforms. Bronze designs at the cuffs and collar detailed the red fabric of the Elemental House. He smiled as he brushed his fingers over the fine embroidery. Despite everything that overwhelmed him, he was making progress. This uniform was proof.

He wanted to share his exciting news and knew exactly who wanted to hear it. He returned to his desk, pulled the pre-addressed letter from his leather bag and a quill from the inkpot, and started writing to his parents.

The more dangerous details were omitted, but an otherwise accurate account of his adventure thus far was given. Sorwin sent them updates, but Zak hadn't communicated with his parents since leaving Densba. He told them of Bernadooth, of the *Swift Star* and her mangy-yet-loveable crew, of Lindomer and the dangerous Rot, of Tor'alan and its splendor. As he wrote, a bubble of emotion burned his throat. Folding the finished letter and wiping misty eyes, he twisted the brass handle on the window.

"*Nuntiumignis.*" The letter burst into flames and zipped around the tiny room before speeding out the window. He leaned on the windowsill, watching it streak through the air toward the Fire Post, wondering how long it would take to travel to far-off Densba.

After donning his new uniform, he went to breakfast. Rumors flew around the mess hall, mainly conjecture about the dark shapes, how they managed to get inside Tor'alan's considerable defenses, and why they were resistant to magic—most magic, at any rate. The stares of many mages followed Zak while stepping through the buffet line, and a hush turned into a revitalized buzz as he passed through the room to an empty table.

He sighed. The attack was no secret, nor was his role in

defeating the creatures. The excitement of his arrival had died down considerably the last two weeks, leaving him able to have an almost regular meal, unperturbed by curious glances and pelted questions. Now, with the renewed attention, it felt like he was starting over again.

Except this time, it was worse. Instead of being a complete stranger, some of the mages now knew him, like Rauffe.

"Oh look, it's Tor'alan's savior," Rauffe said. He loomed over Zak and put one foot on a chair, resting an elbow on his knee. "All a bit convenient, if you ask me. These creatures show up, and only *you* can defeat them. How'd that happen, *Nacusti*?"

Rauffe's lips curled as the gang of cronies behind him cackled.

Zak shoved his flaring anger down and kept quiet. It wasn't worth it. He had no idea where the creatures came from—and neither did anyone else—so he couldn't explain why only *his* magic worked, and even if he could, they wouldn't believe him anyway. Instead, he twisted slightly in his chair away from Rauffe.

But Rauffe wasn't going to let Zak ignore him. "Oi!" He shoved Zak's shoulder into the table. "Why'd you do it? Why'd you conjure all those beasts to hurt all those people? You wanted to save the day, didn't you? Didn't feel special enough, *Nacusti*?"

"Shut up!" Zak sprang up as green fire curled around his fists, losing all sense of himself as that gods-cursed name—*Nacusti*—flew out of Rauffe's *stulmati* mouth. But an iron grip clamped his wrist before he could do anything.

Bazil was at his side.

"That's enough, Werbeggen. Finish your meal at your own table or leave the mess hall—either way, shove off."

The entire room fell silent, mesmerized by the spectacle. Bazil was only one rank above Rauffe, but it must have been sufficient seniority because Rauffe sneered, kicked over a chair, and stalked away with his cronies in tow. Only when they disappeared through the doors did Bazil release Zak's wrist, and with a flick of his own, the overturned chair righted itself.

Zak's fire had died down when Bazil surprised him. "Thanks." He sat behind his plate once again and glared at the nearest tables, whose occupants quickly averted their eyes. Now that the confrontation was over, a slow chatter resumed in the hall. "You may have just put yourself on Rauffe's most hated list right behind me."

"I can handle that *stulmati*," Bazil said, sitting with a full plate. Zak smirked at the Evartian slang. It seemed he wasn't the only one spending time with Shira. "I'm more concerned with what happens when Inguma or I aren't around to interfere."

"I'll be fine. I already beat him in sparring once." *Though the match was far from easy*, he thought.

"It's not you I'm worried about. You were nervous, it was your first sparring match. Imagine what you could do now that Rauffe's been bullying you, now that you're probably mad at him."

Inguma had said something similar, though not as bluntly as Bazil. Is this how everyone thought of him? As a walking inferno of magic that could explode at any moment, and woe be to the ones in his path of fury? And given what just happened—how anger and magic escaped his control with a few prods from Rauffe—could he blame them?

No, I can't. All anyone saw was an untrained, Guardian-born mage that had fought the Consortium at least twice and survived. Many senior mages couldn't claim the same. How could they know the extent of his capabilities, of the potential danger he posed to them? How could *he*?

"Bazil, would you—" he began. But Bazil must have known what Zak was about to ask.

"Of course, Zak. I'm sort of gutted you hadn't asked me to join you for breakfast more often." He winked. "Though we may have to meet a little earlier. I teach basic healing in the morning session." With Bazil nearby, hopefully Rauffe and any other rumor-mongers would be deterred for the next few weeks.

Zak shook his head, wondering how he'd been lucky enough to find another friend who seemed to know what he needed before he did. *That would be an interesting pair.* He imagined the conversations Kal and Bazil would have, which would inevitably be Kal pestering Bazil with as many questions as possible about priest magic. There wasn't a question Kal wouldn't ask.

For the rest of the meal, Zak prized speed over manners, shoveling as much food into his mouth at once as he could. Bazil trailed him from the mess hall not a moment too soon.

Lessons didn't go well that day. Zak lobbed question after question at Sorwin about the creatures and plans to save

Terasi, but his magus had no answers. Instead, he redirected Zak toward practice. It was his first time attempting earth magic, and he couldn't connect with the element. It was supposed to be the easiest to learn after fire, but it felt cold and distant. Fire was warm, ready, and hungry to be cast. After nearly an hour of meditating, Sorwin, with a concerned look, ended the lesson early.

I must look worse than I feel, Zak thought. Sorwin rarely left a minute unused.

As equally terrible as you usually look, Jolsu said.

The break didn't do much for Zak. While sparring, his left guard was weak, and his conjured weapon flickered in and out of existence at the most inopportune times. Once, Bazil mounted a series of easy attacks to loosen Zak up, but a simple overhead swing passed right through his staff, connecting with his skull. Somehow, Olivia seemed both amused and annoyed at his flubs, but he couldn't entirely be sure as she kept their interactions to fleeting, accidental eye contact.

He finally stomped out of court seven after midday, the thunderous *crack* of the door's barrier epitomizing the foulness of his mood. What happened to the surge of optimism from that morning when writing to his parents? How did it disappear so fast?

He skipped lunch—not wanting another dramatic meal in the mess hall and not ready to bother Bazil again so soon—and trudged toward the Temple of Light. He carefully stepped up the wide flagstone stairs, afraid to scuff or mar the bright surface. It was Foursday, and the prospect of seeing Kal put him in a better mood.

At least, it did the first visit.

Zak strode through the main hall, past the healing wards, and up a staircase at the back of the Temple. There was meant to be a visit every Foursday, but Archlumen Sashina had canceled several previous weeks, saying Kal wasn't in a "visiting state" those days.

More than anything, Zak wanted to see Kal today. He wanted to know his friend was okay, that he was recovering. There were so many questions Kal could answer if Zak could ask, and they would be immediate and thoughtful answers, like the ones he always gave back home, before all this chaos with the League and Zandorn. He needed his best friend today.

And Zak wasn't going to get him.

Two priests struggled to pin Kal's arms and legs to the bed while Sashina incanted spells above him, her magic coiling through the air like rose-colored vines.

Kal yelled and thrashed until the magic wrapped around him, and he sunk into a barely conscious state with unintelligible mutters.

"Kal! What have you done to him?" Zak rushed into the room without thinking. One of the priests caught his midriff and held him back a step from the bed.

"Easy, *Nacusti*, we're helping your friend to relax," Sashina said in her calming lower register.

"What happened? Is he still unwell?" Zak stopped struggling, and the priest let go of him with a nod from Sashina. Kal's eyes fluttered as if fighting sleep, a moment away from waking.

"He is, I'm sorry to say. Whatever Renna or Zandorn did to him, we're having a time untangling his mind from the magic. I'm unsure if your...*intervention* helped or hindered his situation."

Zak's stomach somersaulted, never once considering that the unexplainable connection he and Kal shared in the middle of the battle had made things worse. "But I—what have you found out?"

Sashina gently lifted Kal's hand and inspected it. For what, Zak had no idea. "We know Kalbick has a unique essence. He's a *sorgeus*, one who absorbs. Most mages are innately protected by their magic, it repels certain unwanted magical contact. A *sorgeus*' magic does the opposite. It absorbs magic, perhaps to strengthen the mage, yet just as often with ill effects. That is why *sorgeus* are rare; they eventually absorb something they shouldn't and die from the complications."

"You're saying...is Kal going to die?" he whimpered.

"Not yet, though we can't rule it out." Sashina's impartial tone simmered something in Zak. "He certainly absorbed Renna's magic, but something else in him is making a mess of things. It's difficult to parse through the four separate entities."

"Four?"

"Yes: Kal's, yours, Renna's—which I am unfortunately familiar with—and whatever the fourth magic is." She counted on her fingers as she listed them out.

"Can I sit with him?" Zak asked. "I'll only stay a few minutes," he added, seeing Sashina hesitate. Zak couldn't leave his friend. Not today.

"Very well. We'll return in a quarter-hour. I shouldn't find you here when we do." The priests filed out of the small room. "And Zakolor," Sashina rested a hand on the door-frame. "No physical contact, please. We can't risk him absorbing more of your magic."

Zak pulled his hand back as he was about to grab Kal's.

Good idea, Jolsu said. *Would be a shame to have* another *mishap.*

Zak clenched his fists as he ignored the dragon's taunt. Sitting with Kal, even in his lulled state, should have eased his mind, the nearness reassuring they would both be fine. But without any conversation, the silence in the room let Sashina's words swirl round and round in his thoughts, and he wondered if he had made everything worse by trying to help Kal all those weeks ago.

He paced around the small room, nerves and guilt forcing him to move. Kal was the picture of restful slumber most of the time. Yet, an occasional flutter of his eyelids or sharp inhale told Zak that whatever he experienced was anything but peaceful.

This was a mistake. He couldn't watch Kal suffer, and he couldn't be in the room any longer. He went for the door. As soon as he was in the hall, he almost collided with Tansil.

"Archmagus!" Zak said, taking a step back in surprise. "Apologies, I was just—"

"Visiting your friend?" Tansil said with a hint of a concerned smile. "I'm glad the Archlumen let you in today. How is our young Kalbick?" The elf clasped his hands over buttery-colored robes.

Zak glanced back to Kal's door, unsure how to answer. "He's not well." Zak noticed Tansil had been about to step into Kal's room when they almost ran into one another. "Were you going to see him?"

"The Archlumen, actually, and you, as it happens."

"Me?"

"Yes. I promised more answers about Cerevita, and you deserve them. I thought we had a little more time, as is often the fault of my kind. Time is different for elves, you see." Almost proving his point, Tansil's focus drifted off as he stood silently.

"Um, right," Zak said. His voice brought the elf back.

"Well, with yesterday's attack, we cannot delay a moment longer. Meet me in the evening on Onesday in my office, and I'll explain everything I can."

"Of course, Archmagus." He stepped aside as Tansil continued down the hallway.

With a last forlorn glance at Kal, Zak plodded through the Temple and across the Center courtyard, ignoring the fast-yellowing Autumn grass and occasional leaf zigzagging to the ground.

Tansil would explain everything—did that mean he would speak with Cerevita again? If he could, he'd ask how to cure Olivia and Kal. If Sashina couldn't heal them, maybe a god could, or at least knew how.

And what if she didn't? What if she couldn't?

He shuddered the thoughts away, refusing to give up before following every possible avenue. That meant researching the horned bird from his vision and waiting for Onesday evening with Tansil.

Kal twisted and turned, running from the darkness. Light swirled around him, greens and reds dancing above his head as he scrambled down the path. He had no idea where it led, but he knew with a cold certainty he couldn't stop. If he did, he'd be consumed.

A voice—Zak's voice—echoed from somewhere far away. The sound spurred him on and pierced him with sadness.

He remembered everything. Remembered confronting Zak in battle, saying horrible things, and the twist of pain as their magics collided. He had hurt Zak.

What have I done?

The darkness growled—roared—behind him. He ran faster. How much longer could he keep out of its grasp?

CHAPTER 6
DISCOVERY

Doubt crept to the edges of Zak's mind as he meditated. Cross-legged on the green lawn of court seven, the element of earth quaked outside his grasp.

It reminded him of chasing Kal when they were young. They were supposed to take turns; if Zak caught Kal, the roles would reverse, and he would run away. But he never did because Kal was always faster, always beyond his reach. Every time his hand would dart out, stretching for Kal, he'd grab nothing but empty air as his friend lunged away, cackling at his clever game.

Now, the very earth beneath him cackled, or it would if it cared, which, of course, it didn't. It somehow felt unmoving and far away, which didn't make sense. Fire magic was effortless for Zak, and he never considered that the other elements would prove challenging. He had hoped that all magic would come easy to him as the *Nacusti*. He couldn't have been more wrong.

After accumulating a few more sizeable bruises from sparring, his lessons for the day ended in relative silence. Sorwin and Kaleb lingered by the stone bench, trading whispers Zak couldn't hear. Perhaps about his poor progress lately, or perhaps something else. Sorwin's cheeks blushed, but that was normal whenever Kaleb was near.

Olivia approached as he sipped from a waterskin, and he nearly choked as she addressed him directly after weeks of being ignored. "It's Fivesday. Meet Euphemius in two hours near the main gate of the Center."

"Right." He gurgled, water spilling down his chin. He dragged a sleeve across his face as Olivia's expression scrunched in disgust, or was she holding back a laugh? "Will you be there?" he asked. Working for Euphemius would be worth it if it meant time with Olivia.

"Unfortunately," she said before heading for the door. "Don't be late."

"See you there!" Zak waved, but she didn't see. He didn't care. Maybe he could finally apologize properly for Jolsu's binding and offer a glimmer of hope for a cure. That reminded him of something.

"Bazil. What are you doing right now?"

"Cooling down after exercise," he said, pulling himself toward his toes so his body folded in half.

Zak still hadn't learned much about priests and their magic, only that they took their physical health seriously since their magic enhanced their body's abilities. Bazil's dry wit was unique to him.

"I meant after that," Zak clarified.

"Nothing in particular." Bazil flowed upward, arms reaching overhead. "Fivesday is normally my day off, except for helping you train."

"Would you mind helping me a little more? In the Archives?" Zak bit his lip, knowing he pushed the limits of their young friendship. He met Bazil almost two months ago, yet sometimes it felt like they had known each other for years. Maybe it was an effect of seeing each other every day.

"Need help researching a cure for Olivia?" Bazil asked.

"Yes, and maybe Kal...you've helped the Archlumen with his treatment, haven't you?"

"A little, when requested. He's in a bit of a state." Bazil must have noticed Zak flinch at his words. "Sorry, I'll help. You could have asked sooner, you know."

"Yeah, well, you're already doing a lot for me," he said. "I wasn't in a hurry to add 'research assistant' alongside your other titles of 'sparring partner' and 'breakfast escort.'"

Bazil stopped stretching and gave Zak an appraising look. He righted himself, placed a supportive hand on Zak's shoulder, and spoke to him like an older brother. "Zak, you're the *Nacusti*. The whole League is here to help you, and you, it. After what I've seen the last two days, I figure you won't be able to focus much on your training until you help Olivia and Kal, at least a little. And having one of the most talented priests aid your cause doesn't hurt." He said the last part with a hint of a smirk.

"Oh, *most talented* priest, are you?"

"It's better than *breakfast escort*. How dare you?"

Their banter continued as they packed their belongings and walked to the Archives. Somehow, Zak thought most of the mages in the League would *not* volunteer to help with extra lessons and research—according to one of the more colorful rumors, he could easily be a shapeshifting Caries demon in disguise—but he was grateful Bazil did.

Zak led Bazil to the third floor of the circular wooden tower, withstanding several wary glances from archivists on the way to his usual table by the window. Perhaps his habit of falling asleep had garnered extra attention. He slung his bag over a chair and fanned his notes out, walking Bazil through the little progress he made.

"I started with bindings for Olivia, but there's hardly anything on *vitaligos* since they're so rare and old. There are a few references to making one, but nothing about releasing it. I started looking at curses to see if there were any similarities or even *vitaligos* used as a curse, like what Jolsu did to Olivia." He trailed off, waiting for Bazil to absorb the information.

"Smart thinking. I have a few ideas to start with. What about for Kal?"

"His situation has been trickier since I didn't know what ailed him until yesterday. The Archlumen told me he's a *sorgeus*, so we could start there?" His inflection went up, hoping the priest agreed or had another suggestion.

Bazil blew air between his lips. "One friend a *sorgeus* and another with a *vitaligo*? I'm starting to feel not very special."

Zak grinned. "But imagine how special you'll feel when you *heal* their conditions, Most Talented Priest!"

"Oh, you *are* wicked," Bazil quipped. "Alright, if I'm taking these two, what are you researching?'

He absently tapped the table with his fingers, eyes scanning the brass plates nailed to the end of each bookcase, denoting its contents. "I don't have much time. I have to meet Euphemius in a little over an hour, but I have a bird to find."

Without another word, he drifted to the wooden stacks, lacquered edges glinting from the blue glow of the magelight sconces. There was no mention of birds on the third or fourth floors. The fifth had an extensive bird of prey section, but most volumes detailed how to fight, capture, breed, or train them. Few entries had pictures, and of those, none resembled the bird from his dream.

He almost asked for help from an archivist, but their intimidating stares warded him off. Nearly half his time was gone when he found his way to a long bookcase on the sixth floor with a promising nameplate:

Magic, Menace, and Myth: Creatures of Valecium and Beyond

Hundreds of book spines in varying heights, colors, and dinginess clustered together. Most were old and tattered, neglect and overuse wreaking equal havoc. Stacks of scrolls interspersed the tomes, and the tightly wound ringlets of parchment reminded Zak of his favorite pastry from Densba—a crushed citrus tart. His stomach growled as he worked his way down the row, focusing on the titles while ignoring his hunger. The scrolls were more challenging to read. Some had descriptive names on the outside, but most he had to untie and unroll to discover what was inside.

Many books mentioned specific creatures, which didn't help as Zak didn't know what the bird from his dream was called. Several covered geographic areas and countries, and again, he gritted his teeth as he lacked the most basic information to aid his search. All he had was an image: a dark-feathered, horned bird. There had to be something here that could help.

Keenly aware of his thinning time as several more minutes trickled away, he skimmed the shelves faster and faster. A wide book with dark yellow panels caught his attention on one of the high shelves near the end of the curved bookcase. It read simply *BIRDS* in large, embossed letters on the spine.

If this doesn't help, I'm in trouble, he mused. As he slid the tome from its shelf, a thick cloud of dust puffed over him.

He coughed and waved the cloud away, then moved to a nearby table and dropped the tome. It was heavy, like an ingot in his father's smithy, and the *clunk* of the rigid panels against the solid table echoed in the near-silent Archives. Zak half expected to see an archivist sneering at the sound.

Thank Cerevita. He was alone. They didn't need another reason to dislike him.

As he opened the book, a brief tone from the Center's bell sounded. He had precisely half an hour left before meeting Euphemius.

He thumbed past the beginning pages. Since he didn't know what he was looking for, a table of contents and foreword didn't do him any good. A handful of pages in, a grin overtook his face. A third of the lefthand page contained an elegant sketch of a bird resembling an eagle. The name at the top of the page read *Alerion*, and the rest of the text described details like its known habitats, diet, migration patterns, and mating rituals.

This book was *exactly* what he needed!

Zak pushed each page over as fast as he could without ripping the weathered parchment. Sketch after sketch blurred by as he hunted for the horned bird from his dream, his eyes catching on the names every few pages.

Alkonost, anhinga, avocet...

Most of the sketches depicted what Zak would expect to find in a book of birds: creatures with feathers, beaks, and wings. Some were more terrifying, with large claws and jagged teeth. The startling ones with human-like features—such as faces or arms—sent a jolt through him.

Yet, none had horns.

Bank swallow, barn owl, bittern...

His pace quickened as the minutes slipped away. He needed to find something, needed to make progress, needed to move forward instead of standing still.

Bullfinch, cactus wren, caladrius...

In haste, he flipped another two pages before realizing what he found. He pawed the pages back and flattened the book.

There it was—the horned bird from his dream.

The caladrius.

Black ink outlined its shape, and the yellowed parchment filled its interior like all the other sketches. Even without the midnight-hued feathers, he knew this was the bird. The artist skillfully captured its sharp gaze and the elegant curve in the ribbed horns.

The author didn't provide much information on the caladrius. Migration patterns and mating rituals were blank. There was a short entry in the middle of the page:

The caladrius is a coastal omnivorous bird that, except for the telltale horns, can be mistaken for a common dove at a distance. While its size and shape are similar, its nature is very different. Caladrius claim two unique abilities. If willing, it can heal almost any wound, illness, or affliction. Its fickle nature makes the healing unpredictable and may lead to it displaying its second ability, predicting death. If a caladrius is presented to an individual—afflicted or not—and dips its horns before looking away, the individual is marked and will soon die. Exact timelines are debated, but as far as this author is aware, most deaths occur within three to five weeks.

He re-read the passage three times to be sure he wasn't mistaken. The caladrius can help someone avoid death and also predict it.

It can heal almost any wound, illness, or affliction.

Excitement shot through him like lightning.

Olivia! The caladrius could heal Olivia! Her *vitaligo* had to count as an affliction. Could it heal Kal, too? He was *definitely* afflicted with cursed magic.

Was this why the caladrius was in his dream? Were his visions a portent of hope this time instead of a warning? He didn't know or have time to work it out now.

He closed the book and returned it to its dusty shelf, taking a moment to memorize its location in case he needed to find it again. He repeated the caladrius name and the book's location under his breath and moved as fast as he dared through the Archives, being careful *not* to run near archivists, and returned to the table on the third floor.

Bazil was there, poring over three different tomes and

mumbling to himself. Zak scribbled *caladrius* with a quill on a page with jumbled notes, as well as the location of the *BIRDS* book. He couldn't risk losing either of his discoveries to a faulty memory.

"Find something?" Bazil asked, looking up at Zak's flurry of movement.

"Yes! Yes! Yes!" He tried to whisper, but his excitement elevated the last word to a shout. His heart pounded as he apologized to a scandalized reader frowning at him from a nearby table.

"Well? What did you find?"

Lowering his voice, Zak explained. "It's called a caladrius. It's a bird that can heal almost anything! I bet it could heal Olivia *and* Kal."

Bazil crossed his arms and leaned back, the wooden chair creaking against the movement. "Not sure, Zak. From what I've heard, caladrius are pretty rare and temperamental."

His excitement waned a little. "But you've heard of them? Does the Temple have any?" As healers, he thought the priests would be the most likely out of anyone in the League.

"I've heard of them. Read a few reports about their miraculous healing powers. They're really potent. One even managed to cure magtrophitis, which isn't normally possible."

"Magtrophitis?"

"A rare degenerative disease where a mage's essence deteriorates until they can't use magic and eventually wither. Anyway, I think the Temple did have a few caladrius throughout the years, but we haven't had one in centuries."

"We need to find one," Zak stated, almost promising to himself.

Bazil's mouth twitched as his eyebrows raised. "That'll be tough."

"We have to!" He quieted himself again as the nearby reader scoffed at him. "This could be the only thing that helps Olivia and Kal. Unless you found something?" He waved a hand over the books Bazil had open.

"Not yet." The priest shook his head. "But Zak, caladrius are rare *because* their powers are incredible. They've been hunted and captured for thousands of years, and we still know next to nothing about them. They don't breed in captivity, so once one is caught, it eventually dies."

"That's horrible," Zak said. His initial excitement lessened, yet his determination persisted. He couldn't leave any potential cure for his friends unpursued. As his mind sifted through the information to formulate a plan, the bell sounded in the Center once again.

He was late to meet Euphemius.

"Three Fires!" he yelped, jumping to his feet and shoving his notes into his bag.

"Quiet!" hissed the nearby reader, flinging their hands up in frustration.

"Sorry!" Zak whispered as he slung his bag cross-body. "Bazil, I have to go. You don't have to stay here, but would you come back with me next time?"

Bazil gave Zak a playful, dismissive wave. "Nonsense, I don't have anything else to do today. I'll keep searching. I have a promising lead on a runic countercurse."

He squeezed Bazil's shoulder in gratitude as he passed. "I owe you again." His friend's knowledge of healing magic was already proving invaluable.

"I could have told you that," Bazil whispered as Zak left.

Chapter 7
OUTBURSTS

"You're late," Euphemius said with distaste sharper than the tip of his well-polished shoe that tapped the cobblestone street.

"Apologies, Mr. Van Ilia." Zak huffed, breathless from sprinting. He was still five minutes late. Olivia stood to Euphemius' right, arms crossed, looking almost as annoyed as her sponsor.

"This is the first and last time it will happen. Let's go." Euphemius strutted down the main road toward the Market district, a grey half-cape billowing from his shoulders.

The merchant's short legs set a relaxed pace. Zak fell into step next to Olivia and when he caught his breath, leaned over and whispered, "What are we doing?" Even after signing a contract, the details of working for Euphemius remained a mystery.

Olivia frowned. "We're walking."

Had they been on better terms, Zak would have laughed. Olivia's dryness was second only to Bazil. But laughing didn't seem like a wise choice at this moment. Not with their strained friendship. "Well, yes, I meant what should I expect to *do*?"

Her expression softened from hostile to irritated. "Walking and waiting. We follow Mr. Van Ilia; he stops at several locations, and we wait for him to conduct his business. If there's trouble at any point, he'll expect us to step in. But Tor'alan is the heart of the League, so there's never trouble. Not for him, anyway."

"So we just follow him?" It sounded easy, sure, but also dull. Maybe less so if he could keep Olivia talking.

"That's not all we're doing," she said cryptically.

"What do you mean?"

She gave the smallest of nods to the left. "Take a look."

Zak looked at the rows of shops and stands lining the avenue. Nearly every shop owner and many passersby waved and greeted Euphemius. Some the merchant ignored completely; for others, he awarded a quick nod. Only twice did Euphemius offer an "Afternoon." More than a few people greeted Olivia, too. She always gave a nod or smile back.

Then Zak understood what Olivia meant. When passersby noticed *him,* fingers pointed, whispers flew, and curious glances came his way. He had been in Tor'alan long enough for most people to recognize him as the *Nacusti*, and now they saw him working for Euphemius.

This must have been what Euphemius wanted all along, to make him an ornament, a dazzling *object* to further his reputation.

His fists clenched as anger burned in his gut. This was the exact dynamic he had worked tirelessly to avoid with Limba

Dar and High King Marius. Even worse, he was technically *paying* Euphemius to be his prop by working off the cost of Olivia's contract. Accusations formed inside him, but they lodged in his throat before he could voice them.

"You catch on quick, Zak, but it's not worth it," Olivia warned. "You already signed the contract."

"Three Fires," he cursed. She was right, but something else caught his attention. She called him Zak—not *Nacusti*. Did that mean...?

Euphemius turned, heading toward the main square in the Market district and abruptly stopped outside a decadent four-story building with colorful bricks and mosaic tile arches. "Wait here," he said as he pushed through the front door.

A few minutes passed in awkward silence as Zak collected his thoughts and courage. Before he lost his nerve, he turned to Olivia.

"I wanted to apologize—" he started.

"Don't," she ordered.

"But I—"

"How many times, Zak? How many times have you apologized?" She wasn't looking at him. Her eyes continued surveying the street.

"I don't know." At least a few times after the binding, before she stopped speaking to him, and then every chance he had with the possibility of her hearing him. "Maybe a dozen?"

She let out one loud laugh, but he knew it wasn't humorous. "Try doubling that number, and you'll be getting close. Do you know why I haven't accepted any of your apologies?"

"No," he said honestly.

"Because," and then she did turn to face him, leveling a devastating look into his eyes, "Your apologies aren't for me. They're for you."

"No! Olivia, that's not true." He reacted before thinking. He couldn't stand the idea that she believed such a thing.

"Cerevita's grace, Zak, you're *still* not listening." She shook her head, disappointment etched into her frown. "I don't need your apologies. I am *mad* and broken, and words won't fix me. The only one they're helping is you."

Euphemius emerged from the colorful brick building and gestured to Zak and Olivia as he resumed his strut down the street.

Zak followed, his steps uneven as his bewildered thoughts whirled. How could she think that he didn't mean it when he apologized? He took a few deep breaths. *That wasn't what she said*, he thought. She said his words weren't *helping* her, that she was mad and broken.

Maybe his words couldn't help her, but perhaps his actions would.

Zak bided his time as Euphemius stopped at a smattering of vendors and collected payment for various services or loans. If Zak hadn't been so consumed with navigating his situation with Olivia, he would have been impressed with the number of Bronze and Silver Marks that rattled in the merchant's hands after barely an hour.

"Mr. Van Ilia," said a well-dressed man, tipping his hat in greeting as he neared Euphemius.

"Mr. Greyson," Euphemius replied with a similar gesture. "How is business?"

"Oh, fine," Mr. Greyson replied. His hands twitched around the top of his walking cane, and his smile looked forced. "Managing a few...*challenges* at the moment."

"You don't say?" Euphemius' tone was light, but Zak thought he heard some curiosity.

Mr. Greyson's lips tightened. "Indeed, Sir. Those zealots raided two of my shipments and a warehouse. Can you believe it? The sheer audacity, a *warehouse*!"

"It was the Disciples? Are you sure?" Euphemius asked, not hiding his urgency.

Zak leaned toward Olivia and whispered. "Who are the Disciples?" He'd never heard the name before.

Olivia gave him a look but said nothing.

"Quite sure," Mr. Greyson continued. "They left some strange runes behind and a message claiming it was 'for the good of the divine' and that I'd be rewarded for my donation. As if I *donated* a month's worth of shipments they *stole*!"

Euphemius reached up and patted Mr. Greyson's arm in a stilted manner as if it were an unfamiliar motion. "Now, now, Nathan. Go to the Lark's Jewel. I'll be along to see what I can do to help."

For the first time in the conversation, Mr. Greyson looked relieved. "Oh, Euphemius, thank you. If anyone can, it would be you, dear friend." The man walked away, blotting at his face with a silk handkerchief.

Euphemius glared at Zak. "Never speak when I am," he said in a low tone.

He must have heard the whispered question. Zak's anger was stoked again, but he held it back, remembering Olivia's advice from earlier. He already signed the contract, and arguing with Euphemius would only make their time together worse.

They collected a few more payments from vendors and renters—Euphemius was a prolific landlord in Tor'alan—before coming to a halt outside a dark wooden building. Two large, rectangular windows made up most of the exterior wall, and looking through the glass, the interior appeared to be a posh tavern. Glowing crystals on every table bathed the room in a soft purple light. Plush cushions covered every bench and stool while embroidered fabrics cascaded across the vaulted ceiling. Above the door hung a bronze sign depicting two birds in flight. Purple gems glittered where their eyes should be, and below them read *Lark's Jewel* in burnished script.

"This one will take a few minutes. Don't stray." Euphemius spoke directly to Zak before he went inside. A surge of lively music poured from the door as it briefly opened and closed. Zak watched the merchant through the window as he moved through the luxurious space, shaking a few hands before disappearing into the crowd.

And when Zak turned, Limba Dar stood before him.

"I wasn't aware your tastes were so refined, Zakolor." Limba Dar waved at the door of Lark's Jewel.

Zak fought a groan, but after holding back his anger with Euphemius, he had a very loose grip on the annoyance that Limba Dar always inspired. "I'm here for Euphemius," he said.

"Ah, of course. Working off your debt, correct? Well, aren't you fortunate to be employed by a respectable figure such as Mr. Van Ilia." Limba Dar twitched, as if the compliment only hurt him a minor amount. "I hope he appreciates the stature you bring, too."

He didn't respond but started drifting toward the fountain in the middle of the square where Olivia sat, probably amused with herself. She must have seen Limba Dar approaching and decided to let Zak be ambushed.

But Limba Dar—ever implacable—continued. "It's no small thing to employ the *Nacusti*—especially these days. I've received more than a few reports of theft and other crimes from merchants, notably in the east. Apparently, they're blaming a group called the Disciples."

That stopped Zak, his curiosity too powerful to resist. "What do you know of them?"

Limba Dar's twisted smile curled his lips as if celebrating that the hook stuck. In Zak's opinion, he wasn't any better than Euphemius—was arguably far worse. At least Euphemius had obvious goals for wealth and status, but Limba Dar's aims were still a mystery to Zak. He had slithered his way up to Marius' shoulder, whispering in his ear and acting almost as a king by proxy. Why? For the power? Was that all he wanted?

"The Disciples are a small religious group in Weslinton, or at least they were. Recent reports say their numbers swelled under new leadership. They preach of the power and benevolence of the gods, and some claim they would restore the divine to the physical plane given the choice."

"They want to bring the gods *back*?" Zak couldn't believe it, and neither could Jolsu. A wave of vicious rage swelled from the dragon, and Zak understood why. "But the whole point of the Guardian War was to regain free will. Wouldn't returning the gods undo all that sacrifice?"

"Exactly. Free will was the point, and wouldn't you say that the freedom to devote oneself to a god of your choosing falls under it?"

"Not if they *force* everyone to devote. Isn't that what happened before?"

Limba Dar inhaled loud and slow through his hooked nose. "Yes, but perhaps they believe even the gods can learn moderation. What do *you* think, Zakolor? Would you welcome the gods if they returned?"

Zak's brow furrowed. "Why do you care what I think?"

Another painful smile split Limba Dar's face. "You're the *Nacusti*, the last representative of the Contract, which means your opinions are more than just your own. Would you see the Contract upheld, or amended for a different—freer—future?"

The question overwhelmed Zak, and so did the reminder that many in the League were listening, watching, waiting for his beliefs to be known.

If he was honest with himself, he hadn't given his beliefs much thought, but he knew plenty of people who had. His mother was devoted to Cerevita, and so was Tansil. Bazil and many priests stood behind Azubelux, the Father of Light and Healing. Baltenebris was a little more controversial as the Lord of Shadows and Demons, but more than a few summoners weren't shy about supporting him.

Yet the gods lost the war against the mortal races, and the

Nacusti and their Guardians pushed the divine from Valecium. So, it wasn't what the gods represented that worried Zak, it was what they would do if they ever returned.

But Zak didn't want to share any of his fears or beliefs with Limba Dar. Instead, he said, "I don't think I could decide that alone. It goes against the idea of free will."

The thin line of Limba Dar's lips didn't reveal whether he was happy with the answer or not. "Well-reasoned, Zakolor, I can't fault you for that. Perhaps think about it more, if you have time between your studies." He swished away through the crowded square, probably to torment someone else into an existential crisis.

With a new headache lodged behind his brow, Zak wandered over to Olivia at the fountain, no more than twenty paces from the Lark's Jewel. He sat next to her on the curved edge that ran its circumference.

Her posture was relaxed, but Zak saw her eyes, ever vigilant, scanning clusters of people as they went about their business. Most wore heavier tunics, cloaks, and layers of fabric as the Autumn air continued to cool.

Now might be his best chance to tell Olivia some good news. He'd have to ease into it, though.

"Limba Dar was a treat, as usual. But he had some interesting things to say about the Disciples."

Olivia didn't respond, didn't take the bait. He'd have to try a more direct approach.

"What have you heard about the Disciples? The ones that stole from Mr. Greyson."

"That they're religious quacks," she answered. "They

want to destroy the Contract and bring the gods back."

Zak's eyes widened. "What? Are you sure?" It was one thing to discuss bringing the gods back, to allow devoted to worship more directly. It was another entirely to destroy the Contract. Limba Dar hadn't mentioned *that* at all. Was that on purpose, or did he not know? Or was Olivia misinformed?

"That's what recent security briefings that Euphemius attended have said. They think they'll be rewarded and that life would be better under the divine's influence."

Having met Cerevita, Zak could see the appeal. Her presence was powerful, almost intoxicating how she distorted his senses. Even though she seemed kind, imagining her will crushing any mortal that stood before her for too long was easy.

"Don't they know anything about the Guardian War and why the *Nacusti* fought the gods?"

Olivia shrugged. "Probably. Some people refuse to believe a thing without seeing it with their own eyes."

The Disciples unsettled Zak, but he had more pressing news to share with Olivia. "I found something," he said, his voice quiet, as if speaking too loudly would scare her away. Or, more likely, provoke her into yelling at him again.

She neither ran nor yelled but did something far worse. She ignored him, perhaps recognizing the shift in the conversation.

"In the Archives," he continued. Maybe Olivia wouldn't answer, but he wanted to tell her anyway. "There was a book that had a bird from my dream. It's called a caladrius, and it can heal almost anything. If we found one, maybe it could heal you and Kal."

Her eyes darted to his for a moment. "Haven't heard of it. How does it work?"

"I, uh, I'm not sure yet, but I'm going to find out," he promised. A flutter danced in his stomach as Olivia said nothing but gave a single nod. It wouldn't have meant much coming from anyone else, but from her, especially now, it was more than he could have hoped for.

Zak's moment of triumph disappeared when Olivia suddenly doubled over, clutching her hand. Yellow fire erupted from her palm.

"What's happening? Put it out!" Zak leaped to his feet. Using magic would drain her life. She could die!

"I'm trying!" She strained against the magic, almost like it fought to escape her palm. Turning, she thrust her hand into the fountain. The water bubbled and steamed, and after a moment, she pulled her hand back. The yellow fire was gone.

Olivia rested her head on the rim of the fountain bench, catching her erratic breath.

"Was that...did your magic do that on its own?" he asked.

"Yeah," she said. "Do you remember what I told you that day before you disappeared with the *indagomius*?"

"Of course I do." He'd never forget Olivia describing how magic had burst from her before she learned control, how it forced her to run away from home. The pain that threaded through her voice as she spoke of the fear she would accidentally kill her parents, so she spared them the heartbreak of abandoning her by doing it herself. "Why is it happening again?"

She exhaled slowly, and when her eyes looked up at Zak, they glistened. "This is what happens when I don't use my magic. It builds up, and if I don't let it out, it finds its own release."

"But, Olivia, that means—" The *vitaligo* bound her life to her magic. If these outbursts continued...

"I know what it means, Zak. If this keeps up—and it will—I will die."

He couldn't move, couldn't think, couldn't breathe. He knew the binding would be difficult to undo, but he thought he had time to figure it out.

"How long have they been happening? The outbursts?"

"It started a few days ago. This is the third one." She stood, wiped dirt from her knees, and pulled at the bottom hem of her uniform, flattening it back into place.

Zak had so many questions. How much magic did each outburst use? Were they consistent or increasing in frequency and scale? Was it always fire or different magic that escaped?

He stopped the onslaught of silent questions as Olivia's earlier phrase echoed in his head: *words won't fix me*. He didn't want to burden Olivia with the questions and had a feeling their answers wouldn't make a difference anyway. Only a cure would help.

He needed to find a caladrius, and he needed to find one soon.

As he was about to share his determination with Olivia, something small whizzed overhead, flashing a bright red light and blaring a high-pitched tone. Zak covered his ears as it circled the fountain several times, then hurtled off down the street.

Before he could ask Olivia what in the Three Fires that was, the ground shook beneath his feet. His heart jumped into his throat with the vibrations as he braced himself against the fountain's edge. What *now*?

Then he remembered it had been two days since the council meeting. Tor'alan was *moving*.

They were going to Masdaan.

Chapter 8

Wants and Needs

Renna's footsteps echoed through the halls of the old dwarven fortress, her stride smooth and not rushed. It wasn't uncommon for Zandorn to summon her, and it was never wise to keep him waiting, but it had been several weeks since the last call to her father's chambers. Around the time his new pet—the Druid—arrived. Meanwhile, her poor Kalbick most likely languished in a League prison cell.

It wasn't fair that Zandorn had a new plaything when hers was stolen away.

So, her pace was neither fast nor slow as she strode through the final ornate door into Zandorn's private laboratory. Abandoned furniture was piled in heaps, shoved against the wall, and boxed in by two long, polished tables covered in scattered notes, crystals, jars (empty and filled), and magical tools. Some of their names and uses eluded even Renna's extensive knowledge, reminding Renna that Zandorn's genius was the most frightening thing about him. After a century of leading the Consortium with him, she still trailed far behind his brilliance.

At least, that's what she *needed* Zandorn to believe.

She halted a few paces behind Zandorn. He faced the Druid, whose green arms and legs were chained to the moss-covered wall.

"It seems nature is drawn to him," Renna said. The wall had been mere stone a few weeks prior.

"It is! Watch." Zandorn was giddy as he drew a dagger against the Druid's arm. He growled as a thin red line of blood followed the blade and dropped into a glass bottle. Zandorn bent, pouring the blood into a crevice on the floor. Within moments, a small stem sprouted between the worn stone slabs.

"Marvelous," Renna said, not disguising her bored tone.

"Isn't it?" His eyes were bright with excitement, a stark contrast against his greyish skin. "I knew Druids would be important, pivotal, to my work. My sweet Terasi," he said, running a gentle hand down the Druid's face. "You're even more valuable than I realized."

Terasi said nothing, but Renna saw the muscles in his arms and chest flex, their tension giving away his feelings. He was stripped from the waist up, covered in bruises and cuts that marred his tattoos. Half of one of his antlers was missing, no doubt a casualty of Zandorn's experiments. His golden eyes focused on Zandorn, and Renna could almost feel the fiery hate in his gaze.

"Have you retrieved any useful information?" Renna asked. "Besides the anatomical sort, I mean." She had to clarify. Whenever Zandorn was in these overly excited states, he focused solely on the research subject in front of him. It fell to her to drag his attention back to the bigger goals of the Consortium.

"Not yet," he said, flicking the small green stem before walking to the nearby table and pouring a glass of water. "His mind is strong, it will be difficult to break." His lips curled up at the corners, relishing the challenge ahead.

Renna crossed her arms and silently tapped one finger against the silk sleeve of her robe. She missed Kalbick. Gods, how much *progress* she had made with him in such a short amount of time was astounding. After only a few weeks, her beautiful Kalbick followed her every whim with barely a command. He had known what she wanted just before she did and had been ready to do anything to get it for her.

She looked up, and Zandorn studied her, his eyes finally leaving the Druid. *Baltenebris curse him*, she thought. She let her guard down for a moment and he caught her lamenting.

"I know you're upset about losing Kalbick," he said.

This was, by far, the most frustrating thing about living with a genius like Zandorn. It wasn't enough to feel inadequate next to his intellect and power. He also had to demonstrate his superiority by putting the smallest fragments of information together, sharing his deductions as if he had read her mind. The only thing that made it bearable was that Renna—as Zandorn's last remaining shred of family—was his weak spot.

And she knew it.

"If you know, why aren't you doing anything about it?"

she asked, pretending to pick a speck of dust from her immaculate sleeve. No one in Valecium would dare speak to him with such harshness. Or they wouldn't unless they wanted to donate their body, mind, and magic to his experiments. But she could—did—and was rewarded.

Zandorn smiled, and for a moment Renna saw the shadow of the handsome man he had been at one point. Perhaps a century ago, before her mother died, before he began her resurrection campaign. "My dear, I am doing something about it. The time is not right, but we *will* return your precious Kalbick. You have my word."

"Fine," she said, making sure to hide any hope or excitement she felt. It wasn't that she doubted Zandorn; quite the opposite—he always delivered on his promises. But she didn't want to give him the satisfaction of pleasing her right now. "What did you wish to speak about?"

"Ah, yes." He sipped water from the glass before returning it to the table. "I'll need you to continue leading the Consortium and our operations for a few more weeks." His eyes drifted back to Terasi, and Renna understood.

"Of course," she replied.

"You'll get nothing from me," Terasi said in a low snarl.

"Haven't I already?" Zandorn's smooth voice was edged with sweet venom.

"You may break my body, take pieces of it, but my mind will never be yours. I will never help you find what you seek." He leaned forward as he spoke, chains rattling as his arms pulled them taught from the wall.

Renna's ears perked up. *What is Zandorn looking for?* He

shared many of his plans with her, but not all of them.

"We shall see, Druid." Zandorn stood a hair's breadth away from Terasi, silently taunting him in his confinement. "That will be all," he said. He didn't turn from his staredown with Terasi, but Renna knew he spoke to her.

"I'll keep sending the regular reports," she said, bowing before leaving. As she pulled the chamber door shut, Terasi cried out in pain. It reminded her of Kalbick—he had the most beautiful screams. She rolled her eyes in annoyance.

Why did Zandorn have to taunt her with his toys?

Her mood soured, burning a hole in her chest as she strode through the torchlit hallways. Flicking her wrist, the doors to her chambers flung open with a *bang*. Gunther loomed over the long table to the left, spindly white hair falling into his face while carefully placing settings for a meal. The plates looked tiny in his giant palms. Renna had known Zandorn would ask her to keep minding the Consortium, so she set Gunther to prepare for the advisor's meeting before she had left.

Pouring herself a pemberry wine from the serving table on the far wall, she looked out on the lush greenery and gentle waterfall below.

Zandorn had carved the large opening in the wall and crafted the oasis for her when she was eleven. It only cost a few months of complaining about the monotony of living in the dwarven fortress. It was the first time Renna made something happen because she wanted it. Without asking Zandorn to *do* something, she'd still be staring at a solid stone wall. That feeling of satisfaction, of victory, when her demands were met—the rush of getting her way and the elation that she was powerful enough to break any resistance kept her going, especially now, when she was so close to getting what she truly wanted.

And this time, she wouldn't be asking anyone for permission.

"I've always admired this view," Karazul said.

She *barely* jostled her wine in surprise. No one could sneak up on her except this gods-cursed assassin. She blamed his lack of magic, which meant she couldn't sense his presence, but his step was also silent as death. Karazul must have noticed her small movement as he smirked, waiting for her response.

"You're early," she said. The meeting wasn't for another half hour.

"I thought we should talk."

Renna crossed the room to a raised platform with a desk. The curved legs supported a black stained top with elaborate floral embellishments made of the finest Janlakan hardwood. She had killed its previous owner and stolen it herself. The memory always made her smile, and she did so again as she sat behind it, leaning back as she sipped her wine.

"Whatever you have to say, we can discuss at the meeting." She didn't like or dislike Karazul, but his anti-magic abilities deserved respect. Keeping her distance from the infamous mage killer was preferable, especially now that Burvenin was dead. That oaf's greatest value had been keeping Karazul distracted with his buffoonery.

"Unfortunately, that is not the case. What I have to ask

is a little sensitive." He draped himself soundlessly in one of the chairs opposite Renna, the hilts of his swords and daggers glinting in the low light.

She gestured with an apathetic wave, inviting him to speak his piece.

"You know my arrangement with your father. I serve his purpose, and he gives me information on my brother in exchange. I've held my end for several years, and now it is time for him to pay up." He twiddled his fingers on the back of the chair next to him, but his eyes were focused, singular in their intention.

"You'll have to discuss it with Zandorn," she said. "Your deal is with him, and so is the payment."

Karazul smiled, but the motion was practiced and fleeting. "I would, but he hasn't seen anyone in the last month *except* for you. So," he copied her wave from a moment ago, "here I am, asking you instead."

"And what makes you think I know anything?" she asked. Truthfully, she didn't know anything about Karazul's brother or much about his mysterious past. Something in her gut told her to avoid him from the moment he arrived, so she did.

"I don't think you do," he guessed. "But you're the only one who can get to Zandorn right now, meaning you're the only one who can get me what I'm due."

Renna thought for a moment, tapping her finger on the rim of her glass. She hadn't expected this conversation, but it wasn't a problem. Karazul had signed a blood contract with Zandorn, swearing him to service, and those contracts were nearly unbreakable. She wasn't worried about denying Karazul anything because no interaction between them would alter the agreement. But maybe...maybe this was an opportunity she didn't foresee.

"Let's say," she leaned forward, setting her glass on the desk. "That I can get you *what you are due*." She stressed his words, twining her fingers beneath her chin. "What are you willing to do for me?"

She knew Karazul was smart, and he wouldn't come asking for her help without expecting a request in return.

"Whatever the lady wishes, should she make a request within my power to grant." His fingers stopped dancing on the chair as he shifted to match her posture. "Do you know what you want?" There was a glint in his eye, and Renna suspected he enjoyed this game they were starting.

Her lips twisted into a genuine smile.

"I know *exactly* what I want," she said.

CHAPTER 9

CONTROL

Zak wobbled up the spiral staircase to Tansil's office. It had only been a day since Tor'alan lurched into movement, beginning its journey to Masdaan. The initial alarms blaring through the city and the immediate shockwaves were unsettling, but now Zak hardly noticed the subtle shifting as his feet wavered before plunking up each step. He heard it had been several years since Tor'alan relocated, yet most people seemed unbothered in their usual activities.

He steadied himself on the cold stone wall at the top of the stairs, straightened his uniform, and blockaded his mind against Jolsu. It was difficult, but Zak had too many important questions for Tansil to let the dragon's prodding distract him. He had never been to Tansil's office by himself, and his stomach knotted as he knocked and the elf's lilting voice beckoned him inside.

"Ah, Zakolor, good timing." Tansil rose from behind the mahogany desk, waving him over to one of the chairs beside a small table laden with a harvest meal. A tureen of squash and garlic soup stood in the center, surrounded by hunks of sourdough bread, roasted chicken, boiled and seasoned potatoes, apple and pear tarts, and cauliflower acorn puree.

It was a dark evening, and little moonlight penetrated the windowed room. Dozens of candles scattered about provided a soft, warm glow.

A green orb on the other side of Tansil's office caught Zak's attention as he sat. It was no more than a foot wide, and inside a small bronze lizard curled up on a bed of crushed stones, twigs, and leaves. "Is that the lizard found in the forest after Terasi was taken?"

Tansil's bright green eyes followed Zak's across the room. "Yes, it's a curious thing. The orb allows food and some inanimate objects to pass through. It repels any magic or physical approach." Tansil held up his hand, and the tips of three fingers were scorched.

"I'm sorry, Archmagus," Zak said. The harsh wound looked painful.

"Oh, it's no bother. Injuries heal. This orb, though, is perplexing. I can't feel the life energy within the lizard. It's as if the barrier protects the creature from everything outside its circumference." His attention drifted as his expression softened into some kind of pondering.

Zak's sweaty hands fidgeted in his lap. "Um, sir," he started, returning Tansil's attention to the conversation. "You mentioned you'd explain everything about Cerevita."

"I did." Tansil shifted in his seat. "You know the basics about the Contract. Following their defeat in the Guardian War, it barred the gods from the physical world. Lesser known are the details of the Contract and its...allowances. Did you notice the three thrones in the chamber where you met Cerevita?"

"I remember them," Zak said. How could he not? The imposing, oversized thrones were too large for any human or elf to sit in comfortably, and when Cerevita had materialized, he understood why.

"Before the Guardian War, Tor'alan belonged to the gods, and they used the thrones to hold court. They took turns leading, passing the role every century, and the tradition became known as the rotating throne of power. A bit of a misnomer, of course, since there are three thrones, but I digress." The elf gestured for Zak to help himself to the food on the table. He plucked a few berries and cheese and put them on his plate, but they felt more decorative than anything. He was too nervous to eat.

Tansil continued, biting into a plum. " Elves, dwarves, humans...all were unhappy in the Era of Dominion. Not all of the gods supported the policy of forcing devotion, but with Azubelux and Baltenebris championing the cause, none would directly oppose it.

"That was why Cerevita came up with the clever idea to create the *Nacusti*. It appeared as a diplomatic gesture, elevating three elves and three humans to serve as bridges between the divine and the mortals. In reality, it gave the mortals divine power and a fighting chance in the war that soon followed. The mortals barely won the war—only two of the six *Nacusti* survived. Your ancestor, Adrastus Belcour, and the elf Temaway Galeria. With Azubelux and Baltenebris cowed, an agreement was negotiated. Temaway and Cerevita were close, had been for centuries, and they recommended including a small exception to the complete banning of gods from this plane."

Zak held his breath. None of these details of the Guardian War or the Contract were mentioned in any of his schooling back in Densba, or at least he didn't think so. *Kal would know for certain*, he thought. "What was the exception?" he asked.

"That once a month, if called, the reigning god could visit this plane for exactly one hour," Tansil replied.

"The reigning god?"

"Yes, they kept the tradition of rotating power every century. You met Cerevita because she is the reigning god on the throne of power, so she is the only one that can be called, at least until the next Year Festival."

"What happens at the Year Festival?" Zak's heartbeat quickened.

"We enter a new century in 600 E.F., and Azubelux will be the reigning god for the next hundred years." Tansil's tone was flat, matter-of-fact.

Zak jumped to his feet, chair skidding on the floor. "But that's only four months away! How can Cerevita help us destroy the Consortium if she can't be here?"

"Now you understand our urgency," Tansil said. "We may call on Cerevita four more times before she is beyond our reach."

Zak's fury melted his nerves. He thought he was done discovering secrets, especially after he *met* Cerevita, and Tansil promised that Zak would lead the League down this path, toward victory over Zandorn and the Consortium. It was his path, the elf had said, as the *Nacusti*.

But it wasn't true, had never been. He was still being led by Tansil, Limba Dar, Euphemius, and everyone else who remained a step ahead.

"None of this makes sense." Zak fell into his chair, a coldness leeching to his core. "Why did you and Sorwin wait so long to find me? To train me? I could have had *years* of learning from you and Cerevita to prepare."

"Wishes and hubris." Tansil sighed. "I knew your mother, and she wished to keep you far from this conflict between the League and Consortium. And in my hubris, I thought we could win without the *Nacusti* power. Or that we'd have enough time to try."

My mother. Kamira, according to Tansil. But Zak had never known her—she had given birth and then became another casualty in the war. Clairise was the only mother he had known—the only one he needed.

He leveled a caustic look at Tansil. "I want to speak to Cerevita."

"That won't be possible."

Zak slammed his fists on the table, the plates clattering. "You promised! You *promised* I would lead us down this path. Those were *your* words!" Rage blurred the edges of his vision as his skin flashed green.

A long moment stretched between them, but the elf's attention had not drifted. Tansil's stare didn't waver from Zak.

"It isn't possible," Tansil said slowly, "because we already spoke to Cerevita in Autumn. The Contract allows us to call her exactly once per month. The earliest we could speak again is on the first day of Autumnfall."

Zak's heavy breath roiled with anger. "Then we'll speak with her then."

"I would advise caution, Zakolor. If we call her on the first day, we would have to wait the entirety of Autumnfall—a full six weeks—before speaking with Cerevita again. And by then it would be Winterrise. We should wait until our need for guidance is greatest."

"My need is great right now!" Zak countered. "Olivia and Kal need help. They're both on borrowed time. Cerevita will know how to cure them. She has to." He didn't care that he was almost pleading now, his desperation to save his friends more important than his pride.

Tansil nodded knowingly. "I understand, and we will help them. We will ask Cerevita when next she is summoned. All I ask is that we wait until the moment is right."

Zak leaned back in his chair, some of his mental faculties returning in the wake of his anger. Tansil made it sound like he was choosing Olivia and Kal's well-being over the entirety of the League if he called Cerevita too soon. Was that true? What did Tansil want to wait for?

"I'll think about it," Zak said. He couldn't make a decision, not now.

"That is all I ask."

"Archmagus." He stood to leave, too frustrated to stay in the elf's presence. Near the door, Tansil's voice sounded again.

"One last thing, if I may."

Zak fought a grimace that wanted to cover his face and turned.

"The dark shapes that attacked a few days ago. I thought you'd want to know we determined how they infiltrated Tor'alan."

That certainly piqued Zak's interest. "How? Did you find out what they are?"

"This was the first attack that breached Tor'alan's shields, so we thoroughly investigated to find what weakness was exploited. By studying the creature you, Shira, and Bazil captured, we discovered they can manipulate their size and shape to some extent. They shrunk and smuggled themselves through the entrance portal by clinging to mages and soldiers returning from the field."

"Three Fires...they didn't seem that intelligent when we fought them."

Tansil stood but didn't approach, respecting Zak's space. "I don't believe they are. Someone is controlling them—most likely Zandorn. We haven't figured out what they are yet, but they share disturbing similarities with the Rot."

"What do you mean?"

"We've been studying the Rot, hoping to find a way to stymie its spread. The creatures absorb life energy, just like the Rot. They are highly resistant to magic, though not immune like the Rot. Some mages have noticed the parallels and started calling the creatures 'Rotters.'"

"Rotters," Zak repeated. He imagined the grotesque creatures crawling out of the Rot and shivered at the terrifying thought.

"We instituted new inspections for all individuals entering the city. It won't happen again," Tansil promised.

The following two weeks were some of Zak's most challenging. Despite Tor'alan's steady progression toward Masdaan, he continued feeling stuck in place. There were no more attacks—from Rotters or anything else—so Tansil kept one promise for now. But rumors of the Disciples spread through the city, putting everyone on edge.

"Gettin' bolder, they are," Zak had overheard a grocer say to a customer while following Euphemius through the Market district. "Heard about another three raids just this week!"

"What do they think they'll accomplish fighting against the League? Honestly!" the customer had said, shaking her head in disbelief.

Zak pressed Sorwin for details on the Disciples during his lessons. His normally loquacious magus only avoided topics he *couldn't* discuss, which made Zak worry when Sorwin offered nothing on the raids or the mysterious religious group.

"The League is aware of them," Sorwin said. "And we're handling the situation. Perhaps you should focus more on your earth magic rather than rumors?"

Sorwin was right. Zak made some progress with the earth element—he could now form shields and perform basic spells—but he had so much further to go before Sorwin would consider teaching him water or air magic. Besides, between his studies, research in the Archives, worrying about Olivia and Kal, and ignoring Jolsu, Zak didn't have the time or energy for another concern.

He kept hoping for a breakthrough in the Archives, to stumble upon more information about the caladrius or discover an obscure treatment for Olivia and Kal. Even with Bazil's help, progress was nonexistent. The caladrius continued to be their only lead on a cure, but Zak found little mention of the rare bird in any books or scrolls. And, since he begrudgingly decided to listen to Tansil's advice, he didn't call on Cerevita to ask for her help—for now.

After several weeks, Tor'alan quaked to a halt near Masdaan. Zak buzzed with excitement, trying to peer from the upper floors of the Archives to the sand-ensconced city below. He hadn't left Tor'alan in ages, and despite the heaviness of his guilt for his friends and responsibilities as *Nacusti*, he wanted a break, an escape, even if only for a few hours.

He was in luck, as Euphemius sent a Firepost that morning informing him they would venture into Masdaan. A few hours later, Zak met him and Olivia at the Center's main gates after the council meeting—which he fortunately avoided this time.

But before they could set off, Limba Dar waylaid them, rapid footsteps clicking on the stone path as he approached. He held out two envelopes with a wax seal, one for Euphemius and one for Zak.

"What is this?" Euphemius asked.

"An invitation. Baron Woolbin of Masdaan is hosting the

council and a few notable persons tomorrow for a congenial afternoon."

"A bit early for merrymaking." Euphemius tucked the invitation into a hidden pocket. "We haven't even mediated the disagreement with Evartia yet."

"All in good time," Limba Dar cooed in his scratchy voice. "The Baron simply wishes to be a good host for the League. And I trust he's curious to meet our *Nacusti*, too. Just as well you sped from the council chambers before I could hand out the invitations, Euphemius. You saved me the trouble of tracking down Zakolor."

Like you wouldn't have enjoyed the excuse, Zak thought. He looked down at the ornate envelope, a rich cream with brocaded etchings glinting in the sunlight.

Sorwin had encouraged him to attend one or two similar functions in Tor'alan. These were not extravagant events where Limba Dar or Marius would be present to sink their claws into him, but smaller functions with merchants, laborers, and artisans, all people who kept the League running. "You need to be seen to begin changing things for the better," Sorwin had said.

Zak remembered the first event had been in a merchant's manor in the Lion district. There was a stuffy dining room, forced niceties, shaking many hands, small talk, and too-small appetizers. It exhausted him and felt like theatre—a performance in which everyone played a role that ultimately wasn't real.

The memory sent a jolt down his spine as a sudden flash of a similar luncheon with high-status nobles and officials passed through his mind. *This will be so much worse*, he thought. Limba Dar would undoubtedly be there, cloying at the vaguest whiff of power, which was enough incentive to make Zak decline the invitation right then.

He wasn't sure if attendance was mandatory, but what if someone there knew about a caladrius or the Disciples? It could be an opportunity to uncover more information.

Going alone felt impossible. He needed a friend at his side. Sorwin would be there but most likely occupied as the representative of Darlangson. If Olivia went, she'd be trailing Euphemius—and she wouldn't want to keep him company anyway.

"Can I bring a guest?" he asked.

Limba Dar, who had half-turned to leave, tilted his head as his mouth twisted in a greedy smile, almost like he was happy Zak made the request. "It's irregular, but so is the *Nacusti*. I'm confident the baron would accommodate your guest."

Zak nodded, unable to address Limba Dar with a "thank you," though he was grateful nonetheless. He'd ask Bazil to go with him later. If anyone could block the perfunctory rituals of high society, it was Bazil and his no-nonsense demeanor.

Limba Dar drifted back toward the castle as Sorwin exited the large doors, and Zak slid the invitation into a pocket.

It only took a moment of conversing for Sorwin to piece together that Euphemius was taking Zak from the safety of Tor'alan and into the unknown of Masdaan.

"I can't allow this," Sorwin declared.

"This isn't your decision, Magerus," Euphemius smiled

fiendishly at Sorwin.

"Neither is it yours, Mr. Van Ilia. The threat of the Consortium and Rotters is enough to keep Zakolor here, and now we have confirmed the Disciples' activity in Masdaan—"

"All the more reason I need the protection of the *Nacusti* for my business."

"You would risk his life for your *ego*?" Sorwin shouted.

"I would enforce the contract *he signed*." Euphemius' smile faded, knuckles whitening on the grip of his cane.

Sorwin, usually calm and level-headed and thoughtful, looked furious. After a few labored breaths, he continued in a low, dangerous tone, "I will summon the council to stop you if I have to, Euphemius."

"You can try, Sorwin, but we've already parted for the day, so good luck herding us all back together. And besides, you were in the meeting. You heard the same as me that Vermig and General Lupa are indisposed on the front lines, and Limba Dar insists on the presence of the full council to negotiate between Evartia and Weslinton. It will be several days before we are convened again. So, if you'll excuse me." He raised the black cane and gestured for Sorwin to step aside. "I wish to return before night falls. We wouldn't want to be *unsafe*, would we?" He sneered, passing Sorwin, who stood unmoving but offered no further resistance.

"Sorwin, I'm sorry," Zak said, reaching out to squeeze his shoulder. As much as he wanted a change of scenery, this felt wrong. All Sorwin ever did was look out for Zak, and this was how he repaid him.

Sorwin stared at something on the ground as he spoke.

"Don't sign any more contracts without speaking to me first."

Zak winced and nodded. He had disappointed Sorwin before, but this was different. This was the first time Sorwin failed to maneuver a situation to his advantage.

He looked at his magus again. Sorwin had dark rings under his eyes, disheveled hair, and slightly rumpled clothes. He was under immense pressure to continue Zak's training, develop portal magic, and fight the Consortium. Was it all catching up with him? And was Zak making everything worse?

You should make a list, Jolsu suggested. *It'll be easier to track all of your blunders.*

Zak redoubled his efforts to blockade the dragon from his thoughts.

"I'm sending Croi with you," Sorwin said, finally meeting Zak's concerned expression.

"Of course." He couldn't argue with Sorwin, not now. "I'll be okay. Try not to worry." With one last inadequate pat on the shoulder, Zak left Sorwin and caught up to Euphemius and Olivia as they walked toward the entrance portal.

CHAPTER 10
KAPANA

The chaotic trip through the portal from Tor'alan to the ground stirred Zak's insides, and he fought the urge to retch. His excitement about visiting Masdaan didn't help matters. He had never been to a foreign country or city—not really, anyway. Densba was on the Southern Isles, which was part of Regadensia. The Isles had been settled only a few generations ago, and although they were geographically different from the mainland, the culture felt similar between Densba, Bernadooth, Lindomer, and Tor'alan.

The air was warmer on the ground. Little drops of sweat formed on his brow as he walked through the city's outskirts, and packed dirt paths transformed into sparkling mosaic sidewalks at Masdaan's western gate, glinting in the sunlight and throwing rainbows of color onto the tan walls of nearby buildings. The structures were short, many only a single story or two with flat, clay tile roofs.

Masdaan felt different. Masdaan felt alive.

Masdaan felt like *fire*.

He grinned and followed Euphemius and Olivia closely through the bustling streets. Unlike Tor'alan, Masdaan wasn't organized. Narrow roads twisted and turned, and dwellings pushed against one another, leaning at crooked angles. Most people were draped in light-colored fabrics and wore head coverings to protect them from the relentless heat. He pulled at his sticky uniform and wondered if it was this hot all year or perhaps even more stifling in Summer.

In the heart of the city, the crowded street opened onto a large central square. With more space, Zak could see further than a few feet in front of him for the first time since entering the city.

He gasped. An enormous glass pyramid dominated the area. It was bigger than the entire Center in Tor'alan. The glass panels were edged with white mortar or paint—he couldn't tell—and slowly rotated. Air flowed between gaps in the panels with a melodic whistle. Inside, hundreds of small buildings, tents, and booths populated what appeared to be a market.

Euphemius pulled Zak and Olivia aside, out of the flow of bodies moving toward the giant structure.

"I have several stops to make inside the Kapana" Euphemius said.

"Kapana?" Zak repeated, his tone inflecting the question.

"The Glass Dream." Euphemius glared, gesturing to the pyramid with his cane. "Some stops will be short, others long. Keep up, do as I say, and *do not speak* unless spoken to."

Zak was so excited he didn't even bristle at Euphemius' patronizing instructions. He nodded, wide-eyed, as he followed the merchant to the entrance of the Kapana. Olivia's expression read equally awestruck. She also looked paler than usual.

His earlier guess that the Kapana was a market proved true. It was somehow more than that too. Vendors shouted their wares from stalls and tents, and performers danced on makeshift stages. He saw everything from jugglers to puppet shows to fire mages. His mouth fell open as a skilled artist twisted white flames into a wide-petaled flower, then shifted to a fish leaping through waves. He knew magic was powerful and practical; he had never seen it be this *beautiful*.

And gods—the *scents* that flooded the air. It was overwhelming, the sharpness of spice and warmth of sweets pulling his attention as they waded through the throng of stalls and goods and bodies. The Kapana had its own unique heartbeat, pulse, rhythm.

"Wait here, I'll be a half hour." Euphemius vanished through the folds of a large circular tent.

Zak couldn't contain himself for more than a minute. "Want to look around?" he asked Olivia.

"We shouldn't." Her usual confidence was absent as her gaze drifted over the exotic surroundings.

He jingled a few Bronze Marks in his hand. "Any food you want, my treat."

Her eyes narrowed and lips twitched upward. "*Any* food, you say?" She looked around, heading for the nearest vendor.

"Uh, *almost* any!" Zak clarified, stumbling behind her.

They passed by candied sweet buns, sugared cakes, seasoned meats, and steamed vegetables. Zak didn't recognize any of the food, but he wanted to try them all. Most of the vendors shouted prices in Marks, and they seemed reasonable. His wage as an adept wasn't much, but he could afford two treats for each of them. Olivia chose a fish tart and honeyed candy, while he went for a small pemberry pie and corn dumpling.

With appetites sated, they wandered through the market, keeping Euphemius' tent within sight. Zak marveled at the spinning glass panels overhead, and spotted Croi drifting among them.

Somehow, the air was cooler inside the Kapana than outside. The heat should have been insufferable with the glass amplifying the sunlight, but the chilled, melodic breeze ruffled his hair no matter where he moved in the market.

The sound of something spilling turned Zak's head. A man in a brown tunic and breeches splayed on the ground with hundreds of rice grains. Two men in beige uniforms stood over him.

"Watch yourself," one of the uniformed men said, laughing as the pair walked over the man, scuffing their heels in the pile of rice. The fallen man said nothing, but began scooping the rice into its bag when the men left.

"Hey." Zak started toward the men, but Olivia grasped his arm.

"Don't," she warned. "Those are Masdaan mages. Look around."

His eyes slid around the Kapana. He noticed—for the first time—at least a dozen pairs of mages in the same beige uniforms. Some stood guard at different entrances, while others patrolled the narrow market paths. It would be unwise to get tangled with local guards, especially as the *Nacusti*, and definitely while working for Euphemius.

Yet the thought of Euphemius' angry, scrunched face almost made him *want* to get into trouble.

Instead, Zak ignored the guards as they walked away and approached the man on the ground, still scooping his rice.

"Can I help?" Zak asked.

The man shielded his eyes from the sun as he looked up with a suspicious expression. "Why? I can't pay you."

"That's fine," Zak said with a friendly smile. "Just hold open the bag."

The man hesitated, but after looking at the huge pile of rice, he held the top of the bag open.

Zak moved his hands in circles, coaxing the grains to swirl into the air and pour into the bag like water into a pitcher. When the last grain was safely stored, he held out his hand, and the man accepted the help to his feet.

"Thank you, Magus," he said, his unfamiliar accent plucking at the words.

"It's just Zak," he said. He thought he saw Olivia roll her eyes.

"I am Malu," the man said. He hefted the bag of rice, which was almost the same size as him, and started walking away.

"Can I help with that?" Zak asked.

"I don't have far to go." Malu's voice thinned as he strained under the weight of the rice.

"What was that about, with the guards?" He walked next to Malu, at least hoping to prevent anyone else from running into him.

"Dangerous times, Zak, dangerous indeed. Guards are on edge like the rest of us, aren't they? Maybe moreso."

"Dangerous because of the Disciples?" Olivia asked.

Malu gasped and set down the sack of rice, spinning to face Olivia. "Mask your words, Magus! It is dangerous even to *name* them."

"Surely the League and Weslinton are taking care of them?" Zak was surprised at Malu's strong reaction. Weren't the Disciples more of a nuisance than a threat?

"Not fast enough," Malu said. "They raid, steal, and kill. They endanger all Masdaan, all Aghoomi." He picked up his rice and started his slow march again.

"Aghoomi?" Zak asked.

"Yes. Your maps and your League may say Weslinton, but we are still Aghoomi, the land of fire, glass, and spice," Malu spat in a sharp tone.

"I'm sorry, I didn't know there was another name."

"The world is not always as it seems, Zak." Malu put down the sack of rice and fiddled with the door of a wide clay building. Rows of rounded windows contained different creatures: dogs, cats, lizards, fish, birds, and more than a few that Zak didn't recognize. They all paced, swam, fluttered, and chirped as Malu neared the door as if they recognized him.

"Is this your shop?"

"Welcome to Zindost, where you can find a friend for life," Malu said in a well-practiced—if not bored—voice. "Are you in need of a companion?"

Zak followed Malu inside as the man wrestled the bag of rice behind a long counter. "I wish I were," he said honestly, eyeing the menagerie. Sorwin's advice about being ready for a familiar rung in his ears. It wasn't his time.

Malu must be knowledgeable, Zak thought. Looking at the variety of creatures the man cared for, he had to be. He wondered how far that knowledge extended. Hopefully, to a wide range of birds.

Maybe even to rare ones.

As Olivia wandered toward the glass enclosures, he turned to Malu.

"Do you know anything about caladrius?" he asked, keeping his voice quiet, not wanting to get Olivia's hopes up.

Malu's eyes snapped to his. "You ask many questions, Zak." He was silent, scrutinizing for a moment before speaking again. "Who are you?"

"A League mage," he said, pulling on the sleeves of his uniform.

"What else?" Malu countered.

He couldn't tell Malu he was the *Nacusti*. He barely knew the man and he promised Sorwin he'd be careful. He didn't want to use his title, anyway.

"A concerned friend. Olivia," he gestured to her, "is sick, and nothing has helped. I need to find a caladrius to heal her."

"I may know something. What ails her?" Malu asked as he divided the rice into smaller containers.

"It's difficult to explain." More omissions. He didn't want to tell him about the *vitaligo*. Old magic was rare and memorable. Most of the League didn't know the details of her condition, only that something happened that bound her magic. He couldn't risk being specific.

"They are fickle things, caladrius. No guarantee they will heal your friend."

"It might be her only chance. Please, do you know where we can find one?" Zak released the counter, realizing he had a white-knuckle hold on the smooth edge.

"How many Marks do you have?" Malu asked with a sigh.

"Wha–why?"

"Nothing is free. How many Marks do you have?"

Zak reached into his pocket and pulled out an assortment of coins, pushing them with a finger as he counted. "Three Silver, twenty-three Bronze." He had brought most of his money—more than he should have—but he hadn't been sure how much anything in Masdaan would cost.

Malu reached over and plucked the Silver Marks from Zak's palm before he could react.

"Hey!"

"This way, bring your friend." Malu walked around the counter toward the rear of the shop.

Olivia swept toward Zak when he yelled. "What happened?"

"I'm not sure." He shoved the remaining coins into his pocket, not wanting to give Malu another chance to swipe them. "Come on, I think I bought something."

They followed Malu around a corner. The shop was much larger than it looked from the outside. A long interior wall divided the front area from the back, with only a few glazed windows dotting the rough plaster. The air was cool and a little dusty. Towers of wooden crates, clay jars, and metal cages were stacked with perilous negligence, threatening to tumble at the softest touch. Malu stepped through makeshift aisles with an easy familiarity while Zak and Olivia carefully followed him to a locked door.

"What you see in here, you mention to no one. Yes?" Malu said. His tone made it a statement, not a question.

"What will we see?" Zak asked.

A deep crease appeared between Malu's brows. "Agree, or you don't see."

"Yes, fine. We'll keep it secret," Zak conceded.

Malu unlocked the door and led them inside.

It was best Malu *hadn't* told him what was inside, because Zak wouldn't have believed him.

The round room split into sections no more than a few feet wide, each holding what appeared to be tiny landscapes. One had a mountain approximately three feet tall. Another had a lake the size of a puddle. Miniature fields, forests, and streams all rested in their respective slivers of the strange room, connected by a detailed wooden inlay in the middle of the floor.

"This way," Malu beckoned. As he walked toward a coastal landscape with cliffs and beaches, he began to shrink.

"Malu!" Zak gasped, not sure what was happening to the man.

"Come!" Malu yelled back. He was only two feet tall now, and his voice sounded far away like he called from a distance.

Zak twisted to Olivia, her eyes just as wild as his. "What did you do, Zakolor?" She breathed the question.

"Something good, I hope." Before she could protest—or he lost his nerve—he grabbed her hand and pulled her behind him.

He didn't feel any different, but as he ran, the cliffs grew taller and taller. He chanced a look back and the door to the room had doubled in size.

They were *definitely* shrinking.

"Where are we?" Zak called. His footsteps slowed on the wet sand as waves crashed into the beach and salty gusts whipped through grey skies. It was like they walked right into another world.

"The better question is 'what's here?'" Malu said. He cupped his hands around his mouth, and a high-pitched whistle cut through the wind.

Hundreds of birds perched on the cliffs took to the sky, a blur of wings and colored feathers soaring down the rocky face. Zak ducked as the mass swooped overhead, buffeting him with blasts of air. He laughed as he stood, the sheer rush of the spectacle releasing something in him.

Olivia smiled too, and Zak couldn't remember the last time she looked this happy. Her auburn curls danced around her face, which looked thinner than a few days ago. He still held her hand and squeezed, and her eyes met his. Why was his heart beating so fast?

She seemed to remember herself at the same time Zak did, and they unclasped hands and averted their eyes.

Malu had a roguish grin as he approached Zak and Olivia. On his outstretched arm rested a small white bird with elegantly curved horns arcing from its brow to the back of its head.

"A caladrius!" Zak gasped. There was no doubt in his mind this was the bird from his dream.

And not for the first time, he wondered who this strange man really was.

Malu fed the regal bird something from his pocket and it nipped gratefully at the treat. "I must remind you, these creatures are of their own mind. Caladrius may make things better, do nothing at all, or deliver a death note. The choice is yours." He turned to Olivia as he finished his warning.

Zak looked from Malu to the caladrius to Olivia.

Olivia's entire body tensed, and Zak knew she understood the implications. The caladrius might be able to heal her. It could also foretell her death.

He wanted to tell her to seize the chance to be free of her binding, that this could be the end of her curse, her suffering. But he needed to listen to her, truly listen, like she asked him to before.

So he waited.

Barely breathing.

Summoning patience.

And finally, thankfully, she spoke. "Tell me what to do," she said to Malu.

The strange man nodded. "Approach, look into its eyes, and wait."

Olivia moved within a step of Malu and the caladrius and stared into its golden eyes. The bird twitched its head to the side, meeting Olivia's gaze.

Odd, Zak thought. *The caladrius in my dream was black*

with blue eyes. It had the same horns and shape. Did the color matter? The tension between the caladrius and Olivia was thick, like it would burst if he made a sound, so he kept silent.

After a minute that dragged on for hours, the caladrius dipped its head forward, the tips of its ribbed horns nearly grazing Olivia's brow. It picked its head up and took two small steps to turn away.

That was the mark of death.

Olivia was going to *die.*

"No," Zak whispered. He couldn't move, couldn't breathe. This wasn't right. This wasn't how it was supposed to happen.

Olivia is going to die, and it's all my fault.

He looked at her—she hadn't moved yet. Then her shoulders fell, and her head tilted back a fraction like she let go of something that held her together.

"No," he said again. The numbness faded from his limbs and he surged forward, grasping Olivia's shoulders. "We'll fix this, *I* will fix this."

Tears streamed down her pale, gaunt cheeks. For a moment, Zak thought he saw a mixture of exhaustion and relief in the small, joyless smile that pierced her lips. She pushed out of his grasp and ran away, retracing her footprints in the sand.

Olivia is going to die, and there's nothing I can do.

Zak let her go, fire burning in his chest as he spun on Malu.

"What is that thing? It's not a caladrius!" he yelled, pointing at the bird. It squawked and flew away, rejoining its flock on the cliffs.

"I warned you this may happen," Malu said, his tone laced with sorrow or pity.

"No, you said that was a caladrius, but it wasn't. I've seen one. They're black with blue eyes," he spat.

Malu's face hardened as he lunged and grabbed Zak's wrists. "You've seen a black caladrius? Where?" The man hissed with urgency, desperation.

"Get off!" Zak twisted, trying to escape, but Malu's iron grip held him fast.

"Where did you see it?" Malu said, his voice boomed like thunder as the sky darkened behind him.

"In a dream!" he shouted, fear and shock driving the answer from him.

Malu released his wrists, and Zak rubbed them as he stumbled back a few steps. "I should have known. I'm sorry I lost my temper."

Zak barely listened. He fell, scrambling on the sand before regaining his footing and turning to run. Olivia was ahead, where the edge of the beach met the strange room. She grew taller with every step, and Zak hoped she was far enough away to be safe from Malu.

She's still going to die because of me.

Whatever Malu was, he was powerful, and Zak needed to get far away from him.

"Wait, I'm sorry!" Malu called. "I'm sorry. There's something you should know, *Nacusti*."

Zak froze and faced Malu, heart pounding in his ears. "I never told you I was the *Nacusti*."

Malu stepped forward, arms out wide. "You should

know that caladrius are white. At least the kind you were looking for. That," he gestured over his shoulder to the flock on the cliff, "was a caladrius. The *black* caladrius are supposed to be a myth."

"But I saw one," Zak said. His dreams were many things. Confusing, unpredictable, and frustrating, to name a few—but they were not false. Never.

"I believe you," Malu continued. "If you're looking for a black caladrius, you're in for a difficult hunt." The man hesitated as if considering what to say next.

"Who are you?" Zak asked. His fear wasn't gone, not completely, but Malu didn't seem intent on hurting him.

An impish grin curled Malu's lips. "Ah, *now* you ask the right questions, Zak. I won't give you that answer—not now—but I will give you something else as an apology for losing my temper. If you seek the black caladrius, you'll find it in The Yew Tree."

"A yew tree?" It couldn't be that simple.

Malu scoffed. "*The* Yew Tree. The first in Valecium."

"Why there? Where is it?"

The man clicked his tongue, scolding Zak. "What fun would it be if given all the answers? But what better place for the Bird of Death to roost than the Tree of Death?"

"Bird of Death? Caladrius are supposed to be healing birds."

"Oh yes, most caladrius are; the rare black caladrius is death." Malu let out a low cackle.

"Who are you?" Zak repeated, taking another step back as Malu's laugh sent a shiver up his spine.

"A friend to some, a nuisance to others, and a laugh to most." Malu flashed one more terrifying grin. "The world is not as it seems, *Nacusti*." He snapped his fingers, and everything disappeared.

Zak blinked. The first thing he noticed was the noise. People chattering, kids laughing. He was back in the Kapana, glass panels spinning overhead to their slow, melodic tune.

He turned, and where the entrance to Malu's shop should have been was a leatherworker's stall.

"How..." The entire clay building was gone. Malu's last words echoed in his thoughts.

The world is not as it seems.

An illusion? But it was so elaborate, so real. Before he could decipher the cryptic message, a thought crashed into him. *Olivia!* Was she still inside the shop when it disappeared?

He frantically pushed through the crowd, searching the market. She had been ahead of him, she must have made it out.

There—he spotted her auburn curls as she drifted between market patrons and vendors. He caught up to her just as Euphemius emerged from the circular tent. The merchant didn't even look as he waved for them to follow along to his next stop.

Zak walked close to Olivia. Her cheeks were splotched and damp. His nausea from earlier returned, twice as strong. What should he say to her? What *could* he say?

Olivia is going to die.

CHAPTER 11

LAND OF FIRE

Somehow, Zak found sleep that night—either due to the sheer exhaustion of the emotional ups and downs of the day or from the heavy guilt for what he did to Olivia. Or both. He couldn't accept that she would die, but Olivia believed the caladrius' prediction, and he couldn't forgive himself for putting her in the position to witness it.

The black caladrius plagued his dreams, taunting him with its visage. The midnight feathers and bright blue eyes should have shattered his hope for a cure, now knowing it represented death. Yet it was still his only lead to pursue, a symbol guiding him toward the future.

What if it represented Olivia's death?

Terasi was in the dream this time, running across the grove with outstretched hands grasping toward him. The Druid's mouth moved, but Zak heard no sound.

He woke in a daze, head pounding and more tired than the night before. Sleep didn't necessarily mean rest.

That became abundantly clear as he muddled through lessons. The slow progress he had made with earth magic came to a standstill as he could barely form half of a shield. It should have been easy, shields were his talent. But all he could conjure was a thin veil of dust no higher than his knee.

Sorwin took pity on them both—he looked just as ragged as Zak—and let them return to their quarters to prepare for the afternoon's festivities.

Within a few hours, Sorwin collected Zak and Bazil—the latter thankfully agreeing to attend the party—from the Center and led them through the meandering streets of Masdaan. On a small knoll overlooking the Kapana, a mansion glittered in painted tiles, sculpted glass, and blazing fire. An attendant—flanked by two mages in beige Masdaan uniforms—greeted guests and took their invitations as they passed through the arched door.

"Magerus Sorwin," the attendant said, bowing his head and flicking the invitation into an embroidered pouch on his hip. His eyes widened as they landed on Zak. "Ah–*Nacusti*! Divines bless your flames!" His hand moved in a circular pattern before resting between his brows.

Zak had no idea how the attendant recognized him or what the greeting meant. "Yes, you too." He handed the invitation to the attendant and shuffled by as fast as he could.

"I'd prepare for more of that," Bazil said, leaning to whisper in Zak's ear. "Many in Weslinton are devoted to the gods, and with *Nacusti* magic in your veins, you're the closest to divine they'll likely get."

"But shouldn't they hate me? The *Nacusti* are the ones that defeated the gods."

"Some might, but most remember the time before the

Contract. The gods created the Guardians to watch over Valecium, and the Guardians helped make the *Nacusti*. To them, you're a living work of the divine."

Zak swallowed a bubbling queasiness. He didn't want—didn't deserve—the adoration of anyone. At the moment, all he wanted was to survive this gods-cursed party.

A large request for your ineptitude, Jolsu said.

He ignored the dragon but couldn't disagree with his assessment. He *was* inept at high society and politics. "What do I say if that happens again?" he asked Bazil.

"The blessing? Just say, 'And may yours ever burn.' It's part of an old prayer. They'll probably go mad if you do."

"Thanks, I think." He didn't want to excite any religious folks at the party, not with all the rumors swirling about the Disciples becoming more aggressive, but it wouldn't be a bad thing if they thought fondly of him. He needed to build relationships to live up to Sorwin and Tansil's expectation of uniting the League.

More of a dream than expectation, he groaned internally.

Following the string of guests through the mansion, Zak, Bazil, and Sorwin found themselves in an elaborate dining room on the second floor. A stained glass ceiling illuminated by the midday sun depicted images of Weslinton's long history—or Aghoomi, according to Malu.

Green, blue, red, and brown swirled in the adorned tiles on the floors and walls, and a table made entirely of glass ran the length of the room. There wasn't a fingers-width of space left unencumbered by a decadent feast, which was a happy sight for Zak. The last party he attended offered little in the way of sustenance, and he had left hungry. At least he wasn't at risk of that today.

Limba Dar accosted them with his labored smile as soon as they entered. "*Nacusti*! Ah, I see you brought Magus Bazil. A fine addition to our afternoon." His expression flattened noticeably as he looked at Sorwin. "Magerus, I believe the Archmagus was looking for you."

Sorwin frowned. "Tansil? Are you sure? We just—"

"Yes, quite sure. I wouldn't keep him waiting—not that he's impatient, as you know—but that he's *too* patient and may take a month before he gets around to speaking to you."

Limba Dar's words tumbled so fast that Zak had difficulty keeping up. *He's unusually impassioned today.*

He didn't wait for a response but kept pushing through his words like a farmer with a full wheelbarrow, eager to unload the heavy contents. "I last saw him on the terrace. I'll watch over Zakolor and Bazil while you're occupied. There are plenty of individuals eager to meet the *Nacusti*."

Before Zak knew what happened, Limba Dar steered him and Bazil toward the opposite end of the room. Zak shot a look back at Sorwin, trying to say, "Don't worry, I'll be fine," but he wasn't sure if he heard the unspoken message.

Even after a light morning and extra rest, Sorwin looked worn out, and he was no match for Limba Dar's enthusiastic state. He wandered off toward the terrace, picking at the collar of his tunic.

Limba Dar eagerly paraded Zak about, foisting him on merchants and nobles for a quarter-hour. Shock and exclamations followed his introduction, and no less than seven

"Three Fires!" were lobbed at him with gasps and round eyes. Through it all, Limba Dar pulsed excitedly, soaking up the reverence by proxy from the famed *Nacusti*—his energetic spewage drowning any attempt Zak made at speech.

At least Zak was introduced in conversation; Limba Dar apparently didn't deem Bazil worthy of note and ignored him completely. Bazil tensed more and more as the minutes passed excruciatingly slow.

This was the *exact* scenario Zak expected—false theatrics caressing egos and propping up Limba Dar as his keeper. He'd had enough of Limba Dar's frenzy, and as they parted from the most recent gawkers, Zak pushed away, readying a tirade for his and Bazil's sakes, but someone else cut in.

"Why, Limba Dar! You're running those boys ragged. Be still for a moment, let me see you—finally in Masdaan again." A portly man with a sagging, embellished hat strolled up to them. A full plate rested on the edge of his belly.

"Lord Woolbin, it's a pleasure." For the first time since Zak arrived, Limba Dar looked unsteady.

Lord Woolbin? He must be the Baron of Masdaan.

"I was ever so happy to receive your Firepost about organizing this splendid affair. Well, don't delay, Limby, who's this?" Woolbin gestured to Zak and Bazil.

"*Limby*?" Zak couldn't contain a fiendish smile, and Bazil buried a laugh beneath a cough.

Now, it was Limba Dar who seethed, hissing an introduction through his teeth. "My Lord, this is the *Nacusti*, Zakolor Keldin."

"Three Fires! How do you do, my boy?" Woolbin

stopped chewing his drumstick long enough to set it down and extend a greasy palm.

Zak shook it and discreetly wiped his hand against his thigh. "I'm well, Your Lordship. How do you know Limby?" He took a little too much satisfaction seeing Limba Dar squirm, clearly disliking the nickname.

Woolbin didn't notice but almost knocked Limba Dar over with a vigorous arm pat. "This clever crow used to work for me! He's from Masdaan, didn't he tell you? How long has it been, Limby, three years at least? When my cousin Marius visited, he was absolutely beside himself with worry since he had just inherited Regadensia and the League. Of course, he came here for my sage advice, and Limby was in several of those meetings offering guidance. By the end of the week, Marius couldn't fathom leaving without our dear Limby, and, being as generous as I am, I couldn't deny our young king this boon."

Beneath Woolbin's thick layer of self-aggrandizing, Zak heard something important. "You're King Marius' cousin, Sir?"

"Why yes! Didn't Limby tell you?"

Limba Dar, who looked close to keeling over in a mixture of horror and furor, finally found his prickly voice. "*High* King Marius honored me with an offer to serve the entire League. I'll forever be grateful to you for providing the opportunity, My Lord." He offered a stilted bow to Woolbin.

That's one mystery solved, Zak thought. Now he knew how Limba Dar scratched his way to Marius' ear. But the circumstances of their meeting still didn't tell Zak about his goals or intentions. It wasn't that Zak necessarily wanted to know—everyone had their reasons for things—but learning more about Limba Dar could prepare him to avoid future political maneuvers.

"Never mind about that, Limby. I hear you're doing splendid things for Marius." Woolbin took a squelching bite of his drumstick as grease dribbled down his chin. "And you boys, have you enjoyed any of Masdaan since you arrived?"

Zak struggled not to be disgusted while watching Woolbin eat. "Yes, I went to the Kapana yesterday."

"Of course! Our pride and joy here in Masdaan—all of Weslinton, really. You know it was constructed in the Era of Mages? Thousands of years ago! We're lucky those glass panes never break; I'm not sure we have the magic know-how to fix them these days."

Chunks of meat splattered on the floor as Woolbin waved the drumstick as he spoke. Footmen in pristine uniforms continually swooped in, cleaning the tiles mere moments after they were soiled, and Zak suspected the footmen were well practiced in the act.

"It's very impressive magic," Zak said. He didn't want to linger with Woolbin, the taste of diplomacy already bitter on his tongue. But the baron was important in Masdaan—and to the League, as Marius' cousin—and his friendly demeanor and unintentional needling at Limba Dar made him a suitable target for practicing small talk. "During my visit, I heard the name Aghoomi for the first time and wondered if you could tell me more about your land's history. When did the name change to Weslinton?"

Woolbin froze, his jovial bearing disappearing faster than the fallen chunks of his drumstick. "You *dare* utter that name in my presence? What sick game is this? Limba, what poison has your pet ingested?"

The baron's transformation from merry to livid left Zak without words, jaw working but producing no sound, like a fish gasping out of water.

Limba Dar's crooked smile split his face as if sensing Zak's weakness. And now he was a hawk circling his prey. "My deepest apologies for his ignorance, Your Lordship. I will apply the antidote immediately." He shoved Zak to a corner of the room, out of Woolbin's eyeline.

"What happened?" Zak asked, thoroughly confused. "I thought asking about his country would be a good thing."

Bazil had followed them to the corner. "Your curiosity is admirable, but Weslinton's past is controversial."

Limba Dar looked at Bazil in thoughtful surprise. "That is tactfully put for a Regadensian."

"Not all of us are proud of Regadensia's past," Bazil said. "Not the parts with unnecessary bloodshed, anyway."

"Sorry, what?" Zak wasn't following the conversation at all.

Limba Dar sighed. "Aghoomi is the true name of my country. Relations with Regadensia were never healthy but remained stable in the Era of Dominion because the gods didn't allow large-scale warfare. Too many devoted would be lost in the violence, which meant less prayers and less power for them. But after the Guardian War when the gods were no longer here to keep the peace, tensions escalated. It didn't happen all at once, but over the decades, there'd be an argument here, a border dispute there, and we were one rash decision away from war."

"That was when the Woolbins hatched a plan to invade Aghoomi," Bazil said, a sadness knit in his brow.

"Why?"

"Greed." Limba Dar's customary venom returned. "The Woolbins held a duchy on the border of Aghoomi, but it wasn't enough. They saw the opportunity to become kings."

"But one duchy couldn't have conquered a whole country," Zak reasoned.

Bazil shook his head. "They didn't. This was centuries ago, but the Ferns and Woolbins were close even then. They saw the opportunity to turn an enemy into an ally if they conquered Aghoomi and crowned the Woolbins."

"But Woolbin is a baron, and Masdaan is far from Regadensia's border." If the Woolbins really did conquer Aghoomi, why wasn't the baron the king?

Limba Dar rolled his eyes. "Lord Gideon Woolbin is a baron. His Majesty Gyrnavo Woolbin is the king. You should pay closer attention in council meetings, *Nacusti*."

He was right. If Zak had missed the surname of one of the leaders of the four countries in the League, what else had he overlooked? "The Woolbins aren't from Aghoomi. They're Regadensian nobles that conquered the country."

"They are *occupiers*, not conquerors," Limba Dar spat. "If you were in Masdaan for a single day and heard the name Aghoomi, that is proof enough it yet lives."

"But the Woolbins would see Aghoomi buried beneath

its own sand," Bazil said. "That's why they erased the name from maps and records and replaced it with Weslinton."

A strange, weightless sensation washed over his understanding. "So my mentioning Aghoomi to Lord Woolbin..."

"Was akin to slapping him *and* his ancestors in the face," Bazil said. "But the problem isn't that you offended a baron. It's that you offended a cousin to *two* kings."

"Marius and Gyrnavo." Zak groaned, burying his face in his hands.

From the little he learned of Lord Woolbin in their short time together, Zak had no doubt he would run to his cousins to lament the abuse he suffered from the oafish *Nacusti*. How had he mucked up a simple conversation so spectacularly that it was about to become an international fiasco?

A stunning spectacle. Even I *couldn't have predicted this magnificent of a blunder*. Jolsu's bliss rippled through Zak, conflicting with his own shame, making him shudder.

He couldn't believe what he was about to say, but Zak knew it was the right thing to do. "Limba Dar, I'm sorry for embarrassing you in front of Lord Woolbin. And I'm sorry that Aghoomi has suffered. What the Woolbins and Ferns did wasn't right."

Limba Dar looked at him, not with the greedy eyes he usually wore, but with a quizzical, evaluating gaze. "If you're truly sorry, there's someone else you should meet. Stay here, I'll return momentarily."

As Limba Dar's thin frame darted between partygoers, Zak let his thoughts drift on the currents of chatter and music that filled the crowded dining room. He wallowed for a few minutes as his gaffe grew heavier.

Bazil had the good sense not to attempt cheering him up but settled for plying him with a mountainous plate of meats and sweets. Zak was too nauseous to eat but held the plate anyway, hoping its solidity would ground him and push away the overwhelming numbness paralyzing him.

The plate didn't help, but confusion did. The more he reflected on the conversation, the less he understood Limba Dar.

He was from Weslinton—Aghoomi—which meant he had good reason to despise the Woolbins. Yet he had worked for Lord Woolbin, whose family invaded his country. Now, he worked for Marius Fern, whose family supported the invasion—made it possible, given their resources. Why? What did Limba Dar stand to gain by working for either of them? How could he stomach it?

He had to suspend his thinking as Limba Dar reappeared with a stern-faced man.

"Zakolor Keldin, I'd like to introduce Magus Fanum Ket, Eelikuh of Weslinton."

"*Benevita, Nacusti*." Fanum Ket bowed at the neck. "I hear you are interested in our...history in this country." His voice was deep and smooth, the opposite of Limba Dar's.

"*Benevita*, Magus. I certainly have a great deal to learn." Which was, as Zak now painfully understood, an understatement.

Fanum Ket's dark features lifted in a warm expression. "That is an admirable attitude, *Nacusti*. I believe we should never cease learning."

Zak cringed at the use of his title. "You would get along well with Magerus Sorwin, then. Please, call me Zak." He made a point to introduce Bazil, not wanting him to think he had been invited to the party just to follow Zak around and be ignored.

"*Benevita*, Bazil," Fanum Ket said. "I'm unsure what Limba Dar has shared with either of you, but I am the Eelikuh, similar to your Archs in the League. I guide our country's mages—all those who remain, anyway, and have not joined the League."

Now that Zak looked closer, he saw the resemblance of Fanum Ket's fitted trousers and flowing tunic to the Masdaan mages' uniform. "It's an honor to meet you."

Zak held his tongue, afraid to make another misstep, and hoping Fanum Ket would guide the conversation—which he did. They carefully waded through safe topics like the wonders of the Kapana, the weather, and the confusing twists and turns of Masdaan's ancient streets. Fanum Ket was kind and solid, like a sun-warmed boulder. But something else underneath the exterior gave Zak pause, something that said this man was tense, coiled, ready to lunge at any threat.

He felt dangerous.

Maybe it was his magic or his title. If being Eelikuh was similar to being an Arch, only the most powerful mages would qualify. Maybe he had lived a hard life, was accustomed to struggle that forced him to prepare for the worst. Whatever it was, something about the man put Zak on edge.

But on the surface, Fanum Ket shone with a brilliance of polished brass. "Limba Dar mentioned you're an elemental mage, as am I." He sipped from the glass in his hand. "And that you're gifted in shield magic."

Zak clenched a fist behind his back. "Limba Dar is well informed." *More informed than I realized.* He wanted to ask Sorwin if he supplied these details to the council or if Limba Dar collected the information independently.

"That he is," Fanum Ket smiled. "He also tells me the two of you discussed the Contract and how it limits the devoted."

"It came up before." He shifted his weight, uncomfortable with the conversation's turn. *Is this why Limba Dar wanted me to meet Fanum Ket? To talk about the Contract?*

"And what are your thoughts?"

This felt perilously similar to his conversation with Lord Woolbin. Two conversations wove together at once: the words they spoke and those they didn't. Except this time, he was very aware of how easily his ignorance could offend Fanum Ket.

Sweat beaded on his lip. "Limba Dar must have also told you I am not devoted and that even though I am the *Nacusti*, I could not decide the Contract's fate on my own." He was confident that was true; the council, at least, would voice many opinions if the matter was ever up for debate.

"But if it *were* up to you, if your hand was forced to choose a side, would you uphold oppression or bend for freedom?" Fanum Ket's brown eyes sharpened, fiery as they studied Zak.

Bazil was the one to speak. "That's not a fair question, Eelikuh. The Contract *gave* freedom to many. You present conflicting choices."

Zak disguised his sharp intake of breath, thinking Bazil's bluntness to be ill-timed. It was partly why Zak brought him, to fend off stuffy nobles, but he didn't expect to meet anyone like Fanum Ket.

To his relief, the Eelikuh shrugged and held up a hand. "I merely seek to understand the *Nacusti*. My role as Eelikuh is to understand the world's mighty magics and determine if they are friend or foe."

"Weslinton is a member of the League of Kingdoms," Zak said. "Of course we're allies."

Fanum Ket looked disappointed. "Allies are not the same as friends. After your discussion with Woolbin, I'd hoped you had learned something about my country."

Abnormally silent until then, Limba Dar interjected. "Well, Eelikuh, let us give the *Nacusti* a chance to enjoy the festivities. I'm afraid I took *too much* of his time today." He was unreadable, but his hand shook as he held it open to guide Fanum Ket away.

With a nod and a bow and a cold "*Benevita*," Fanum Ket followed Limba Dar back through the crowded room.

"Are you alright?" Bazil asked.

Zak couldn't quite relax, still surrounded by the crowd of unfamiliar people, but his shoulders lowered, sore from tension. "I think so."

"Good." Bazil flicked Zak's ear.

"Hey! What was that for?" He cupped his ear. That *hurt*.

"For being a *stulmati*." Bazil sighed. "Why did you come to this party today? What was your intention?"

He didn't know what Bazil was after but trusted his

friend enough to follow along despite the ear flicking. "Sorwin's always telling me "people are the reason and the cause," which I think is some strange way of saying I need to build more relationships to understand them—"

Bazil's hand flashed as he flicked Zak's ear again.

"Knock it off!" he hissed, keeping his voice low to not draw attention.

"I asked for *your* intention, not Sorwin's. Try again."

Zak grunted, annoyed, and suddenly felt sorry for Bazil's acolytes if *this* was his teaching method. "Fine, my intention was to find someone with information about the black caladrius. And that was a failure since I was busy offending as many influential leaders as possible."

Zak hadn't told Sorwin about Malu or Olivia's encounter with the caladrius. He didn't think Malu meant any harm to him or the League—he had trapped Zak, had him prone and at his mercy, and had let him go. So Zak told himself it wasn't his news to share, but in truth, he didn't want to burden Sorwin more than he already did.

But he had to tell *someone*. And Bazil was already helping him hunt down a cure for Olivia, so he deserved to know.

He rubbed his ear and told Bazil about his and Olivia's misadventure in the Kapana. "What do you think Malu is?"

"Azubelux light me if I know," Bazil said. "Something old and powerful, by the sounds of it. Not a mage alive that I know of that could shrink worlds and disappear like that."

A few moments passed between them before Bazil frowned. "Zak, you brought me to this party as a friend, so as your friend, I must tell you that you messed up today. I know you're going through a lot with Olivia and Kal, and the pressure of expectation hangs unfairly from your shoulders, but it isn't going away. Today was an opportunity for you to release some of that pressure by building inroads with leaders in Masdaan and Weslinton, and you did a bang-up job of squandering it."

"I'm sorry, Bazil." He was right about everything. If things had turned out differently, Zak could have connected with Lord Woolbin and Fanum Ket, two very influential figures in Weslinton. Instead, he did the social equivalent of nudging them down a very steep hill, where they tumbled all the way down and stood up, bruised, confused, and angry. "And I'm sorry you came to this crummy party and were ignored and insulted."

Bazil softened as his strict magus persona melted. "Don't worry about me, Zak. I'm tougher than that. But we should be concerned over Limba Dar and Fanum Ket."

"I thought there was something strange about Limba Dar working for Woolbin *and* Fern. It doesn't make sense."

"Did you notice how Fanum Ket always said 'my country' or something similar? He never said 'Weslinton,' almost like he couldn't bring himself to."

"You don't think..." Zak hesitated, glancing to make sure no one was nearby. The party was still in full swing, and the quartet played a lively song that drew a scattering of partners to a vigorous dance. He whispered anyway, hoping Bazil could hear him over the clamor. "Do you think they support the Disciples?"

Bazil, who rarely showed his emotions, went through

several forms of disbelief, intrigue, and worry. Still, he reined them in and kept judgment from Zak's guess, instead asking, "Why do you think they might?"

"Well, you heard them. They're both interested in reducing or destroying the Contract. Wasn't it odd that *after* I apologized to Limba Dar about Woolbin and Aghoomi, he said he wanted me to meet Fanum Ket?"

"Yes, that was interesting timing." A deep contemplation settled over Bazil.

"And that was the second time Limba Dar broached the topic with me. What if they support the Disciples and seek allies in the League?"

"That is a serious charge, Zak. What if you're wrong? What if they are devoted and not Disciples? There is a difference. I am devoted, and if given the choice, I would wish to be closer to Azubelux."

"But you wouldn't at the cost of all free will in Valecium, would you?"

"Well, no. That defeats the purpose."

"Exactly!" Zak ran a hand through his hair as his thoughts buzzed with a quickness. "I don't know if I could say the same about Limba Dar. Look at all he's done to maneuver to Marius' side."

Bazil shook his head. "Even so, we have nothing of substance that says either of them could be involved with the Disciples, only our fears. I wouldn't bring this concern to anyone without proof."

It was a fair point. It would be incredibly irresponsible to accuse Limba Dar of treason without anything to back up the claim besides, "I just know it." Perhaps his dislike of the man clouded his objectivity, making connections fit together when they otherwise wouldn't. No, he couldn't mention this to anyone except Bazil—not yet. But he wouldn't be idle, either.

"I won't for now, but I'll keep a closer eye on Limba Dar."

"We both should," Bazil agreed.

CHAPTER 12

BOILING POINT

The following day, council members filed into Lord Woolbin's dining room again, finally assembling to mediate the schism between Evartia and Weslinton. Limba Dar and King Gyrnavo insisted on meeting in Masdaan since Weslinton complained first, and Lord Woolbin volunteered to host the affair. Zak noticed Woolbin purposefully ignored him while greeting other guests and pointedly diverted his attention if it ever drifted close to Zak.

That will take some fixing, he thought.

Much of the party decor remained from the previous day, though the glass table had been cleared of the feast and looked even longer flanked by rows of cushioned chairs. Zak sat next to Sorwin and felt the strain of their tiny schism. They hadn't spoken much in the last few days.

The council members were already arguing. Zak was there to symbolize unification, and he grimaced, feeling every bit the prop Tansil and Marius needed him to be. If they genuinely believed in his power and ability to unite the League, they wouldn't waste his time with this squabble over fish.

They wouldn't demand so much of Sorwin. They would let both of them focus on his training.

They wouldn't ignore Olivia and Kal.

Zak's anger flared for his two friends and their very different circumstances, plunging them toward the same fate.

What if the black caladrius represented both *of their deaths?*

A soft touch on his shoulder made him turn and meet Sorwin's worried eyes. Even as exhausted and frustrated as Sorwin appeared, Zak knew he never stopped caring for him.

But Zak couldn't keep draining Sorwin's energy; he needed to be less of a burden and more of a boon. He tried releasing the tension in his body—not for himself, but for his magus—and they shared a nod, and Zak thought they silently told one another *I'm okay, I promise.*

King Gyrnavo reddened from shouting accusations across the table. "It doesn't matter where the fish are now. Your people were the FIRST to trespass!"

Minister Qor sat with folded arms. "By that logic, Janlaka should inhabit the *entire* river since our city was established first. That means Masdaan has been trespassing for thousands of years." She seemed to control her anger on the surface, but the subtle tapping of fingers on her elbow betrayed the facade. Zak imagined the politician—who had led the Evartian revolution—was more accustomed to arguments than the king who occupied Aghoomi.

Assessing the rest of the table, most council members appeared in various states of boredom, annoyance, or anger. Sashina sat stone-still. Vermig's face darkened from his normal tomato-red to plum-purple. General Lupa ignored the deliberations and spoke to a captain at his side. Tansil and Marius seemed to be the only two paying attention, though Tansil had a far-off look that could have meant he didn't hear a word. Euphemius wrote in a ledger, quill scratching across thick parchment.

Then there was Limba Dar, sitting at the far end of the table, light from above casting long shadows over his sharp features. He was near the only entrance to the room besides the twin doors on the opposite end leading to the terrace.

That was odd. Limba Dar *loved* being the center of attention. He sprang at any chance to put himself in the middle of council meetings. In fact, he had orchestrated this entire discussion, advising Marius to move Tor'alan and demanding they wait until the whole council was present to mediate. Zak thought the man would revel in his success, jumping in to negotiate and brag about his influence to bring the League's most powerful people together on *his* recommendation.

Why, then, was Limba Dar hiding in the corner?

"Compensation for *thousands* of years?" King Gyrnavo's voice became squeakier by the moment, filled with fury. "Evartia wasn't a country when Janlaka was established, so you have no claim to such a demand."

Minister Qor stopped tapping her elbow. "And from what I hear, the Woolbins have no true claim to Weslinton. Or should I say Aghoomi?"

An audible gasp rippled through the lavish dining room, which suddenly felt cavernous. The council paid attention now, waiting to see what Minister Qor's bold insult would yield.

King Gyrnavo rattled with rage, unable to form words. Surprisingly, Marius—generally meek and avoidant of conflict—spoke up.

"Limba Dar, you're from Masdaan and have served the League diligently. Perhaps you can act as a bridge for this conversation?"

Zak prepared to roll his eyes and bury his disgust—Limba Dar relished this type of invitation, when he didn't have to force himself into a conversation but was sought for his expertise.

But Zak was in for another surprise as Limba Dar looked nervous, hands fidgeting and voice quaking. "Oh, Your Majesty, I wouldn't dare overstep my role. I'm simply the one that brought you all together. I'm sure King Gyrnavo and Minister Qor can continue their deliberations."

What in the Three Fires was happening? Did Limba Dar just *deny* an opportunity for power?

Marius scratched his jaw, perhaps confused as well, but he didn't quit the idea. "I respect your humbleness, but I'm sure we could all do with a fresh voice and guidance."

Limba Dar squirmed and then abruptly stood, chair skidding harshly against the tiled floor. "Perhaps a break, then? To let tempers cool and calm minds return."

"Sound judgment, thank you, Limba Dar." Marius addressed everyone at the long table. "Let us resume in a half hour."

A chorus of chairs and rustling fabric filled the air as the council and local officials stood, clumping to speak in hushed tones. King Gyrnavo wasted no time stomping over to Marius, towering over him with arms flailing, no doubt delivering a mad speech about disrespect. Lord Woolbin hurried over to a footman standing at attention near the wall, probably to order refreshments during the break.

Zak was stunned by Limba Dar's behavior. Humble and nervous were never words he would use in association with Limba Dar, but that was how he appeared today, the opposite of his usual self.

Pushing his suspicions even further, he watched Limba Dar slip from the room unnoticed by nearly everyone. There was a host of influential people in the room, and this break provided the perfect opportunity for Limba Dar to sink his greedy claws into any of them. But he chose to leave.

Something is wrong, he thought.

Should he follow Limba Dar? It would be risky since he was unfamiliar with the mansion's layout. But Limba Dar wasn't—he most likely knew every nook, cranny, and secret in this ancient building after working for Lord Woolbin. It would be too easy to catch Zak pursuing him, and it might not even be worth it. What if he was simply going outside for fresh air?

Still, he had to do something. Despite what he and Bazil agreed to yesterday, he couldn't keep quiet any longer. Limba Dar was up to something, and Zak had a terrible feeling it was spinning out of his control.

The only person he could tell was Sorwin.

Stulmati, he silently cursed himself. Hadn't he just sworn *not* to burden his magus more?

Breaking a promise in less than an hour is quite the achievement, Jolsu chirped.

I don't have a choice. Zak didn't have the energy to argue with Jolsu or block him out.

He had to tell Sorwin about his suspicions. But as a compromise, he didn't have to share everything, just enough to pique his interest and stoke his own misgivings. Which wouldn't take much, Zak reasoned, since Sorwin vehemently disliked Limba Dar already.

When he turned to tell Sorwin, the sound of shattering glass pierced the chamber.

"Rotters!" someone yelled.

As Zak looked up, thousands of shards of glass fell toward him. The mosaic ceiling had broken, and dark shapes poured through the opening.

Tansil reacted first. His ice-blue magic shielded the entire council, protecting them from the glass.

Rotters oozed down the walls as the doors to the room burst open. Several guards lay dead at the feet of a mob. They wore striped black, white, and green bandanas covering the lower halves of their faces.

"Burn the Contract!" a man in the front shouted, raising a sword as he charged into the room. The mob echoed the chant, surging behind him, the metal of their weapons flashing.

For a moment, everything slowed as the room erupted into chaos.

Tansil, Sashina, and Vermig worked in unison. Sashina put up a rose-colored shield while Tansil's faded as he manipulated branches and vines that sprung from the floors and walls, pinning the charging mob in place. Vermig summoned a demon that looked like an armored bull. It lowered its horns and pushed the mob back into the hall.

The first wave of Rotters made it to the floor. They toppled League mages and Masdaan footmen scattered around the room, leaving their drained corpses behind and throwing themselves against Sashina's shield. It held but winked dangerously as if it would give out at any moment.

"Sorwin!" Tansil shouted above the mayhem.

"I know!" Sorwin answered as if they shared the same thoughts. "Zak!" he shouted.

And Zak realized *they* must have the same connection because he immediately knew what Sorwin was asking.

Zak's magic was the only thing that could destroy the Rotters.

His whole body thudded with a quickened pulse as he spun and shouted, "*Ignis*!"

Emerald flames burst from his palms, engulfing the nearest Rotters crawling up the edges of Sashina's shield. They hissed and screamed as they burned to ash. But for every ten he destroyed, twice as many streamed down the walls and slithered toward him.

"There's too many!" Zak shouted, but Sorwin didn't hear him. He had moved too far away, protecting the rest of the council that couldn't fight or wield magic.

The acrid taste of burned flesh flooded the air. *What do I do?*

"You're holding back, *Nacusti*."

Zak turned his head as he kept up the stream of fire.

A few paces away, Vermig cupped a *lapidaemas* in his hands as countless demons streamed from the stone. They flew and scurried to the hall, all limbs and claws and teeth and horns, the different shapes and sizes joining the fray with the mob. "You need to let go," Vermig said.

"I'm not holding back." He wasn't, he couldn't be. His power surged through his arms, fueling the thick spouts of flames.

"You are," Vermig said, wincing from the incredible effort of summoning a horde of demons. "And you have been since that day."

Zak knew precisely what day Vermig meant. It was the day he rescued Kal, only to leave him trapped between worlds. The day he saved Olivia, only to curse her to a slow, painful death. The day he almost lost himself to his own power.

No, not his power—Jolsu's.

He's right, the dragon said. *You've held us back since that day. You haven't embraced our power once.*

Heat flooded Zak's insides. He didn't have words for the tumult of emotions tearing through him. *It was never 'our' power. It was always yours,* he said to Jolsu.

It's that belief that limits you, Parignis.

"No!" Zak yelled, and as he did, his skin flashed green as his flames pulsed up the nearest wall, decimating half the Rotters in front of him. Zak gasped, releasing the spell. What did he just do?

"That's it!" Vermig called. "Let go, *Nacusti*."

He didn't have time to understand how Vermig saw

through him, saw straight into his fears. Had he been holding back? He was terrified of what he almost became that day, how far he pushed Jolsu's power—*his* power. What would he have become if he had kept going?

Rotters flooded down the walls, stacking themselves against Sashina's weakening shield. Reverberations of battle from the hall made a cold harmony with the certainty in his mind.

He couldn't ignore his power anymore.

He couldn't be afraid of what he might become.

He couldn't fail again.

He *needed* to be the *Nacusti*.

All the pain, guilt, frustration, and anger Zak had carried for months pooled in his chest—like it did that day—and he released it all with a feral scream.

Emerald flames scorched the air around him, manifested by his shout. They burned through the Rotters on the shield in a second and then collected into a fiery ball. Wings and a body folded outward, and a dragon made of fire swooped around the room.

Rotters fell from the ceiling and walls as the flames passed through them, high-pitched cries fading as their sludge-like bodies charred into ash.

The council and mages within the shield cheered as the endless stream of Rotters stopped. They were gone. Zak had destroyed them all.

The fiery dragon landed on the floor next to him. It was smaller than Jolsu had been when they spoke in his mind, but it had his likeness. At that moment, Zak forgot all his anger toward the dragon and beamed at the magnificence of their power. He turned to Vermig. "How did you know?"

The Archalium smiled, and as he opened his mouth to answer, a figure appeared behind him. A hand grabbed his chin, and a blade slid across his throat. Vermig's eyes widened as he clutched at his neck, red already pouring down his front.

"No!" Zak shouted, and the fiery dragon roared, lunging toward the figure.

The man held up a hand, and the dragon dissipated like a candle being snuffed. "Cute trick, *Nacusti*," said the figure.

"Karazul." Zak recognized the voice at once.

"You remember? I'm touched." The assassin removed the striped bandana covering his jaw and bent, pulling something from Vermig's pocket.

No one else was nearby. Sashina had dropped the shield when the Rotters were gone and rushed to tend to the injured. The battle with the mob still raged in the hall, where Tansil, Sorwin, and the rest of the mages must have been.

Zak flung flames at Karazul, but the assassin batted them away. He swore, feeling his magic fade. The fire dragon had taken more out of him than he realized.

"This time, I'm not here for you, *Nacusti*." Karazul backed away, shaking the prize he plucked from Vermig in the air. His sharp eyes and sharper grin boiled Zak's blood. A watery surface rippled on the wall behind him as he walked backward into the portal, disappearing.

Zak rushed to Vermig's side, calling for Sashina. She swept in, turning the mage over. Her hands moved fast around the wound in a rosy glow, but Zak saw the absent glaze in Vermig's eyes.

The Archalium was dead.

Zak huddled over his tea, the spicy ginger searing his raw throat. He had cried for almost an hour after Sorwin whisked him back to Tor'alan, away from the chaos of Masdaan and into the safety of Inguma's firm presence. After a quick word with Sorwin and one glance at Zak, she took him to the kitchens, away from the prying eyes of the mages in the Dormitory and the mess hall.

He sat at a small table in the corner, usually reserved for staff to take their meals. Inguma sat across from him but said nothing, save for the occasional direction to place food and drinks. He didn't eat but clutched the mug of tea, its heat the only feeling in his otherwise numb body.

He had seen death before and had even killed to defend himself. But Zak had never witnessed the murder of someone he *knew*. Every time he closed his eyes, he saw Karazul's blade at Vermig's throat, the cold metal slashing a warm red line. The image made everything feel somehow so real and so pointless. Why was life so fragile? What chance did he have of making a difference in this war? Why couldn't he save someone right in front of him?

What was the point of trying?

"You weren't alone, Zakolor," Inguma said, peering at him over her blue half-moon glasses. Her lavender hair was covered in a tight cloth wrap.

"What?" He only half heard her through his loud thoughts.

"In Masdaan. The room was full of soldiers and mages, not to mention all three Archs. You alone weren't expected to save Vermig."

"But I—"

"No," she said, reaching across the rough tabletop to squeeze Zak's hand. "It is okay to feel sad, to grieve, but you cannot carry the guilt of his death."

He said nothing, staring down at his tea. *But someone should*, he thought. And as he sat there, out of tears and sunk low in the mires of grief and shock, something happened. A spark caught inside him as his thoughts slowly churned.

Too many coincidences led to the council being together in Masdaan, in that room, at that moment. This didn't happen by accident, and one man was responsible.

Limba Dar.

He was the puppeteer who pulled all the strings for weeks to organize the meeting, but it still didn't make sense to Zak. Why would Limba Dar work his way through Masdaan, up to Marius' side, just to attempt to destroy the council? Did he hate the Woolbins and Ferns that much? Fanum Ket certainly seemed to; did he convince Limba Dar to betray the council?

The picture may have been clearer if they knew who controlled the Rotters. Tansil suspected it was Zandorn, and so did Zak. It was difficult to imagine anyone else with the knowledge and ability to create the creatures.

Yet the Disciples were involved in the attack. It was their mob that stormed the mansion, not the Consortium. Did that mean they were allies now? It would explain how Karazul arrived at *just* the right moment to kill Vermig and take something from his corpse. Why did the Consortium target Vermig? Or why did they *only* target Vermig? Even Karazul would have had difficulty dealing with all three Archs, but he could have done more damage in the chaos of the battle with his blades and anti-magic. Wouldn't it have made sense for him to kill as many council members as possible?

He also had a chance to capture Zak, whom Zandorn supposedly still desired. Why didn't he try?

He fought a groan creeping up his throat. He had been training ferociously and was *still* vulnerable, a burden.

"Zakolor," Tansil's soft voice called from the nearby doorway.

Zak startled as he looked up to the Archmage's bright green eyes. They cast a soft glow on his dark brown hair and maroon robes. The elf always moved with unnerving silence, but Zak had been so lost in his thoughts that he didn't see him approach.

"Archmagus," he rasped, clearing his throat.

"Magus Inguma, thank you for watching over Zakolor. We have matters to discuss, so I will relieve you. *Benevita*."

"Of course, it was no trouble, Archmagus. *Benevita*." Inguma left with a nod and concerned smile toward Zak.

"Now, Zakolor. I am sure you have many questions, and I'm afraid I will disappoint you as I have few answers. Yet myself and several others spent the last hours piecing together what occurred, so I will provide what I can."

Tansil's swift clarity brought Zak's wits to him. It was

unlike the pensieve elf.

"How did this happen?" It seemed too simple a question, but Tansil was nothing if not thorough. He would know how deep Zak's need ran.

"There was a rally near the Kapana that began roughly at the same time as our meeting. It was the latest in a string of increasingly common events across Weslinton in recent months. It's the Disciples, calling the devoted to action in the name of freedom. A seductive song, one that many did not resist. This particular rally grew violent, and when word reached them that the entire League council—including King Gyrnavo—was in Lord Woolbin's dining room, well..."

"They stormed the mansion."

Tansil's brown hair waved as his head shook. "We should have been more prepared. Soldiers and mages were stationed everywhere, yet they found our weakest points and broke through, a relentless river bolstered by the stormy rapids of zealousness."

That could be the link, Zak thought. What if Limba Dar wormed his way into Lord Woolbin's house as a spy for the Disciples and then moved on to Marius Fern when luck presented the chance?

If that was true, Zak couldn't keep his suspicions to himself any longer. This attack may be all the proof needed to confirm Limba Dar's betrayal and treason.

"Sir, what if the mob *knew* where to attack? What if someone told them?"

"We have considered it, of course. We don't have enough information yet to say either way."

"It's Limba Dar," Zak said. He spent several minutes telling Tansil everything he could—though truthfully, there wasn't much: the way Limba Dar stalked him around Tor'alan, the conversations where he tried to wheedle out Zak's beliefs on the Contract and the gods, how he introduced him to Fanum Ket and *his* zealousness, and how peculiar Limba Dar acted during the mediation—including how he slipped from the dining room moments before the attack began.

Silence scratched at Zak as he waited for Tansil to react, to say something, even if it was to tell him his theory was foolish. Instead, he said something much more chilling.

"Limba Dar is gone."

"Gone?"

"Missing," Tansil clarified. "I thought perhaps he ran and hid when the attack began and hadn't found his way back yet. He wouldn't be the first to lose himself in an ambush. But it has been hours, and he remains unaccounted. And you say he left before the attack began."

"So, he could be responsible."

"Perhaps. I must thank you, Zakolor. I know that wasn't easy to withhold and even less to share. Though I'll ask that, for now, we keep this between us until I can properly investigate Limba Dar."

"I understand, Archmagus." His hands balled into fists on the table. "But if he is responsible, he can't get away with this."

"If he is responsible, we *will* find him." Tansil's eyes glinted with something fierce. Zak remembered that Tansil and Vermig, despite their many differences, had been friends. Whatever pain Zak felt over his passing, Tansil must have felt tenfold.

"Of course." If there was one thing Zak understood, it was avenging friends.

Tansil sighed, and the weariness looked foreign on the usually aloof elf. "There is one thing I can confirm with certainty. Zandorn is controlling the Rotters. It was difficult to detect before since the Rotters are resistant to magic, but when they attacked in such vast numbers, I sensed Zandorn's magic and intent woven between them. The Consortium sent the Rotters and Karazul."

Even though Zak believed Zandorn was behind the Rotters already, hearing it stole the air from his lungs. "That means—"

"That the Consortium and Disciples are working together? It would appear so. We have much to understand about today and our loss, but for now, I am bold enough to ask too much of you."

Zak froze, unsure what Tansil meant. A moment passed, and he thought the elf's attention drifted—but he seemed to be collecting his thoughts before he spoke again.

"I need you to forget about the Disciples, Limba Dar, Vermig, and every distraction you may now carry. I need you to focus on being the *Nacusti*, and I need you to speak with Cerevita. Now."

Chapter 13

A Gods-Blessed Chance

Zak stuck close to Tansil's heels as the elf led him down the innards of the Center castle, passing guards stationed at doorways and stairwells, and pausing only to disable protective enchantments. He watched as the final door shifted, and light and dark figures etched in stone retreated from the blossoming green of nature. The heavy barrier opened with a surprisingly light push.

He hadn't returned to the throne room since first meeting Cerevita. He had been a wounded mess, needing Bazil to support half his weight to walk. He felt worse now, even without a wound, distraught over Vermig and the Disciples. Tansil's instruction to set everything in his mind—his life—aside became clearer. How could he speak to a god with grief pulling at him?

A glimmer caught his eye as their footsteps echoed through the large room. A pedestal stood off to the left, its glass cover winking in the torchlight. There was something inside.

"What is that?" Zak asked. He drifted toward the pedestal without thinking.

Tansil followed, standing beside him as they looked down at the glass together. "That is the Contract."

He said it so simply and matter-of-fact that it took Zak a moment to comprehend.

This was *the* Contract.

The one that stopped the Guardian War.

The one that his ancestor, Adrastus, fought to create.

The one that Jolsu sacrificed himself for.

The one that bound the gods.

Looping, graceful lines of ink slid across the page. It was shorter than Zak imagined. Even with small writing and large parchment, all the text fit into one page. Despite its encasement in the charmed pedestal and secure room, Zak could have mistaken the Contract for any regular document—except for the pure *magic* radiating from the yellowed page. It had called to him from across the room. He couldn't believe he hadn't noticed the document during his first visit.

His hand hovered above the glass, over the signatures at the bottom of the page. The two on the left were the *Nacusti* signatures.

Adrastus Belcour.

Temaway Galeria.

Zak's breath caught as he saw the three names on the right.

Azubelux.

Baltenebris.

Cerevita.

"If they could do this," Tansil said softly, gesturing to Adrastus and Temaway's signatures. "If they could force *gods* to sign the Contract, I *know* you can defeat Zandorn and the Consortium."

"It sounds simple, put that way." Zak knew Tansil meant well, but his words didn't help.

"It never is," Tansil agreed.

"Weren't there six *Nacusti* at the beginning of the war?"

"Freedom is never free. There is always a cost." Tansil turned from the Contract and walked toward the thrones at the end of the room.

The cost is already too high, Zak thought as the faces of Kal, Olivia, Terasi, and Vermig flashed in his mind.

It could always be higher, Jolsu said. Zak didn't feel the dragon's normal wave of venom or smugness, but a trickle of sadness instead.

Tansil had already inserted the *cordeus*—the god's heart—into the throne when Zak approached. It sparkled with every color Zak recognized, and many he did not. He shielded his eyes from a bright flash of light, and when he opened them, a woman with green skin and flowing brown hair that reached the floor sat in the towering green seat.

Finally, Zak was face-to-face with Cerevita again.

"*Benevita*, Mother." Tansil bowed in greeting, and Zak copied the movement.

Cerevita nodded, acknowledging them. "*What news?*" she asked. Her powerful voice filled the room and Zak's thoughts as if she spoke *through* the world.

Tansil had prepared Zak for this meeting on their walk from the kitchens. With only one hour of Cerevita's time, they didn't have a second to waste. The elf spoke fast—a departure from his usual flowing pace—summarizing the day's events with the Consortium, Disciples, and Vermig.

"The Consortium stole Baltenebris' *cordeus* from the Archalium," Tansil said. "What could they be planning, Mother?"

Of course! Zak thought. Karazul had taken the *cordeus* from Vermig after the assassination. Each of the Archs carried the heart of their god. Zak wondered if that was another detail of the Contract.

"*It is powerful,*" Cerevita said. Her expression was almost neutral, a little austere. "*Its applications are near limitless.*"

"Could Zandorn pierce the veil with it? Will it aid his ritual of resurrection?" Tansil asked.

"*It is possible.*"

Tansil and Cerevita discussed the implications of losing Baltenebris' *cordeus* for several minutes as Zak waited. He struggled to keep his patience as his hands fidgeted with the hem of his uniform. Eventually, Cerevita turned her attention toward him.

"*Nacusti,*" she said. Her deep brown eyes fixed on his face. "*Do you recall our previous conversation?*"

"I do," he said. "Mother?" He wasn't sure how to address her. It hadn't come up the last time.

Her green lips spread in a dazzling smile, and Zak mirrored the expression. Her presence was everywhere, all-encompassing, as if her essence pushed at his from all sides.

In the back of his mind, he started to understand *how* the gods had reigned over mortals for thousands of years. Even with her power restricted by the Contract, Cerevita was an ocean, one he would happily drown in, and Zak was barely a raindrop.

"*You may call me Cerevita. Unless you keep the faith?*"

"I'm not sure." He thought he didn't, but his nerves and Cerevita's presence bungled his thoughts, so he looked to Tansil for guidance.

"Do you pray at her altar?" Tansil asked.

"No. My mother does."

"Gods gain power from their devoted," Tansil explained. "And it was custom for devoted to identify themselves in conversation. Clairise—your mother—would use 'Mother' when speaking to Cerevita. You should use 'Cerevita.'"

"*You recall our conversation,*" Cerevita continued. Zak's eyes snapped back to hers. "*Then I must ask* why *you resist your Nacusti power? Why do you not heed my advice and embrace what you are?*"

"I—" Zak's throat burned, thinking of Vermig's similar words hours earlier, before he died. "I'm afraid," he said, speaking as honestly as possible.

"*Fear is natural, young one, but is not a reason. Why do you resist your power?*"

Zak hesitated. "But, I *am* afraid. Afraid of what I'll become, so I held back."

"*No.*" Cerevita's voice thundered through him. "*Why do you resist your power?*"

"Because I'm afraid!" Zak said, heat rising in his cheeks.

Was he angry or terrified?

"*Why do you resist your power?*" The room darkened as if storm clouds hung overhead, a tempest threatening to swallow him.

"Because it isn't MINE!"

His words echoed through the chamber, and no one moved. He had squeezed his eyes closed and now slowly opened them to look up at Cerevita. The darkness receded, and calm returned to her as if she hadn't just pushed him off an emotional cliff.

"*Jolsu, what have you done?*"

Nothing, Cerevita. Zak heard the dragon's words in his mind, but they must have reached Cerevita somehow, too.

"*You have sacrificed and suffered more than your share, Jolsu-Ko. You lost your body and your jyrnen in the war. Would you let that be for naught?*"

Jolsu said nothing, but Zak felt him retreat from their bond as if trying to hide from Cerevita.

"*What did he do?*" Cerevita directed the question to Zak this time.

"He placed a *vitaligo* on my friend Olivia," Zak said. "What's a *jyrnen*?"

"*A flight, a dragon's family.*"

Zak almost felt sympathy for Jolsu. He knew the dragon had given up his freedom to bond with Adrastus but didn't consider what else he lost. Still, it didn't change what he did to Olivia.

"*This is the barrier in your bond. You need to move past it together.*"

"Unless you can heal Olivia, I can't move past it." Zak almost forgot he was speaking to a god, his desperation to save Olivia overpowering any lingering nerves and Cerevita's presence. "And even if you can heal her, forgiving Jolsu is impossible."

"*I cannot heal her, not with the Contract in place. But there is someone who may be able to heal both your friend and your bond.*"

"Who?" Zak's heart leaped. He may be close to an answer for Olivia, mere seconds away from finally having a cure.

"*Temaway.*"

Tansil gasped, and Zak had almost forgotten the elf was there. He had been so silent. "But that's impossible!" he said. "Temaway is gone. He perished a few years after the signing."

Zak was equally as shocked. If Temaway was alive, he wasn't the only *Nacusti*.

"*You doubt my knowledge of my devoted?*" Cerevita asked. It wasn't really a question.

"No, Mother." Tansil took a step back. "If he's been alive all this time, why hasn't he come forward? He could have ended this war before it began."

"*You assume much, child,*" Cerevita said to Tansil. And Zak realized that compared to the god, Tansil *was* a child. His centuries of life were barely a fraction of Cerevita's millenia. It made Zak feel even smaller. "*Step forward.*"

Tansil did as told without hesitation.

"*Do you willingly accept this gift?*" Cerevita asked, leaning forward on her throne.

"I willingly accept this gift," Tansil answered.

Cerevita reached out, the end of her green finger nearly the same size as Tansil's torso. She brushed it against his forehead, a small flash of light passing between them before she withdrew.

"*You will be able to find Temaway now. Go to him and ask your questions. You may bring Olivia, but the secret of Temaway's existence must remain between the three of you.*"

"We understand. *Benevita*, Mother," Tansil said with another bow.

Why was Tansil saying goodbye? Zak was about to speak up when Cerevita started fading, her waning form becoming more and more transparent by the second.

"*Embrace your power, Nacusti.*" Her voice sounded far away, like the rumble of distant thunder.

Zak stood still as she disappeared. Their time was up, and it had passed too fast. He had a dozen more questions; he didn't have a chance to ask about Kal or the black caladrius. Even though he didn't get everything he wanted from Cerevita, he was certain of three things.

He needed to bond with Jolsu to defeat Zandorn.

He wasn't the last *Nacusti*.

He had a gods-blessed chance to save Olivia.

Chapter 14

Nacusti Secrets

Zak surveyed the scattered belongings on his bed. *I have no idea what I'm doing*, he thought.

"Pack for two weeks," Tansil had instructed the night before. "Expect to be gone for several more."

The last time he packed for a journey was when Sorwin took him from Densba. Somehow, that felt longer ago than a few months. A few years, at minimum.

He crammed his (freshly laundered) uniforms into the rucksack with a few extra tunics and breeches. A hooded cape was rolled and strapped to the outside, while a knife, waterskin, and two books made it inside before he secured the straps.

As he did a final check of his room and stowed the rest of his belongings in the rusted trunk at the foot of his bed, a Firepost burst from the crack under his door. The vibrant flames of the spell lit the small room in a red glow before the letter settled on his desk. Zak had jumped, startled when the fire suddenly appeared. He unfolded the parchment.

It was from his parents.

He read several pages of Clairise's neat script. She congratulated Zak on passing his adept exam, asked him if he was eating enough, and maybe he should take extra portions at meal times—just to be sure, and encouraged him to keep listening to Sorwin, that even though she didn't know the man well, she was sure he wanted the best for Zak—he had promised her as much before they left. There were also several updates on his father—Ageric—and Densba. Nothing happened in the small town, Zak knew, but the way Clairise wrote about the local harvest festival and the townsfolk made his heart ache.

He missed his parents. He missed his *home*.

He couldn't go back, not now that he knew exactly what he needed to do to defeat Zandorn and save his friends. But he *could* carry a small piece of them with him. Opening his rucksack, he carefully tucked the letter inside one of his books for safekeeping.

Breakfast was easier than it had been in weeks. He revisited the entrance to the kitchens that Inguma had shown him, asking the staff if he could take a few things. They didn't seem to mind—still paid him little attention at all, which suited Zak perfectly. He plucked a few pastries and fruits from bowls on one of the counters, eating as he rounded the building and waited, half-hidden behind the rough stone wall.

When Bazil approached the mess hall, Zak waved to catch his attention. He explained with as little detail as possible why he would be gone for a few weeks, so Bazil wouldn't need to escort him to breakfast. He didn't want to lie to his friend, especially when he was constantly helping Zak. But he promised Cerevita he would keep Temaway a secret, and luckily Bazil was more than understanding, saying, "Keep your secrets, *Nacusti*. I'll be here when you return." With a wink and a playful punch to the shoulder, Bazil strode through the mess hall doors.

Unfortunately, the conversation with Sorwin was much more difficult.

At Zak's request, Tansil agreed to convince Olivia to accompany them on the journey to find Temaway. Zak figured Olivia wouldn't listen to him after what happened with the caladrius. He also wanted to be the one to tell Sorwin he was leaving, even if he couldn't tell him *why*.

"Explain it to me again," Sorwin said, pacing a small trench into the grass of the training court.

Zak had already told him twice, but perhaps a third time would deliver the message. "I'm leaving Tor'alan with Tansil and Olivia. I don't know how long we'll be gone, though Tansil seems to think several weeks. The official reasoning is that Tansil is showing me the front lines and the Rot as part of my training. He wanted you to know that isn't the real reason, but that—"

"He can't tell me the real reason," Sorwin cut in.

"Yes," Zak said. He chewed his lip, searching for words of comfort or explanation. But nothing came. He settled on, "I'm sorry."

"You say that a lot." Sorwin's hands were on his hips, fingers drumming as he stopped pacing. "Agh, Zakolor." He ran a hand through his wavy hair. "I should be the one apologizing. I haven't been myself lately. I have been pushing you too hard. Maybe time away is what you need..."

"Sorwin, you've done more for me than any magus should for their apprentice. I wouldn't be ready for this journey without you."

Sorwin nodded, and the tightness in his shoulders eased. "I'm no stranger to secrets, not after two decades of working with Tansil. I tried making things different between us. I wanted us to be more open, more honest."

"You have," Zak said, catching and holding Sorwin's eye. "And I promise I'll tell you everything as soon as I can."

After a few more clumsy attempts at reassurance and a hug goodbye, Zak closed the door to court seven, the thunderclap of the protective barrier echoing as he left.

The large doors of the western stable stood open as Zak approached. He found it odd that "western" remained in the name, given Tor'alan's unique system for directions. Perhaps "foreport stables" was too much of a mouthful.

Tansil and Olivia stood to the side, away from the bustle in and out of the timber frame building. His brow furrowed seeing Olivia. She looked even more sick, a pale shadow of herself. *More outbursts*, he thought. He almost asked if she should stay behind, if the journey would be too challenging. But he knew better than to question Olivia's decision.

She was here. That meant she was going.

The pungent mixture of animal smells thickened as Tansil led them through the stables. "The quickest way to our destination is by wing," the elf said. He stopped outside two stalls with tall, arched openings.

Zak stared at the creatures inside. "Wyverns," he whispered, awe taking his breath.

He barely saw them when Sorwin led the group to his rescue a few months ago. Their blue and brown scales looked soft in the morning light. They had powerful rear legs and sharp leather wings jutting from their smaller forelegs. Serpentine necks and tails reminded Zak of the lizards he chased as a child.

As he approached, the wyverns' heads twisted toward him, their jaws snapping as a surprisingly high-pitched sound jumped from their throats. They seemed *afraid* of him.

They are, Jolsu said. *To them, you smell of dragon.*

Zak looked to Tansil, and the elf understood. "Not to worry, we can soothe Burgo's mind. I suspect he'll be more calm after a few days."

"Burgo?" Zak asked.

"Your mount, of course." Tansil opened the stall and held up a hand.

The nearest wyvern—Burgo—was already saddled. His large eyes focused on Tansil's hand as his head lowered slowly and hot air from his nostrils ruffled Zak's hair as he let out a contented sigh.

"How do we..." Zak started to ask.

"Olivia has some experience with wyverns. Follow her lead," Tansil said.

Zak watched a silent Olivia move into the stall and strap her pack to the back of the saddle. He wasn't sure how angry she was with him, but it felt different than before. She seemed more drained than anything, and that only added to Zak's worry.

She took his rucksack and fastened it to the saddle as well, tossing a leg over the beast as she settled into the first seat. Zak climbed up and sat in the seat behind her, his face warming from their closeness.

Tansil led Burgo through the rear doors of the stable to an open area reserved for exercise. A few horses in the yard whinnied and shied from Burgo, almost like the wyvern had done with Zak. As they approached the middle of the area, Tansil stepped to the side so Zak and Olivia could see him.

"It will take a few days to reach our destination. We'll stop only once during the day and once for the night." As he spoke, large wings unfolded from his back in a glitter of magic. Feathers of white, brown, and grey mixed together and reminded Zak of an owl.

Without further explanation, Tansil crouched and launched himself into the air with a beat of his wings.

A moment later, Burgo did the same.

Zak could have sworn he left his stomach on the ground as the wyvern took flight. Air rushed past as he fought to sit upright from the force. Luckily, their saddle was designed for two riders. He gripped the horn in front of him with all his strength. After a long minute, Burgo stopped climbing and leveled his path to the west, wings beating a fast yet even pace.

Once he was sure he wouldn't be sick or fall to his death, Zak picked his head up. The view was incredible. The Karanadee twisted below, its waters shimmering in the morning light. Masdaan and the Kapana looked small, which felt impossible. Desert sands rippled like stagnant ocean waves, extending far to the south.

After a few minutes, a broad smile lit his face, and Zak realized he *liked* flying. The sound of air whipping in his ears, the elevated view, the steady rhythm of wings...it was its own magic.

He felt something peculiar from Jolsu too. It was joy, real, authentic joy. Not the usual acidic smugness that came with his antics.

You missed flying. Zak observed more than asked.

Almost as much as I miss my jyrnen, he said without hesitation. A sliver of sadness snuck through their connection.

Couldn't we fly together? He recalled his transformation when fighting Burvenin when he had pulled on Jolsu's magic. Scaly green wings had sprouted from his shoulders.

Perhaps.

Zak didn't push further. Short as it was, this was their first real conversation, the first time he had felt happiness from the dragon. Something had changed in Jolsu since speaking with Cerevita, and he hoped it wasn't temporary.

Hours flitted past as they soared through the sky. They flew higher than most birds and dipped through the occasional cloud, water droplets dampening Zak's hair and uniform. Sometimes, he closed his eyes, enjoying the wind on his face and the up-and-down cadence of Burgo's flight.

He was almost thrown from the saddle when they landed for lunch. Even with the soft leather beneath him, the jarring of the wyvern's powerful legs meeting the earth nearly bounced him off. He walked with a ginger step for the half-hour they stopped.

In the second part of their flight, Zak was bold enough

to release his grip on the horn. He leaned forward and thrust his arms out against the strong force of the air as it tried to wrench him backward. He laughed as gusts danced around and through him, but the wind carried the sound away.

Below, sand gave way to grassy plains, and the occasional tree became more common as they neared the Weslinton border. Finally, as the sun fell closer and closer to the horizon, Burgo tipped his wings into a descent, landing on the silted coast of a large lake. Zak managed the landing much better the second time, keeping the bouncing and bruising to a minimum.

He dismounted from Burgo first and held a hand up for Olivia. She hesitated but took it, gracefully sliding down the wyvern's side. She hadn't spoken all day, not even to Tansil when they stopped earlier.

Leading Burgo a short distance away and unsaddling the beast, she leaned on the sturdy leather as she set it down, breathing heavily.

Zak knew she wouldn't accept his help, so he hid his worried glances as he collected firewood.

Tansil conjured supplies in a flurry of movement and magic. A mound of freshly butchered meat appeared before Burgo, and the wyvern dove into it hungrily. Wooden poles dug into the ground as a brown canvas strung itself between them, creating a small barrier from the lakeside breeze. Bedrolls unfolded, stones rolled across the ground into a circle for the fire, and chopped vegetables threw themselves into a pot that already boiled with stock.

A few months ago, the display would have been enough

to convince Zak that Tansil was more god than elf. Now, he knew enough about magic to understand Tansil conjured these objects from somewhere and that he wasn't creating them. Most likely, he organized provisions before they left Tor'alan. Conjuring was advanced magic, and Zak hadn't attempted it yet, but it did bring a question to mind.

"Why do we know how to conjure but not make portals?" he asked Tansil, stacking his collected firewood. "Isn't it the same idea, moving objects between places?"

"The same idea, but different fare and means," Tansil said.

Zak waited for more of an explanation, but none came. He realized how accustomed he was to Sorwin's exposition, how he freely shared knowledge and asked questions. Tansil was certainly not Sorwin. Knowledgeable, perhaps moreso than anyone in the League, but he wasn't friendly or warm, and Zak silently berated himself for taking Sorwin for granted.

"So it works differently?" Zak prompted.

"Yes," Tansil said. As if to prove the point, he conjured a ladle with a flourish and dipped it into the soup.

Three Fires, Zak thought. "How is it different?" he pressed.

Tansil slowly stirred the simmering broth, focusing on something far away. "Conjuring moves objects between places. If anything, conjuring is similar to teleportation—where a mortal moves through space. But we cannot conjure living things, and a mage can only teleport themselves. Portals *connect* distant points together, where any number of objects or creatures may pass through the door, which is a different magic entirely."

"But we had portal magic in the past, didn't we? Who built the one in Tor'alan?" Zak thought about the city's entrance portal and how it felt like his body stretched and twisted as he traveled through it. He shuddered at the memory of the unpleasant experience.

"It is old magic," Tansil said. "Portals used to be common. Difficult magic, of course, but millennia ago, a web of doors connected all of Valecium and was the pride of mages. That was before the Era of Gods, before they sought dominion over mortals, before they erased portal magic from the world."

"Why did they take portals from us?"

"Why did they do anything? For control, for power. They thought portals gave us too much freedom. Perhaps they were afraid of the places we could go."

Zak fell silent, mulling the information in his thoughts. Everything Tansil said was factual and objective. He thought it odd that the elf seemed so devoted to Cerevita when she appeared yet spoke so callously of the gods now. Perhaps that was the elven way—Zak didn't know any other elves to compare. Or perhaps that was just Tansil.

He lost the thread of his thoughts as Olivia drifted into the light of the fire, ladling a small bowl of soup before sitting. She hadn't had an outburst of magic all day. That was good. Each time magic clawed its way out of her meant hours, days, or weeks the *vitaligo* took from her life. He wasn't sure how much time she had left. It was hard to tell, but looking at how fast her health deteriorated, it couldn't be much. A year? A few months?

Maybe *only* a month.

Zak tensed, the spoon he gripped pressing into his palm with a sharp pain. He was running out of time. Zandorn had figured out how portals work, which was a decent explanation of how the Consortium always seemed to be a step ahead of them. Zandorn had found Zak first, found Terasi first, and used the Disciples right under the council's nose.

It was more than portals, though. Zak had enough experience with the Consortium to know Zandorn had to be a brilliant strategist. Everyone said he was a genius with magic, so that wasn't a far leap.

He collected the bowls and cutlery from the meal and washed them at the edge of the lake, light from the moon and stars dancing in the ripples of the water. One small comfort of this journey was being back in nature. He hadn't realized how trapped he felt in Tor'alan these last months. As much as he loved learning magic and his life in the capital, he couldn't breathe in the city like he could out here. The freshness, the freedom, the space.

Nature felt like home.

It is, for us, Jolsu said.

And Zak agreed.

The next day was uneventful. Hours and hours of silent flight with a short midday break. Zak's body ached all over. In his months of daily training, Zak had developed a wiry, strong physique. But he was accustomed to movement, and the constant tightening of his muscles as he clung to the saddle put dozens of knots in his arms and legs.

Finally, something happened on the morning of the third day.

After two hours of flying, Tansil descended to the ground near the edge of a forest. Burgo followed, and Zak was grateful when he and Olivia slid off the wyvern's back.

"We're close," Tansil said, his owlish wings disappearing.

"Where are we?" Olivia asked. It was the first time she spoke on their trek.

"Near the Anguis River. Cerevita showed me this place. I don't know where Temaway is exactly, but we'll find him in this forest. A word of caution: this is elven territory. We're not welcome here."

"Wouldn't you be?" Zak asked. He knew the elves closed their borders to humans centuries ago, but Tansil was an elf.

"Certainly not," Tansil answered with a hint of a sad smile. "There's a reason I'm the only elf in the League. That's a story for another time." He placed a hand on Burgo's head, and the beast seemed to calm. Tansil conjured some food for him, explaining he'd return for Burgo later, and promptly headed for the nearest break in the treeline.

Zak unclipped their packs from the saddle, shouldering his own and holding Olivia's in his other hand. Olivia reached for hers, but he held it firm in his grip.

She gave him a confused look for a moment before understanding turned into annoyance. "I can carry my own bag," she said.

"I know," he said. "But I have it."

"Zakolor." Her tone was a warning.

He didn't heed it. "Come on, let's go!" He jogged to catch up to Tansil.

She said something under her breath he couldn't hear, but Zak smiled when she kept pace behind him and didn't try to take her bag back.

A small victory, but he was satisfied nonetheless.

They followed Tansil for another hour. The elf picked a careful path through brush and trees, sometimes pausing to look and listen. To what, Zak didn't know, but he seemed to make decisions based on whatever he saw or heard.

As they walked, Zak started to feel something.

Impossible...I didn't dare believe it. Jolsu stirred, and the dragon's disbelief and excitement ran through their connection.

What is it? Zak asked.

I feel them, don't you?

He didn't know how to describe it. It was an energy, an awareness of some kind. It was similar to how he felt Jolsu in his mind, but there were two *new* beings.

With a sudden confidence—a *knowing*—he turned right and forged a new path through the underbrush.

"Zakolor?" Tansil asked, turning back.

"This way," he said. Zak was almost running now, the two bags jostling against his shoulders.

He darted past trees and skipped over streams. The feeling grew stronger, he knew he was getting closer. He slid past two boulders that formed a passage between them. On the other side, he stopped in his tracks, panting from excitement and exertion.

An ancient elf sat a few paces away.

Zak knew it was an elf from the pointed ears and bright green eyes—the same as Tansil's. The similarities ended there. Where Tansil's features were dark and sharp, this elf was light and round. Grey and white hair reached his waist, running over a brown and green robe.

"About time," the elf said. "I thought you'd be here sooner."

"Temaway," Zak said.

The elf nodded as Tansil and Olivia made their way through the passage.

"Is that all of you?" Temaway asked. He groaned as he stood, leaning on the staff he gripped between gnarled knuckles.

"It is," Tansil said, eyes wide with shock.

"Then let's be on our way." Temaway turned and started hobbling away.

"W-wait! Where are you going?" Zak asked.

Temaway didn't stop but called over his shoulder. "I should think you'd like a meal before saving all Valecium."

Chapter 15
Nature's Ward

There wasn't a path—at least not in the traditional sense—but a trail of grass thinned from years of comings and goings cut through thicker vegetation. Temaway followed it, and Zak followed him with Tansil and Olivia close behind.

Zak marveled as the forest parted around Temaway. Low branches swayed above his head as he passed, sizeable rocks and boulders shifted, and bushes and smaller plants actually *plucked* themselves from the ground and planted their roots elsewhere.

As they walked into a small clearing, the world closed behind them—trees, stones, and plants bending back to cover the trail as if it didn't exist. And in that moment, Zak understood what he saw, understood how Temaway had hidden for centuries and been presumed dead.

Nature *protected* him.

"Incredible," Zak said, awe lining his voice.

A large, hollow tree stood at the other end of the clearing. A branch big enough to walk on spiraled around the outside, leading to various openings in the thick bark. Temaway puttered through different areas of the camp, removing his cloak and draping it on a rope strung between two trees already laden with other garments, then sat on a stump next to the firepit, poking it with the end of his staff as flames erupted.

"How is it possible?" Tansil asked, pushing past Zak to stand near the fire, staring at Temaway. "How have you been alive all this time?"

"There are many mysteries in the world, *Parignis*," Temaway answered. He put a flat stone in the fire, pulled a knife from his belt, and started chopping ingredients for the meal he promised.

"Then de-mystify it," Tansil said bluntly.

"It was Cerevita, wasn't it?" Zak ventured a guess, and both elves looked at him with very different expressions. Tansil's eyes widened as his brow furrowed, perhaps feeling another sting of betrayal from his god. Temaway gave Zak a playful, knowing wink.

"Follow the thought, *Nacusti*," Temaway encouraged. "Why?"

"I don't know. But this place," he gestured to the clearing, "it's Cerevita. I can feel her magic. She's protecting you." He knew it was true. It felt like its own world, shrouded in a cocoon of nature, in *her* power.

"'A debt repaid' is how she would phrase it," Temaway said.

The earth by the fire moved, piling itself into a gently curved bench. Zak, Tansil, and Olivia sat, waiting for their enigmatic host to explain further.

He didn't, of course.

"What does that mean?" Tansil asked, his posture rigid.

Zak found Tansil's frustration with the tight-lipped ancient elf ironic.

"It means the gods are surprisingly simple. Cerevita asked much of me in the era leading up to the Guardian War and during the conflict itself. I have always been her devoted—happy to serve—yet she saw my deeds as cause for compensation." Temaway placed several fillets of fish and chopped vegetables on the stone in the fire. They sizzled, releasing a delicious scent as he sprinkled seasoning on top.

"Your reward for defeating her brothers in the Guardian War was solitude?" Tansil scoffed, and his frustration flowed into anger. "Why did you accept? Why did you stay here when Valecium needed you countless times—needs you right now? You could have stopped this conflict with Zandorn as soon as it began!"

"Archmagus!" Zak had never seen Tansil rattled. He always remained calm in the shouting matches at council meetings and never took the bait for an argument. Now, he was starting one with the mage that could save Olivia.

Temaway seemed unbothered, continuing to putter through his dinner preparations. "Life is a balance of growth and loss. I was born in the Era of Mages, survived the Era of Gods, and ushered in the Era of Freedom with Adrastus and Cerevita. After so much life—so much growth and loss—I was ready to be alone. I was ready for less."

Zak felt a wave of emotion from Jolsu, a mixture of sadness and empathy. And he realized that Jolsu must have felt the same for centuries, that he was *grieving*.

"I'm sorry," Zak said, to Temaway and Jolsu. It felt woefully inadequate, but he was at a loss for any other words.

"Life is never something to be sorry about," Temaway said, a sudden fire in his eyes as he spoke. "That is *why* we fought, to let life flourish again."

"You said Adrastus *and* Cerevita." Olivia's voice cracked from disuse. "She fought against the other gods?"

"Not directly. Yet she is the goddess of life, and the Era of Gods was a dominion, a mockery of life. It was Cerevita's idea to create the *Nacusti*."

It's true, Jolsu said. *She sent Temaway to all the Guardians to ask for our sacrifice.*

Temaway's head tilted toward Zak when the dragon spoke. "Ah, *benevita*, old friend."

Zak gasped, realizing Temaway could hear Jolsu. "But why didn't Cerevita fight in the war if she wanted to end the Era of Gods?" Tansil had told him of Cerevita's hand in helping the mortals by creating the *Nacusti*, but he didn't understand why she hadn't fought in the war herself.

The old elf turned the fish and vegetables on the stone slab. "Perhaps you should ask her when next you speak. I know she didn't risk sending you here for history lessons."

Zak looked to his companions. Tansil had fallen silent, stewing in anger. Olivia looked exhausted, the travel and her condition weighing on her.

It was up to Zak to get what they were after.

"We need help with two things," he said. "Removing Olivia's *vitaligo* and training Jolsu and me to bond."

"Two sizeable requests," Temaway observed.

"Can you help?" Too much desperation snuck into the question and he gripped his knees with shameful strength.

"With removing a *vitaligo*? To my knowledge, it hasn't been done."

Zak thought he saw Olivia fade into an even paler hue. "But it could be?" This was his last lead for a cure. If it didn't work...

"Certainties are rare. Most things are plausible if not probable."

"Does that mean yes?" Zak asked. He began to recognize a few more similarities between Tansil and Temaway. Namely their annoyingly vague responses to questions.

"It means I'll look into it," he said. His green eyes flitted over Olivia before settling on Zak. "You and Jolsu, I know I can help. But first, we eat." The warm scent of cooked herbs drifted to Zak's nose as Temaway dished the food into wooden bowls.

It was an awkward meal. Tansil and Olivia were both quiet (the former from anger, the latter from weariness). Temaway hummed a little as he ate, his toes tapping in time with the tune. Zak didn't know what to say to any of them, so he palmed his bowl in silence, pondering all Temaway had said as he ate.

He had the feeling he could ask the elf *anything*, and he would know the answer. The Era of Mages ended over three thousand years ago, which meant Temaway had to be even older. He couldn't imagine living so long, seeing and experiencing the varied versions of Valecium through the centuries.

Zak eyed Tansil as he pushed his food around with a fork and wondered if he felt young compared to Temaway, maybe as young as Zak felt compared to Tansil.

Temaway finished his food with a satisfied sound and set his bowl on the ground. A small plant with wiry vines picked it up and carried it away, waddling lopsidedly on its roots. To where, Zak wasn't sure, but he didn't have a chance to ask.

"No time like the present, *Nacusti*." Temaway lurched to his feet with a groan and beckoned Zak with a wave.

For some reason, it didn't bother Zak when Temaway called him *Nacusti*.

He set his bowl on the ground, as Temaway had, and followed the old elf to a small alcove tucked into the protective treeline of the clearing.

The alcove felt important. Sacred. As Temaway's hands drifted over flowers and branches, they leaned toward him as if craving his touch. A stone plinth supported a wooden statue of Cerevita. Except, it wasn't a statue at all. It was a *tree* growing in the *shape* of Cerevita. With a gesture, Temaway conjured two plush cushions and placed them at the base of Cerevita's altar, sitting on one and nodding for Zak to claim the other. Zak did so and his sweaty palms stuck to his uniform as they ran nervously over the fabric.

Sitting across from Temaway, staring into the elf's glowing green eyes, he was faced with stark reality.

I'm not the only Nacusti.

Temaway wore an impish smile like he could read Zak's thoughts. Maybe he could?

"We'll start with evaluating your connection," Temaway

instructed. "Where have you spoken to Jolsu?"

"Where?" Zak parroted. That was an odd question. "In my head?" His upward inflection didn't make it sound like an answer.

"True, but where specifically? We seek your *inriloc*, the place of connection with your Guardian. Have you spoken to Jolsu and been somewhere else?"

The answer came to Zak immediately. "Near a seaside cave, on my home island." He'd never forget waking up in the shallow water of the coast, hearing Jolsu's voice, and seeing the dragon's mighty form.

Temaway's eyes twinkled in the low light. "Then begin meditating and find your *inriloc*."

Zak had a knot in his stomach as he closed his eyes and, for the first time, reached for his connection with Jolsu. He had spent months pushing the dragon away, trying to bury him in the darkest corners of his mind. It felt strange to do the complete opposite now.

And it wasn't only strange, it was difficult. He could feel Jolsu's presence, but as he reached for the dragon, he slipped away, like water running through his fingers. Zak tried picturing the beach—his *inriloc*—tried listening for the soothing ocean waves and smelling the salty wind.

Nothing came to him.

All he saw was the inside of his eyelids. Jolsu's emotions hovered at the edge of his awareness, a little curiosity and trepidation and annoyance. The dragon wanted to be left alone, and in truth, Zak wanted nothing to do with him either, but he didn't have a choice. Cerevita's words were clear:

if Zak wanted to defeat Zandorn, he needed to embrace his *Nacusti* powers.

Countless minutes dragged on while he meditated and tried to connect with Jolsu, but eventually, Temaway must have taken pity on him.

"I see," was all the elf said—as if Zak's failure to find his *inriloc* spoke volumes. "Let's try this."

The alcove blurred into view, and for a moment, Zak thought he opened his eyes. The light was different, darker than it should have been.

Temaway sat across from him on his cushion with a majestic bird perched on a low branch over his shoulder. Its feathers looked like wildfire, a dozen colors flaring along the lines of powerful wings and four large tail feathers.

"This is Vess," Temaway said, introducing the bird. "She's a phoenix."

"*Benevita, Parignis.*" Vess' voice was high and plucky, like a fiddle string.

"*Benevita*," Zak echoed. He knew where he was now. "Is this your *inriloc*?"

"A version of it," Temaway said. "I thought a familiar place, even one as new as this, would be less jarring for both of you."

"Both?" Zak's voice trailed off as he looked to his right. Jolsu's enormous body towered over him, emerald scales glittering even in the dark light of the *inriloc*. Zak tensed at the sight of the dragon. Jolsu seemed to notice, and his serpentine head twitched so one of his gold eyes peered down at Zak.

"Now that we're all here," Temaway started. "Why don't

you tell me why your connection is more brittle than a dead twig."

Olivia knew Tansil was upset. In the years she had known him, she had never seen him give in to anger, frustration, and betrayal like he did today. He was justified in all his feelings—it wasn't every day you found out your god had been lying to you for hundreds of years—but it conflicted with his usual aloofness. She admired his ability to remain distant and objective. Now, he seemed too *human*. So, as Tansil made excuses to leave the clearing and check on Burgo, Olivia thought a bit less of him.

She handed her half-empty bowl to a red flower waiting at her knee, leafy appendages carrying it out of sight. From her seat on the earthen bench, she could see Zak and Temaway's outlines in an alcove. Neither moved—both sat with their eyes closed—and she figured they must be meditating.

Good, she thought. *That'll keep Zak busy*.

Finding herself alone next to the soft crackle of the fire, she reached into her pack and brought out a fresh sheet of parchment and a quill charmed to write without ink. Her hand grasped the quill and hovered above the page, shaking.

It was a funny thing, knowing she was going to die.

At first, when the caladrius foretold her death, she was distraught. And she still was. But then she thought maybe it was better to know. Most people didn't get the advance notice, the warning of their impending doom.

But then reality set in.

There was so much she wanted to do, so much she wanted to say. Not many people were important to her—just a few—but suddenly, *knowing* she likely had only weeks left to live, she felt the need to get her words out while she could.

So the quill waited for her words, but none came. She glanced at Zak and Temaway again. They hadn't moved. It occurred to her how opposite her situation was from Temaway's. His life was long, eventful, full of challenges and victories. Hers was short, painful, full of challenges and losses.

The blankness of the parchment was loud, almost mocking her ineptitude at voicing her thoughts. Her fist curled around the quill. What *should* her last words be, anyway? What final message did she really expect to share?

She began packing the quill and parchment away when a sharp pain pierced her core. Doubling over, she gasped and could have sworn she was being torn apart from the inside.

Not now! she thought, falling to her knees and clutching her body as if enough pressure would push the pain away.

But it wouldn't, and she was alone. Tansil had left, and Zak and Temaway were deep in meditation. Could she call out to them? Would it matter? She tried anyway, but her throat constricted, and all that came out was a weak wail.

As she collapsed to the ground, her head in the dirt and the flames of the fire blurring her vision, she wondered if this was the last thing she'd feel.

"Is that the whole of it?" Temaway asked.

"Yes, Magus," Zak said.

He had told the elf everything, from Sorwin finding him in Densba and Burvenin taking Kal to the battle with the Consortium and Jolsu binding Olivia, and even their recent encounter with Karazul where, for a moment, it felt like he and Jolsu connected. Zak's anger flared when he finished, the wounds reopened with the telling. What little progress on bonding they might have made during the journey to find Temaway disappeared.

"Jolsu?" Temaway's tone made the name a question.

"The girl was dying, so I saved her life," the dragon said.

"You *condemned* her to death!" Zak whirled on Jolsu, but the dragon was still except his curling lip.

"Your priest could not heal the mortal wound," Jolsu snarled. "Would you have had her die in that field instead?"

"That wouldn't have happened! Bazil or Sorwin would have...we would have done something." His confidence faltered. What *would* have happened without the *vitaligo*? Zak's anger hadn't let him think about it. He had been too consumed with blaming Jolsu for Olivia's binding. But did Jolsu actually save Olivia?

No. That was impossible.

"Why did you do it, Jolsu?" Temaway's calm voice cut through the vitriol between Zak and his Guardian.

Jolsu's tail twitched as he hesitated, struggling to say

something. Zak had never felt the dragon off balance before. He was about to answer when his head whipped to the side, toward the center of the sanctuary. "Temaway," Jolsu said in an unfamiliar and soft voice.

"I feel it," Temaway said. Whatever caught Jolsu's attention, Temaway must have recognized too.

"What's happening?" Zak asked, completely lost.

Suddenly, Jolsu and Vess disappeared, and the dark light of the *inriloc* shifted abruptly into the darkness of early evening.

Zak blinked. They were back in the physical world.

Temaway quickly moved toward the fire he had cooked dinner on, surprisingly spry for an ancient elf. Zak followed, his legs tingling as they reawoke, still unsure what interrupted their meditation.

Then he saw Olivia.

She writhed on the ground, sharp gasps escaping her lungs as bursts of yellow magic poured from her body.

"No, no, no!" Zak ran to her side, grasping her hand as she thrashed in pained throes.

"Hold her steady," Temaway said.

Zak tried to pin Olivia's shoulders and arms to the ground. Pain blossomed as he caught an elbow to the cheek, but he didn't care. All that mattered was Olivia.

The elf pulled a jar from his robes, dipped his fingers inside, spread a brown ointment on Olivia's forehead, and began muttering something. She calmed, her breathing slowed, the flow of magic ceased, and her thrashing subsided.

Zak sat back, not needing to restrain Olivia anymore, but

held tight to her hand.

"We've tried everything, even a caladrius," Zak said. Temaway's eyes studied Olivia, and his brow pinched in concern. "You're our last hope, Temaway. Cerevita said...can you help? Can you heal her?"

It was probably only a few moments, but the silence stretched impossibly long while Zak waited for an answer.

Finally, Temaway rocked back on his heels, grunting as he moved his old bones to sit on a stump by the fire. He looked sad as his attention remained fixed on Olivia, the line of his mouth tight and curled downward, his eyes glassy.

"I understand now," the elf said.

Zak's heart thumped as if it might burst from his chest.

"I cannot promise a cure," Temaway continued. "But I can promise to try."

"That's all I ask," Zak said, mist clouding his eyes.

He squeezed Olivia's hand, her steady breath of sleep reassuring him they had time. Enough time for one last chance, one last hope.

Chapter 16

Forest Groves

Sorwin pushed through the forest, stepping carefully around dry leaves that had fallen from now-bare branches. A small squad of soldiers and mages followed in his wake, a silent wave washing through the wood.

They were hunting.

A day prior, the League received word from the city of Lindomer. The Consortium had been spotted nearby, and Sorwin was dispatched to investigate, along with Kaleb and Shira. Usually, Sorwin didn't like missions like this, a glorified chase to find-and-destroy the enemy. He found them tedious and unnecessarily bloody. Now, he welcomed the reprieve from his work. He and Tansil had made little progress on developing portals in the last months, and with Tansil away, his progress faltered entirely.

Tansil.

To say Sorwin felt frustrated with him was an understatement. He was used to Tansil's secrets, elven aloofness, and lack of basic empathy. He took it all in stride as part of their relationship, seeing it as the tradeoff for learning from one of the greatest living mages in the world. But when Tansil's secrets started infiltrating his and Zak's relationship, a quiet rage gripped him.

He wanted things to be different between him and his apprentice.

He wanted them to be *better*.

And now, Tansil had whisked Zak and Olivia off to who-knows-where for who-knows-what, and they wouldn't return until who-knows-when.

Sorwin paused at a signal from Kaleb and heard the squad halt as well. Twenty paces ahead, the major scouted for threats before resuming the hunt.

Kaleb was a welcome distraction, albeit a flustering one. Every time Sorwin laid eyes on him, his face flushed and burned, his body pulled toward him involuntarily. In their conversations, his words either came out stilted and broken or rushed, like he had only a moment to get everything out before he lost Kaleb's attention.

But he never did. No matter how flustered or nonsensical he sounded, Kaleb's dark eyes never left Sorwin's. In fact, Kaleb's gaze often found him in Tor'alan: walking through the Center, outside council meetings, and especially in court seven. He stole glances at Kaleb leaning casually against the stone wall, eyes fixed on Sorwin while he finished Zak's magic lessons. The curves of his bare, muscled arms in his sleeveless tunic made Sorwin want to—

"Am I interrupting?"

Sorwin almost shouted as Shira's voice whispered near his ear. "Baltenebris blast your demons!" He cursed his friend in a harsh undertone and looked to his left, where he *should* have seen Shira, but she was invisible, one of the many impressive—yet currently annoying—powers of Shira's demons.

He could hear the smile in her voice as she spoke. "There is such a thing as waiting too long, Sorwin. Even the best tea shouldn't steep forever."

"Hmph." She had caught him pining, and she was right; he couldn't wait forever if he wanted something more.

But Kaleb wasn't tea. If he were, he'd be the first glorious sip that warmed even the chilliest bones. He was more than that. He was a sunburst shooting through grey clouds. He was an afternoon in the countryside. He was a good book next to the crackling hearth in his study.

He was perfect, and that made him terrifying.

As Kaleb motioned for Sorwin and the squad to move up to his position, his heart skittered as he crept forward and crouched next to the major, chest warming as their shoulders brushed, like he had just swallowed the *hottest* tea.

Focus, Sorwin chided himself.

"There's a group ahead," Kaleb said. "Shira, are you here?" He looked around, unsure where to address the invisible mage.

"Yes, Major," she answered from somewhere to the right.

"Did Ubba find them?"

Shira had sent her tracking demon ahead of the group when they entered the forest. A moment of silence passed while she conferred with the imp. "They're half our number. They seem to be searching the grove for something past the treeline."

"Now is the time, then," Kaleb said, addressing the squad. "Use our numbers to our advantage and work in pairs. Capture targets alive if you can—we need to question them—but don't take any unnecessary risks. You know what to do if it comes down to you or them."

Silent nods and gestures rippled through the squad as they paired off and slunk away, circling the grove ahead to prepare for the ambush. Sorwin felt a firm but gentle grip at his elbow.

"You're with me, right?" Kaleb asked.

"I am." Sorwin felt the words spill out before he knew he had spoken. *More than you know.*

"Good," Kaleb said. His black hair blended into the darkness of the early evening. He hesitated momentarily, his jaw working as if he was going to say something.

"What is it?" Sorwin prodded.

Kaleb's lips twitched into a rare smile. He was always serious, and Sorwin savored the few moments his stoicism gave way to something softer, happier. He squeezed Sorwin's arm again as he said, "We'll talk later."

Three Fires, Sorwin thought, his heart leaping into his throat. *Perfect and terrifying.*

Sorwin couldn't form words—something that *never* happened to him except around Kaleb—but simply nodded. He was sure a mixture of dumbstruck and dazed painted his expression. He thought he heard Shira's snorting laugh a few paces away, but the pounding pulse in his ears drowned out everything around him.

He collected himself as he followed Kaleb through the

brush to the edge of the grove, adrenaline for the ensuing battle temporarily pushing any romantic thoughts from his mind.

Ubba's scouting was efficient—peering through the foliage, there were eight Consortium members. Some were on the ground looking skyward, and others climbed the wide yew tree branches.

"What are they looking for?" Kaleb wondered aloud in a whisper.

"Not sure," Sorwin said. A thought of Tansil, Zak, and Olivia on their secret mission flickered through his mind. "But we might know *someone* who could tell us."

A broad man in the Consortium black-and-blue wandered to the edge of the grove opposite where Sorwin and Kaleb crouched. Two of their squadmates took advantage of the opportunity and pulled him into the brush. Sorwin thought they maintained their cover for a moment, but a shout sounded from one of the yew trees.

Someone had seen their comrade taken.

That was when the chaos started.

Vivid light erupted in the grove, flames and spells flying between the squads. Sorwin launched to his feet and blocked a fireball with an orange shield. Kaleb intercepted a charging axeman, twisting around the man's guard to slam the pommel of his sword into the side of the man's head. He crumpled to the ground as Sorwin and Kaleb moved into the fray.

A mage hurled three more fireballs at Kaleb. Sorwin pulled at the earth, erecting small barriers that caught the blasts as Kaleb ran, closing the distance to the Consortium mage in mere moments. The mage danced back as she parried Kaleb's blades with bursts of magic. He slid from the force, feet digging small trenches in the ground.

With a series of gestures, Sorwin coaxed the roots of a tree to coil around the mage's legs, pinning her in place. It didn't last long as she covered her hands in flames and grasped the roots, burning them away. But Sorwin didn't need long. He only needed a moment.

In that moment, he had closed his eyes and reached deep into the earth with his magic. He found a reservoir and made a dozen channels leading up to the grove before him. With a flick of his wrist, water shot toward the sky in streams, covering the area in geysers.

The mage had only used fire and pure magic energy, and Sorwin guessed she couldn't use other elements.

When she blanched at the sight of the water, he knew he guessed right.

He gathered the water around the mage, trapping her in a liquid sphere. Air bubbles escaped as she thrashed in the suspended water, her magic pushing against the spell. But he was far stronger, his will burying hers. Sorwin lowered her to the ground, and the water receded below the mage's chin. She gasped for air, coughing as the water solidified into ice.

With his opponent trapped, Sorwin's gaze swept through the grove. A few of the Consortium squad members lay motionless on the ground. Shira had one pinned beneath a cat-like demon the size of a small horse. Kaleb tended to an injured League squad member. As far as he could tell, Sorwin had trapped the only mage among them.

He leveled his attention on his captive. "What are you looking for here?"

The mage spat at Sorwin's feet, muttering a few colorful phrases.

"Of course, how rude of me," Sorwin said. "I didn't introduce myself. I am Sorwin Darlangson." He stepped toward the trapped mage as she paled a few shades lighter. "I see you recognize my name. Then you know you are outmatched. So," he twitched his fingers, and icicles sharp as knives slowly grew from the icy prison, angling for the mage's throat. She had to tip her head back to avoid the cold blades. "I'll ask again: what are you looking for here?"

He didn't enjoy the fearsome magerus role, but it was necessary. Perhaps, with all his pent-up frustrations, it was a little easier today.

The mage tried to look around for her comrades, but the ice restricted her movement. "You'll find out, but not from me. Not until *he* wants you to." Her voice was rough and gravelly.

"Are you sure?" He pushed the ice blades further, drawing a bead of red that dripped down her neck.

She winced and *smiled*.

He realized too late what she was about to do.

A fireball burst from her mouth and slammed into the nearest yew tree, engulfing it in a violent red flame. Wild light danced in her eyes as she looked at Sorwin and yelled, "For Zandorn!" Blue fire consumed her in a flash, melting the icy prison and leaving nothing behind but ash and water.

The cry echoed through the grove, and Sorwin turned to

see the remaining Consortium squad members burst into the same blue flames, each of their captors backing away as their prisoners disintegrated.

A long, heavy silence filled the grove, broken only by the crackling blaze of the yew tree. The squad slowly collected around Sorwin. Kaleb came up behind him, the soft pressure of his hand pressed on his lower back.

His eyes drifted to the faces of his squad mates, each reflecting his knot of sorrow and anger. None of their squad had died, only sustained minor injuries, but somehow, this felt like a loss.

They were so *close* to capturing Consortium members. It was a rare opportunity. The nefarious group was elusive and excelled at cloak-and-dagger tactics. This had been a chance to discover what the Consortium plotted, and Sorwin failed.

Add it to the list, he thought.

Shira became visible, releasing her demons in swirls of light that darted back into her *lapidaemas*. "Well," she started, hands finding her hips as she surveyed the squad and the grove. "We know two things: they're searching old groves and won't return to this one."

"How do we know that?" Kaleb asked.

"Why else would they set it ablaze? Whatever they were looking for wasn't here, and they wanted to let Zandorn know. That tree is a message," she said, pointing at the burning yew.

"Shira," Sorwin said in a low voice. Her words lifted him agitation enough for pieces of a puzzle to connect in his thoughts. "You've seen Zakolor's dream, haven't you?"

"Part of it. Why?"

"The bird. Zak said it was in a grove. Did it look like this one?"

Shira looked around again. "A bit. Some of the same trees and the odd spacing of an untended grove." Her eyes widened and snapped to Sorwin. "Do you think...?"

"I do," Sorwin said. The puzzle took shape, and became much less puzzling. Maybe the day wasn't a total failure. "I think the Consortium is hunting a black caladrius."

Terasi grunted through the pain, not wanting to give Zandorn the pleasure of hearing him scream. He had a few times—it was impossible not to over the torturous months—but he was proud it happened on no more than two occasions.

"This would be easier if you just *told* me the right grove," Zandorn said in his silky voice. "Though I do rather enjoy our time together." The mage's hands gripped Terasi's skull and pressed it against the stone wall of his prison. It felt like the inside of his head was on fire as Zandorn ripped through his memories. He had already found two groves. There were only a few more, but—

No. He needed to think about *anything* except the groves. He expanded his mind, searching for nearby plants, trees, and nature. He found a small oasis during his first days of captivity, a lush forest wedged between cold mountains. It was surprising to find it there when nothing grew in the Wastelands; a bright spot of life in a desert of death. He pushed his mind there, trying to lose himself in the roots and branches, sliding along the leaves and brushing over soft petals.

It didn't always work. Often, Zandorn would follow, pulling his consciousness back to his body and cutting through his thoughts like a wildfire through a forest, leaving destruction and pain behind. Terasi didn't know what was different about today, but cool relief flooded over him as Zandorn's hands pulled away.

Terasi blinked and saw beads of sweat on Zandorn's brow. "Even you have limits, *Calinus*." He must have drawn more strength from the plants than he realized.

Zandorn said nothing but picked up a dagger from the nearby table and slashed down Terasi's right arm, easily splitting his green skin. This was part of their ritual. Zandorn cut him every time they parted. Sometimes, Terasi accrued several in a single day. He was so accustomed to the pain that now he barely winced.

As Zandorn left the room, Terasi slumped, his chains rattling. His head drooped forward as a trickle of blood raced down to his palm.

Luckily there were no mirrors or water or reflective surfaces to catch a glimpse of his visage. At one point, his druidic body represented the pride of nature. Dark green skin covered strong muscles, tattoos told the story of the earth he cared for, and golden-brown antlers curved gracefully to the sky. Now his emaciated frame paled with marred runes and a lightness in his head from his missing antlers, hacked off for Zandorn's dark experiments.

Terasi hadn't tried to escape before because he thought it pointless. Zandorn sealed the room from outside magic and kept Terasi's locked in. Most of it, anyway. A few times he reached for the *Nacusti* hoping their magics would resonate, but his efforts yielded no results.

His captor had tried to break his spirit and limit his power. But no seal or spell could contain nature.

And that gave him an idea.

Perhaps he could do more than suffer with pride. Perhaps he could warn the world of the Consortium's plans. He had been imprisoned long enough to hear more than a few important details. Zandorn had shared much of them himself, his cockiness and confidence in the Druid's inevitable demise burning his sense of caution away.

Perhaps he could take advantage of that.

Emboldened by his recent victory, Terasi reached for the oldest, strongest roots in the small oasis, falling down their twining paths to see just how deep they ran.

CHAPTER 17

THE CURSE OF COST

Zak flexed his clawed hands. Green scales dotted his arms up to his elbows, winking in the low light of the *inriloc*. After days of effort, this was the progress he and Jolsu made.

It wasn't enough.

In another time or place, Zak would have been elated. His arms looked like small copies of Jolsu's forelegs. He partially transformed into a *dragon* without suffering the untethered ferocity from before, when he fought Burvenin. That transformation had been fueled by desperate rage. This one felt calm and controlled.

But with the pressure of time slipping away, he couldn't celebrate this small success. Olivia's condition worsened by the day, and Kal's probably did too. And Zandorn could move against the League at any second. The helplessness Zak felt when facing Karazul flashed through him, stinging his heart. He relived the moments of the assassin's blade sliding across Vermig's throat, the fleeting seconds slowed down and drawn to impossible length in his memory. If he wanted to end the war and save his friends, he needed more power.

What he had now wasn't enough.

His scales faded and claws shrunk back into fingers. Temaway and Vess looked at him, and Jolsu sat stiffly to his right.

"You will progress faster if you forgive one another," Temaway said. The elf had an uncanny ability to almost read Zak's thoughts, and he wondered if it was the culmination of living for thousands of years or an obscure magic he wielded.

Jolsu shifted his weight between his front legs, long talons piercing the rough earth. Zak had learned the movement meant the dragon was annoyed, and he felt the same.

"I didn't do anything," Zak said. "He's the one that hurt Olivia."

"Are you certain?" Temaway asked. He sat on his cushion, unmoving as his green eyes bore into Zak.

"Yes," Zak said. Of *course* he was certain. He hadn't done anything to Jolsu. The dragon had earned his anger.

"So you've asked Jolsu? Spoken to him about how he feels?"

"Well, no." Zak's confidence faltered as his eyes darted to Jolsu. The dragon looked annoyed, but there was something else present in the tilt of his head, the way he avoided Zak's gaze. Had he done something to Jolsu? Not on purpose, but inadvertently?

"What do you know of the connection between Guardian and *Nacusti*?" Temaway leaned slightly toward Vess as he spoke.

"Not much." Zak answered honestly. "I can feel Jolsu's

power sometimes, and I know when he has strong feelings. His voice is in my head." Embarrassment prickled across his skull while he rattled off the meager list. "There wasn't exactly anyone around to ask...you're the first *Nacusti* I've met."

"Indeed," Temaway said. "Then consider the opportunity before you." He gestured to himself, Vess, and Jolsu.

There was no judgment in his voice. In Zak's short time with Temaway, he realized what was different about him: he had no ego. He made no attempts to impress or impose, to sway or to swagger. He simply *existed* and seemed perfectly content with that.

The only irritation from Temaway's lessons was how he framed the conversation to get Zak to ask his own questions. Between the mental and magical exercises, he had a splitting headache at the end of each day.

Zak couldn't bear the thought of asking Jolsu a question. His stomach soured at the idea. Instead, he addressed Vess. "What is it like to be a Guardian with a *Nacusti*?"

The phoenix twitched her head. Her feathers—a mix of reds, yellows, oranges, and even hints of purples and pinks—reminded Zak of the painted skies at both sunrise and sunset. "A blessing and a curse. Sometimes one, sometimes both," she said in her high voice.

"How is it one or both?"

"We are not strangers to responsibility. Guardians had many duties in the Era of Gods, and we sacrificed willingly to free the mortals of Valecium. Our power tipped the balance in your favor, and we were glad of it. Yet being stripped of our bodies and autonomy is a heavy weight to carry."

"You live through us," Zak said. He wondered how it must feel to have no control over where he went or what he did. In a small sense, he did know. His time in Tor'alan was scheduled down to the minute, and he had little choice but to comply and play the role of the League's savior.

He may have *felt* like he had little choice, but he did—in fact—have a choice. He could run away at any time. He could wake up tomorrow, decide he had enough, and make his way back to Densba, back to his parents' loving embrace. There would be consequences, to be sure, yet he could still make the choice.

But Guardians could not.

They had no bodies of their own, only their thoughts and feelings and magic, but little else. The *Nacusti* tied them to the physical plane, for better or worse.

"Is there no way to restore you to your bodies?" Zak felt strange asking the question, but he had to know. Maybe he could set Jolsu free if they defeated Zandorn.

Vess' wings bristled at her sides. "None worth the cost."

"What do you mean?" The phoenix was almost as cryptic as the elves.

"She means," Temaway said, "that we tried—for a few centuries—to develop a spell that would return her sacrifice. But magic is a balance, a transaction of cost and benefit. To give new life to the Guardian, the *Nacusti* must perish."

As Zak looked at Jolsu again, he realized what he saw.

Sorrow.

Zak was his prison and his keeper. Jolsu had been trapped for centuries, and to the dragon, Zak was nothing more than the newest cell. His fate was to live for eternity in Adrastus' descendants, none of them willing to sacrifice their life for the dragon, as Jolsu had sacrificed for all Valecium.

A tear itched as it slid down Zak's cheek. He wiped it away with the back of his hand and, perhaps for the first time, he understood Jolsu.

The dragon's yellow eyes observed him. He said nothing and sat more still than any statue, but somehow, he seemed a little smaller to Zak, not as imposing.

"Let's end there for today," Temaway said.

The odd light of the *inriloc* faded, and so did the images of Vess and Jolsu, though their presence remained in his mind. The blaze of late afternoon burned Zak's eyes as he blinked them open. Autumnfall pushed into Temaway's sanctuary, the air colder and crisper, and the sun set earlier every day.

"I had no idea," Zak said. He hadn't moved from his seat on the cushion.

Temaway grunted his way to standing, more than a few joints popping as he did. "Of course you didn't," he said. "That's why we ask questions, to learn. And you asked some good questions, if I may say so." The old elf stretched his back and lifted his staff from where it leaned against a nearby tree. "Shall we? I'm curious to see what Olivia managed for dinner. After a few hundred years mostly alone, it is a welcome change of pace not to prepare every meal."

Dinner was a silent affair, save the sounds of the fire and Temaway's gentle humming (he made most meals musical). Tansil kept to himself, reading notes on his portal theories between bites. Even though she made the carrot stew, Olivia pushed her food around disinterestedly. It had been several days since her last outburst, and Zak wondered if she was waiting for the next inevitable fit.

Temaway stopped humming and tilted his head as if listening to something. "We have a guest."

Zak jumped to his feet, assuming the worst. His stew splashed on the fire, spewing a burned smell of food. "Is it the Consortium?"

Temaway gave him a curious look. "It's Pordu."

Tansil and Olivia said nothing, but their attention focused on Temaway. Before Zak could ask who that was, a rustling sounded at the other end of the clearing, and a small Druid stepped through the brush. Her green skin, short antlers, and brown clothes blended in perfectly with the leaves and bark. If she were standing still, Zak wouldn't have spotted her. He sat back down as she approached.

"*Benevita* Pordu," Temaway said.

"*Benevita Clarignis*," Pordu replied. She touched her hand to her mouth and then cast it to the sky.

"Carrot stew?" A nearby tulip offered a bowl to Temaway, and he plucked it from the flower to hand it to Pordu.

The druid shook her head. "No, I am not here to stay, only to deliver a message." Her lips held a firm, severe line. Temaway gestured for her to sit, and she moved to the nearest tree stump stool, not bothering to address Zak, Olivia, or Ta nsil.

"What news?"

"You are aware Zandorn is targeting old Druid groves?"

Pordu asked.

"I felt the disturbances."

"Then you felt the patterns emerge. He is methodic, searching for something. We didn't know what until a few days ago, but now we do. He seeks the black caladrius."

The air in Zak's lungs froze as if it had turned to ice. *This is it*, he thought. *What my Sight tried to warn me of is happening*. Maybe the months of opaque dreams would finally make sense.

"How do you know?" Temaway asked. His wrinkled face looked stern and unfamiliar.

"ter-Terasi sent us a message."

"You spoke to Terasi?" Zak interrupted. The mention of the Druid that saved him pushed the initial shock from his chest.

Pordu looked at him for the first time. Her features marked her as a Druid, but she seemed very different from Terasi. Both spoke with direct and cutting words, but she lacked the undercurrent of caring in Terasi's tone. "Not spoke, received a message." She turned back to Temaway. "He found deep roots that grew below the Rot."

"Where is he? Is he okay?" Zak needed to find out everything he could about Terasi to save him. He would never have been captured if he hadn't been defending Zak.

What little patience Pordu seemed to have faded fast. Her eyes darkened as she looked at Zak again. "He is far from 'okay,' *Parignis*. He is in the clutches of death itself, in the heart of the Rot. He risked everything to send us the key to Zandorn's plan."

Zak swallowed hard. He was confident his knees would have buckled beneath the Druid's words if he had been standing.

"The black caladrius is real?" Tansil asked. His notes and stew settled on the bench next to him.

"Quite real and quite rare these days." Temaway tapped a finger against his chin.

Zak remembered something he had learned about the black caladrius. "Why is it called the Bird of Death?"

All four faces around the fire leveled their gazes on him.

"Where did you hear that name?" Pordu asked.

"In Masdaan." Zak flinched under Olivia's warning eyes. She had asked Zak not to tell anyone about their encounter with the caladrius and Malu, but he may no longer have a choice. He had only told Bazil. But he needed to understand the black caladrius, especially if Zandorn wanted it.

"From who?" Pordu pressed.

"A merchant named Malu." It wasn't strictly a lie; Malu *was* a merchant who sold pets and familiars, but Zak knew he was something more, too.

Upon hearing the name, several things happened simultaneously. Olivia folded her arms across her front, Tansil and Pordu muttered curses, and Temaway let out a single, barking laugh.

"What?" Zak asked, directing his question to Temaway. Based on his reaction, he seemed the most likely to answer.

"Malu is a trickster god," Temaway said. "I assume 'nothing was as it seemed' when you met him."

Zak nodded, having difficulty forming words. "How?

With the Contract?" It shouldn't have been possible to meet a god in Valecium. None except Cerevita, anyway.

"Not all gods succumbed to the Contract," Tansil said. "It was namely the Three: Azubelux, Baltenebris, and Cerevita. Most other gods followed the Three back to the divine plane—or were forced to by their hands. Though if anyone were going to escape, it would have been Malu."

Some of Malu's words started to make more sense to Zak.

A friend to some, a nuisance to others, and a laugh to most.

A trickster.

Zak's headache worsened with the onslaught of information. He needed to focus on one subject at a time. "What is the black caladrius, and why does Zandorn want it?"

It was Temaway's turn to bear the weight of the group's attention as four pairs of eyes shifted to him.

"Bird of Death is an erroneous yet memorable title. The black caladrius was prized and feared because of its ability to *negate* anything. Magic, life, the very fabric of the world, nothing could withstand its power."

"That sounds like Karazul's anti-magic," Zak said. His stomach twisted as the assassin's name passed his lips.

"It is similar, from what I've heard," Temaway agreed. "Though the black caladrius' power worked differently. The bird could not use its gift, but a single feather could enact the ability. It came at a cost, one the bird paid with its life. It was a curse, really, to carry such power and be a victim to others who sought it. Between those using the birds' power and others hunting it out of fear, it was thought to be extinct millennia ago."

"But at least one lives," Pordu said. Her gaze had fallen to the fire, and its light danced along the inky lines of her tattoos. "Zandorn has been searching for groves with the black caladrius in ter-Terasi's mind. Druids are connected to the earth, we know its secrets. It is only a matter of time before he finds what he seeks."

"Then we must do all we can to stop him." Temaway stood with a renewed vigor. "Let's go, *Nacusti*."

"What? Where?" Was Temaway leaving in the middle of their conversation?

"To finish what we started. You should come too, Olivia." The elf gestured at her, and Olivia's eyes widened.

"Before you go, *Clarignis*, another warning. Your efforts with the *Parignis* have not gone unnoticed. I fear you will not be protected here much longer."

"Thank you, Pordu. How long do you give us?" The elf seemed unbothered by the idea that the Consortium could descend on his sanctuary at any moment.

"Anywhere from a few hours to a day, two at most. Their portals make their movements unpredictable." Pordu stood, clasping wrists with Temaway. "*Benevita, Clarignis.*"

"May the Mother guide your roots," Temaway said. As Pordu turned and left as swiftly as she entered the clearing, Temaway looked at Zak and Olivia expectantly. "Well, you heard the Druid. We haven't a moment to lose." He turned in a ruffle of robes and strode toward the alcove with Cerevita's altar.

Zak and Olivia exchanged anxious glances. To Zak's surprise, it was Tansil who spoke. "Go with him, both of you," the elf said. His sharp features cut a concerned visage. "This may be your best—and last—chance to get what you both need. I'll see to fortifying our protections."

"What exactly did you have in mind?" Zak asked Temaway, stumbling behind the elf toward their cushions. Olivia reluctantly followed.

"We're going to fix your bond tonight." Temaway conjured a third cushion for Olivia as he settled on his seat.

"How?" Zak knew enough about magic and elves to know there was always a catch.

Temaway's impish smile twitched the corners of his mouth. "By cutting to the heart of your barrier. Olivia and Jolsu need to meet."

Olivia's ashen complexion paled even more, and Zak thought he would be sick.

Chapter 18
Inriloc Talk

There weren't many things that scared Olivia. She was used to others shying away from *her*, darting glances and rushing passersby, afraid to get caught in the storm of her wild, unpredictable magic. At least, that's how it had been for years, moving from village to village each time she inadvertently destroyed something. The destruction itself didn't prod her on, but the fear she saw in villagers' faces. Fear of what she could do and how she could hurt them. That ended when Sorwin found her. When she learned control. Discipline.

Now, her body shook involuntarily, rebelling against her control. Her life slipped further away each day, each outburst stealing precious years she wouldn't live. That wasn't why she was shaking, though.

It was the *anger*.

Meeting Jolsu meant meeting the one who cursed her to this torturous march toward death. She had fought for her existence for years and painstakingly tamed the magic within her, only to have her future stolen by one little, devastating spell.

What would she say if she faced the dragon? It was odd knowing he existed, feeling the effects of his twisted magic, but never having met him or heard his voice. On the one hand, she knew Zak needed Jolsu's power, and the League did too. Zandorn and the Consortium were killing Valecium, and Olivia wanted to stop them.

On the other hand, she wanted revenge on Jolsu.

Weighing her limited options, Zak and Temaway stared at her, waiting. *Cursed Nacusti*, she thought. She was never really mad at Zak for what happened. She blamed him, of course; he was the only one she could direct her anger toward. But she knew it wasn't his fault, and his constant apologies and research and botched remedies somehow made her *like* him.

Maybe there was a fine line between annoyance and affection.

Against her better judgment, she sat on the offered cushion, tightening her muscles to prevent the trembling. "What do I do?" she asked.

"Take our hands and close your eyes. We'll do the rest," Temaway said. He held out his ancient hand, and Zak held out his young one.

Olivia let out one long, pained sigh before grasping both of them and scrunching her eyes closed tight.

The strange light of the *inriloc* stretched over the alcove.

Zak saw Temaway, Vess, and Jolsu staring at Olivia, her face pinched as if waiting for a jolt of pain. He gently squeezed her hand. "You can open your eyes."

She did, and her expression was unreadable while her attention flitted around the alcove, piecing together where she was. It was a place that was the same and not the same. Her eyebrows lifted as she spotted Vess, then lowered as her gaze settled on Jolsu.

The dragon didn't move, speak, or snarl. He simply returned Olivia's dangerous glare. Zak wasn't sure if that was a good thing or not.

"I assume you heard what Pordu shared?" Temaway directed his question at Vess and Jolsu. The phoenix twitched her head in a movement that resembled a nod. The dragon blinked twice. Temaway took that as an answer. "Then you realize we have precious little time to sort this out. Who will start?"

It was Zak's turn to look around. Olivia kept her gaze away from Jolsu, like when she expertly avoided Zak for the better part of a month. He felt sweat on her palm, which he still held. Jolsu shifted his weight between his front legs. Both remained silent.

Zak and Temaway shared a look. The elf's mischievous smile had a hint of understanding, maybe even pride. His bushy eyebrows arched up, offering a silent invitation.

"I will," Zak said. He took a nervous, shaky breath as he felt the weight of attention upon him. He gathered himself and what courage he could muster before turning to Olivia. "I'm sorry," he said, which must have been his thousandth apology to his friend.

He could tell she fought the urge to roll her eyes, maybe thinking the same thing. "I know," she said.

"No," he continued. "I've been apologizing for the wrong thing. I was apologizing for your *vitaligo*, that it happened. I should have been apologizing for putting you in danger to begin with."

Olivia stirred in her seat but said nothing. She looked confused, so he pressed on.

"That day, we went to Tansil's office to recharge the *indagomius*. I was feeling..." he swallowed a lump in his throat, "many things. I wanted to prove to you I was good enough, *strong* enough, to defeat Zandorn. I should have waited for Tansil, but I was reckless. That decision led to us being in the field with the Consortium, to Karazul running you through, to you needing the *vitaligo* at all." His jaw clenched, thinking of Karazul. He was determined to make the assassin pay for all the pain he caused.

"That's what you were holding onto?" Surprise softened Olivia's voice. "Zak, I was told to help Sorwin find you. But even before Euphemius gave the order, I was volunteering. You didn't force me to do anything. I would have been there anyway."

He searched her face—unsure what he sought—finding steadiness and sadness. Strange, that they both released the other from responsibility, yet still pained over the memory.

His eyes slid away from Olivia and onto Temaway—the elf giving him a supportive wink—before he looked up to Jolsu. The dragon was still and silent.

This one was trickier than Malu.

"I'm sorry I shut you out and ignored you." Zak's voice sounded thin, and he cleared his throat before continuing. "I'm sorry you don't have a body of your own. I'm sorry that you lost your *jyrnen* and sacrificed everything to save Valecium from the gods. I'm sorry your reward was a punishment, spending an eternity trapped inside mages. I'm sorry none of this has been fair, and you deserved better." Nerves quickened his pace and made him forget to breathe. He was almost panting by the end of his speech.

Jolsu's tail twitched. He lowered his giant head to be level with Zak's. "You assume much responsibility, *Parignis*. You do this all for her?" He nodded toward Olivia, the brilliant green of his scales glinting with the movement in the grey light of the *inriloc*.

Zak's resolve didn't waver. He sat up straighter under Jolsu's massive eye. "For her, for the League, for Valecium, for myself, and for you. We need each other, Jolsu. Whether we like it or not, we're family—*jyrnen*."

The dragon's lip curled—was that a smile or a grimace? "Hatchling steps, *Parignis*." He raised his head again and, this time, rested his golden eyes on Olivia.

For a long moment, nothing happened. The silence and tension between Olivia and Jolsu's standoff was unbearable. Zak almost said something, but then he saw a change in Jolsu. The dragon's face softened—as much as his scale-hardened face *could* soften—and a stream of hot air blew from his nostrils.

"I didn't know about your condition," Jolsu's deep voice

rumbled. "I will admit I enjoyed the discomfort the *Nacusti* suffered these last months at your expense, but I cast the *vitaligo* to save your life. You were dying, and even then, I could sense how much Zakolor cared for you. I intended to save your life, not cause your slow death."

"If that's how you help people, you're terrible at it," Olivia spat.

Zak gasped, but Jolsu remained calm.

"Helping was never my strength. It was always Nel's."

"Nel?" Zak asked.

"Nelvowig. My *sodalis*, my mate. She was the true leader of our *jyrnen*."

"Your mate's name was *Nelvowig*? Brutal," Olivia said.

"Olivia!" Zak chided. Despite himself, he fought back a snicker. It *was* an odd-sounding name.

A grumble sounded in Jolsu's chest as he leaned back and thumped his tail on the ground. "It's a strong dragon name!"

Zak saw a playful flash in Jolsu's eye and knew enough of the dragon's real anger to see he feigned offense. Olivia must have caught on too as she laughed.

The pair of them—Olivia and Jolsu—seemed very alike, both short of patience and preferring few words to many. Jolsu never said sorry, and Olivia never said she forgave him. Neither seemed to need specific words uttered but reached a silent understanding. Zak didn't want to ruin the mood and the progress they made, but he needed to ask one last question.

"Jolsu," Zak said. "Is it possible to remove the *vitaligo*?"

The levity faded from the alcove as a weight settled onto

the dragon once again, reverting him to his statue-esque posture. "If there is, I do not know it. The binding was never meant to be undone."

"There may be one path left to unravel the *vitaligo*," Temaway said.

Zak barely registered his disappointment with Jolsu's answer before hope again surged. If he felt this thrashed around, he wondered what Olivia must be enduring. "What do we do?"

Temaway clutched his chest and let out a yelp, afflicted by something unseen as he bent forward. Zak rushed to his side, placing a hand on the elf's back and arm. The thinness of the flesh hanging on his fragile bones startled Zak. Temaway was ancient, but this close to him—even in the *inriloc*—Zak observed his drawn and tired features with new concern, saw ligaments straining from the effort of holding his frame upright. He was deeply unwell. How had Zak not seen it before?

"It will have to wait a few moments." The elf's breath rattled, and Vess flapped her wings, clearly distressed.

"What's happening?"

Temaway placed shaky hands on his knees.

"The Consortium," Temaway said. "They're here."

Chapter 19

THREE FIRES

The dark light of the *inriloc* disappeared as Zak opened his eyes to utter turmoil.

Fire tore around the edges of Temaway's sanctuary. The hollow tree at the end of the clearing blazed, half turned to ash already. An icy blue barrier arched over the alcove, protecting Zak, Olivia, and Temaway. It was Tansil's magic. He stood in the middle of the clearing, hurling spells and orders.

Flowers, shrubs, saplings, and rocks fought against the Consortium. They climbed, kicked, slapped, and pelted the soldiers with anything they could throw (sometimes themselves, in the case of the rocks). Burgo circled overhead, swooping to snatch a soldier before they could dive out of the wyvern's path. A sickening crunch sounded as powerful jaws closed on the man's neck. Burgo dropped the body and twisted in the air, looking for new prey.

The bizarre army created such confusion and disarray that they seemed to be winning the conflict.

For a moment, anyway.

Gouts of colored flames burst from the far end of the

clearing, devouring everything they touched. More than twenty soldiers and mages charged through the opening, reinforcing those already fighting.

And there, sauntering in behind them all, was Karazul.

Zak ran to Tansil's side, fury burning his gut. Temaway hobbled behind, the elf's arm slung over Olivia's shoulders.

"Time to put your training to purpose," Tansil said before Zak could ask what he needed. The Archmagus was incredible—an extension of nature as he wove the elements against his foes. A wall of water pushed a line of soldiers back, a gust of wind stilled the air in another's lungs, and a sharpened stone shot straight through the armor and flesh of two others. His dark hair flew wild behind him, a reflection of the fierce battle.

"No," Temaway said, standing beside them with Olivia's help.

"I can help. I can do this!" Zak's arm flailed at the approaching Consortium soldiers. Did Temaway not believe in him?

"I know you can, *Parignis*," he said. "You made more progress than I dared hope. But this is my home—Cerevita's last gift—and I *will* defend it with my life." Temaway found a hidden well of energy as he stood up straight, his wrinkled brow furrowed in determination. He handed his staff to Olivia and stepped forward. Even Tansil wavered from his spells, his attention diverted to steal a glance at the ancient *Nacusti*.

Zak didn't know what to expect, but the memory of the elf's signature on the Contract reminded him of one thing.

Temaway had fought the gods and *won.*

"*ter-amis,*" Temaway's voice thundered across the clearing louder than any natural voice should. Stillness froze the battle as all his plant and earthen defenders focused.

An unspoken command must have passed between them as they rushed together at the same time, colliding. No, not colliding, *building*. Rocks fused, plants twined and twisted, and trees sprouted more branches and foliage. A lumbering figure unfolded, its full height rivaling the nearby forest canopy, with empty sockets where eyes should have been carved into a dirt-clod, snarling face.

It was the largest golem Zak had ever seen.

More than a few soldiers took wary steps back, staring at the gnarled golem, but it was too late.

Heavy fists of wood-rock-earth swung, launching bodies through the air and crashing through the half-burned treeline. One daring mage tried to shackle the golem's leg with a ring of earth. But the golem *was* earth; it absorbed the material and stamped on the mage, squashing them beneath its clumped foot.

As the golem tore through Consortium ranks, Karazul waded into the fray, teeth visible through his devious smile. Zak knew the assassin enjoyed this, the thrill of testing his abilities. He reveled in the challenge of deadliness.

Zak hoped he was outmatched.

The assassin broke into a run, dodging the golem's limbs that sought to crush him. The creature was big and destructive but slow. It had pummeled half of the Consortium soldiers, but as Karazul turned out of the way of the latest attack, he put his hands on the golem and pushed. His antimagic flooded through the creature, and it fell to pieces, a rain of dirt, stone, and twigs.

The mountain of debris collapsed. Zak waited, thinking the tiny creatures would stand and resume the fight, even if the magic that bound them into the large golem had been destroyed. But their tiny bodies were still, unmoving.

Karazul hadn't just pushed the magic from the golem. He pushed the life out of every creature inside it.

"No..." Olivia whispered.

And Zak felt the same loss. They had befriended those flowers and rocks during their time in the sanctuary. Most had helped them gather food or taught them strange dances to accompany Temaway's even stranger music. Zak stepped forward, unable to restrain his rage, but Tansil's hand shot across his chest, halting him.

"We'll only get in his way," Tansil said. And even though Zak knew he was right, it felt wrong to stand by and do nothing.

Temaway hadn't been idle. While Karazul fought the golem, the elf cupped the air before him. Violet, red, and yellow fire curled down his arms and collected in his palms. In a blinding flash, the ball shot up and stretched fiery wings from its center, taking Vess' shape. The phoenix shrieked a battle cry and surged across the clearing.

"Incredible," Zak said. It looked similar to the spell he performed on accident in Masdaan when he created a likeness of Jolsu out of fire. This spell was far superior—far *stronger*. He could feel it. Vess looked real, like her form was physical and not a manifestation of magic.

The bird took Karazul by surprise. His eyes widened at the sight of her and he rolled a second too late to avoid the sunrise-colored flames jetting from her wings, clipping his right leg and forcing him into the base of a burning tree. He slammed hard into the charred wood.

Vess tilted her flight and passed over the wreckage that was the golem. Her wings beat softer as embers floated down on the rocks and plants. Tiny sparks alighted, and one by one, the small creatures that had given themselves to defend Temaway emerged from the rubble. Zak smiled, a happy bubble in his chest as the dazed creatures waved stems, petals, and pebbles of thanks to Vess.

"The phoenix," Temaway said, his voice still unnaturally loud, "is one of the only known creatures to master the Three Fires. Even the gods struggled with that feat." He took slow steps toward Karazul.

A handful of Consortium soldiers retreated from the clearing, fear-stricken by Temaway and Vess. Burgo flew overhead, pursuing them.

The assassin shook his head, slowly recovering from Vess' attack. As he stood, he pulled a dagger from somewhere and flung it at Temaway before running toward the elf.

The dagger *burned* in midair. Not even ash was left behind.

"Most know the Consuming Fire, the easiest to master." Even though Temaway didn't raise a finger or speak a word, Zak knew the magic came from him. This was Thought casting, what Sorwin tried to teach him. The elf continued his slow march forward, and Zak worried as the distance between him and the assassin closed.

If Karazul laid one hand on Temaway, it would be over.

Mere steps away, Karazul drew a sword and sliced at Temaway. The blade bounced off a barrier that appeared inches from the elf's throat. The assassin used the momentum to twist and thrust the blade toward Temaway's ribs but again met resistance as it turned harmlessly away.

A torrent of air buffeted Karazul, pushing him back as his heels dug trenches into the earth. He held his arms over his face, the wind so strong his eyes nearly closed.

Temaway was like the eye of a storm, marching a slow, determined path of destruction.

But Karazul wasn't without power, either. Doubled over and fighting against the gale, the assassin pulled a small statue from a pouch at his belt, put it to his lips, and whispered something. Black smoke spewed from the figurine and poured all around, blocking him from view. While the assassin disappeared, two giant beasts took shape.

Shadoweres.

Zak recognized them immediately. The wolf-like beasts attacked him and Sorwin twice after leaving Densba.

Temaway didn't break his stride as Vess swooped low, a wake of fire streaming from her wings. One Shadowere succumbed to the flames and burst into smoke. The other dodged, jumping out of the way in time. It ran at Temaway, maw wide with knife-sharp teeth baring toward the elf. A few paces away, it erupted in sunrise fire, yelping as it turned to smoke.

Then, something happened.

Suddenly, Karazul was behind Temaway. The assassin stabbed his blade toward the elf's flank. A barrier appeared again, but Karazul followed the blade with his free hand and pushed, shattering the magic. Without the barrier, the blade pierced Temaway's right side.

"Temaway!" Zak shouted. It all happened so fast and so slow. *Not again,* he thought. Not another life, another death on his hands. Temaway could have lived another thousand years in peace if Zak had never come here.

The elf smiled with bloodied lips, and held up a hand, stopping Zak's shocked steps. Karazul gripped the elf's shoulder and retracted his sword, thinking the fight ended.

He was wrong.

"The second fire is much more difficult," Temaway said. He faced Karazul, who froze in apparent shock. "The Curing Fire."

Vess, who had been larger than a horse-drawn cart, shrunk to the size of Sorwin's hawk, Croi, and landed on Temaway's shoulder. The elf coughed as blood seeped from the gash in his flank. The phoenix dipped her head, and a gentle blue fire curved through the air. It drifted gently around Temaway's side and sealed the wound before fading away.

"You...you're a *Nacusti*," Karazul said. He seemed to search for words as he put the pieces together. "You shouldn't exist." Zak had never seen the assassin *scared* before. He enjoyed the sight.

"Neither should you, Niltris." Temaway had a dangerous coil in his grin.

"What did you name me?" His sword arm faltered.

"You have held many names over the years, haven't you?" Temaway continued, ignoring the assassin's question. "I had my suspicions. Rumors of a man with anti-magic penetrated even my secluded sanctuary."

"You know me?" Karazul asked. "Where do I come from? Where is my brother?" He jabbed his blade toward the elf, accentuating his questions. His face scrunched, and Zak felt as confused as the assassin looked. Did Karazul not know who he was?

Temaway nodded, a heaviness in the movement. "Yours is a sad story, and your brother's even moreso. But it is not my tale to unravel. And your current deeds do nothing to garner favor. Instead, you shall yield to the third: the Creating Fire."

Vess exhaled a dark orange flame. The sight of it set shivers up Zak's spine. It was potent and pure, but the intent in the flames was clear as they twisted through the air.

Before Karazul could move or gasp, the orange fire circled his head, joining itself to make a fiery crown. The assassin's eyes rolled back as he dropped his sword and crumpled to the ground.

No sooner than the assassin fell did Temaway also collapse, bending to a knee. Vess disappeared in a wisp of smoke, and Zak, Olivia, and Tansil rushed toward the elf. Tansil eased the ancient elf back to recline against his thighs. His breath came shallow and quick, a glistening on his forehead matted his hair.

"You overdid it," Zak said. He couldn't believe he was scolding the elf, the veritable *legend*, in front of him.

Temaway grunted a breathy laugh. "You would too if your home was threatened."

Zak thought of Densba, of Burvenin's attack the night Kal was stolen. If he had any control of his magic back then, he would have given everything to defend his family, his friend, his town. He couldn't disagree with the elf. He glanced at Karazul, the orange flames floating around his head.

"What did you do to him?"

"The Creating Fire has many forms. That," Temaway pointed a bony finger at the orange crown, "is a powerful *senligo*, a binding of the mind. He is trapped in his own nightmares for now. It will not hold forever, not against him." He cast his eyes up to meet Tansil's. "You will want to find a safe place to hold him."

Tansil tipped his head in agreement. "You knew him, called him by another name."

An impish smile flitted across Temaway's lips. "I suspect he'll have many questions when he wakes. Do not dismiss them—or him—too swiftly. He may yet be an ally in your war."

"Him?!" Zak couldn't restrain himself. "Temaway, he's done terrible things in Zandorn's name. I think you confused him with someone else." The absurdity of Karazul fighting for the League and against Zandorn was too much to entertain.

"I am certain of his nature, but the decision will be yours."

As much as Zak questioned the elf's judgment of Karazul, he was astonished at the power and control he wielded. He single-handedly defeated the assassin that no one in the League could stop. Not even Sorwin or Tansil.

The elf coughed. It was the rough, rattling sound of someone deeply unwell.

"Temaway..." Zak said, his voice thin.

One of the recovered flowers wobbled over with a waterskin. Temaway took it and drank, handing it back with a gracious nod. The rest of the little creatures trickled into a circle around Temaway.

"We haven't much time. You found the path to walk with Jolsu and took the first steps. Will you continue?" His light eyes flicked across Zak's, searching.

"I will," he said. Relief pushed the tension from Temaway's face. "But, the spell you did with Vess. Can I learn that?"

"You can, and much more. You and your dragon can achieve nearly anything together."

Such simple words with so much difficulty beneath them. Temaway must have read his apprehension as the elf patted his hand.

"Remember that Jolsu fought in the Guardian War, too. He knows what is possible. Let him guide you."

"I will," Zak said again, making the promise. A wave of sadness and pride came from Jolsu then, sensing the end of his old friend.

"Olivia." Temaway's voice grew quieter every time he spoke.

She had been sitting on her heels and, upon hearing her name, leaned closer to the elf.

"After a few thousand years of life, one develops many skills. The one I am most proud of is learning hearts. Our time together was short, but your heart is strong, determined. You have lived in pain, suffered injustice, and resisted the temptation of wickedness. Yours is a righteous heart, one of love, and I would see it beat in this world as long as it can."

Temaway reached for Olivia's hand, and she offered it. He squeezed tight around her fingers as tears spilled down her cheeks.

"There is one way I know to save you from the *vitaligo*," the elf continued. He looked up at Tansil. "*Is shalri?*"

Zak didn't understand what he said, but Tansil conjured a small knife with the flick of his wrist and handed it to Temaway.

"There is a reason the Belcour bloodline never lost the status of *Nacusti*," he explained. He gripped the wood of the knife handle, drawing the grey metal against his palm. "The *Nacusti* were made from the sacrifice of Guardians. And it is only through sacrifice that another can be made." He held the blade out for Olivia and raised his hand, a red line blooming against his light skin.

Olivia's eyes darted from the blade, to Temaway, to Zak, and back again, confusion giving way to horrified understanding. "I cannot. You'll die," she said in a harsh voice barely above a whisper.

"Take me in, *Parignis*." He gestured at his sprawled, weakened body. "I greet death already. But this way, there is no reason you should too."

Zak's gaze settled on the knife as he discerned the meaning behind Temaway's words. "If Olivia becomes a *Nacusti*, it will break the *vitaligo*?"

"The gift must be given willingly and accepted willingly, otherwise it will not take." He offered the handle of the knife to Olivia once again.

If things were different—if Temaway weren't dying—it would have been a difficult choice. If Zak was in Olivia's position, he couldn't trade another life for his own if they were hale and hearty. But Temaway *was* dying, fading from the world before their eyes. Zak wanted to shout with all the strength in his lungs for Olivia to take the knife, to accept the elf's gift.

Instead, he waited, sweaty palms pressed together in his lap.

"Can't Vess heal you with the Curing Fire?" Olivia asked. "Or me?"

"There are limits to even the most powerful magics. The Curing Fire cannot halt nature's progress. I have seen nearly four thousand years, and even elves wither eventually. Nor can the fire untether your chains."

"I don't understand," Olivia said. "If Vess can't heal me with her magic, how could becoming a *Nacusti* fix the binding?"

"Nothing is gained without sacrifice," Temaway said. The lines in his cheeks slackened as his smile began to falter. He was fading fast.

"I don't know." Olivia shook her head, the pressure of time not lessening the weight of her decision. Her misty eyes looked skyward, seeking an answer or an escape.

"Olivia." Tansil gripped her shoulder. "This is your decision, but know you are not responsible for Temaway's life. He is leaving this world with or without you accepting his gift. You need only answer one question: do you want to live?" The younger elf's dark features were more tender than Zak had ever seen. Not warm, exactly, or friendly—but a fierce kindness, a genuine concern for Olivia's life.

Tansil truly was Cerevita's devoted.

"I do," Olivia said. "I do want to live." Something in her started to change, loosen.

"And will you find a better chance elsewhere?" Tansil pressed.

"I—" She looked at Zak, and all he could do was remember the weeks he spent digging for cures in the Archives, her countless tests with priests and healers, and their failed run-in with Malu and the caladrius. He gave a single shake of his head, answering her unasked question. "I don't think so," Olivia said.

"Then this is it." Tansil took the knife from Temaway and placed it in Olivia's hand.

She stared at the blade, and Zak knew she felt its heaviness. She slowly curled her fingers around the smooth wood of the handle, making her decision. Olivia drew the blade against her palm and held it up, mirroring Temaway's.

The elf smiled as he pressed his hand against hers, grasping it lightly so their cuts met. "For what it's worth, I think you made the right choice. And I am happy Vess will live on with you."

"Thank you, Temaway," Olivia whispered.

"One last thing," he said, pulling a worn leather journal from an inner pocket of his robe. "You'll need this later. Vess will explain."

Olivia laid the journal in her lap. Questions played in her eyes, but she held them back, save one. "What do I do?"

"The words will come to you," Temaway said. He took a deep breath and took one last look at all their faces, his playful smile returning for a moment. "I'm happy it ended this way."

Tears drenched all of their cheeks now, and Zak wiped his eyes as his vision blurred.

"Where branches end," Temaway said.

"Retrace to crooks," Olivia responded.

"And chase below."

"Where deep roots grow."

"Replant the two."

"To bloom as one."

"My life for thee."

"Your life for me."

The stillness of the following moments was peaceful and sad. Temaway's chest no longer rose and fell. Olivia gently lowered his hand to rest at his side. She looked at her own for a moment, and when Zak caught her eye with a questioning gaze, she shook her head. Nothing about her seemed different, and none of them knew what to say or do.

The flowers, rocks, shrubs, and saplings, who had held a silent vigil throughout the ordeal, crept forward. They lifted Temaway from Tansil's lap and carried him with reverence toward the hollow tree at the end of the clearing. The strange sounds of nature came from the surrounding forest.

Birds fluttered and sang sorrowed notes. Deer pranced and stamped the ground. Trees bent and swayed, their boughs drooping low.

Nature was honoring Temaway.

The procession of little creatures swarmed around their friend, their guardian, and set him with care at the base of the hollow tree. It had been Temaway's home, and now it would be his place of rest.

The tree, which had been half burned in the Consortium's attack, sprouted new life. Foliage and branches jumped from its ashen bark, growing rapidly so it filled out even thicker than before. The tree's strong branches lifted the elf and placed him inside on a bed of fresh leaves. The openings of the tree started to fill in and close, the green of new growth shifting to a lighter color, similar to Temaway's features.

And then the elf was gone, hidden inside the tree to enjoy the peace he more than deserved.

"*Benevita,*" Zak said through a tightened throat.

Chapter 20

BINDS AND BONDS

Slowly, the attendees of Temaway's ceremony departed. The birds' song quieted as they flew away. The deer picked careful paths through the underbrush, and the trees righted themselves, branches returning to natural angles and heights. Temaway's little creatures stayed, hugging and pawing at the tree that was no longer hollow but full of the memories of their friend.

Zak couldn't watch them, afraid he would never stop crying if he did. Instead, he wiped his face, burning and itching from tears, and turned to Olivia. "How are you feeling?"

"Fine, I think. The same."

"Did it take?" Tansil asked.

"I'm not sure." Olivia looked down at her palm, running a thumb over the thin cut.

Tansil watched her for a long moment before assessing the rest of their surroundings. "Stay here, both of you," he said. "I'll find Burgo and check for any lingering Consortium soldiers." He crouched momentarily near Karazul, checking the spell that held the assassin. Satisfied, he jogged from the clearing and doused the remaining fires from any trees as he went.

There was no sign the magic worked and that Olivia was a *Nacusti*. No colors or flashes of light emanated from the spell. The only evidence was that Temaway was gone, but he had already been dying. How did they know if he passed from the spell or not? Zak thought he still felt a flicker of Vess's magic, but he couldn't be sure. He already missed Temaway. He could ask the ancient elf anything and get an answer or a nudge in the right direction.

Then Zak remembered Temaway's final piece of advice.

Jolsu? Zak reached through their connection. *Did it work? Is Olivia a Nacusti?*

When he focused on their bond, Jolsu's thoughts and feelings were stronger in his mind than ever before. The dragon was thinking about the past, remembering something painful. He quested toward Olivia with his power, and she must have felt it as she sat up straighter.

It worked. Vess is with Olivia, buried deep. The ritual is difficult for Guardians. It will take time for their bond to grow.

Zak relayed the message to Olivia but withheld Jolsu's feelings. It must have been unpleasant to witness the same ritual he underwent centuries ago, when he sacrificed his body. He left the dragon alone with his memories, sensing he didn't want to discuss them.

"I don't feel different," Olivia said. She flexed her hands into fists, testing her strength. Biting her lip, she focused on a single finger. After a moment, a tiny yellow flame appeared at the tip. She immediately stopped the spell and doubled over in pain.

"Olivia!" How could she be so reckless?

"I had to check," she said through gritted teeth. "The binding is still intact."

"It will take time. Maybe your bond has to be stronger before the binding is undone," Zak guessed. He didn't know if the bond would break the binding, and Temaway didn't have time to explain his theory.

"Maybe there's something in here," Olivia said. She opened the journal Temaway had given her.

Unfamiliar lines and shapes in dark ink covered the yellowed pages. Zak couldn't read the writing, but there was much of it.

"Is it Elvish?" he asked. Maybe Tansil could read it when he returned.

"No. I've seen Elvish in some of Tansil's notes. This is something else." She shut the journal, putting her frustration into the gesture.

"We'll figure it out, *Nacusti*." He tried to replicate Temaway's impish smile as he threw the title at someone else for the first time.

Olivia's mouth opened a little, but no sound came out. It was the first time he had seen her speechless, and despite the loss they just endured, Zak *laughed*. It was a deep belly laugh that came from his very core. All the pain, frustration, dead-ends, and loss melted away. He laughed even harder when Olivia pushed him in the shoulder and he toppled over, cackling as he squirmed on the ground. Then Olivia joined in, her shoulders shaking with the happy sound.

For a moment, it felt like they were two young friends sharing a joke instead of two young mages who needed to save Valecium.

"You're right," Olivia said, her voice raspy from tears and laughter. "That does feel weird. I'm sorry I ever teased you with the name."

"You get used to it, sort of." He still didn't like being called *Nacusti*, but he slowly accepted that was how the world viewed him. And now, how it would view Olivia. It was too soon to celebrate—the *vitaligo* still threatened Olivia's life. But he had hope that this time they had finally found her cure.

After a few minutes of scattered talk and questions about being a *Nacusti*, Zak left Olivia to watch over Karazul while he walked the perimeter of the clearing, snuffing the few remaining flames from the Consortium's attack. He couldn't use water magic yet, but the fire responded to his will as he coaxed them into embers, then nothing at all.

When he finished, Tansil returned with a limping Burgo. He had crashed hard during the battle, bruising a wing and gashing one of his powerful rear legs. Tansil patched him up with some salve and minor pain relief spells, but he admitted healing wasn't one of his strengths.

They all agreed to wait in the ruined sanctuary for a few hours, at least until dawn. The darkness of the night would slow their progress toward Tor'alan anyway, and Olivia, Tansil, and Burgo needed the rest.

A few hours later, when faint golden sunbeams pierced

the thinning blanket of Autumnfall leaves, their circumstances hadn't improved.

"I doubt Burgo can carry you both with his injuries," Tansil said, frowning as he patted the wyvern's blueish-brown neck. The beast made a soft whine in his throat. "We may have to wait a day."

"We shouldn't stay here any longer." Olivia surveyed the damage in the sanctuary. "This place protected Temaway, not us. That must be how they found it in the first place, by tracking our magic. They'll return when they realize we have Karazul."

We can fly, Jolsu said.

What? The dragon's unexpected suggestion surprised Zak. *Are you sure?*

"Then we'll start on foot," Tansil said. "I received a Firepost while searching for Burgo. Tor'alan moved back to its previous location."

I'm sure. The question is, are you ready?

Zak hesitated for a moment. The last time he grew wings, the appendages burst from the middle of his back in a painful fit. But he hadn't known Jolsu back then—he had been a mysterious voice, and Zak had turned to his power in desperation.

It will be different this time. We *are different,* Jolsu said, sensing Zak's apprehension.

"How far is it from here?" Olivia asked.

"Only a few hours south by wing, a few days walking."

This time had to be different. Zak needed to trust Jolsu. He promised Temaway he would try. *I'm ready. What do we do?*

Use both our magic and wills and say the word.

Zak thought of his magic like an ocean, deep with a rhythm like the tide. When he reached for it, he found Jolsu's magic too. He had never felt the entirety of it, only pieces in moments. Jolsu's power felt like the sky, bright and cold and vast. When he pulled, it came easy, like his own magic, and somehow, he knew this was the work of their bond.

"*Pennilma*," Zak said aloud. The words came to him from somewhere—maybe Jolsu—as he thrust their magic into the spell. Glittering light pulsed over his shoulder, and when he looked, mighty emerald wings appeared. He stretched them out to the side in a rush of air, a giddiness lifting his face.

Burgo snarled and cowered while Tansil and Olivia jumped back in surprise. They both quickly pieced together what he planned to do.

"Zakolor—" Tansil said.

"Don't you—" Olivia started at the same time, but Zak didn't let either of them finish.

"A few hours south, you said? Let's see if you can keep up." He flashed his new Temaway-esque smile and bent his knees, thrusting himself straight up, copying what Sorwin and Tansil did whenever they flew.

After a few heavy beats of his wings, Zak wondered if this was a terrible idea.

Flap faster! And harder! Jolsu urged.

"I'm trying!" He couldn't breathe. All he heard was the wind and his pulse drumming in his ears. He careened in every direction, unable to level his flight. The ground called to him, willing him to touch his feet back down. Why did he feel so heavy?

Your wings must work together!

Suddenly, there were branches all around him. He curled his arms in as twigs and leaves tore at his uniform and skin, leaving dozens of tiny cuts while he crashed through the treetops at the edge of the clearing.

Let me show you, Jolsu said.

The dragon's will gripped his wings. They bent and relaxed, curving before thrusting powerfully down. The leathery wings pushed the air with such force that his body lifted from the mess of branches. Then they did the movement again, and again, and again. With each flap, he rose higher and higher, fierce wind gusting against him as he picked up speed. The treetops started to shrink, and soon, he could see miles in every direction.

We're flying! He yipped and hollered even though the whipping air swallowed the sound.

We are, Jolsu said. The dragon's joy filled Zak's chest as much as his own.

He dipped his head, looking to the ground below. Olivia climbed on Burgo, the injured wyvern shaking his wings in preparation for the flight ahead. Tansil's owlish wings draped from his shoulders as he threaded a grip under Karazul's arms and leaped to the sky. The elf must have worked some magic on the assassin to lighten his weight.

Good, Zak thought. He didn't mean to *actually* leave his friends behind, but excitement got the better of him in the moment. Jolsu slowed their flapping wings, leaning them into a glide until the others caught up. When they did, Olivia rolled her eyes at Zak, and Tansil had what could have been an amused look.

In a few short hours, the floating city came into view. Tor'alan looked even more majestic from the air. The morning light reflected off the roofs and streets, and the Center's white stone and shocking veins of orange and purple glittered.

While he was momentarily lost in its beauty, Zak almost wished the city was further away. He didn't want the flight to end. He reveled in the freedom, the feeling of his wings against the crisp air currents. But he knew he needed to land, to resume the responsibilities that awaited him back on the ground.

"Oh gods," he said. He had to *land*.

Ending the flight hadn't occurred to him. As his panic surged, he felt amusement from Jolsu.

You'll be fine, the dragon said. *Do not stop all at once.*

A flicker of light blue magic pulsed from Tansil. It was difficult to see against the morning sky as it shot straight toward Tor'alan and collided with the barrier protecting the city. The ordinarily invisible barrier shone a bright gold around the large opening the elf's magic created, a window for them to pass through.

Zak followed Burgo, who followed Tansil, each banking left as the barrier closed behind them. The timber frame of the stables came into view below. Tansil floated nearly straight down to the grassy yard as Burgo tilted into a circular descent.

Zak approached the ground at an angle but quickly realized his mistake as his speed increased. He pulled his chest up, trying to get his legs underneath instead of behind him. He would have had an easier time pulling against a solid brick wall. His heels connected with the grass just in time, digging into the ground as he skidded across the yard. He wasn't stopping fast enough. His wings disappeared as he launched forward, smashing hard into the dirt.

Pain radiated all down his front as he grunted his way to standing. A few stablehands chuckled as he brushed chunks of dirt and grass from his uniform and hair. He scowled at them but knew he wasn't intimidating as they laughed harder, and his cheeks warmed from embarrassment.

Flying was fun. Landing was not.

A worthy first flight, Jolsu said. Zak could hear and feel the dragon's mirth.

Luckily, his friends didn't witness his clumsiness. Tansil's back was turned to help Olivia down from Burgo. Olivia was a new shade of pale as she leaned against the Archmage and slid down the wyvern's scaly side. She let out a cry and crumpled as soon as her feet touched down. Yellow magic pulsated around her entire body, and cracks in the ground darted through the grassy yard. The entire island seemed to tremble as Olivia's power erupted.

Tansil—quick as a shadow—stepped behind her. His lips moved as his hand cupped her forehead. Olivia sank back into the elf's arms, unconscious. The yellow magic faded, and the trembling ground stilled.

"Not again," Zak rushed to Olivia's side. The binding

was still in place, but Zak foolishly hoped the outbursts would stop now that Olivia was a *Nacusti*.

"She's in a light sleep, but it won't hold long," Tansil said. "Take her to the healing wards. Sashina will be able to do more."

"The Archlumen couldn't heal her before," Zak reminded Tansil. He brushed auburn curls from Olivia's face, which twisted in pain in the magic-induced sleep.

"Correct, she cannot remove the *vitaligo*, but she can ease the next outburst."

Is there nothing more to be done? Zak wondered. "What will you do?"

"I'll assemble the council. They need to know everything that transpired with Temaway. And we have to discuss what to do with him." Tansil pointed at Karazul, whom he had left on the ground while helping Olivia.

"Should I..." Zak left the question unfinished as he looked at Olivia again, worry washing through him.

"No, not this time," Tansil said. "I'll handle the council. You are the only one with an inkling of what Olivia will be going through. I should think she'll need you now and in the coming days."

It wasn't like Tansil to release Zak—or anyone—from duty. Obligation to the League always came first for the elf. Perhaps his short time with Temaway had changed him.

Zak moved one arm behind Olivia's back and the other under her knees. He stood, lifting her with Tansil's help. She was light in his arms, too light. A frown pinched his brow as he tore his eyes away from her and back to the elf.

"Thank you, Archmagus." He hoped the honorific conveyed his sincere thanks. He couldn't imagine leaving her side to sit in a council meeting.

"On your way, Zakolor." Tansil gave a nod and firm smile as he swept from the stable yard, robes rippling behind his fast stride and Karazul floating unconscious in his wake.

"We're almost there," Zak whispered to Olivia as he ambled through the stables and down the stone streets toward the Center. He attracted confused and worried looks from townsfolk with Olivia's limp body in his arms, but he paid them no heed. All he could think about was Olivia. "You're almost better. We're so close to healing you." Her eyelids fluttered but remained closed.

When Zak met Temaway and realized he wasn't the only *Nacusti*, it hadn't felt different. It didn't sink in because Temaway was a legend. He felt far away because of his long life and unfathomable power. Now, one of his closest friends—someone he cared for deeply—was a *Nacusti*, and everything had changed. A wet tear dripped down his cheek.

"Don't leave me alone," he begged Olivia.

Chapter 21
DISTRACTIONS

Only a few days had passed since Zak delivered Olivia to the healing wards. He tried to stay by her side, but Sashina wouldn't have it. She shooed him from the Temple's halls, only allowing weekly visits to Olivia and Kal. Failing to see any other choice, he begrudgingly accepted the arrangement and negotiated to keep them on separate days at least.

On Twosday, he caught up with Bazil at breakfast. Zak welcomed the priest's company as new rumors incited upon his return.

"Where did he go for so long?" he overheard a mage not-so-quietly whisper at the next table.

"The front, apparently. There's been a few battles with the Consortium near Lindomer."

"To see what? We've got Rotters and murders right here in Tor'alan!"

Murder? Zak thought. Then he remembered.

Vermig.

He had rushed from the city with Tansil and Olivia so soon after Vermig's assassination he hadn't considered the turmoil they left behind. The death of an Arch—one of the three most powerful mages in all Valecium—was no small matter.

"A new Archalium was voted in a few days ago," Bazil said. "It was the first assembly the Den of Darkness had in a while. Interesting to see all those summoners in Tor'alan together but," he shivered, "demons give me the creeps." He chomped on a brittle strip of bacon. "You'll likely meet her in a council meeting soon."

"Who?" Zak had stopped listening, thinking instead about Vermig and how quickly everyone seemed to be moving on. *We don't have a choice, I guess. The war continues on...*

"Rinka, the new Archalium. Are you okay?" Bazil focused on him with a sideways look.

"I'm fine just...a lot happened while I was away. I want to explain everything to you—can we meet in the Dormitory instead of the Archives later?"

"Sure, I actually wanted to share a few ideas on cures I found for Olivia—"

"We found one, we think," Zak said sheepishly, ashamed he didn't mention *that* part of the journey before leaving. He hoped Bazil didn't waste too many hours in the Archives on his behalf.

"Oh, right. Well that's good! Isn't it?" Bazil was hesitant, perhaps from Zak's own lack of confidence.

"I hope so."

Later that afternoon, Zak visited Olivia. She was thinner, and her complexion faded to a sickly gray. The less Olivia used her magic, the more it tried to escape. The priests applied potions and salves to lessen the physical toll, but the outbursts had become stronger and more frequent.

On Threesday, he had an abysmal Sight lesson. He couldn't quiet his mind or focus on the image of the black caladrius at all. Not when he knew Olivia's health failed in the healing wards while he sat on Shira's purple couch. The small, overheated sitting room was suffocating.

That evening, he went to Sorwin's townhouse. Their daily lessons had been awkward, clouded with unasked questions and untold answers. Zak needed to clear the air between them. He didn't like withholding the truth from his magus and owed it to Sorwin to be honest.

He wandered from the Center to the Lion district in the north, where most nobles lived. When he knocked on the solid wood door, Sorwin opened it, and the smile on his face shifted into a look of surprise.

"Zakolor! What brings you here tonight, this late?"

"Hello, Sorwin. I'm sorry to stop by unannounced. I thought we should speak about everything." His words trailed off as he heard another voice carrying from several rooms away. "Is someone else here? Should I come back another time?"

Sorwin looked over his shoulder, blushing into a deep maroon. "No, I mean—yes, someone is here, and no, you shouldn't come back. Now is fine. We should speak." Zak had seen Sorwin in many states and moods in the months they knew each other. Often happy or excited, occasionally troubled or annoyed, but he had never seen Sorwin *flustered*.

It was quite amusing.

Sorwin pulled Zak inside the townhouse and waved the door shut. He pushed him ahead as two pocket doors parted, revealing a study.

"H-hey!" Zak tripped into the room as Sorwin hurried to shut the doors behind them. "Sorwin, what's going on?"

"What? I thought you wanted to speak, so here we are! What say you?" He was out of breath, and how he placed his hands on his hips reminded Zak of his mother when she was upset.

"Sorwin," he said slowly, "who is here?" He came to end the secrets between them, and it seemed Sorwin intended on keeping something from him.

Before Sorwin could answer, the pocket doors slid open to reveal Kaleb standing with a steaming dish of something savory.

"Zakolor," Kaleb said with a nod, his dark hair picking up the light from a nearby sconce. "I thought I heard you. Good to see you again." It had only been a few hours since their afternoon lesson in the training court.

Speech eluded Zak momentarily as confusion turned to understanding. He realized, with a bit of shame, that he knew frighteningly little about Sorwin. He knew he was a High Magus, the Prince of Darlangson, and a council member for the League of Kingdoms. But when it came to personal details, he knew next to nothing. His magic was bright orange, yet he favored cool colors like blue and lilac. He loved learning and teaching. He liked most foods.

Tsk. You have some work to do, Parignis. For once, Jolsu wasn't wrong.

When no one said anything, Kaleb interrupted the silence again. "Will you be joining us for dinner?" He held up the dish in his hands. "I made mushroom casserole. I'm not sure it's my best—I had to clean the entire oven first. The disuse of the thing was pungent." His disapproval settled on Sorwin, whose complexion closely matched the scarlet of the fabric-covered walls.

Sensing his presence interrupted the evening—and knowing both Sorwin and Kaleb were too kind to turn him away—Zak knew the best way to show his appreciation to his magus. "No, thank you for the invitation. I just need a moment of Sorwin's time, then he is all yours." He added a wink, and the way Sorwin's eyes bulged, he thought his head might explode.

"I see you're both enjoying this," Sorwin squeaked in a higher register than normal. "I'll join you in the dining room shortly, Kaleb." With another wave of his hand, the pocket doors clicked shut.

"I'll just be on my way then." Kaleb's muffled voice carried through the thick doors.

Zak absently tapped the edge of the desk that stood behind him. "I'm sorry for interrupting your evening, Sorwin. I hope you know that, well, I'm happy for you." He offered what he hoped was a sincere smile. He didn't want to risk pushing Sorwin's patience for jests any further.

"Thank you, Zakolor." Sorwin sighed. "The truth is, I'm unsure there's anything to be happy about yet. This is our first..." He gulped.

"Date?" Zak offered with an impish curl to his smile.

Sorwin nodded, looking at something on the wall. "It's odd. My whole life has been a series of battles. Growing up as a royal in a palace leaves little room for mystery or surprise. Every second of my life was planned years in advance. I fought for autonomy, for the freedom to explore and learn. I fought to come to Tor'alan to study with Tansil. I fought to represent Darlangson on the council. I fought for you, Zakolor, that we may be Magus and Apprentice." He shook his head, almost laughing as his tension broke. "So when this—when Kaleb—came along, I expected to fight. And it's all been so easy, maybe too easy. I think I'm still waiting for the fight to com e."

"I think I know what you mean." An image of Olivia in her sick bed flickered in Zak's mind. "And maybe the fight will come, maybe it won't." He closed the distance between them with two steps and rested a hand on Sorwin's shoulder, their eyes meeting. "But one thing you should do is enjoy the time you have right now. We never know how much or how little is left."

Then Sorwin's familiar smile brightened his face. "When did you become so wise?"

"I have a good magus," he answered with a shrug.

"Well, I know you didn't come here to discuss my troubles, romantic or otherwise. What do you need?"

Words poured from Zak like a surging stream after a heavy rain, a constant flow and sometimes jumbled and crashing. He didn't want to take up more of Sorwin's evening than he already had and didn't want to leave any secrets unshared. He told him everything, from the encounter with

Malu, to the white and black caladrius, to his meeting with Cerevita and the events with Temaway. A pang of guilt racked him as he finished, realizing the extent of things he hid from Sorwin.

To his surprise, Sorwin didn't react negatively or much at all. He nodded along, listening to Zak's account. It was as if he already knew some of the events or perhaps suspected a few. Maybe Croi was an even better spy than Zak gave her credit.

"I knew there was a connection with the groves. I couldn't see it at the time," Sorwin said. He flung open the doors of a glass-fronted cabinet and rifled through books, scrolls, and oddities. More than a few fell to the floor as he pulled a long parchment from the back of the lacquered cabinet. Unrolling it on the desk, the small objects that had fallen floated through the air and rested at the parchment's corners to keep the worn paper from curling in on itself. It was a map of Valecium, an old one.

"Look, here and here." Sorwin pointed to yellowed spots on the map with inked trees. "These are both old druid groves, which would have yew trees. From what Malu told you, the black caladrius will be found in a yew tree."

"*The* Yew tree, apparently," Zak said, remembering Malu's words.

"Right, and these three groves were places the Consortium visited recently. There are only two more similar groves, which means–"

"We know where Zandorn will strike next!" Zak finished Sorwin's thought, and they shared excited smiles as they connected the puzzle pieces together.

"Maybe not exactly where, but it's more information than we've had in a good long while."

"Zandorn is always a step ahead. We finally might be able to surprise him."

Sorwin carefully rolled the old map up, sliding it into a leatherbound tube that leaned against the cabinet. "I'll share this with Tansil first thing tomorrow. I'm sure we'll need your help to convince the council to send mages and soldiers to the remaining groves as soon as possible."

Zak agreed and left Sorwin to his time with Kaleb, slipping through the Center and up to his room without a sound. He barely slept that night as energy buzzed in his entire body, thinking about his and Sorwin's discovery. If this worked and they had a real chance to get an edge on Zandorn, maybe defeating him and the Consortium wouldn't be impossible.

It was never impossible, simply difficult, Jolsu said.

You're right. The best part of bonding with Jolsu was the dragon's change in demeanor. It was comforting to have his wisdom and deep voice in the back of his mind, offering guidance rather than quips and cruelty.

I could easily offer guidance and *quips*.

I don't doubt it.

The next day was Foursday. After lessons—which included numerous sideways glances and blushing from Sorwin to Kaleb—Zak visited Kal. He was propped up in his bed, blonde hair dull against the stark white room. Dark rings circled his clouded eyes, the lingering effects of the draughts and spells the priests used to sedate him. Zak sat in a chair beside the bed, his knee bouncing as he tried to still his fidgeting hands.

"I'm glad the Archlumen let me in today," Zak said with a concerned smile and tip of his head, angling to catch Kal's eye.

"Lucky you, finding your way to my prison." Kal crossed his arms.

"It's not a prison, Kal. You're unwell, you need care." The priests had warned Zak that his friend's mood was sour, unstable. They thought it resulted from his confinement to the healing ward, but Zak thought it was something more. Back home, even on his worst days, Kal was neutral, never caustic.

"Not a prison?" Kal moved to stand, but chains at his wrists and ankles rattled taut. The metal kept him locked to the bed.

"It's for your safety. Your fits are violent, and they can't use magic to restrain you for long. You end up—"

"Absorbing it, I know." Kal shook his head and looked out the single window in the bright room. "All this time, I thought living in Densba was a curse. I knew I had talent but no means to pursue it. Turns out the nearly magic-free village might have been the one thing that kept me alive this long." The fog lifted as his eyes sharpened, and he turned them on Zak. "Except, Densba wasn't entirely magic-free. You were there. Why didn't I absorb *your* magic?"

Zak hadn't considered that before. "Maybe the jade prevented it?" They both knew of the necklace's magic-binding ability. "I'm not sure, but whatever the reason, I'm glad of it. Seems my magic only made your situation worse."

"Yes, thanks for that." Kal's tone was dry and scathing. His new casual cruelty cut sharper than any blade.

Offer distraction—not reminders, Jolsu advised.

It wasn't a bad idea; Zak was getting nowhere. Perhaps a story could lighten Kal's spirit.

"I met Temaway Galeria," Zak said. "One of the *Nacusti* that fought in the Guardian War and wrote the Contract."

"He's still alive?" Kal's eyebrow arched, sounding surprised. That was better than hostile. "Wasn't he old when the war started? That was six hundred years ago. He must be ancient."

"He had lived almost four thousand years," Zak said, nodding slowly as his heart ached. "He was odd but kind and fierce." He told his friend of their arrival in the sanctuary, of the funny little creatures that kept close to the old elf, of his last battle to defend his home and defeat Karazul. Kal listened, the edge of his words giving way to curious questions. Zak hurried to answer them, afraid to leave too much time silent for fear that his friend would slip back to his darker mood.

"Did he ever tell you about the Contract?" Kal asked. "It seems unthinkable, making an agreement powerful enough to bind the gods."

"He didn't speak of it much," Zak said. When he saw Kal frown, more words spilled forth. "But I saw it once!"

"You saw the Contract?" Kal gasped and leaned forward.

"I did! It's in the Center." Zak had him now.

"Where in the Center?"

"There's an old temple underneath the castle. Tansil told me it used to be where the gods held court. Their thrones are still there, and when I met Cerevita—"

"You *met* Cerevita?" Kal sighed and ran a hand through his straw-like hair. He looked overwhelmed with all the information. "We'll get to that in a minute. Finish telling me about the Contract."

Zak's smile widened, knowing his friend couldn't resist discovering knowledge. He was similar to Sorwin in that way, driven by what he didn't know. The more he spoke, and the more Kal asked, the more it felt like his old friend had returned.

Chapter 22

Into the Eyewood

The sand and water map of Valecium shook with the chorus of shouts in the council chamber. Sorwin watched as the mage holding it aloft grit his teeth. It wasn't a difficult spell—or didn't require much magic—but it wasn't meant to withstand the ruckus of a dozen people disrupting its gentle flow with pitched voices.

"We have explained it thrice over. What more do you need to believe us?" The normally stoic and controlled Tansil sounded exasperated. The elf had changed in his time with Temaway. Sorwin didn't quite understand what was different, but he was looser somehow.

"Facts, for a start." General Lupa pounded a fist on the octagonal table, and the floating map shuddered. "We can't send soldiers traipsing to every grove between here and Evartia!"

"There are two groves and only *one* in Evartia," Tansil shot back.

“Allow me, Archmagus,” Sorwin said.

Tansil waved a hand, conceding to his efforts.

Sorwin stood, glancing at Zak briefly. The three of them had tried explaining the situation to the council several times and seemed to be making no progress. They finally had an advantage over Zandorn. They knew two places he would strike, and soon. Sorwin wasn’t about to let League politics and Tansil’s new temper squander the opportunity.

“This has been a long, tiresome conflict with the Consortium. All of us in this room—save Tansil—were not alive when it started a century ago. But we are present now and will be the ones to finish it if we act.”

Grumbles and murmurs sounded beneath his words, but Sorwin didn’t let them deter him. He pressed on. “Here is what we know. Zandorn is targeting ancient Druidic groves. There weren’t many created, and even fewer stand today—five in total. Three have already been attacked. The first near the border of Gort’haal and Regadensia.” As he spoke, bright orange lights illuminated the locations on the map. “Second, northeast of Lindomer.” He had been present for that one but failed to stop the Consortium. “And third, near Accipia.” He swallowed hard, hoping no one in the small town had been hurt. He hadn’t visited his childhood hideaway in many years. Too many.

“That means there are two left,” Tansil said. “One far to the east on the coast of Evartia and one directly north of here, in the Eyewood.” Two icy blue lights appeared on the map.

“The Eyewood is in Nalawin.” King Gyrnavo leaned forward, scratching his brown beard as he studied the lights.

"You'd have us trespass on elven lands? You know better than most the dangers of their justice, Archmagus."

That was bold, Sorwin thought. No one mentioned Tansil's exile in front of him. Gyrnavo must still be angry about the mess the council made in Masdaan. Though, no one gave a sour pemberry about fishing rights anymore, and Sorwin was determined to remind the League they had much bigger problems.

Tansil's lips tightened into a thin line. "We would trespass no more than a few hours if all goes to plan."

"The plan being that we find and capture a black caladrius?" High King Marius asked in a squeaky tone.

Sorwin pitied Marius. He wasn't made of strong stuff to begin with, but ever since Limba Dar's disappearance, he had become meek and paranoid, weaker than a midday shadow. But he followed the conversation today, which wasn't always the case. "Precisely. We know Zandorn is after the bird, and if we capture it first we can dissolve his plans and perhaps turn it to our purpose. Say, fending off the Rot." It wasn't outlandish if the fabled black caladrius powers were half as potent as legends claimed.

"We have reports of Consortium forces massing in the west in Gort'haal. Would you have us ignore them in favor of stalking these groves?" General Lupa's face reddened every second the conversation continued.

"Of course not." Sorwin kept his voice slow and even. "But we know they seek the black caladrius, so we must recognize the tactic as a distraction."

"And we know this because of a few burned groves and

one child's unreliable Sight?" Rinka's clear monotone cut through the chatter, quieting the council. The new Archalium's gray hair was pulled into a tight bun, accentuating her severe features.

"I'm not a child." Zak stood, eyes narrowed at Rinka.

"Your reaction says otherwise." Zak opened his mouth to retort, but Rinka continued. "Shira informed me of your lessons and inability to see past the bird figure. We're to take your word that it is a creature thought to be a myth?"

"No," Sorwin said. "You're to take mine." He nodded to Zak, who sat again with blushing cheeks. Pride for his apprentice swelled in Sorwin—he stood up for himself, but leaving Zak to spar with Rinka would be irresponsible. She seemed every bit the dissenter that Vermig was, perhaps even moreso with a shrewdness her predecessor lacked.

Rinka touched the opal at her chest, hanging from a thin silver chain. Dozens of colors—her demons—swirled in the stone, bright against the black of her fitted robe. "And what do you say, Prince Sorwin?"

She knew he disliked his royal title.

He smiled, though it didn't reach his eyes. He wasn't as easily ruffled as Zak. "The Consortium has attacked three groves, we have confirmation from Zak *and* Shira of a vision of the black caladrius, and word from a Druid that confirms Zandorn is hunting the bird." He nodded to Tansil, thankful he had relayed Pordu's warning to Temaway. "The evidence clearly shows that Zandorn will pursue the last two groves. Our discourse should be how we approach both, not if we should."

"I agree." Minister Qor shifted in her seat. "We can investigate the grove in Evartia with local forces, though a few mages from Tor'alan would be welcome."

From there, the conversation changed, and a plan began to take shape. King Gyrnavo would handle The Disciples. The group remained a threat after the attack on the council, and scouts had tracked them to the desert south of Masdaan. He would continue the search for Limba Dar and prevent their forces from joining with the Consortium in the west.

General Lupa would take a host to the border near Gort'haal to meet the gathering army. Tansil and Kaleb would lead a joint investigation of the Eyewood grove. Minister Qor would investigate the grove on Evartia's coast with support from Rinka and a few senior summoners. Sorwin was surprised the Archalium volunteered to help, but it seemed she wasn't about to go against the council's consensus, no matter how tenuous.

The meeting dissolved, and each leader turned to their assignments and preparation. The further operations would take days or a week to organize, considering the time for messages and travel. The closest investigation was Tansil and Kaleb's in the Eyewood. It was only a few hours north of Tor'alan, which meant there wasn't a moment to lose. Sorwin's stomach knotted. With the day half gone, they needed to move swiftly to find the grove by nightfall.

The Center bustled with activity. Mages and soldiers trotted between buildings carrying orders and supplies for the pending expeditions. Zak had less than an hour to prepare to leave. It was made clear that he and Shira were needed in the Eyewood to locate the black caladrius. If the bird hid in the grove, the closer they came to finding it, the stronger Shira's Sight would be. Her skill matched with his raw power gave them hope and an edge over the Consortium. And, if they didn't find anything, they would be whisked to the east to search Evartia's grove.

After running to the Dormitory to change and pack his leather bag, Zak went to the healing wards to tell Olivia the plan before leaving. He figured she would want to know.

Sashina was there. He thought she would stop him for a moment, but she offered to walk with him to Olivia's room instead. When Zak asked if she was joining one of the investigations, she shook her head. "One of us needs to stay in Tor'alan this time. With Tansil and Rinka both leaving, that means me."

Zak nodded and was secretly grateful. Of the three Archs, he selfishly wanted Sashina—who oversaw Olivia and Kal's care—to stay.

He steeled himself as he entered Olivia's room. She was more unwell every time he saw her, and today was no different. The air in her lungs rasped, and her auburn curls hung limp and grayed. When he asked how she was feeling, she made an annoyed sound and said, "Sorwin has taught you better than to ask questions with obvious answers."

When he finished telling her the plan, she stared at the barren wall opposite her for a long time. Her eyes were difficult to read, but they held traces of sadness and regret. He waited, but when it seemed she wouldn't speak, he stood. *Perhaps she wants to be alone*, he thought.

"Keep Bazil close," she said as he reached the door. "Someone has to watch your back and cover for your mistakes."

Zak smiled. "I will. And when I get back, we'll start your *Nacusti* training."

"I'll hold you to that threat," she said.

He looked in on Kal before leaving, but his friend was in one of his fitful sleeps. Adjusting the strap of his bag on his shoulder, he descended the Temple steps and made a silent promise to sneak in extra visits when he returned.

Kal ran, but he was so tired. His surroundings grew darker, even as the red and green lights chasing him grew brighter. They closed in on him, and his feet were heavy.

Maybe I can stop, just for a moment.

But he knew what would happen if he did. He knew that would be the end.

Within a few hours, Zak dismounted a horse at the edge of the Eyewood. Initially, he was disappointed when he learned he wouldn't be flying—it was *all* he wanted to do after that first flight, and he could feel Jolsu's desire to be airborne again too. But flying would have quickly outpaced the soldiers and other mages, so he rode on horseback.

Ignoring his chafed thighs, he went to find Tansil. Navigating the tumult of bodies—fifty soldiers, two dozen mages, and a horse for each—he realized stealth and surprise would not be weapons they leveraged.

Zak almost stopped when he saw Rauffe filling basins with water for the horses. Their eyes met, and to his utter shock, Rauffe gave him one curt nod, as if to say, *We're allies for now, Nacusti*. He nodded back, unsure what else to do, and luckily Bazil was at his side a moment later, strong-arming him through the rest of the crowd toward Tansil and Kaleb.

A brown and gold streak to the right caught his eye, and those around him gasped. Some drew weapons, and more than a few colored flames flickered around mages. They relaxed when they realized it was a bird—Croi—taking flight to scout the forest ahead. From the bits of conversations he overheard as he followed Bazil, everyone expected to face the Consortium before the day was done, and a jittery energy buzzed through the company with the impending battle inching closer and closer.

Zak moved in the direction Croi had leaped from and found Tansil giving instructions to Sorwin, Shira, and Kaleb. He smoothed the red fabric of his uniform as he sidled up to listen.

"We'll divide into small groups and fan out, combing the Eyewood. With Croi in the sky and Zakolor and Shira using their Sight, we should be lucky to find the grove within an hour."

"And what if the Consortium interrupts the search?" Kaleb asked.

"When they interrupt," Sorwin corrected. "Our smaller groups will be close enough to condense on the attack."

"Precisely." Tansil's attention flicked to Shira. "And we wouldn't turn down any advance notice, either."

"Of course," Shira said. "Though with my focus on searching for the caladrius, I may see little else."

Tansil nodded. "A tradeoff we'll need to make. Haste is our tactic to avoid the Consortium, but also the elves. I don't want them to find us inside their borders." His eyes darkened as he spoke about his kin. Why did he fear them?

Zak didn't have time to wonder or ask as Tansil gave further orders. "Sorwin and Kaleb, divide the soldiers and mages into small groups. Shira and Zakolor, prepare what you need and begin searching. We'll all be right behind you." With a nod and a turn, the elf disappeared in the throng of League forces.

"I won't be far away," Bazil said. "I promised Olivia I'd keep an eye on you."

"Of course you did," Zak said with a smirk, despite the queasiness churning inside. "Thanks, Bazil."

"Apprentice," Sorwin said, approaching as Bazil stepped back. He squeezed Zak's shoulder. Somehow, this gesture had become their way of communicating support, luck, concern, care, and many other unspoken things. Zak was glad of the comfort and familiarity, something he had so little of since leaving Densba and his parents.

"Magus," Zak replied. He didn't need to say more. All the

hours of training led to this moment: a chance to finally help the League defeat Zandorn.

As Sorwin and Kaleb melted into the regiment to organize the search parties, Zak turned to Shira.

"If this works, Sorwin will pester us to write a book." Shira's hand idly stroked Ubba's chin as he perched on her shoulder. The imp sneezed a few times, scrunching his face.

"If this works, he can pester all he wants," Zak said. It was true. What they were about to attempt was history-making. As far as he knew, Sight magic was used to delve into the past or foretell the future, not to track creatures, and certainly not by two mages with different Sights. Now, they'd find out if all their practice over the last months would pay off.

They waded through tall grasses that thinned as they neared the edge of the Eyewood, stopping a few paces from the treeline. Zak had been in the same forest a few weeks ago, only several miles to the west. That was where Temaway's sanctuary had been. This part of the forest felt different, wilder, and unsafe. Maybe it was the absence of Temaway's magic or Zak's fear of what lay ahead.

Closing his eyes, Zak reached for his magic and felt Shira do the same at his side, the bright purple of her magic mixing with his green. He focused on the image of the black caladrius and his desire to find it. Scenes unfolded before them: versions of themselves walking into the forest, picking a careful path to the left, searching for several minutes, and finding nothing but squirrels and vegetation. The images faded as they reached the limit of Shira's Sight.

"To the right we go," Shira said. "Keep a nose out for any

magic, dear." She gave Ubba another scratch on his chin as he chirped his agreement.

They kept up the pattern of Sight and search for a half hour: moving through the woods, pausing to See what they might encounter, then adjusting their path as needed. It was tedious and tiring work, and Zak's energy drained with each vision. He started to worry about what would happen if—when—the Consortium ambushed them.

You have my power now, remember, Jolsu said. A wave of confidence followed his words. The dragon was just as determined to stop the Consortium as Zak.

Small groups of soldiers and mages searched the woods behind and around him. Whenever he and Shira changed direction, the others did too. He noticed they never left the sightlines between each other, always keeping one group visible to the left and right. This must have been the approach Tansil mentioned—spread out, yet close enough to react to any danger.

Finally, Zak saw it: the clearing from his dream. He saw himself finding it in the vision, and now he knew exactly where it was. He opened his eyes and sprinted forward.

"Zakolor!" Shira hissed a warning as she chased behind him.

He couldn't wait, couldn't contain the confusion of excitement and fear. The dream that had plagued him for so long was about to come true.

Bursting through dried brush, he found it. The grove, the bush he had hidden behind in his dream. It was all there, right in front of him. There was a large pond off to one side. He hadn't seen that in his dream. But this was the right place. He knew it. Across the clearing was the yew—The Yew—the first in Valecium, where the black caladrius would perch.

Except it wasn't there.

He frowned as Shira and the nearest search parties caught up to him.

"Zak! Don't take off like that. We don't know where or when the Consortium could—" She cut her chastisement short, and Zak knew she recognized the clearing too.

"We found it," Zak said. "Now we wait." He settled behind the bush, crouching as he had in his dream.

"We wait? Are you sure?"

"I'm sure. It's too bright, too early. The black caladrius will come, but not yet." He couldn't explain it further. It was a feeling he had, a deep *knowing* that if they waited, the bird would find them.

Shira seemed to accept his words. Whether for his confidence or lack of alternative, he didn't know. She gestured to the nearest search parties to hunker down. The message passed from group to group in hushed whispers, and soon, dozens of mages and soldiers huddled behind trees and shrubs, waiting.

And waiting.

And waiting a little more.

As more minutes drifted by, Zak felt the uneasiness of the group fester. Conversations that started as whispers became more frequent and louder, and shadows darted between hiding spots. Some stood, stretching tightened muscles or spying on the clearing for any hint of the caladrius. Even Shira gave worried glances toward him, her earlier faith faltering. Zak couldn't blame any of them. They didn't See what he saw, couldn't possibly know what he knew.

When the group seemed about to break from anticipation, it happened.

"This is it," Zak said. Word passed down the line, and within a moment, the restless soldiers and mages quieted.

The light faded fast behind the trees across the clearing. Autumnfall neared its end, and a thin mist settled above the pond with the chill of the evening. A stillness gripped the grove, nature's usual sounds and movement absent from this place of reverence.

A small figure interrupted the tranquility, black wings swooping and fluttering to land on a twisting limb of The Yew tree. Ribbed horns flashed as a tiny head twitched and preened beneath dark feathers.

Zak let out a shaky breath.

He had found the black caladrius.

Chapter 23
Not Alone

Zak's dreams—visions—hadn't progressed beyond this moment. He always woke when he found the black caladrius. The deep sense of knowing persisted, heavy like a stone anchoring his thoughts to purpose. He hadn't seen what happened next, but he *knew* what to do.

As he went to step toward the clearing and out from his hiding spot, Shira's iron grip clenched his arm. "What are you doing?"

"I'm getting the caladrius." He nodded toward the bird in the tree as if it was obvious.

"How?"

He didn't understand how he knew what needed to happen, which made it difficult—and a little annoying—to explain what he would do.

Maybe I won't explain, he thought.

"Do you trust me?" he asked Shira.

Her expression softened. "Of course, Zakolor. I only meant to help—"

"Stay here with everyone else. I know how to get the

caladrius, but I must do it alone. Then we can all go home." He was a little surprised at the sound of his own confidence.

Shira nodded and passed the message to the nearest soldiers and mages. As Zak walked slowly across the clearing, he heard Tansil and Sorwin slip into the space next to Shira, undoubtedly asking what he was doing. But she must have convinced them to wait since no one followed.

An unnatural silence blanketed the clearing. Even though it was nearly Winterrise, there should have been some activity in the surrounding trees and pond. Birds chirping, insects clicking, frogs croaking. Instead, only his abnormally loud footsteps crunched on the frost-hardened grass and leaves, carrying him closer and closer to The Yew tree.

The black caladrius perched in one of the lower branches. As Zak neared the tree's base, he could reach the bird with an outstretched hand. But he shouldn't need to. The pounding in his ears was deafening as he stopped a few feet from the tree and the bird, the two symbols that haunted his dreams for months now stood before him.

"Someone—" he started, voice cracking as he addressed the bird. He cleared his throat and tried again. "Someone is after you. They're called the Consortium. They'll be here soon to capture you and use your magic. I don't want them to, and I don't want to see you hurt. If you come with me, I can protect you."

While he spoke, the caladrius continued to preen, but a blue eye focused on him. He couldn't explain why, but he knew he had to tell the bird the truth, that somehow it could understand him. If he was honest about his intentions, it could decide what to do.

The caladrius fluttered to a lower branch, eye-level with Zak as its head twitched, studying him. Except for the horns and startling irises, it almost looked like a small crow, but Zak knew better. He could see the intelligence—the awareness—in its stare. He held out his arm and matched the bird's stare, instinct urging him forward. For a moment, neither moved, frozen as they tested one another in a battle of wills. Then, the caladrius hopped onto his arm.

He had done it. He had earned the bird's trust.

Finally, we're a step ahead for a change.

With the near-weightless bird perched on his shoulder, Zak turned with a triumphant blossoming in his chest. He was about to breathe deep for the first time all day when Renna sauntered from the woods.

"It's not how I would have proceeded, but I suppose it was impressive nonetheless," she said. Her maroon robes and pale skin were bright against the darkness of the trees like she was cast in her own moonlight.

Zak backed away, stumbling toward the opposite end of the clearing, where he heard the League forces leaping from behind bushes and trees. His stomach wrenched as he tried to remain calm and in control. The last time he saw Renna, she stole Terasi and nearly killed his friends.

Delay her for a few seconds. You aren't alone, Jolsu said. He was right. The League was nearly upon them.

"You can't have the black caladrius." He fought to keep his voice from wavering and gestured to the charging squads behind him. "You're outnumbered."

"When has that ever mattered?" A predatory grin slashed her face as she continued her slow, determined march toward him. Her power and stride reminded him of a twisted version of Temaway when he fought Karazul, overwhelming confidence that she was stronger than her foe. "But alas, you are wrong about several things. I will *take* the black caladrius, and I did not come here alone."

Four swirling pockets of energy ruptured the air behind Renna. Soldiers and mages poured from three of them, charging straight ahead. Dark shapes spilled into the clearing from the fourth, slithering and jumping over one another.

"Rotters." Zak cursed. He had to deal with them. His magic was one of the only effective means of destroying them. Before he could move toward them, he was swallowed by the line of League soldiers and mages.

Chaos engulfed him as metal clanged, shouts and spells flung through the air. He lost sight of Renna and the Rotters in the mass of bodies. The clash of League and Consortium forces pushed and pulled at him like violent storm waters. Someone clipped his left side, and he fell hard to the ground. The black caladrius squawked and flew from his shoulder.

"No!" He tried to stand and see where it went, but a foot caught him in the ribs. Pain shot through his side, and winded, he fell back down.

Couldn't anyone see him? Didn't they charge forward to save him? Feet danced around his field of vision, threatening to stamp on him. He curled his limbs in, making himself small, calling desperately for the earth. It heeded, and a dome of packed soil and stone grew over him, plunging him into darkness.

It was quieter, but muffled voices still sounded through his barrier. A few loud thumps made him jump. Someone must have run into the outside wall. He swallowed a lump in his throat and wiped the wet corners of his eyes.

You're rattled. Jolsu said. *Catch your breath. You aren't alone.*

That's the problem, Zak said. *There are too many people. How do I move? How do I find the black caladrius again?*

No, Parignis. It isn't the League I speak of. You aren't alone because I am with you.

Zak's chest stopped heaving as he pushed upright to his knees. How could he continue to be so foolish? Jolsu had been present since they left Temaway's sanctuary, guiding him with advice and support, reminding him that he wasn't alone. When would he start listening?

Now. He would start listening *now.*

What do we do? he asked the dragon.

We fight. Jolsu's power and courage surged into Zak. The energy and emotion weren't his, but they weren't foreign. Not anymore.

Jolsu was part of him.

Fortified by his Guardian, the barrier receded to the earth as Zak stood. The sounds, sights, and smells of battle assaulted him: weapons clanged, vibrant flames and colors flashed, orders and spells were shouted, and a burnt metallic tang clouded the air. It was overwhelming, but he was more prepared for the chaos this time.

He needed to get out of the fray and find the caladrius.

Most of the soldiers near him were Leaguians. There was more space by the pond. He pushed a halting path through the host of bodies toward the water.

A sword arched down from the left. Zak stumbled back in time, the blade landing heavily in the mucked dirt. The Consortium soldier's face was pure bloodlust as he hefted the sword and charged again. Zak scrambled back. He couldn't get to his feet in time to dodge!

A flicker of white shrouded the soldier from view, and suddenly Bazil was there. His hands moved faster than Zak thought possible, striking the soldier's wrist, throat, and torso in less than a second. The soldier grunted and fell unconscious.

Bazil turned and pulled Zak to his feet with ease. "Some would think this was your first battle, *Nacusti.*" Even in the middle of combat, the priest kept his composure.

"It's my third, at least." He had to yell over the blare of fighting. "How did you—"

"Not here, it's not safe." Bazil pushed away a soldier who backed into him. The man flew through the air and collided with a group of Consortiumites. "Follow me!" Bazil ran toward the pond, apparently having the same idea as Zak.

Zak followed in awe. Consortium soldiers attempted to block their path, but Bazil's fists quickly opened guards, wove past shields and blades, and hindered anyone threatening him. The priest didn't carry any weapons, but with his speed and strength, he didn't need any.

"How are you doing this?" Zak asked, breathless from the run across the embattled clearing. They made it to the pond and had respite for a moment.

"This is a priest's magic," Bazil said. "We do not weave elements or tame demons. We master our bodies." He said it matter-of-fact, as he held his open palms up as all the proof he needed.

"Why haven't you shown this power before?" In all their sparring sessions, Bazil never once used this magic.

"It wasn't needed. We trained for your benefit, not mine." His eyes darted over the skirmish, then back to Zak. "We can discuss this later. Where is the black caladrius?"

Zak nodded. It was time to focus. "It flew off when I fell. I think it went this way." He pointed to the opposite side of the pond.

"Then let's go."

While they ran along the banked edge of the pond, Zak looked over the battle. It was difficult to tell who was winning. The vibrant uniforms of the League clashed with the dark black and blue of the Consortium. He couldn't see Shira, but Tansil and Sorwin dueled Renna outside the main skirmish. The struggle between them seemed even, and somehow, Renna still kept the portals open behind her.

The portals. Zak had forgotten about them in his panic. Three of the portals were quiet. One still poured Rotters into the clearing like an endless stream of dark ooze.

Zak halted immediately. He had to destroy them before he found the caladrius. Bazil had continued running but trotted back when he noticed Zak had stopped. He nodded as Zak explained his plan. "I'll help the soldiers while you take care of them." He disappeared into the fray, and Zak ran toward the Rotters.

Three mages held back the flood of Rotters with shields and fire, but their efforts weren't enough. The creatures pooled in the limited space, hissing at the flames and chomping at the barriers. They *ate* the magic, gaining strength with each devoured spell. The smaller creatures started fusing, globbing onto one another until they became two giant Rotters, taller than a house. One loosed a deep, throaty noise as it swung a slimy fist, crushing a barrier and the mage beneath it.

Horrified, Zak skidded to a stop and flung his arms toward the creature. "*Ignitelum!*" Spears of green fire flew through the air. Two pierced the Rotter in the shoulder and the side. It roared as some of its mass melted away and stomped toward him.

He called the earth to wrap around the Rotter's back foot. It stopped for a moment, but the Rotter was amorphous. It shrunk its leg to slither from the bind and turned, hammering fists into the ground, shaking the earth as Zak ran and dove out of the way.

He needed a big spell to deal with the equally large creature. While it readied another attack, Zak reached for the well of his magic. "*Ignitempesta!*"

Emerald flame swirled, growing into a twister of fire that thrust into the monster's oozy flesh. It howled as chunks hardened and broke off, crisping in the air from the heat of the flames. It collapsed in a pile of sizzling ash, smoke wafting from the remains.

Zak panted and wiped the sweat from his brow. The spell had taken a lot of magic, but he didn't have time to rest. Another giant Rotter battled the other two mages, and the portal was still open, pouring more creatures into the clearing.

They wouldn't make any progress until that portal closed.

You need to get Sorwin. He'll know how to close it, Jolsu said.

"But how? I can't leave—those mages will die. I can't be in two places at once."

You cannot, but we *can.*

Of course! He had witnessed Temaway call Vess—manifesting her in the physical plane. The words came to his mind as if he always knew them.

Use as much of our magic as you can. Whatever you put in the spell is what will sustain me.

Zak focused, gathering his and Jolsu's magic together. It thundered through his chest, his veins, his outstretched arms. He had never channeled so much power before, and it was terrifying and euphoric as he spoke: "*Customateria!*"

Swirling green energy streamed from him. Muscled legs sprouted, wings stretched, and a scaly neck and head with jaws and dagger-like teeth formed. It was Jolsu, but he was not made of fire like he had been in Masdaan. This time, he was made of pure magic. The dragon looked like green glass, not solid like Vess had been, but present nonetheless. Zak smiled.

He had conjured a dragon.

Power radiated from the visage of his Guardian. *Go now, find Sorwin. I will slow the Rotters as long as I can.* Jolsu roared and galloped toward the Rotters, and Zak felt the disruption of the battle as soldiers and mages stumbled back from the enormous dragon.

If Zak was tired before, he was ragged now. He put as much magic as possible into calling Jolsu, but he couldn't rest, couldn't stop. Exhaustion had to wait. He needed to find Sorwin and then the black caladrius.

The former wasn't difficult. Sorwin and Tansil still dueled Renna and had found room to fight, or perhaps the others shied away, afraid of getting caught in the devastating magic hurling between them. Demons scurried and flitted over rendered earth, and spells flashed the area with light.

Zak crept as close as he could to the battle, barely keeping up with the dizzying exchange. "Sorwin!" he called. "Sorwin! The portals!"

Sorwin parried two attacks with an orange shield, looked at Zak briefly, and then disappeared altogether. Several seconds later, Zak jumped as Sorwin reappeared right next to him in a cloud of smoke.

"Sorry," Sorwin said. "There's little time. Tansil can hold for a moment, but Renna is too powerful for either of us alone. What about the portals?"

"It's the fourth one. Rotters are still coming through. It's endless. We need to close it."

Sorwin looked toward the portals and gasped. "Zak is that—"

"Jolsu," Zak answered.

Sorwin smiled and squeezed Zak's shoulder. "Well done, Apprentice. We just might win this day yet."

Zak couldn't help but feel a surge of pride. This was it—he was finally making a difference.

The portals, Zakolor. Jolsu's deep, gravelly voice called.

Zak turned, looking toward the visage of Jolsu as it breathed spouts of fire on the Rotters. *How are you still with me, when you're over there?*

I'm always with you, Parignis.

"How do we close the portals?" Zak asked, turning back to Sorwin.

"Leave them to me." Sorwin's brow furrowed. "I must ask too much of you, Zak." He gripped his shoulders and looked down into Zak's eyes, though he wasn't much taller anymore. "Find the black caladrius and fly back to Tor'alan. We can suffer any losses today except that. If the Consortium gets the black caladrius, I fear this war is lost."

Zak bit back a retort. He wanted to argue, to say he could help more in the battle before finding the caladrius. But if Zandorn obtained the power of the black caladrius, he could undo *any* magic, including the spells that protected Tor'alan, the heart of the League.

Instead, he nodded and turned toward the tree line in the direction he thought the caladrius had flown off. Before he left, he made a request of his own to Sorwin. "Do what you can to stop Renna, for Kal."

"I will," Sorwin said. With a final, meaningful look, his apprentice sprinted toward the forest and disappeared.

Sorwin allowed himself a moment to think. He couldn't close the portal. At least, he didn't know how to do it properly. Could he disrupt it? It was magic, subject to the customary laws. Or was it? There was still so much he didn't know about portals, still so much he and Tansil had not discovered.

Tansil. He turned and watched the elf blast two demons from the sky. He held out against Renna for the moment, but he wouldn't last much longer on his own. There was something strange about the woman and her magic. It felt familiar somehow, though he had never fought against her before. But gods, the sheer *power* she wielded. Every spell hit his shield like a boulder.

"Cerevita's grace..." he cursed. He didn't have time for his thoughts to wander. Whatever he was going to do, he had to do it now.

He shifted to the astral plane again and ran across the clearing. The silence jarred as he moved unencumbered. The chaotic battle didn't exist there. He shifted back to the physical plane a few paces behind the portals. As Zak said, three stood quiet save the gentle swirl of energy. The fourth was active, with a growing pool of Rotters crowding beneath it.

The manifestation of Jolsu raged against the Rotters, covering them in green fire and stamping on the smaller ones with clawed, scaly limbs. The dragon turned and swatted a giant Rotter with his tail, knocking it over before pouncing on it, agile as a cat.

The sight was magnificent. Dragons disappeared from Valecium centuries ago, and Sorwin never thought he would see one. While Jolsu wasn't entirely corporeal, he looked every inch the size and shape a real dragon would have been if what Sorwin read in books was to be believed.

He refocused on the swirling blue portal. Stopping any powerful spell was tricky business. Closing a portal with only half a notion of how it functioned was potentially lethal. Nonetheless, Sorwin found himself smiling. *Not all learning is done within the pages of a book.* Sometimes, it was important to get one's hands dirty. And that seemed inevitable with a portal spewing Rotters.

"*Magus expurgo!*" he yelled. A bolt of magic sizzled against the blue portal, but it remained open. Clapping his hands together, orange light appeared at the portal's edges. Sorwin gritted his teeth and pushed with all his might, trying to force the portal closed, but it didn't yield. Next, he flung fire, water, and pure magic energy, but his spells passed through the portal and disappeared.

A crease pulled at his brows. *The real problem isn't the portal*, he thought. *It's the Rotters.*

Reaching for his magic, he pushed as much energy into the spell as he could "*Tegofortis!*" An orange barrier appeared around the portal and stemmed the flow of Rotters. The creatures cried out, slapping sludgy appendages against the wall. It worked for a moment, but then Rotters on both sides of the barrier started eating the magic, and when it was gone, they poured through the portal again.

Jolsu snarled and spouted fire at the nearest Rotters, burning them to ash. *Hurry up, Magus. My form won't keep much longer.*

Sorwin gasped. The dragon's deep voice rang clearly in his head. It was unsettling at first but also fascinating. Is this what Zak heard when he had that foggy look like his thoughts were far away?

He bit his lip. *Think!* He couldn't dispel the portal. Forcing it closed didn't work. All of the magic he tossed at it passed straight through. Not even Jolsu's dragon fire disrupted its flow.

"Wait—the flow!" Sorwin studied the slow swirl of the blue energy in the portal. It was consistent, purposeful, *intentional.*

For months, he and Tansil had theorized and experimented to figure out how portals work. Portals were essentially doors—and they managed to open a few—but they always slammed shut after a few moments. They struggled to discern how to *keep* one open. Funneling massive amounts of magic into the spell hadn't seemed to matter.

Seeing the active portal in front of him, suddenly, it all made sense. They had tried to sustain portals with stagnant magic, like bricks holding up a wall or bridge. But it needed a constant flow of magic to be propped open, like a waterwheel needed a current to keep it stable, productive.

His discovery was monumental; portals were a significant strategic advantage for the Consortium. Once he and Tansil worked out the finer points together, he was confident they would level that edge. For the moment, though, one thing became clear.

Sorwin knew *precisely* how to close this portal.

Sprinting at full speed, he leaped over the pool of Rotters—slimy limbs grasping for his legs. When Sorwin was halfway through the portal, blue lightning rippled across his entire body as he disappeared. A booming *crack* like thunder sounded across the clearing, and the portal instantly closed. Sorwin reappeared a few paces away, stumbling to lean against a tree, chest heaving.

With the reinforcements cut off, Jolsu decimated the remaining Rotters with emerald fire. *How did you do it?* the dragon asked.

Sorwin answered with his thoughts. *I disrupted the flow of the portal with a teleportation spell. Not one of my more elegant ideas, but it worked*. He left the other three portals alone, unsure his body could withstand tearing another portal apart. They seemed inactive for the moment, anyway.

Well done, Magus. Jolsu stepped on the last Rotter, the creature squealing as it disintegrated. *This form will exhaust momentarily. Help the elf—I am with Zakolor*. The dragon leveled a golden eye at Sorwin before his edges blurred, and he faded from sight.

"'No rest for the brilliant.'" He smirked, quoting his sister's favorite phrase. If he lived through the day, he promised to write her a long letter detailing his discovery. Or better yet, maybe he would open a portal to Darlangson and show her. She always pushed him to be better and share more of himself. For now, he settled for pushing off the tree and jogging back to the battle with Tansil and Renna.

We will do all we can, he thought. *We're counting on you, Zakolor*.

Chapter 24
Greatest Fear

Zak threw himself to the ground as a tree to his left exploded. Splinters sprayed the air and he scrambled down a slope and collapsed against the incline.

You can't keep dodging. That spell would have maimed you, Jolsu said.

I know, but I can't hit the cursed thing! Zak peeked over the rocky edge of his hiding spot and saw the demon, its wispy, yellow body floating slowly through the air, hunting. It looked like a yellow cloud, if clouds had red eyes and could combust objects with breath alone. Zak had been looking for the caladrius when he ran into a Consortium mage and the demon.

Fire didn't work. Try something different.

The demon had split its gaseous form around his fiery attacks. Earth magic would be even slower than fire. He silently cursed himself for running off before finding Bazil. It was unfortunate Zak hadn't learned water or air magic yet. He could have doused the demon or blown it away with a gust of wind.

That's it! Zak thought. He didn't need air magic. He just needed *air*.

He crept along the shallow ridge until he had more room. "*Pennilma*," he whispered. In a faint glittering light, scaly green wings appeared on his back. He climbed over the ridge and stayed low, sneaking until he was directly in line with the demon.

It must have noticed him. Before he could get its attention, red eyes glared through the yellow fog. A hole, something like a mouth, formed in the middle of the cloud as it expanded, took in air and then expelled it in a burst of magic.

Zak rooted himself with solid legs, stretched his wings as far back as they would go, and thrust them forward in one powerful motion. The gust from his wings sent the spelled air back toward the demon, its red eyes widening before it exploded. A loud *bang* sounded, and yellow fog curled as it diffused into nothing.

Ha! Now you're thinking like a dragon, Jolsu said.

Zak grinned, but he didn't have a chance to appreciate the praise. The mage that summoned the demon heard the explosion and appeared between two trees to Zak's right.

She snarled, seeing the last wisps of the yellow demon fade. Her arms blurred with movement and launched firebolts at Zak.

He jumped back from the first one and blocked the next three with a fire shield. "*Igniaveru!*" A dozen darts of fire shot from Zak's hand toward the mage.

She spun—and to Zak's surprise—so did his spell. The fire darts circled the mage and flew back toward Zak. He gasped but couldn't get a shield up in time and instinctively brought his arms up in a meager defense.

He felt a tug as one of his wings curled and blocked the spell. But how? He hadn't moved.

Jolsu.

Think more *like a dragon, Parignis. We do not fear fire.*

R-right. He peeked at his wing, leathery skin and green scales unblemished from the attack. Dragonhide never burned.

The mage prepared another spell, dark shadows twisting along her arms. Zak doubted his wings could resist *that*. He reached out with magic to the branches above the mage and pulled down hard. Log-like limbs snapped and fell, dropping her in an instant.

Steadying his nerves, he listened for other threats. He heard nothing nearby, only faint echoes of the League and Consortium battle some distance away. Finally, he could search for the black caladrius again.

How could he track it without Shira and their visions guiding him this time? Maybe the finding spell? "*Invepati* black caladrius," he said. But nothing happened. No light appeared to guide his way. Then he remembered that spell only found items the caster owned. *That would have been too easy*, he supposed.

He thought for a moment. He was in the Eyewood, an ancient forest rumored to be home to the first Sight mages. Maybe he *could* rely on his visions?

Quieting his mind and closing his eyes, he stood still as a mountain. He let his thoughts drift as he sought the weightless feeling that accompanied the connection with his Sight. It was getting easier after all the practice with Shira, but he hadn't managed an intentional vision on his own yet. After a few minutes, he heard a twig snap, and his eyes flew open, the muscles in his arms and legs tightening to meet the threat.

A small brown hare hopped from behind a nearby tree.

Zak blew air between his lips and paced back and forth. His concentration broke, and he doubted he could get it back—it was a wonder he found it at all. He was running out of ideas.

What would a dragon do? he asked Jolsu. It wasn't challenging to think like a dragon when one lived in his mind.

Dragons hunt from the skies. Joslu flexed the wings that still hung at Zak's shoulders for emphasis.

It's worth a try. Zak crouched and sprung into the air. Jolsu guided his wings, lifting him into the air. It felt more natural this time, more familiar, and a sudden energy surged in his chest as he flew above the forest.

He leveled out, arcing in a wide circle. Most of the trees were barren with only a few scattered pines dotting the sea of branches. Zak squinted. Even without foliage, he struggled to see anything through the thick forest canopy.

Let me, Jolsu said.

A trickle of the dragon's magic passed through him as his vision blurred. He panicked—flying without eyesight was terrifying—but it quickly refocused and he calmed. It was different, sharper, and with a golden tint. A pair of cranes flew in the distance, and when he looked, an odd glow hung around them. Some of the trees below had the same glow, and so did a few rabbits, squirrels, deer, and other creatures he could now see with astonishing clarity.

What is that? he asked.

Magic, Jolsu said.

Of course. Magic is in all things. *Is this how you see? It's beautiful.*

Sometimes. Search quickly. We cannot see the magic for long.

With his enhanced vision, locating the black caladrius was much more manageable. After circling in the air twice more, he spotted the bird on a branch of a tall pine, huddled near the trunk where the needles didn't grow.

Jolsu angled them into a swift descent, and Zak swung his legs forward to catch himself, landing far enough away not to startle the caladrius. Its blue eyes tracked Zak as he approached. He put one foot slowly in front of the other with his hands out wide to show he meant no harm. Hopefully, the bird still trusted him after their first encounter ended unexpectedly.

He was mere steps away when a metal cage appeared around the black caladrius. It squawked in surprise, flapping its wings as it tried to escape, but the new prison held fast.

"You're even better than expected," said a smooth voice.

Zak whipped around. A stranger with grayish skin, a scar running from his eyebrow to his neck, and raven-black hair that matched his dark robes stood before him. Zak staggered when he saw the man—for he didn't feel like a stranger at all.

"Zandorn," Zak said. A chill ran up his spine.

"We meet, at last, Zakolor. You have been very elusive all

these years."

"I didn't have a choice." Fear wavered his voice as his whole body tensed.

"Ah, of course. Our Tansil whisked you away to the Southern Isles when you were only an infant."

"Because you killed my parents!" Zak's anger flared.

The edges of Zandorn's lips curled up. "Not personally, I assure you. I believe that deed belongs to my dear Renna. However, I'm not interested in history but in more recent events. You can't deny your complacency the last few months, simply agreeing with whatever your masters decide is best."

What was happening? How was Zandorn here? Everything unraveled before him, and half of what Zandorn said didn't make sense. The caladrius' cries grew louder as the cage floated down from the tree and rested in midair next to Zandorn. His long fingers gently caressed the bars of the cage as the caladrius became more manic.

"Tell me, how did you find the caladrius this time? If I'm correct—and I usually am—your Sight wouldn't have led you here."

How could he possibly know that? Zak wondered. He took an involuntary step back, and Zandorn's smile deepened.

You have to get away, Jolsu said. *He's too strong and too cunning.*

I can't leave the black caladrius!

Zak looked from Zandorn to the cage several times. This man—mage—had waged war against Valecium for a century and found a way to make himself immortal while destroying more and more of the continent with the Rot. How could

Zak hope to get the caladrius and escape from someone so powerful?

"Aren't you going to answer?" Zandorn's silky voice developed a sharpness. Apparently, he wasn't accustomed to waiting.

Zak's thoughts raced. He knew he had one chance, and only one. Flexing his wings and fists, he reached out to Jolsu.

Dragon, are you ready to fight?

Hmph. You are a fool, Parignis. But Zak felt something beneath Jolsu's words, conveyed through their new, stronger connection.

Pride.

I am ready, with fire and claw.

Zak smiled in the face of his greatest fear. With a flick of his wrist, he called to the cage with the caladrius, which flew into his hands. "*Bracteaveru!*" Zak shouted. Hundreds of dead leaves rose from the forest floor and pelted Zandorn, obscuring him from view.

That wouldn't be enough to slow him for long. Gathering as much magic as he could, he cast another spell. "*Custo-materia!*"

Jolsu's visage appeared next to him and—without wasting a moment—immediately breathed a torrent of emerald fire, lighting the hundreds of leaves ablaze as they swirled and dove toward Zandorn.

Go now! Jolsu urged.

Crouching and clinging tight to the metal cage, Zak sprung into the air, his wings beating hard. He was barely a few lengths above the ground when a strong wind blasted him into a tree. He gasped, the air knocked from his lungs as he crashed through branches and fell back to the earth.

The black caladrius cried out as the cage tumbled from his grip. Zak's wings disappeared as his concentration on the spell broke. He groaned and lifted his head. Zandorn stood silhouetted by fiery leaves floating harmlessly down, untouched by any of his attacks.

Jolsu was nowhere to be seen.

What happened? Zak asked. He coughed as he tried to stand, feeling the sting of dozens of cuts and bruises.

I don't know. He dispelled everything, *all our magic, in a single moment.*

Zak felt the dragon's confusion and fear mingling with his own. He froze halfway to standing when he heard Zandorn's cackling laugh.

"I thought Sorwin would have taught you better manners, *Nacusti.*" Zandorn took measured steps toward Zak. "By all accounts, the Hawk mage is a gentleman."

Two giant fists of soil and stone erupted from the earth and clamped on Zak's wrists. He yelped as the firm grip threatened to crush his bones, yanking his arms wide and lifting him off the ground. He twisted and fought, grunting as his skin tore against the rough stone, but it didn't matter. The fists didn't move nor loosen.

Zandorn stopped a pace away, the black caladrius and its cage once again floating next to him. He was close enough that Zak could smell the spiced scent of herbs mixed with something burnt and metallic which stung his nose.

He couldn't move, but Zak still had his magic. He

opened his palms, and green fire swirled through the air, streaming toward Zandorn.

Zak's fire collided with a dark barrier, parting harmlessly around the defensive magic. He yelled as he tried to kick Zandorn, but two more fists burst from the ground and grabbed his legs.

"You struggle beautifully, *Nacusti*." That cold, pointed cackle sounded again, and Zak's entire body shivered involuntarily. He was trapped, alone in front of Valecium's most dangerous mage.

You're never alone, Parignis.

"Now, what to do with you." Zandorn crossed his arms, theatrically strutting back and forth. Suddenly, he rushed forward and pushed a dagger against Zak's throat. "I could kill you now!" His eyes were wild, and Zak thought he would do it, that he would die with a simple slide of the blade.

"But no, that would be shortsighted." Zandorn pulled back.

Zak's throat burned as something wet dripped down his neck. If he had any chance of getting out of this trap, he needed to buy time and hope that Sorwin or Tansil found him.

"I thought you needed me alive," he said.

"I thought so too, for a time. Now I'm not sure."

"What changed?" It took all his willpower not to scream and cry, to keep the terrifying man talking.

"Research, of course. Magic is constantly changing, surprising..." His attention drifted for a moment before his gaze snapped back to Zak. "Are you distracting me? Oh, you *are* clever."

Zandorn flipped the dagger in his palm and shoved the butt of the weapon into Zak's gut. Pain blazed, and his body instinctively tried to contract, but he couldn't move with the stone fists holding his limbs.

His captor took another step back, evaluating Zak differently. "Look at how far you've come in such a short time. Why, a few months ago, you didn't even know you had magic, and now you're conjuring dragons. No, I cannot kill you—not now—that would be a waste. I could capture you, keep you, study you." He stepped forward again, dragging the dagger along Zak's left arm.

Zak screamed as the blade cut slow and deep into his flesh.

"Yes, I could learn *so* much, peeling back your secrets."

The dagger twisted and dug deeper, and Zak thought he would pass out from the pain.

"But I think I won't."

The blade lifted, and Zak's arm burned as tears slid down his cheeks. He gasped for breath through gritted teeth, giving voice to his hatred. "I *will* kill you."

Zandorn's smile widened. "That's it! Use that desire. Keep getting stronger, *Nacusti*. Then, when the time is right, you will seek me out on your own, and finally, this century of painstaking effort will be fulfilled."

Zak didn't know what to do, what he *could* do. His body was bruised and bloody, his magic didn't bother Zandorn in the slightest, and he was still trapped in the stone fists. All his lessons, all his training, all his effort to be stronger...none of it mattered.

He was a fool to think he could beat this mage that was no longer a man. Zandorn had become something other, something darker. Something much more powerful.

You do not face him alone, Parignis. Ready yourself!

What?

A bolt of lightning tore through the air, blasting into Zandorn. It ricocheted off his shield, but Zak saw the surprise on his face before they both turned toward the attacker.

Sorwin stood on a slight rise, his blue tunic torn and half shredded. Tansil appeared at his side a moment later in a similar, shambled state.

Hope fluttered in Zak's chest. They were both alive—and here. They had been fighting Renna. Did they leave the battle? Or did that mean—

"The day is ours, Zandorn. You have lost," Tansil said.

"Have I, *Magus*?" Zandorn spat the word at Tansil. Zak had forgotten that he was the elf's apprentice a long time ago, before his wife died, before he left Tor'alan, before he founded the Consortium. "Perhaps you should reconsider your definition of victory. I hold the black caladrius and the *Nacusti*."

"Not for long." Sorwin took a step forward and raised a hand. There was movement behind him. Night had fallen, and Zak could barely see, but the darkness melted away as lights shimmered down the line of the small hillock. Nearly thirty soldiers and mages stepped forward, readying steel and spells. He saw Kaleb, Shira, and Bazil among them.

Something inside Zak lightened at the sight. The League

had won the battle.

Zandorn stepped back and plucked the caladrius' cage from the air, holding it close to his side. Zak thought he would be afraid, being outnumbered—surely even *he* couldn't hope to defeat so many foes at once. Or maybe he'd be angry that his torture had been interrupted, his plan foiled.

But instead, he cackled that horrible laugh and smiled.

"You have always lacked vision, Magus, unable to see what isn't in front of you. You labor under the idea that this was the only battle fought today. I wonder what you should find upon your glorious return to your precious Tor'alan?"

Confusion rippled down the line of soldiers and mages, heads turning with whispered questions. What did Zandorn mean? Was he bluffing, or did something happen to their city?

A portal appeared behind Zandorn.

"Do not let him escape!" Tansil shouted, bounding down the slope. The soldiers and mages charged after the elf, seizing the best opportunity they might have to stop Zandorn and end the war.

With a casual indifference, Zandorn strolled toward the portal and paused, the blue light dancing across his face as he turned toward Zak. "You especially should hurry, *Nacusti*, if you want to say goodbye to your friends." He stepped through the portal, and the magic door closed behind him.

As soon as Zandorn disappeared, the stone fists crumbled. Zak's knees buckled as he fell, his whole body shaking.

"Zakolor!" Sorwin was at his side, Bazil too. Both checked over his injuries, healing cuts and bruises.

"How did you find me?" Zak asked.

"Jolsu," Sorwin said. "He spoke to me earlier and told me where to find you. He must have kept our connection open."

Did you? Zak asked Jolsu.

When we fought near the portals, I left a sliver of magic with Sorwin. If anything went wrong, I wanted to be able to call him to us.

Good thinking. It was an understatement, but Zak's attention was elsewhere, replaying Zandorn's words.

If you want to say goodbye to your friends.

Friends. Plural.

"What did he do to you?" Sorwin gingerly lifted Zak's left arm.

He looked down, examining the deep gash from Zandorn's dagger, and even Zak knew it wasn't an ordinary wound. The cuts were intentional and formed a shape of some kind. "I...don't know." He blinked, met Sorwin's gaze, and clutched his shoulder as tightly as possible. "We have to go. Now. Kal and Olivia—I think they're in danger." He told Sorwin what Zandorn had said a moment ago, and his eyes widened.

"Can you heal me enough to fly?" Zak asked. He didn't plan on waiting for permission to rush off to Tor'alan. He was going with or without Sorwin's help.

"We can heal you," Sorwin said, nodding to Bazil. "But I think I have a quicker way to return to Tor'alan."

"Good, then let's hurry." Zak didn't ask what was quicker than flying. He only cared about getting back as fast as possible.

Zandorn may have taken the black caladrius, but Zak

would not let him take his friends.

Chapter 25

No Choice

Olivia wasn't sleeping. She never could in the healing wards, not with the drafts and the echoing footsteps from the hallway. Whoever decided to use stone for most of the building was daft—in her opinion—or maybe hadn't spent much time convalescing.

Either way, she was awake when the consistent low murmurs from beyond her door suddenly grew to yelling. Several people ran through the halls, frantic footfalls stamping, followed by an explosion.

She jumped. It wasn't uncommon for some treatments to be more disruptive—she'd been subject to a few herself—but that sounded more serious.

"Cerevita's grace," she cursed. She lurched from the bed, muscles sore and tight from disuse. The stone floor was frigid against her bare feet as she reached the door, leaning against the wall for support.

Poking her head into the hall, nothing appeared amiss. A young priest scurried past her door, an acolyte judging by her uniform.

Lucky, Olivia thought. One of the older priests probably wouldn't tell her anything. "What's happened?"

"Father's Light!" The priest startled and dropped the bandages and herbs she carried. Shaking, she bent to collect the supplies.

Olivia slowly lowered herself against the doorframe to help. "Are you all right?" she asked, catching the young priest's eye. Her expression was vacant and terrified.

"It's the Archlumen," she said in a raspy voice. "She's been attacked!"

"What? When?" It seemed unlikely. Who would attack one of the Archs in the middle of Tor'alan, in their own magical house?

"Just a moment ago! She was tending to the *sorgeus*—er, Mr. Keldin's friend, when he suddenly attacked!"

Olivia stood as they finished collecting the supplies from the floor. *Mr. Keldin*, she thought. Clearly, this acolyte thought highly of Zak. *I'll have to remember that moniker next time he annoys me.* "How is the Archlumen?"

The acolyte fumbled, her arms full once again. "Drained and a bit banged up. He must have done some awful magic to overpower Lady Sashina."

"Overpower? She didn't subdue Kalbick?"

"No, Magus, he ran right after the Archlumen collapsed. I'm sorry, I have to go—I was sent to bring these supplies to the bishop healing Lady Sashina right away."

Olivia nodded for the priest to be on her way and closed the door, hearing the acolyte almost trip down the hall in her nervous haste.

She knew little about Kalbick and his condition, but several things were clear. He spent a good deal of time with the Consortium, was afflicted with dark magic, and just attacked one of the three most powerful mages in Tor'alan—and won.

Awful magic, indeed, she thought.

Nothing good would come of whatever he was doing or wherever he ran off to. She wasn't sure if the priests had raised an alarm or sent anyone after him yet. It was likely they were in shock, tending to their leader.

Someone needed to pursue Kalbick.

Forcing herself to move a little faster to warm up her muscles, she strode to the far wall and donned her uniform, sword, and boots—all of which she insisted be kept there. She'd been cooped up in the healing wards for weeks, with only occasional trips to the courtyard to break the monotony of her plain, drafty room. A big part of her was all too happy to leave.

A small part wondered if she would live if she found Kalbick and he attacked her.

Well, I don't have long anyway. May as well do some good on my way out.

The fresh air was crisp and cold as she descended the broad front steps of the Temple, pausing for a moment to look back at the building. She didn't need to figure out which room was Kalbick's. On the second floor, halfway down, the wall was shattered where a window should have been, and dark smoke billowed from the opening.

He definitely came this way. She surveyed the manicured lawns, absent of any obvious trail to follow. *But where did he go?*

That was when she heard the first whisper. *The Mother,* the voice said.

Olivia spun as fast as she could, thinking the voice was behind her. But no one was there. The Center was unusually quiet with so many mages and soldiers in the Eyewood.

The Mother...

"Who's there? Who is that?" The voice was faint.

The Mother...

Was insanity part of becoming a *Nacusti*? She hadn't experienced any changes since Temaway's gift, at least nothing good. Her health still worsened with each outburst. Maybe she had been too hard on Zak in the past if *this* was the type of thing a *Nacusti* dealt with.

The Mother...

"Yeah, alright, I hear you," she said. It didn't matter if insanity or death found her first. She wouldn't go without a fight. And besides, she had endured worse things than mysterious voices.

There was only one being "The Mother" could be referring to: Cerevita. She didn't have a lead on Kalbick's trail, so she listened to the voice and started toward the castle.

The only place Cerevita could be was in the throne room. But how would Olivia get there? Dozens of guards and enchantments barred the path. And if the voice was helping her to track Kalbick, surely he couldn't get through them all either.

She neared the first stairwell that led down to the twisting bowels of the castle and the gods' throne room. There should have been two guards posted at the top, and there had been, but their bodies were splayed on the ground.

"Kalbick," she said. It had to be.

Without hesitating, she launched herself down the flight of stairs, taking three at a time. Her body screamed at her. It had deteriorated significantly with the outbursts getting stronger and more frequent, more and more of her life draining away each time. It didn't matter—*couldn't* matter—right now.

She seemed to be the only one on Kalbick's trail. The guards and enchantments would be the least of her concerns. *Hopefully, some of them hold.*

With each turn she took, unconscious guard she stepped over, and absent enchantment she noticed, Olivia grew more agitated. How was one mage—who was bright but relatively uneducated in magic, according to Zak—shattering Tor'alan's most potent defenses? Tansil himself laid these charms.

Sorgeus, the voice whispered.

Of course. He's absorbing the magic, not dispelling or defeating it. But why? Was he searching for something, or had his mind simply cracked under the pressure of his affliction? Olivia couldn't be sure, but at least the voice *did* seem to be helping her. Maybe it was Vess she heard?

One less thing to worry about. For now.

She panted, finally reaching the throne room. The tall stone doors had already been thrown open. Stepping carefully inside, Kalbick stood on the left side of the room, leaning over a pedestal with a glass casing. Light linen bedclothes hung from his bony frame, speckled with fresh droplets of blood.

"I was told to kill you," Kalbick said, his back to Olivia. "Or, more specifically, I was told to kill someone close to Zak."

Olivia grasped the hilt of her sword but kept it sheathed, taking slow steps toward Kalbick. It would be best if she could get close enough to injure him without magic. "Why didn't you?"

He tapped the glass on the pedestal, and it shattered. Then, he stood straight and turned to face Olivia. Dark circles ringed his eyes, and he was paler than a corpse.

She hesitated for a moment. *He looks as bad as I feel.*

"I thought it was too cruel, even by Renna's standards. She doesn't see how much Zak is already suffering. But now you're here, and I wonder if you'll give me a choice." His eyes flicked to her hand on her sword.

"Is Renna controlling you? Is that why you attacked the Archlumen and came down here?"

"Ah, see—you are *not* giving me a choice. I can't have you telling Zak." Kalbick raised his arms as dark blue smoke twisted around them.

Olivia took a step back and released her sword hilt. *This is going to hurt.* She reached for her magic and a deep, cutting pain lanced her core. The *vitaligo* was as strong as ever.

She put up a shield in time. Kalbick's smoke crashed into her yellow magic, filling the throne room with darkness.

"You are *weak*, Olivia Pratinos." Kalbick's voice echoed around the room like it came from the smoke itself. "If I could drain some of your magic, maybe you could live. But no, I might absorb the *vitaligo* too."

She scowled. How did he know about it? Zak must have told him. Regardless, he wasn't wrong. She felt weak. If she hoped to stop Kalbick, she needed to end this fast, but she couldn't pinpoint where he was in the smoke.

"What are you doing here?" she asked. "Why don't you want Zak to know Renna is controlling you?" Maybe she could get him distracted or angry. Then perhaps he would make a mistake.

A blast of blue fire rolled off her shield. Her magic blinked momentarily, dangerously close to giving out as she winced against the pain. Her life drained away for every second she held the shield.

When Kalbick answered, he ignored her first question. "Do you know Zak at all? What do you think he would do if he knew Renna controlled me still?"

"He would try to save you. We all would." Her breathing grew heavier, and a cold sweat dampened her brow.

"Yes, and I cannot risk that."

"Why?"

"He is too important, not worth my life."

"Why?"

"BECAUSE HE IS MY BROTHER!" A colossal face—Kalbick's face—swirled from the smoke and screamed toward her shield. Its mouth opened as if to devour her and her magic.

Olivia conjured a wall of water and pushed it forward, soaking the face and the rest of the smoke in front of her.

But more gathered behind her. Giant smoke hands emerged from the dark cloud and grabbed her shield. One by one, the tips of the fingers pierced the barrier until the yellow magic splintered in a loud *boom*.

Olivia skidded across the drenched floor, thrown backward from the force. She tried to rise, but her palm slipped in a puddle of water. Her body was giving out. She had used too much magic, too much life. Maybe she could have stopped him if she had been at full strength. But with the *vitaligo*...

It was all she could do to prop herself up on one elbow. The remaining smoke dispersed, and Kalbick strolled up to the pedestal and plucked a parchment from the pile of broken glass.

He rolled it up and waved it at her, wearing an annoyingly smug smile. "You used to be strong, Olivia. I can see why Zak loves you."

Loves? Her surprise must have been obvious on her face.

"Oh, you didn't know?" He approached, squatting next to her.

She reached for her sword once again, but Kalbick was quicker. He wrenched it from her fumbling hand and tossed it behind him, metal clanging against the floor.

"It's okay," he said in a taunting whisper. "I don't think he knows either. At least, not how *much*, anyway. But it was so *boring* listening to him go on and on about you whenever he visited me. It was impossible to miss his feelings for you." He looked down at her, lips curling up. "I had intended to let you live. I didn't want to hurt Zak, but you decided your fate. Maybe it is for the best. You would only hold him back."

"And what do you think Zandorn and Renna will do? They won't treat him like a prince. They'll kill him."

His hand moved so fast that Olivia didn't see it, but she felt the sting of his backhand on her cheek. "I will NEVER let them do that. They will use him, and he may endure some pain, but he will live. And when all of this is over, when Zandorn and Renna have what they want, we'll be together again like before. Like brothers."

Kalbick stood and walked away, pausing at the door. "I'll tell him you fought valiantly until the end. I think he'll like that."

Olivia's elbow slipped, and she lay flat on the floor, looking up at the high-arched ceiling. The room spun, and for some reason, the pain that usually wracked her entire body quieted, like it was far away. Was she floating? No, that couldn't be right. But there was water—why was her hair wet?

The fire, said a voice. It sounded high-pitched and friendly but far away, like her pain.

Yeah, it was nice knowing you, too, she thought. Then she gave in, succumbing to the darkness blurring the edges of her world.

CHAPTER 26

ASH AND PARCHMENT

"Are you sure?" Tansil asked.

Sorwin nodded. "I saw one of Renna's portals up close. I figured out what we were missing in our experiments."

Zak lost what little patience he had as the two mages debated. "Let's try, at least."

Tansil's expression hardened. "You barely survived a brush with Zandorn. It would be unwise to go leaping through untested portals. You could end up in any of the six planes or another world entirely."

"But I'm fine! And Olivia and Kal might not be."

"You would trust Zandorn's word?"

"You did in the past." It was harsh but true. Tansil had been Zandorn's magus when he began practicing necromancy. The elf was caught unawares, trusting in his apprentice. Zak didn't have time for Tansil's caution. Every second that slipped by was one less he had to get to Tor'alan. "I trust Sorwin. We need to test the theory at some point, right? Let me do it now."

The elf sighed and waved a hand in defeat, turning to give orders to the soldiers and mages milling about the dark forest. A few magelights hovered above, casting various hues over the group.

"You *can* do this, right?" Zak asked Sorwin. He was in a hurry to save his friends, not to get lost in the cosmos.

Sorwin tapped his finger on his chin. "Yes, I think if—of course." His head bobbed once, deciding something. "Ready when you are, Zak."

"I'm coming too," Bazil said, walking toward Zak and Sorwin. He wiped a patient's blood from his hands with a cloth and stuck it in a satchel at his waist.

"I couldn't ask you to—"

"You're not asking, I'm telling."

"Well, consider me told." Zak smiled and shrugged. He supposed it would be foolish of him to start denying Bazil's help now, after everything. Besides, having one of the League's best healers nearby could prove crucial if Olivia or Kal were injured.

While they spoke, Sorwin had been casting. Zak jumped as a twisting blue door opened a few feet away, the energy crackling and swirling in its center. It looked identical to Renna's portals.

"You did it!" Zak shouted. Up close, the portal was *loud*. He ran toward it, not wanting to lose his nerve or give Tansil a chance to change his mind.

"Wait, Zakolor! One of you has to come back to—" Sorwin's voice abruptly faded as he stepped through the portal.

Zak had been through Tor'alan's entrance portal several times. On numerous occasions, Sorwin had explained to him how that portal and the one he had just stepped through differed, but he never remembered all the theoretical information. One thing he *did* remember was that the portal in Tor'alan connected two points by weaving through physical matter, the island of Tor'alan. The portals they were researching—that Sorwin had figured out—connected two distant points by weaving through nothing at all.

Going through the Tor'alan portal was unpleasant enough, but this was horrible. His entire body felt like it ripped itself apart, stretching and contorting with the crackling and swirling of magic, burning his skin as he traveled between two places that were nowhere near one another. He screamed, or cried. Maybe both—or neither—he couldn't be sure. But whatever he was doing, it didn't help.

The only good part was that it ended in less than a second.

He stumbled onto the raised dais at the entrance of Tor'alan, falling to his knees. Bazil fell beside him in the same state. They both panted like they had run a dozen laps around the training court.

"You brilliant Magus," Zak said, his voice breathy. It worked; Sorwin opened a portal and sent them safely—albeit painfully—to Tor'alan. He must have had the idea to connect the portal he opened in the Eyewood to the entrance portal in Tor'alan.

Zak stood on shaky legs, taking a few halting steps. "Go

back through, Bazil, and tell them it worked."

"I'm not doing *that* again!" Bazil's turquoise magic flashed around his body. "I can't believe that didn't leave any actual wounds."

"Hurry back, in case Kal or Olivia need healing. Good luck!" Zak called.

"You want me to go through *that* two more times? Hey! Argh—Azubelux light you, *Nacusti*!"

Zak didn't look back or apologize for leaving his friend with the dreadful portal. He didn't have time. He had no idea what Zandorn's warning meant, but he made it sound like something happened while they battled in the Eyewood, which meant he could already be too late.

No, he thought. *Have hope. Hope is stronger than worry.*

He felt the truth of his thoughts as his legs pounded the cobblestone streets. His magic was drained—and so was Jolsu's. They had used much of their energy earlier, and Zak's body had sustained much damage from Zandorn. His arm still burned with the strange cut, even under the bandages and dressings Bazil had applied. Despite it all, Zak's legs carried him toward the Center faster than he thought possible.

As soon as he passed through the gate in the circular wall, he knew something was wrong. A cloud of dark smoke rolled above the Temple, and part of the healing ward wall lay scattered on the otherwise immaculate lawn. And, oddest of all, a large barrier had been raised around the entire building.

Why? Zak thought. *Why would the priests need to keep anyone out?*

The Den of Darkness and the House of Elements were

intact. Whatever had happened, whatever Zandorn orchestrated, only affected the Temple. No one else was in the Center, or at least not in the courtyard. A lot of soldiers and mages had gone to the Eyewood, but there should have been *some* people about.

Movement near the castle caught Zak's attention. Someone exited the front doors. He squinted and was surprised to see it was Kalbick.

"Kal?" Zak called, confused. *Why was he out of bed?* "Kal, did you see what happened?"

He jogged toward his friend, whose linen tunic and breeches were torn and singed and covered in blood. Kalbick held a rolled parchment at his side.

Zak's thoughts whirled. *Was Kal feeling better? Healed? Did he fight off Zandorn's forces? Why else would he be out here in the middle of the Center, looking like he just fought for his life?*

But when Zak came within a few paces, a portal opened behind Kalbick. His friend gave him a wave and a sad smile before stepping back and disappearing into the swirling blue magic.

"Kal..." Nothing of what he saw made sense. Did Kal know how to open portals? And where did he go?

Olivia, he thought. He needed to find Olivia.

About to turn around and head toward the Temple to find a way through the barrier, Zak caught a glimpse of a guard face-down through the open doors of the castle. Kalbick had come from there—did he do that?

He checked the guards—they were unconscious but

alive. Zak followed the path of destruction and bodies, winding his way down the labyrinthine passages. His feeling of dread intensified as every protective enchantment he should have encountered was gone, destroyed. He stepped into the throne room.

"Olivia!"

He almost collapsed seeing her on the floor, but he had to be close to her. He rushed to her side, carefully threading a shaking arm under her neck and pulling her into a tight embrace.

"No, no, no, no, no..." She wasn't breathing, and her skin felt too cold. He brushed her auburn curls back as tears fell from his eyes, splashing onto her closed ones.

This wasn't happening. It couldn't be happening.

"Jolsu!" he cried. "Jolsu, do something!"

A wave of sorrow came from the dragon. *I cannot, Parignis. Death is beyond me.*

"She's not dead!" he screamed. Rage and pain twisted inside him. He held a palm to her cheek as his sobs came faster and harder. Footsteps sounded behind him, but he didn't turn away from Olivia.

"Zak?" Sorwin's voice echoed in the large throne room. "Oh, Zakolor." He came up behind Zak and squeezed his shoulder as more footsteps entered the room.

He looked up and saw Bazil and Tansil standing nearby through tear-blurred eyes. "She can't be gone...I...I was too late."

"Zakolor, I'm so sorry." Sorwin pulled gently at his elbow. "Come, let her rest, and we'll—"

"No!" Zak said, wrenching his arm from Sorwin. He buried his face in the crook of Olivia's neck. "I shouldn't have left, I shouldn't have left," he cried over and over.

That was the only sound in the chamber for minutes until Tansil broke the refrain.

"Zakolor, step away—quickly now!" The elf's harsh whisper cut through Zak's grief enough for him to sit up.

A bright yellow fire burned at the tips of Olivia's fingers and the edges of her boots. It grew, climbing her limbs toward her torso, where Zak held her.

"Quickly! Away!"

Confused, Zak lowered Olivia softly to the floor as Sorwin and Tansil each looped one of Zak's arms, pulling him to stand. He wiped his watery eyes with a sleeve so he could see better.

The fire encased her entire body, but it didn't give off any heat. It roared as it grew bigger and brighter, and soon Zak couldn't look at her. He shielded his eyes from the light, half turning away.

Then it flashed and quieted.

When Zak looked back, a pile of ash rested in place of Olivia's body.

Zak's throat tightened again, but before another rush of tears and sobs came, the ash *moved*.

An arm burst from the pile, and Zak and his three companions jumped back. Then another arm emerged, and a body sat up, then stood. The ash fell in a dusty cloud, and when it cleared, Olivia's soot-stained form stared back at t hem.

"Well?" Olivia said. "Aren't you going to help me clean up?"

Zak leaped forward, throwing his arms around her and squeezing her in the tightest hug. He had no idea what happened, but he didn't care.

Olivia was alive.

"Zakolor! I can't breathe!" she gasped.

He pulled back for a moment, noticing the brightness of her eyes against her ashy cheeks. He traced a thumb over her eyebrow and pulled her closer, tight against his chest. "You were gone," he said. "And I thought—"

Olivia kissed him, and everything else melted away. All his fears, all his sadness, all his aches and pains. Nothing existed except for her, her warmth, and this moment. He didn't know he had been waiting for this for so long until, finally, their lips parted, and all he wanted was to kiss her again and again.

His eyes fluttered open, and he managed one word. "How?"

She stepped back from him with rosy cheeks. "My Guardian is a phoenix. You know they can reincarnate, right? Apparently, Vess can use her reincarnations on me, too."

"Does that mean you died? It wasn't the Curing fire?" Tansil asked.

Olivia nodded, then smiled. "I did. And that means..." She held her arms out wide, and bright yellow fire blazed around her.

Zak gasped reflexively, thinking she would be in pain. But she stood solid with no wince or cries or any sign of her life draining away.

"The *vitaligo* is gone," she said as the fire disappeared.

Bazil insisted on thoroughly checking over Olivia. As far as he could tell, she was alive, healthy, free of her *vitaligo*, and a *Nacusti*.

That meant the caladrius had been right. Olivia *did* die. But none of them knew she would be reincarnated.

That also meant Zak wasn't alone.

He wasn't the League's only hope.

Now, there were two *Nacusti*, and they both had a score to settle with the Consortium.

When they were sure she was okay—and Olivia wouldn't suffer more ministration—Tansil and Sorwin's questions began, hoping to understand what had happened. Olivia answered as many as she could, recounting how she learned of Sashina's attack and followed Kal's trail through the gauntlet of protective charms and guards to the throne room.

"But, why did Kalbick come down here?" Sorwin asked.

"I saw him holding something, a parchment, right before he disappeared in the portal," Zak said. A question prodded his thoughts. "Why did Kal go all the way back up the stairs and outside before opening the portal?"

"One of my more subtle charms he didn't break," Tansil said. "We didn't know how to open portals of our own until today, but we knew how to deter them. No portals can open within the castle walls."

"He took something from over there," Olivia said, answering Sorwin's question. She gestured to a pedestal at the side of the room, smashed glass strewn around its base.

The throne room was in such disarray from Olivia and

Kalbick's battle—and he had been overcome with so much grief earlier—that Zak hadn't noticed it at first. But when he looked closer, he immediately recognized the pedestal.

"No," Tansil whispered.

Kalbick had stolen the Contract.

"If Renna is controlling Kalbick, then Zandorn will have the Contract in his possession by now," Sorwin said.

"But why?" Bazil asked. "What could he hope to do with it?"

All the pieces started to fall into place. For months, Zak had wondered at the meaning of his vision, of why the black caladrius kept appearing in his dreams. Everything that happened in the last few hours made Zandorn's plan abundantly clear. "He's going to destroy it."

"Impossible," Tansil said. "It is made of *Nacusti* and divine magics. Not even Zandorn could break it."

"He might not know how right now, but I think he'll figure it out," Zak said. He looked at Tansil. "You said Zandorn needed me, my power, for his experiments. But when he had me trapped, he said he wasn't sure if he *did* need me anymore. That must mean he found a way to get power somewhere else. I think he will use the black caladrius to destroy the Contract and appeal to the gods."

"Cerevita was one of the few gods that supported mortals in the Guardian War," Sorwin said. "Most of them signed because they had to. If the Contract is destroyed, a legion of vengeful gods will be loosed upon Valecium, and they'll be indebted to Zandorn."

"We could face another Era of Dominion. One far worse

than the first," Tansil said.

A heavy silence filled the chamber, and Zak shivered as he peered at the thrones of power, too large for any human or elf to fill.

Chapter 27

Heart's Desire

Renna stood on a vast platform deep in the Consortium's stronghold. When she was young and still had a child's curiosity, she had learned as much as she could about the fortress and the dwarves that had built it. She scoured chiseled tablets and crumbling scrolls, hunting for secrets within the tunneling structure.

The platform had once been a plaza, hosting daily markets and ritual festivals. She had often wondered how different it was back then, the bustling of dwarves about their business, perhaps a stray human or elf visitor come to sample Pywell's renowned craftsmanship. It wouldn't have been uncommon back then, the three races mixing. The time she envisioned was before the Guardian War, before the dwarves sealed themselves away in Gort'haal and the elves hid amongst the trees of Nalawin.

Before Cerevita and the *Nacusti* mucked up the world with their Contract.

Now the platform served as a muster point where forces assembled before and returned from raids. She watched as the tattered remnants of her soldiers—some unconscious, carried by their brothers and sisters in arms, most bleeding from somewhere—stumbled through the portal.

They were lucky she let them return at all after their abysmal performance against the League.

As the last soldiers staggered away to lick their wounds, another portal opened and Zandorn stepped through the swirling blue door. Renna's attention was immediately drawn to the dark bird in the metal cage under his arm.

"You have it," she said. There was no surprise in her voice—there was never any doubt they would retrieve the black caladrius. But she was a little upset it hadn't been her.

"Yes, dearest daughter." His neutral tone contrasted with the shadow that darkened his face. "Your playing with Tansil and Sorwin forced my hand."

"They were more competent than anticipated." Which was true—individually the two mages didn't hold a candle to her flame, but together they were annoyingly compatible and fended off her attacks. At least, the attacks and magic she was willing to display. *A miscalculation that will not be repeated.*

"Hmm."

"I thought you wouldn't want them dead, not yet," she said. It was important to keep Zandorn distracted. If he needled too close at her failure he may discover that she had held back, that she hadn't embraced her full powers, that she never had in Zandorn's service, and she wasn't ready for him to learn that, not until *she* decided it was time.

But keeping a genius at bay was no small task. She had done so successfully for nearly a century, keeping him blissfully unaware that his daughter was more powerful than him, than anyone in Valecium. She only needed a few more months of secrecy, and then everything she ever wanted would be within her grasp.

Zandorn played his part of father well, falling into her machinations once again. "It would be ideal for Tansil to witness my triumph over death, and prove once and for all that he was in the wrong all those years ago, that his rigid morals were the only thing standing in the way of mastery over magic."

"And you shall, with your prize in hand." She gestured to the black caladrius, the key to both of their desires.

He held the cage aloft as the bird squawked and fluttered, perhaps sensing the desire they both held for its power. After a moment, Zandorn reached over to Renna, fingertips gently tracing from temple to chin. "Your mother would be so proud of you, dearest."

The tenderness unbalanced Renna more than any harsh word could. It was a thing not often shared between them, and a sharp intake of breath was all the response she could provide. Lying about her mother was the one thing she could never do. Not because of any objections she harbored, no—for decades she wished she could feign love, pretend she desperately missed the woman who birthed her, the one that had died when she was only a toddler.

In truth, Renna couldn't care less if her mother was brought back to life. But Zandorn did, and she needed Zandorn to keep pursuing her resurrection in order to get what she wanted. So in the rare moments her mother was a subject of conversation, she often turned away and pretended it was too difficult to discuss—because it was, but not for the reasons Zandorn assumed.

Luckily, another portal opened a moment later, interrupting the uncomfortable exchange.

Kalbick appeared, ragged and disheveled, but whole—eyes blazing with a ferocity she hadn't seen in him before.

"You returned to me!" She rushed forward. This was *her* Kalbick, and he was home.

"I heard your call, felt your magic," he said. He swayed, unsteady on his feet.

Renna placed a palm on his chest and felt his body heat through the thin linen shirt. "They poisoned you with their magics." She frowned. *Didn't they know what a treasure he was?*

Zandorn stepped toward them. "All can be undone in time, dearest. What's important is that your pet is returned, and he's brought us a gift. Right, Kalbick?"

She looked down and saw a roll of thick parchment clutched in Kalbick's fist. It radiated power, and Renna was shocked she hadn't noticed it immediately.

"The Contract, Kalbick." Zandorn's tone made it an order, and he held out a hand.

Kalbick looked down at the parchment as if he were surprised to see it too, then thrust it toward Renna.

She couldn't hide her teeth in the wide smile that split her face. Zandorn had asked for the Contract, but Kalbick handed it to *her*. And when she took the parchment and gave it to Zandorn, she knew he hadn't missed the significance of that seemingly innocuous moment.

Kalbick belonged to *her*, and no one else. Not even Zandorn.

"What happens next?" she asked, wanting to keep Zandorn's mind moving.

He unrolled the Contract, stroking it with his slender hands as the black caladrius floated in its cage nearby. "This will be more difficult without Karazul's anti-magic. I will need time to research and plan. It may take longer than I first thought, but by the Year Festival I will be ready."

Perfect. The timeline for her plans still worked then, too. "Should we make efforts to recover Karazul?" She didn't particularly want to as she wasn't bothered by the assassin's absence. And she preferred him gone if his abilities would speed Zandorn's progress to a pace that didn't suit her needs. But part of her success in hiding her truth from Zandorn all these years was her willingness to make his desires come to fruition.

"Not yet. Let us see how I proceed, and let the League hold him, if they can." Without another word or farewell or gesture, Zandorn wandered off, already studying the powerful document with a familiar intensity.

If they can hold him, indeed, Renna thought. She smiled at the idea of Tansil attempting to restrain the troublesome Karazul.

She fished in the pocket of her robe and pulled out Baltenebris' *cordeus*, the prize she had the assassin steal from—what was his name? *Vermig*. At least Karazul served a purpose before getting himself captured, and now, she wouldn't have to hold up her end of their bargain. He could find his own answers about his brother, if he ever escaped.

The dark gem glittered in the low magelight, purples and blacks and scarlets twisting in its seemingly endless depths. "So much power." She held the gem out for Kalbick to see, and his eyes stuck to it immediately. "Imagine what we can do together, Kalbick, with the heart of our god."

Karazul wondered if he was floating. He couldn't see anything, and he thought he should be afraid, but he couldn't *feel* anything—not fear or joy, nor his hands or feet or eyes—and no sound penetrated wherever he was.

Nothing surrounded him.

What happened? He wracked his memory but struggled to recall anything, as if the sea of nothingness were a syrupy layer slowing his thoughts. Fragments returned. He had been fighting someone...an elf...a *Nacusti*! Had the mage cursed him somehow?

Then from the nothingness came a light, and it grew like the morning sun, small and warm at first, and then suddenly blazing, overwhelming in its brightness and heat.

Shadow followed the light, rushing just out of reach as if it would perish if the two should meet. And it would, Karazul knew. The light would suffer no darkness or shade.

But when earth began appearing, rocky and green and uneven, the shadow hid well behind tall trees and stalwart mountains. And with the trees came plants and rivers and oceans and air and creatures of all shapes and sizes, filling the nothingness with life, substance.

What is this? he wondered. The world assembled around him, and the nothingness receded, but didn't disappear completely. It hovered at the edges of his awareness, claiming the spaces between things, almost scurrying out of sight when he searched for it. But nothingness didn't need to scurry, it wasn't there. Was it?

There was one more thing, and Karazul knew it was the last to arrive because when it did, everything was connected, whole. Within every beam of light, every shadow, every creature and fragment of life, there was a presence, an energy, a thing so powerful it wove all others together.

Magic.

Chapter 28

SEED OF HOPE

"Good, he's still caught in the *senligo*," Tansil said.

Zak and Olivia had followed the elf from the throne room into a smaller chamber down the hall which had been converted into a makeshift cell for Karazul. It was one of the safest places in Tor'alan to keep the dangerous man, or so they thought, before Kalbick slashed through most of the guards and protective enchantments. He watched as the assassin's chest slowly rose and fell, the crown of orange flames circling his head.

"How long will it hold?" Olivia asked.

"There's no way of knowing." Tansil held out a hand near the flames, almost like he checked for its heat. "Not long, if I were to venture a guess. Temaway was powerful, and so is this binding, but Karazul's gift seems to break down most magic eventually. I think I'll know when our borrowed time nears its end."

"We need a plan for when he wakes," Zak said.

"Indeed. But one will not be made this night. There is

far too much to do, and you two," Tansil leveled a firm look at Zak and Olivia, "must see yourselves to the Dormitory immediately. Facing Zandorn and fiery resurrections are more than enough to earn what sleep you can."

Zak, for one, was not about to turn down the offer. And neither it seemed was Olivia as she followed him up the meandering path from the bowels of the castle. They passed several guards—who had fallen to Kalbick—being revived, and the rest were being carried to the Temple for healing. He wondered if the barrier surrounding the healing wards had been lowered, but Zak had a feeling the priests wouldn't do so until Sashina recovered and Kalbick was accounted for.

Kalbick. A pang wracked him, draining what little strength he had left. How had he lost his friend again? *Zandorn and Renna will answer for what they've done to him.*

A faint rumbling of agreement came from Jolsu, as well as his exhaustion. He sensed the depth of Jolsu's feelings, his desire to preserve the Contract at all costs, and that now meant destroying Zandorn was more important than ever.

Zak and Olivia passed Sorwin in the vestibule of the castle, organizing a group of mages to begin the tedious work of assessing and replacing the broken enchantments. "And be sure to add a countermeasure for draining *and* abolishing the charms," he said.

He's preparing for Kalbick and Karazul. Zak gave a grim nod. Despite the horrible thought of his best friend attacking Tor'alan again, it comforted him to know that Sorwin was his ever-prepared self again.

An emergency council meeting was being organized, and

Tansil appeared just in time to wave off an attendant that attempted to corral Zak toward the chambers. With another thanks, Zak and Olivia darted out the large front doors of the castle and headed toward the Dormitory, a yellow magelight floating above their heads. Olivia beamed at the little orb, giddy with the excitement at using her magic again.

There was an awkward warmth between them. Neither knew what to say, but once, Zak caught her eye and she blushed, and his cheeks warmed too. They walked so close to one another that their hands brushed a few times, each brief moment of contact with Olivia's warm skin sent a jolt through him, tightening his chest so he could barely breathe.

But as they moved up the Dormitory steps and into the quiet entrance hall, questions assaulted Zak's mind.

What actually happened when Olivia was resurrected? Did she kiss me, or did I kiss her? Did we mean to, or were we both overwhelmed in the moment? How does she feel now, about the kiss, about me? Should I say something, or wait for her to mention it?

He paused, and she did too. Their rooms were up opposite stairwells, and it made sense to part ways in the hall. But neither of them moved for a minute that seemed to stretch into an hour. Zak could have—should have—asked any of the questions that crossed his mind to find out how Olivia felt. Each was more terrifying than the next, and as his heart pounded in his ears and the silence became deafening, he instead settled for a much less effective option.

"So," he said.

"So," she echoed, fidgeting with her belt exactly how she

had for weeks when she avoided his gaze.

What now? The warmth between them quickly chilled, and all that was left was the awkwardness of an unrecognized, intimate moment. "I'm glad you're better."

"So am I," she said.

"And now you're a *Nacusti!*" He gently punched her shoulder. "I'm not alone now, we'll be quite the pair."

Olivia's eyes widened, and so did Zak's when he realized what he said.

"No, that's not—I meant—"

"R-right," Olivia stammered, backing away and tripping up the stairs. "Well, Tansil said get to bed, so better be off!" She sounded chipper, or overly happy, both of which were decidedly *not* Olivia.

But Zak was in no position to argue, needing to escape before he passed out from lack of breathing or his head finally exploded from the mounting pressure between his ears. "Yep! Tansil's orders!" And with a wave he turned and sprinted up the opposite stairs, taking them three at a time.

When he reached his room and closed the door, he leaned against it, heart thudding. After a moment, the fog began clearing from his thoughts and he realized what a *stulmati* he had been.

He had run away from a girl he liked, whom he might have kissed, or might have kissed him. And besides that, he'd have to see her every day. She played an integral part of his training regime, and now that she was a *Nacusti* he imagined they would spend even more time together.

But how, when they apparently couldn't even look at

each other without falling over themselves?

Zak paced his room, wondering what to do. He reached for the door, ready to fling it open and run to her room to apologize—assuming she would open the door at all, or not slam it in his face from pure shock or terror—which he wouldn't blame her for doing.

Yet before he twisted the handle, a Firepost slipped under his door. He snatched it out of the air and waved the smoke away as he unfolded the parchment.

Nacusti training starts tomorrow—court seven. Don't be late.

Sitting on the edge of his bed, he breathed a sigh of relief. Maybe training wasn't the fear, but the solution to their awkwardness. Igniting the tip of his finger with a bit of magic, he scribbled a reply.

I wouldn't dare miss it, Nacusti.

"*Nuntiumignis,*" he said. The folded parchment blazed in fire and soared under the door.

You chose a good one, Parignis. As exhausted as Jolsu was, he had enough energy to poke at him still.

Shut it, wyrm. But there was no venom in his rebuke, and Zak smiled, knowing the dragon felt the warmth of their new friendship.

They had used a lot of their magic, but Jolsu's especially in battling the Rotters and Zandorn, which was very draining after many years of using *no* magic. Underneath the tiredness, a complexity of relief and sorrow pulsed. Jolsu still felt guilty about the *vitaligo*.

Zak shared his happiness, excitement, and forgiveness along their connection. Despite the rockiness of their path together, one truth rang loud in Zak's thoughts: Jolsu saved Olivia. The *vitaligo* had kept her alive when no healer could have. For that, he would always be grateful to the dragon.

As he crawled into bed, his own exhaustion set into his battered body. Yet, as he lay still, his mind raced and returned to their predicament.

At that very moment, Tansil and the council discussed how the League would address the loss of the black caladrius and the Contract and start planning for the worst: a second war with the gods.

He chewed his lip. The only option Zak could see was to stop Zandorn before he could destroy the Contract. The League couldn't afford to wait. They had to attack, find Zandorn's stronghold, and deal with him directly. Until tonight, the struggle between the League of Kingdoms and the Consortium over the last century had been contained to skirmishes and mostly minor events, excluding the progression of the Rot. Lives had been lost, and certainly damage and fear had been wrought. But with the battle in the Eyewood and the theft of the Contract, the conflict had escalated.

The war had officially begun.

Somehow, in the mire of his thoughts, Zak fell asleep. He dreamed of Terasi. It was different than before, when the Druid would grasp toward him but never quite reach him, soundlessly delivering whatever message he mouthed.

This time, Terasi stood in the courtyard of the Center, a clear figure. Or, mostly clear. Zak frowned at the wispy and blurry edges of the Druid. The shape looked familiar, almost like—

"You're alive!" Zak wasn't dreaming. The Druid's spirit stood before him. He rushed toward Terasi and stopped, looking down at his own wispy arms. He wasn't sure if spirits could hug or touch—and he didn't know Terasi that well—but he felt a deep sense of responsibility for his capture.

"I am, but I do not have much time. You answered my call. Let us fly. I have much to show you." Terasi turned and floated away.

Zak urged his spirit to follow the Druid. He had only done this once before—on accident, when he spied on Karazul and Burvenin—yet controlling his spirit was easy, natural. All it took was a little willpower and intent, and off he floated.

They left Tor'alan and headed west, and it looked like they soared between two skies: the faint glow of villages and cities against the dark countryside below mirrored the glittering stars and velvety air above. Flying as a spirit wasn't quite as exciting as flying with dragon wings, but there was considerably less wind—none, in fact—so Zak didn't entirely dislike the experience.

Though the dark night hid much, Zak noticed when the low valleys of Regadensia became tainted with the Rot, and soon everything was covered in the sickly darkness. No plants grew, no animals ran, no birds flew within its borders, and any trees left were eroded and collapsing into dust.

Terasi's specter drifted down toward a single, enormous

mountain. It appeared alive in the sea of Rot, with dense pockets of greenery bristling along ridges and a single waterfall pouring into a wandering stream.

The Druid paused. "This is Pywell Mountain. You must remember this place, *Nacusti*." He waved a gossamer arm at the mountain. "This is where Zandorn hides, where you must come to defeat him."

"This is what we needed! Terasi, you're brilliant!" Zak cheered, but the Druid's grim expression remained set.

Zak tensed as Terasi hurtled toward the rocky sides of the mountain, but his spirit passed straight through. When it was Zak's turn, he closed his eyes and pressed ahead, instinct telling him to expect a painful impact. But, of course, he felt nothing. He wasn't really there; at least, his body wasn't. That was tucked safely away in his bed back in Tor'alan.

On the inside of the mountain, he followed Terasi through a series of rough tunnels that perhaps had been used by miners at one point. These gave way to more lavish halls and chambers with intricate stone carvings, adorned columns, and sculpted iron sconces set into the walls.

The mountain fortress was a hive of activity. Soldiers marched through the halls with different supplies—sometimes prisoners, by the way they dragged chained people behind them. Zak grimaced, wanting to help the poor souls. He nearly lost control and launched forward when Kalbick rounded a corner.

"Leave him," Terasi said. His command was firm but kind.

Zak stopped and shot Terasi a wild look. "You don't

know what he's done. He's my friend and needs help, but he needs to answer for what he did to Olivia and the League."

"It is not fair of me to ask, I know," Terasi said. "But you must come with me now. I do not have much longer."

Without warning, Terasi dropped straight through the floor. Zak hesitated, looking toward the hallway where Kalbick had disappeared, then dove after Terasi.

There, chained against the far wall of the large room, was Terasi's body. Countless gashes covered the Druid, some crusted with scabs and some dripping red lifeblood. His green skin was yellowed and purpled with bruises, and the beautiful antlers Zak remembered were sawn off haphazardly.

Zak would have cried at the sight if he could. But spirits couldn't cry, not really.

"Terasi..." was all he could manage. How had the Druid—a beacon of life—been defiled and reduced to this state? His chest wheezed as it hitched, rising and falling in uneven spurts.

"Do not feel sorry for me," Terasi said, "for I am Druid, I am nature, and there I shall return." Despite his words, the Druid did not look upon his own body. "I needed to show you Zandorn's location and to show you there is no point trying to save me."

"But now I know where you are, and Sorwin can open portals—"

Terasi held up a hand, cutting off Zak's excitement. "There is no point, *Nacusti*. Now that Zandorn has the black caladrius, he will have no more use for me. Focus on defeating him and the Consortium so my death matters." Again, the

Druid floated away, up this time, and motioned for Zak to follow.

Zak felt oddly detached as they hovered at the top of Pywell Mountain, their spirits immune to the cutting gales that blasted the snowy peaks. For a while, nothing happened. At first, Zak thought he should be mad. Terasi said he didn't have much time, and now here they were, floating in silence in the sky. But the Druid was dying, and Zak wasn't immune to the shock of losing another life to this asinine war, and so his mind wandered.

He hadn't experienced a real Winter before. The Southern Isles were chilly in the colder season, but already the gusts of late Autumnfall in Regadensia were far more frigid than anything he had felt on his island home. What would snow feel like?

Dawn approached. The dark skies lightened to a miserable gray, and far in the distance, the Darlangson Mountains emerged. The early morning light made the starkness of the Rot even more apparent, the vastness of it daunting. It flowed—unbroken—as far as he could see.

"How will we ever cross that?" Zak asked, not directly to Terasi, but no one else was around.

"You will find a way," Terasi said. "You must. You cannot defeat Zandorn without coming here."

"Why?" Zak asked.

"His power is here. That which sustains him, keeps him immortal. I have felt the echoes of his power, but I do not know what it is. You will need to find out yourself."

"Not by myself," Zak said. "I am not alone."

Terasi tilted his head, acknowledging him. "Wisdom suits you, *Nacusti*. You may live to be a *Clarignis* yet." He surveyed the dark landscape. "I must make one last request of you. When we met, I traveled with a small creature. She looked like a bronze lizard, and I left her in the forest near where we fought the Consortium. Did you find her after the battle?"

It had only been a few months since that day, but it felt much longer. "Yes, the League found her, and she's safe with Tansil—the Archmagus." A faint memory of the lizard's terrarium in Tansil's office came to Zak.

"Good, then this at least will be easy. You must go to her, *Nacusti*. She will prove helpful in defeating the Consortium."

Confused about how a lizard would help, he simply nodded. He wasn't about to deny the Druid's final request.

They were silent for a few moments longer when Terasi turned to Zak. "*Benevita, Nacusti*."

"*Benevita,* ter-Terasi." He didn't know exactly what it meant, but he remembered hearing Pordu use the name and thought it would bring some comfort.

A weak smile curved Terasi's lips as his spirit faded away.

Zak blinked his eyes open—his real eyes. Back in Tor'alan, in the Dormitory, in his room on the second floor, third door on the left, in his bed. Already, his nighttime spiritual jaunt fogged in his head, but as he wiped his damp cheeks, he knew everything he saw and heard had been real.

Terasi was gone.

Zandorn hid in Pywell Mountain.

He moved slowly as he dressed, his body still recovering from yesterday's exertion and injuries. But he couldn't stay in bed. He needed to tell Tansil and Sorwin what he had learned from Terasi, and then he had to follow through on his promise to train with Olivia. So he carefully pulled a plain tunic over his bandaged arm (the wound from Zandorn's blade still refusing to close) and slid into wool breeches and his boots.

The Center buzzed with talk about the battle with the Consortium. And from the hushed whispers and pointing as he walked through the courtyard toward the castle, it was apparent everyone knew about his confrontation with Zandorn. He looked longingly at the mess hall but knew he'd never get through a meal without being harassed with questions, and he wasn't ready to bother Bazil for help yet.

He groaned. It would be a hungry few weeks waiting for the excitement to wear off.

He climbed the long staircase to Tansil's office and knocked, but there was no answer. The door was unlocked, so Zak let himself in, thinking the Archmagus might not have heard him.

No one was there. Or, almost no one. On the far left wall, on the table converted into a makeshift terrarium, trim trees, waterways, and grasses mixed to form a miniature world, and in the middle the bronze lizard stared up at him.

The last time Zak saw the lizard, it had a protective shield around it that Tansil couldn't break. It was gone now.

It must have been Terasi's magic, he reasoned. With the Druid gone, perhaps the spell broke.

He walked over to the lizard hesitantly, unsure what to do or why the lizard was important. It barely moved as he neared, yet its big golden eyes fixed on his green ones.

Jolsu stirred. *It cannot be.*

What?

I thought they were all destroyed, all gone.

What? Zak repeated. *What destroyed?*

Get closer. Reach out your hand, Jolsu instructed.

He sighed, annoyed that Jolsu ignored his questions, but he did as the dragon asked. As he reached out his hand, the lizard tipped its nose up and grazed his palm, an odd warmth prickling his skin at the touch. A bright light flashed, and Zak instinctively pulled back to cover his eyes. When he opened them, the lizard was much bigger, at least twice the size, and it spoke.

Finally we meet, Father, she said.

My daughter—you are alive! Jolsu said, and Zak felt the flood of joy from his Guardian rush through him.

"What just happened? Did the lizard just *speak*?" Zak asked aloud. Somehow, that seemed much more alarming than Jolsu's voice in his head.

I am no lizard. The bronze not-lizard's tail twitched, and she stood taller. *My name is Elpida, and I am a dragon.*

GLOSSARY AND PRONUNCIATIONS

CHARACTERS

Ageric Keldin (uh-jare-ick): Zakolor's father

Bazil Ben (bas-ill): priest and Zakolor's friend

Bill Solura (bihl): Kalbick's father

Burgo (burr-goh): wyvern

Burvenin (burr-venn-in): Magerus, general of the Consortium

Cerevita (suh-reh–vih-tah): Goddes of Life

Clairise Keldin (clare-eese): Zakolor's mother

Croi (kroy): hawk, Sorwin's familiar

Elpida (ell-pih-duh): bronze lizard, Terasi's companion

Euphemius Van Ilia (you-fem-ee-us): merchant, member of the League's council, Olivia's sponsor

Fanum Ket (fah-numb keht): Eelikuh of Weslinton

Lord Gideon Woolbin (gidd-ee-in): Baron of Masdaan

Gunther (gun-thur): Renna's servant

King Gyrnavo (gear-nah-voh): King of Weslinton

Inguma Foucher (in-goo-mah): Magus in the House of Elements, director of the Dormitory

Minister Jeppida Qor (jep-id-uh core): Prime Minister of the Republic of Evartia

Jolsu (jole-soo): dragon, Zakolor's guardian

Joryl (jore-ill): Densba council leader

Kalbick Solura (kal-bihk): Zakolor's best friend

Major Kaleb Deidaku (kay-lub day-dah-koo): member of League's army

Karazul (care-uh-zool): assassin working for Zandorn

Limba Dar (limb-buh): advisor to High King Marius

General Lupa (loop-uh): leader of the League's army

High King Marius Fern (mare-ee-us): leader of the League's council, King of Regadensia

Malu (mah-loo): notorious trickster and owner of Zindost, a pet and familiar shop

Marralee Solura (mare-uh-lee): Kalbick's mother

Nathan Greyson (nay-thin): merchant, friend of Euphemius

Olivia Pratinos (oh-liv-ee-uh): elementalist, Euphemius' ward, and Zakolor's friend

Pordu (poor-dew): Druid, friend of Temaway

Rauffe Werbeggen (rawf): adept in the League, rival of Zakolor

Renna (wren-uh): Zandorn's daughter

Rinka (reen-kah): newly elected Archalium

Sashina (sosh-in-uh): Archlumen, leader of the Temple of Light

Shira Motchit (sheer-uh): summoner, Sorwin's friend

Sorwin Darlangson (soar-win): Prince of Darlangson, Magerus, Zakolor's magus

Tansil Windover (tan-zill): Archmagus, Magerus, leader of the House of Elements, elven

Temaway Galeria (tehm-uh-way): one of the six original Nacusti that fought in the Guardian War and co-authored the Contract

Terasi (teh-rah-see): Druid

Archivist Tinora (tin-ohr-uh): works in the Archives

Ubba (ub-uh): Shira's imp

Vermig (vir-miig): Archalium, leader of the Den of Darkness

Vess (vehs): Temaway's Guardian, a phoenix

Queen Ymona (ee-mohn-uh): former Queen of Evartia

King Yuri (yuhr-ee): former King of Evartia

Zakolor Keldin (zak-oh-lore): Nacusti

Zandorn (zan-doorn): Magerus, leader of the Consortium

PLACES

Accipia: a village near Sorwin's castle that was a hideaway in his youth.

Aghoomi: one of the oldest nations in Valecium, renamed Weslinton after the Woolbins took over.

Bernadooth: largest port city in the Southern Isles, on the northern tip of Carshandyn.

Carshandyn: the largest of the Southern Isles, where Densba and Bernadooth are located.

Darlangson: western kingdom and member of the League. Home to Sorwin.

Densba: small village on the southern side of Carshandyn, where Zak is from.

Republic of Evartia: eastern country and member of the

League. Recently underwent a rebellion, overthrowing its previous twin monarchs and establishing a democratic republic. Led by Minister Jeppida Qor.

Eyewood: forest in the south of Nalawin, rumored to be the birthplace of Sight magic.

Florinshire: a village on the plains of Darlangson, reportedly where Zak's true parents were hiding when he was born and they were killed by the Consortium.

Gort'haal: southwestern country and land of the dwarves. They were furious with the destruction of the Guardian War and soon after buried themselves in their mountain home. No dwarf has been seen since.

Janlaka: city on the northern bank of the Karanadee, known for its famous hardwood and carpentry.

Kapana: the glass dream, a famous monument housing one of the largest markets in Valecium.

Karanadee River: waterway that serves as the border between Evartia and Weslinton.

Lark's Jewel: a lavish and mysterious tavern in Tor'alan.

Lindomer: port city on the southern tip of Regadensia.

Masdaan: city on the southern bank of the Karanadee, known for its spices and glass works.

Nalawin: northern country and land of the elves. While a few stray elves interact with the outside world, the country closed its borders centuries ago, isolating itself from the rest of Valecium.

Pywell Mountains: hiding place of the Consortium, where Zandorn has found a way to survive in the Rot and extend lifespans beyond the mortal coil.

Regadensia: central kingdom and member of the League. Led by High King Marius Fern.

Tor'alan: capital of the League. The floating city usually resides near the middle of Regadensia.

Wastelands: formerly a country, the land was devastated as a result of the Guardian War.

Weslinton: eastern kingdom and member of the League. Led by King Gyrnavo.

Zindost: Malu's pet and familiar shop.

MAGIC

Anima mea telum: appear, weapon of my soul

Aquatelum: water spear

Bracteaveru: leaf dart

Customateria: appear, Guardian

Daemateria: appear, demon

Dormiligo: sleep binding

Dormio: sleep

Fumus: smoke

Ignis: fire

Ignitelum: fire spear

Ignitempesta: fire storm

Invepati: find the path

Magus expurgo: cleanse of magic

Nuntiumignis: fire message

Pennilma: wing of air

Relentesco: slow

Senligo: thought binding

Sylvaligo: wood binding

Tegofortis: strong shield
Tegoperignis: fire shield
Visus accipiter: sight of the hawk
Vitaligo: life binding

OTHER

Archalium: leader of the Den of Darkness, carries Baltenebris' cordeus.

Archlumen: leader of the Temple of Light, carries Azubelux's cordeus.

Archmagus: leader of the House of Elements, carries Cerevita's cordeus.

Benevita: blessed life, an old-fashioned but still used greeting and parting phrase.

Black Caladrius: bird of immense power thought to be a myth. Its feathers have the ability to negate anything in existence.

Caladrius: bird with powers to heal most wounds and illnesses, as well as foretell death.

Calinus: dark one, term for destroyers of nature.

Clarignis: bright one, term for esteemed mages.

Cordeus: heart of a god, a powerful magic artifact.

Devoted: mortals that pledge themselves to a god.

The Disciples: a radical religious group seeking to destroy the Contract.

Eelikuh: leader of mages in Weslinton.

Familiar: an animal that bonds with a mage. They generally require a high degree of skill and self-awareness of any mage seeking their companionship.

Far Sight: a type of Sight magic that peers into the more distant future.

Firepost: a means of long-distance communication where letters are delivered in a blaze of fire.

Fire Post: iron posts that create a network for Fireposts to travel between.

Indagomius: a pair of charmed gems used for tracking magic.

Inriloc: a mental space for mages to meditate, also serves as an important meeting place for Nacusti and Guardians.

Is shalri: elven term meaning "a knife"

Jyrnen: draconic term meaning "thunder, family, flight"

-Ko: suffix denoting royal dragons

Lapidaemas: demon stone

Magtrophitis: a degenerative disease that atrophies a mage's magic and life force.

Nacusti: Guardian-born

Near Sight: a type of Sight magic that peers into the more immediate future.

Parignis: Little Fire

Rotters: amorphous creatures that are highly resistant to magic.

Sorgeus: a rare mage that can absorb magic, either to their benefit or detriment.

Stulmati: Evartian slang for idiot.

ter-: prefix meaning "sibling," often used among Druids.

ter-amis: earth friends

MAGICAL HOUSES

Magical Houses are both physical structures and orders of mages organized by the primary form of magic they study and use. Each of the three houses has a patron god and is led by one of the Archs.

Temple of Light: Governing body for priests and any mages studying physical magic. In the Era of Dominion, the structure held monuments and altars for the entire pantheon and was dubbed the Temple of Light, as all mortals needed the gods to guide them, much like a lantern in the dark. The name stuck in the Era of Freedom as Azubelux remained the patron god for the order. Led by the Archlumen.

Den of Darkness: Governing body for summoners and any mages contracting demons. Originally an acronym, the Demonic Entropy Nexus (D.E.N.) was shortened to Den for its likeness to a cozy dark room often found in larger abodes. Baltenebris is the patron god. Led by the Archalium.

House of Elements: Governing body for traditional mages and any mage studying elemental magic. Elemental magic was the first to be used in Valecium and is often thought of as the "original" magic. The first magic colleges were Elemental, and the tradition of collecting and housing apprentices during their studies sustained through the eras. Hence, the Dormitory is under the direction of the House of Elements, despite its semi-regular incineration due to the reckless use of fire magic. Cerevita is the patron god. Led by the Archmagus.

THREE FIRES

Fire magic holds a special place of power in Valecium as it is useable by all mages with relatively little study. While there are varying forms it may take, the pinnacle of excellence is in pursuing the mastery of the Three Fires. Few have achieved it, even among the gods. The most famous user of the Three Fires is the phoenix.

Consuming Fire: a fire so strong that it destroys anything it touches, leaving not even ash behind.

Curing Fire: a fire so pure it heals almost any wound and burns many types of diseases.

Creating Fire: a fire so wild it pushes the boundaries of life and imagination, manifesting the caster's true desires.

ERAS OF VALECIUM

Era of Mages: the first age in Valecium, when elves, dwarves, and humans openly studied magic and built the great nations.

Era of Dominion: the second age in Valecium, when the gods forced mortals to become Devoted and restricted their magical studies.

Era of Freedom: the third age in Valecium, when mortals fought the Guardian War and created the Contract to free themselves from the gods.

CALENDAR

The Valecium calendar has four seasons, each lasting three months. Each month has six weeks, and each week has five days. The Year Festival is both the end of one year and the beginning of the next, lasting for a full five days to transition. Each nation and people celebrate a little differently, though many involve feasts and revelry.

Year festival (one week)
Springrise
Spring
Springfall
Summerrise
Summer
Summerfall
Autumnrise
Autumn
Autumnfall
Winterrise
Winter
Winterfall

Weeks are five days, each day is numbered:
Onesday
Twosday
Threesday
Foursday
Fivesday

ACKNOWLEDGEMENTS

Writing this second book could not have been more different from writing the first. I went from on-and-off writing across thirteen years for *Zakolor* to a single year for *The Black Caladrius*. And, as you can imagine, the drastically different timeline demanded drastically different support. It takes a village to publish a book, and I'm so thankful for mine.

Kourtney, you went above and beyond as an editor—in ways I have sworn to keep secret and safe. Your humor, dedication to craft and storytelling, and just pure fun that you brought to this process are more valuable than you know. Thank you for everything, and I'm excited to dive into Book 3 with you. P.S. I think you may be the only person who loves Sorwin more than I do!

Kelly, you wonderful artist! Thank you for navigating the murky (for me) waters of cover design. I came in thinking I knew what I wanted (again) and quickly realized how out of my depth I truly was (again). Your calm approach and patience guided us to a beautiful place (again).

Jane and Kimani, thank you for reading *Zakolor* and beta reading *The Black Caladrius*. You dove into Valecium "eyes first," and the world is all the better for your input. Thank you to my critique partners Kam and Alice for getting into the weeds with me. Your detailed feedback pushed my writing further and faster than I thought possible.

Kenz, Paul, Calvin, and Sylvie—you show me what true love can look like, how it can be shiny and worn, lived in and tender and tough all at the same time. I learn something every time I'm with you.

Mama, your sharp attention to detail makes you the best copy editor I could hope for. Thank you for always lending a hand and being my first cheerleader.

Papa, thank you for always supporting me and asking when the next book will be finished so you can read it. Your eagerness for the journey fuels me more than you know.

Alfredo, you have absolutely no idea what I'm rambling about half the time (through no fault of your own), and you support me anyway. Thank you for the love you give each and every day. Te amo mucho.

Thank you to all my friends and family, too many to name, who have asked questions, read the books, posted or shared online, or just generally offered your support, loud or quiet, near or far. I love you all so much.

And of course, thank you Reader, for none of this would matter or even exist without your love of far-off places and daring adventures. My heart is bursting with gratitude if Zakolor and friends have made their way into yours, even for a moment.

Until next time. *Benevita*!

ABOUT THE AUTHOR

J. R. Douglas began writing as a teenager when daydreams introduced recurring characters. While he keeps busy working in adult education, tending his garden, and trying to stay healthy with some yoga, he plans to continue sharing the world of Valecium through the Nacusti Chronicles. J. R. lives in upstate New York with his partner, Alfredo, and their sweet dog, Samson.

www.jrdwrites.com
www.jrdwrites.substack.com
Instagram: j_r_douglas

Printed in the USA
CPSIA information can be obtained
at www.ICGtesting.com
CBHW030857181024
16013CB00004B/15